James E. Fisher,

Follow your dream

Bill J ___ 5/2/08

DREAMQUEST

DreamQuest

Bill Pottle

Writers Club Press
New York Lincoln Shanghai

DreamQuest

Writers Club Press
an imprint of iUniverse, Inc.

For information address:
iUniverse, Inc.
2021 Pine Lake Road, Suite 100
Lincoln, NE 68512
www.iuniverse.com

Illustrations by Charles DeGuzman
charlesdeguzman@hotmail.com
310 823 3062/303.340.3976

ISBN: 0-595-26804-8

Printed in the United States of America

To Valena, with love

CONTENTS

▼

Chapter 1:   Of Cows and Chickens......................................1

Chapter 2:   Sunrise..15

Chapter 3:   A Really Mean Guy 29

Chapter 4:   Bureaucracy..42

Chapter 5:   The Queen of Darkness..................................50

Chapter 6:   A New Friend...59

Chapter 7:   A City Rejoices..70

Chapter 8:   And it All Came From a Hug.............................84

Chapter 9:   Another Sword of Power and an Old Friend................94

Chapter 10:   More Bad Guys 109

Chapter 11:   More Questions 123

Chapter 12:   Escape 147

Chapter 13:   Someone's in Love…....................................156

Chapter 14:   The Survivor..168

Chapter 15:   Freeton Forever 177

Chapter 16:   A Battle at Night 196

Chapter 17:   The Plan..205

Chapter 18:   The Trap 219

Chapter 19: Into the Heart of Evil 235

Chapter 20: The End of Breshen 243

Coming in 2005 259

Acknowledgements:

The author wishes to express his sincere thanks to the many people who contributed their time and energy to make this story come alive. First and foremost, Connie Pottle gave invaluable advice on manuscript preparation and helped open the world of publishing in a way that only a librarian could do. Jeri Kladder gave a thorough editing of the first complete draft of the story, and provided many useful suggestions in terms of writing style and story content. Sherry Lai has also been a great help, teaching me to reach for the stars while still keeping both feet on the ground. The author is deeply indebted to Charles DeGuzman for his cover art and the interior map. The author would also like to thank his family, for always being there and supporting the project, even though it took many long years to complete. Finally, thanks are due to the many other people who helped read and edit the story throughout the years. Each of you has touched it in your own unique way, and helped to add your mark to the final polished version.

The Lands of Daranor

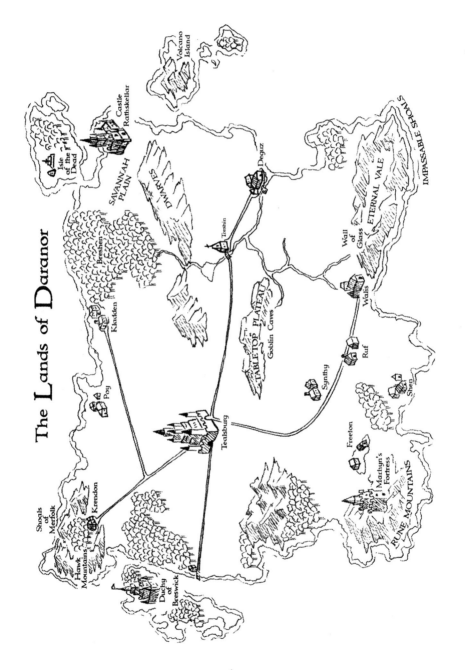

CHAPTER 1

▼

OF COWS AND CHICKENS

All his life young Tarthur had wanted to be a hero, and now was his chance, he thought as he dove out of the way of an arc of fire that exploded the pillar behind him. He felt pebbles bounce against his back.

"I've got to be more careful next time," he thought, "that fire almost hit me."

He dodged another blast, and this time came face to face with Darhyn himself, the Death Lord of Daranor, embodiment of all evil, death, and hatred. The Death Lord laughed slowly, and brought his hand up over Tarthur. Tarthur saw a web beginning to form around Darhyn's fingers, and then grow bigger, coming to ensnare him. Tarthur grabbed his dagger and plunged it straight into the Death Lord's breast. Tarthur felt nothing as it slid in. The Dark One screamed in agony, and then faded away into nothing.

If he had been able to think about it, the boy would have been terrified, but as it was, Tarthur was too stunned to think. He began to run away, for already the shapes of other, darker things were beginning to form in the mist.

He ran out of the main chamber, where a massive iron door swung open for him. Another door remained closed ahead, so he took a turn for the right, for on his left, a hideous ogre dripping with blood, sweat, and slime was hunkering after him. Tarthur ran, and he ran. He didn't know how far he went in that twisted labyrinth, only that every time he turned he would alternate between right and left turns.

He knew there were many monsters chasing him now. He didn't see them, but he saw shadows and heard heavy, panting breathing and he almost felt their moist breath and cold claws digging into his back. They had come to destroy the one who had killed their leader.

Tarthur could think of nothing other than finding a way out. Everywhere he turned, however, seemed to lead him only further down and deeper into the winding catacombs. Suddenly, he felt an even greater urgency to get out alive. The monsters were almost on top of him now. He rounded a corner…

…And found a dead end. He turned to retrace his steps, but saw that where he had entered was already blocked off. He looked down at the corner to see if there was any way out, but instead his eyes spied a small, beat up old chest. Hurriedly, he jiggled the lock with his dagger, and fortunately it popped open.

Inside was a yellowed scroll.

Tarthur wondered what magic this might be, but he was only a young kid. He had never used magic before. He reached around frantically in his tunic for his quill and scroll to copy it down, but it was useless, they had been lost in the harrowing flight from the Death Lord's chamber.

Suddenly, out of nowhere, a voice came, "*Here Tarthur, take these,*" and placed a quill and scroll in Tarthur's hands. Never one to question a gift, Tarthur quickly copied down the old scroll on the other one. Now, the monsters were practically on top of him, and he had nothing left to try. Raising the scroll and staring at the characters that he had never before seen, Tarthur began to read out loud.

Huge waves came crashing down upon everyone in the room without warning. The monsters were completely swept away, but as Tarthur was wondering how it was that he survived, how he stood amidst the maelstrom with a dry tunic, he felt a massive presence take hold of him and begin to shake. He fought it as hard as he could, but try as he might, he couldn't escape. Tarthur was losing air quickly. His vision was beginning to gray around the edges, and he couldn't hold his balance…

＊   ＊   ＊   ＊

"Tarthur, Tarthur wake up!" Tarthur stopped struggling, and found himself far away from the horror, in the small mountain village of Krendon, staring up into the brown eyes of his friend and companion, Derlin. Tarthur breathed in a sigh of relief. "I had a terrible…"

"Dream, I know." Derlin finished. The boys had been close ever since they were small, and could often finish each other's sentences. "When you didn't show up at breakfast, I wondered where you were. I came back and saw you wildly thrashing around for your quill pen and scroll. So I handed them to you, and you started writing down all these weird symbols. I've never seen anything like them before." Derlin finished the sentence with a hint of worry in his voice.

Tarthur looked at the scroll, and indeed it did have strange shapes and markings written all over it. Some of the characters were black, and some were in other colors like blue, red, brown, and green. The ink jar on the small table beside his bed was filled only with black ink, and the quill had been dry the night before. Tarthur had never been one to worry a lot about being literate, but as he looked at the scroll, he knew that those letters were nothing like the ones that that old wandering bard had attempted to teach him. Tarthur quickly rolled up the scroll, and started to fasten it in place with a tie, but it stayed where it was on its own. Tarthur told Derlin about his dream, at least what he remembered of it, and while they played heroes in the forest with sticks as swords and routinely killed the Death Lord without so much as a hindrance, this time somehow seemed different.

"This is definitely strange," Derlin wondered out loud. "I think we should go see Zelin."

Tarthur nodded his head in agreement. "I think we should go right away."

"Wait," Derlin said, putting a restraining hand on his shoulder. "We still have to take care of our punishment. I think we should do that first, since you know we'll just get into more trouble if we don't do it quickly. Not to mention, we have to do the rest of our chores too. I'm already finished with mine, but what do you have to do? It's a Saturday in August, you know."

Tarthur thought for a moment. "Well, I have to feed the chickens, and…"

"I already fed them," Derlin cut him short. "They were clucking like mad when I walked by, so I took care of it myself."

"Well, I guess then there's always Old Betsy."

Derlin grimaced with visible pain. "Yeah, it's better that we get it over with."

The barn was close to Tarthur's quarters, so they were there in a matter of minutes. The two walked slowly inside, with the look of two who wished that they were coming out, their task already completed. Most of the cows mooed softly when they walked by, but one snorted her disgust. Old Betsy was the meanest of the entire herd. She had one brown patch on her left side, and two black ones on her right. Everyone in Krendon knew that to be saddled with the task of milking Old Betsy required the performance of some dastardly and heinous crime. She could claim no particular owner, as no one would take her, but her milk always went to Baron Ercrilla, the landlord who owned the town.

Tarthur cautiously approached from the left flank, and then reached down and began to milk. Meanwhile, Derlin gave her flowers to distract her. As usual, the boys recounted the adventure that had resulted in their punishment.

"We're so unlucky," Tarthur mused. "What are the odds that that cranky old knight…what was his name again?"

"Erso," Derlin returned.

"Yes, that's it," Tarthur remembered. "Yeah, what are the odds that he just happens to come upon us in that abandoned part of the forest, just when we're reenacting old battles? Sword fighting is definitely a skill we need to know."

Derlin nodded in agreement, dodging one of Betsy's vicious hooves. "Maybe next time we should ask the baron before we borrow his swords."

"Oh, come on, Derlin. You know better than that. You know how adults are. You sneak into their house, take their things, and then break them a few times and they'll *never* trust you again."

"You're right, Tarthur," Derlin nodded again. "You know, I guess it must be that the baron is jealous because we're training to become the greatest heroes the land of Daranor has ever seen, and he probably couldn't even become a Royal Knight."

"This darn cow is as stubborn as a mule!" Tarthur uttered as he was sent sprawling into the hay by one of Betsy's patented kicks.

Derlin looked on the bright side. "Well, at least we got a half pail." Derlin was always an optimist. Tarthur usually was too, but it's hard to be optimistic when you've just gotten kicked into a pile of hay by a stubborn milk cow.

They were all set to leave the barn and head straight for Zelin's chambers, but suddenly Tarthur remembered how hungry he was. Since the punishment included being sent to bed the previous night without dinner, it was almost twenty-four hours since Tarthur had last eaten. (His last meal had been lunch Friday, and now it was almost lunchtime Saturday.) Surely, the cooks had already cleaned up breakfast, and while they might make an exception for that snotty baron's son, as sure as the cow Betsy was stubborn, there would be no breakfast for Tarthur—unless, as he put it, he and Derlin 'permanently borrowed' some.

"Derlin, what are they cooking for lunch today?"

"Oh I don't know, some of that thin gruel-like soup I think. But Tarthur, why do you ask…" Derlin trailed off as he saw the familiar look in his friend's eyes again. "Tarthur, oh no you don't…you know that Baron Ercrilla always likes his mincemeat pies right when he returns from his hunting trips…"

"Well, that's illogical," Tarthur countered. "He should eat what he catches, if he's any good at hunting. And it's our job to encourage him in that behavior. Besides, it'll only take a few minutes."

As they walked from the barn to the kitchen, Tarthur watched the children of Krendon. Most of them were joyful, and Tarthur loved them. Maybe being an orphan had made Tarthur want a family more than other children his age. His parents had given him life, his name, and little else. His mother had died during childbirth, and his father had died soon after in a hunting accident. But some said that he had died from grief in losing his beloved. Tarthur's mother had had long, flowing, golden hair, and his father's was brown. Tarthur himself had sandy blond hair and his mother's sky blue eyes. Most of the village children looked up to Tarthur and admired him, in spite of vehement objections from their own mothers. Yet, strolling down the walk came the one village youth that Tarthur despised over all other life forms. It was the dreaded Mortimer, the only son of Baron Ercrilla.

Morty, as Tarthur called him simply because he hated it, approached, and began to speak in a sarcastic tone. "Tarthur, being as though your presence was lacking when we broke our fast this morning, I was inclined to think that you so much enjoyed milking Betsy the cow that you endeavored at it for hours." That was the way educated people talked, and Morty had plenty of education. He had a tutor, who would come for a few days a week, sometimes staying the whole day, making Morty sit there and recite useless facts, and perform strange feats like the diagramming of sentences. Tarthur couldn't imagine anything worse than that.

They started out as friends, since they were almost the same age. Over time, however, they had grown into rivals—they had too much in common. Both could command the interest of the other members of the town, especially the children and the females, although it was for very different reasons. Morty captivated for his money and power, and Tarthur for his recklessness and audacity. Eventually, most had come to like Tarthur better than Morty. Competition had blossomed into jealousy, and then Morty played the first of the ongoing war's cruel jokes.

A herd of sheep grazing in a small pasture just outside of town had been spooked by some small monster, probably a griffin or snake or such. The herd had charged off of the edge of a cliff, taking their shepherd with them as they fell. Tarthur was nearby, and had heard the man's cries for help. He had dragged the man back to town, only to find that he had already died. Morty met him at the gate, and then acting as judge, jury, and executioner, he had Tarthur beaten and made to go for two days without food on the charge of spooking the sheep.

Tarthur, of course, retaliated. He wasn't able to get back at Morty with methods such as these, since he had no influence, but he did quite well in this war.

Derlin stepped forward and shoved Morty while Tarthur stepped on his foot. "Why don't you keep your big, ugly nose out of our business?" Derlin didn't like Morty either, and besides, his nose was big and ugly. It jutted out from his face like a lone mountain peak, with two gigantic caves in it.

Morty flexed his fist to strike, but checked himself. He was no match for Tarthur in physical combat, and if he did anything, surely Derlin would step in. But oh…it would feel so good to get one hard punch in. No, he thought. He was exposed with his dad's bodyguards away with the hunting party. He would get them back with some other, more sinister idea. Derlin too, he would pay for that insult to his face. Morty abruptly turned, and walked off.

"I don't like it, Tarthur, he's planning something."

Tarthur nodded in agreement. "Yeah, I know that look in his face. But who cares? The hunting party is gone today, and tomorrow—well, things will be different with this whole dream business."

Soon the kitchen was in view, and Tarthur and Derlin skirted the front by fifty yards so they could approach in the cover of the woods. The trees were just beginning to turn into a vast array of bursting colors. In a month or so the leaves would reach their peak, falling to give a spectacular carpet to anyone who would take the time to notice.

Walking quietly, the boys soon arrived at the side of the kitchen, and stared up at the windowsill. The sill was old and wanted repainting; it was yellowing and cracking around the edges. But it was on top of the sill where the prize rested. A beautiful mincemeat pie wafted its succulent aroma toward the boys, calling out to them. Tarthur felt his mouth water and his stomach start to turn. Several fine animals had died for that pie. It certainly was a pity that they didn't serve the likes of this to Tarthur and Derlin more often. The pudgy head cook Judith had been infuriated at them ever since that unfortunate pastry incident a few years back.

Tarthur, now in his element, looked around to make sure no one was watching them, then darted up and grabbed the pie as he and Derlin raced away on foot for the safety of the inner forest. On the way, they congratulated themselves on a job well done, for they were sure not a soul had seen them. They were close, only one had, but for Tarthur it was the worst one of all. Stepping from the shadows of a nearby building, Morty chuckled and walked confidently into the kitchen.

*   *   *   *

"Wow," Tarthur groaned, delighted. "That pie was incredible. I'm almost envious of Morty for being able to eat that well."

Derlin nodded in agreement. It had been a good pie. But now, however, they had other things to worry about. "Now," he began in a slightly irritated voice, "if there are no more objections then perhaps we can visit Zelin?"

"None that I can think of." (Tarthur, being the forgetful type, had forgotten that he had to sweep out the blacksmith's shop. But as he was away with the baron's hunting party, no harm was done.)

The two soon completed the short walk to Zelin's chambers. Krendon was a small town; everything was within a short five-minute walk of everything else. It was nice that way. Of course, the forest bordered almost everything, making it handy for the boys' getaways.

The dream had really disturbed Tarthur, however. How had the pen written in color? Was there magic at work? And the dream had seemed so real, not like the other times that he imagined that he had killed the Death Lord. This time he felt like he had actually done it, and the monsters had frightened him like never before.

Zelin's yard was neatly kept. Tarthur had a friend named Girn, who was in charge of keeping the grounds for Zelin. Tarthur liked Girn, but he didn't see him around much anymore. He walked up the stairs leading to the wizard's house. Zelin was extremely old and wise, and you only went to see him for the gravest problems. He was a kindly old man, adored by all the people. Tarthur lifted the knocker…

*   *   *   *

"They did *what*???!!!" Judith's shriek filled the room, causing the other cooks to cower in fear. Morty's smirk was unaffected.

"That's right," he said. He had really gotten them this time. There would be no food for Tarthur and Derlin for a while. Just wait until his dad heard about this.

"All my hard work gone to naught!" Judith bemoaned her loss. "Well, why didn't you stop them, idiot boy?! I'll beat you with this rolling pin to teach you a lesson."

Morty stood there calmly, unfazed by her temper. "Might I so humbly remind you that my father could have you thrown out into the streets to beg for food like a common cur?"

Judith caught herself. It was all too true. While she was on relatively good terms with the baron, he did legally own the entire town. It would not be worth it to risk everything. Still, she wanted to pummel the little snot.

"You're thinking about this in the wrong way," he coaxed her. "Tarthur and Derlin are the ones to blame, for it was they who stole your magnificent pie. I, of course, attempted to dissuade them from their self-destructive course of action, but—alas, my efforts were fruitless. I told them what they were doing was wrong, but what did they do, but spit at me, and say, "Take this spit to Judith, for if she were here I would likewise spit into her ugly face." They told me that they would take their snot and put it into your excellent soup (which, may I say you do a delightful job preparing) to make it taste better."

Judith was absolutely fuming by this time. Morty was having no trouble coaxing her on. "This is not to be borne by such a fine cook as yourself. Since the proper legal authorities are out of town presently, you yourself must deliver the beating, for the scoundrels deserve no less."

Taping the pastry roller in her hand expectantly, Judith stormed out of the kitchen, and Morty followed after to watch.

*   *   *   *

"Come in." The voice came from inside before Tarthur had even let the knocker fall, even as the door swung inward by itself.

The inside of the room was a sharp contrast with the neatly kept outside. Objects were scattered all over. There was an old rusty sword there, an unstrung harp here, and a scarecrow in the corner. Suddenly the scarecrow spoke.

"Welcome boys, Tarthur and Derlin from the look of you. What brings such carefree youth as yourselves to my dwelling?" Tarthur saw that what he had at first mistaken for a scarecrow was in fact Zelin himself. Now that he knew it was him, Tarthur had no idea how he had originally mistaken the wizard for just another part of the clutter. Embarrassed, he was unsure how to proceed.

Zelin noticed him looking around hesitantly at the mess. "Yes, people wonder why I don't keep it tidy, but then I can never find anything when I want to. I think it's much better this way."

Tarthur had to agree. He was never one to be accused of spending too much time to keep his room up to sanitary conditions. Zelin's easy manner made him feel comfortable even though he had been there only a few minutes.

"Well," Tarthur began, "we're here because of this." He handed Zelin the scroll.

Zelin carefully unwrapped it, and his face showed a look of mild surprise. He unrolled the whole thing, glanced over it, and then let it fall from his hands.

The sternness in his voice startled Tarthur. "Where did you get this?"

"I…I just had a dream. I was fighting the Death Lord, and then I killed him with my knife, and when I was running away I found it in a treasure chest and I copied it down."

"Did you read it in your dream?"

"Yes, I did. And it caused huge waves to crash down on the monsters there, killing them all. That's when Derlin woke me."

"Water waves, you say?"

Tarthur nodded, and then unable to contain his excitement any longer, burst out. "What is it? Have we found something important and magical? What does it say?"

Zelin raised his hand to ward off Tarthur's questions. "I'm not sure. It may turn out to be something, and then again, it may turn out to be nothing. But for right now…can you boys fetch the farmer Addyean to me please? Tell him that it is important. I would rather speak with him for the moment."

"Okay," Tarthur answered, a little perplexed. Then he shrugged it off. He was excited, yet also a little worried. What could the scroll say? He'd probably find out the answers to his questions soon. He hoped so at least.

Tarthur and Derlin were good friends with Addyean, for while he was an adult, and therefore boring, he never was condescending when he spoke to them. He treated them just as he treated anyone else. He was a simple man, and had come to the village a few years ago to claim land after his father had passed away. Soon they were at his house, and not finding him there, they set out into the fields to look for him. Krendon was in the mountains, and there was not much level land for growing crops. Thus, it wasn't long before they found him.

"Hello, boys," he greeted cheerfully. "I'm glad you came to help. We need that row over there done before lunch; we're trying to finish harvesting this section today."

"Uh, actually, Addyean, we're here because something happened and Zelin wants to talk to you."

Addyean stopped for a minute. "Me? What does Zelin want to talk to me for? Wait a minute, this better not be one of your crazy schemes. If you're lying, you'll harvest the *whole* field. Now, does Zelin really want to talk to me?"

Tarthur nodded, going back in his mind and remembering that yes, Zelin did definitely want to talk to him. Harvesting the whole field would not be a good punishment. (As if any punishment was.)

"I'll answer the summons then," Addyean replied. "You boys just stay here and work."

Tarthur was about to pick up the handle of the sickle, but oddly enough, the shabbily made article broke. Oh well, how could he harvest if he had no tools?

$$* \qquad * \qquad * \qquad *$$

"But why? This makes absolutely no sense. Why would he summon him?" Addyean was frustrated. There were so many things that didn't make sense.

"Perhaps he considers him a threat, and wants to destroy him or enslave him before he can become strong enough?" Zelin was equally lost for ideas.

Addyean thought for a while more. "Do mistakes ever happen? I mean, could it have been meant for someone else?"

"It's highly unlikely, but possible, yes. Most likely, it was completely random. Or, Tarthur could be working for him, and telling us of these stories of the Water Orb."

"I think that is unlikely," Addyean countered, while holding up his hand to still admit the possibility. "But in any case, where do we go from here? Do you really think that something could be starting?"

Zelin stared ahead almost as if he hadn't heard. "What puzzles me is that Tarthur said he killed him, that he faded into the mist. Suppose he did defeat him there? This could be an unprecedented opportunity. Just the possibility of that is worth following up."

The two were full of questions, firing them off back and forth so fast that the other would never have had a chance to answer them, if indeed they could. Zelin made an exception for Addyean's next question. "What was with the gigantic wave, anyway?"

"I think that he may have somehow stumbled onto the spell that controls the Water Orb. The boys are familiar with forest lore, are they not?" Addyean nodded, not quite understanding.

"Good," Zelin replied. "Girn!" With this call, a young, quiet, shaggy-haired boy burst in from another room. "Girn, you are familiar with the boys Tarthur and Derlin, are you not?"

The young boy nodded. He had lost both his parents when he was little, and he almost never spoke. He had started off as another one of Tarthur's admirers, and had actually become one of Tarthur's closer friends. But Girn was always younger and smaller, and had the problem of having a small amount of morals. So he often preferred not to accompany the boys on some of their more brazen outings. Girn's speed was unmatched in the village, and this made him a valuable asset as an apprentice. He worked hard, and Zelin had picked him out personally. So, in time, his friendship with the boys had waned, but he was still looked upon as a welcome ally.

"Go to Yrean, the tailor and tell him to make two traveling cloaks, forest green, and have Judith prepare a couple of sacks of food. Get at least a week's worth." Zelin motioned in the air by Girn's face, and a scroll materialized and fell into his hand. Then, Zelin flipped him a shiny coin, which Girn swiftly caught as he raced out the door.

∗   ∗   ∗   ∗

"I wonder what it could be," Tarthur said aloud, the excitement starting to affect him. "Probably I've discovered some important secret of the world. Don't worry, Derlin, when I'm a famous hero, I won't forget you."

"Zelin looked worried, Tarthur. I don't know him that well, but he seemed like something serious could be wrong. And why won't they tell us anything?"

Tarthur shrugged. "Maybe they really don't know. We'll probably have to go to one of the big cities to find out. Maybe we'll even get to meet the king. He'll say, 'Tarthur, I award you this medal of bravery for exceptional courage. Why, you could fight the Death Lord in your sleep. And so you did! I think I'll make you a Royal Knight of the highest order.'"

"Well, something important must be happening. Look, someone is running this way." Derlin pointed as a figure still too far away to be recognized charged at them.

"Wait a minute…is that…oh no! Run, Derlin!" Coming at them at breakneck speed, waving a rolling pin viciously through the air, was none other than Judith herself, with a furious look on her face. But it was too late.

"I'll beat you little cretins senseless! Look at what's happening to the youth these days! You better be able to grow new legs, because I'm going to break the ones you have, and then we'll see what you have to say about my soup!"

"You will not trouble us," Derlin stood up. "We are on private business with Zelin."

It would be a lie to say that Judith was not incredibly startled. This was the second boy today to boss her around. It wasn't so much that she accepted their excuse but more that she was just shocked. "Zelin, what do you two thieving liars have to do with him?"

"We are NOT liars," Derlin countered. "And you practically forced us to steal that pie by starving Tarthur."

"And a good pie it was!" Tarthur cut in.

"Quiet," Derlin reprimanded. "I was winning the argument."

All three were cut short by the appearance of Girn.

"I...I b...bear a summons." Tarthur could tell that forming the words was difficult for Girn. He turned to collect Tarthur and Derlin, and to bring them with him. "Now, wait just a minute," Judith was not about to just let them go like this. "There must be something going on here."

Girn nodded. "Y...you are all...also to make them a...a wallet of food. By...tomorrow." Judith could not believe her ears, but he did have a piece of paper telling exactly what was to be done, signed by Zelin himself. Judith resolved to take it up with the baron later when he returned.

As the boys walked silently to Zelin's house, Tarthur and Derlin were both thinking the same thing—they were getting food packed for them. That could only mean one thing, that they were to go on a journey. But where?

They soon arrived at Zelin's house, and walked silently into the room.

Zelin and Addyean were seated in a pair of stiff-backed chairs, and Tarthur and Derlin took the two remaining chairs. Girn left to go take care of the cloaks. As there were only four chairs, he assumed he was not invited.

Silence reigned for a moment, and then Tarthur broke it. "So, do you know what it is? I mean, we're going on a quest, right? I bet it's something important." Derlin was embarrassed and forced to give his friend a look that told him he better shut up quickly.

"I will begin by telling you a story," Zelin said calmly. "It is a story about the beginning. When the world was young, the Creator established a delicate equilibrium, a balance that existed between all things. Everything was good, and so he rested. The power in the world was divided into four elemental forces, which separated on the first day. All creatures could share in them, but eventually each element grew close to a special group. Air dwelt with the eagles that nest in the high reaches of the Rune Mountains, Fire to the firebeasts that perished long ago, Earth went to all creatures, and Water to the mermen."

"One day, there was a man named Frehu. He was a righteous man; he gave to the poor, and helped build many of the towns that are in existence today. Yet, he saw the power of the elements and he wanted to control them. Fool!" Zelin cried out. "He delved in lore that he should not have. He sought to control the elements by enchaining them. The spell he used was permanent. Fire, he imprisoned in a single tongue of flame that never goes out. Earth was locked in a grain of sand. Air, is kept in a feather from Firewing, the mighty eagle. Lastly, Water forever flows in a glistening orb. He fashioned four spells that would allow the user to unleash this awesome power."

"When he enchained the elements, the Creator saw what was happening and took part of his world away into what has now become the Eternal Vale. The rest of the world is where we live today. He sealed off the Eternal Vale with a wall of glass, so none may enter. Still, Frehu tried to enter, and in the end his own power collapsed inward on him, destroying him completely. Yet for all this, the trouble was not over, for Frehu had an apprentice named Darhyn." At this name, Tarthur felt a shiver run down his spine and thought that the room had become a shade darker. "Darhyn hated what had been done to his master, and so with this hate building within him, took two of the elements, Fire and Water, and began to wage war, in an attempt to destroy the world."

"Many valiant people fought against him, and eventually he was defeated, but not destroyed. He sleeps in a palace in the Savannah Plain. For some reason or another, we have absolutely no idea why, he called you, and we believe that you may have found the spell that controls the Water Orb."

"So, what do we do now?" Tarthur wondered.

"That," Zelin replied, "is what Addyean and I have been trying to decide. Unfortunately, we really don't know too much of anything right now. We may have a great chance, we may have nothing, and then again, we may be walking into a trap. But for now, we must find out more. And we must keep this a secret. The four of us present know, and Girn, Judith, and Yrean know something is happening. I would like to keep that number as small as possible, which is why I am sending you boys alone. You will not be missed much around here like Addyean or I will, and you can travel swiftly and secretly. Now, you go to see the mermen. They, if anyone, will know about this event and they might know something more about the spell, so we can determine if this, in fact, is it. My friend Tustor, the merwizard, will be able to tell you if it is authentic or if it is just some strange thing that was hidden in the Death Lord's castle. You may tell him, but no one else. There are powerful beings in this world that can sense the use of magic, and have ways of prying into your hearts. This must be kept secret, at least until we find out more."

Tarthur was excited. "Where are the shoals? When do we leave?"

"It's not far from here, only two days walk north, so I'm not expecting any problems."

Tarthur was surprised. Mermen only lived two days north? His master, the blacksmith, didn't even believe that mermen existed. If he had known that, Derlin and he would have tried to visit them before.

"You should be ready to leave in the morning, before first light." Addyean finally spoke. "If there is anything you need in the way of provisions, I'll take care of it. I want to remind you boys that this is certainly a serious thing. You should go, find out what you can, and return right away. We are putting a lot of trust in you; I don't want anything to happen."

Tarthur nodded. "You can count on us, sir."

CHAPTER 2

▼

SUNRISE

There weren't any goodbyes said the next morning. The boys simply gathered their belongings and set out early before the sun had come out to warm the land with its rays.

Tarthur and Derlin began walking northward into the forest, whistling happily. While it wasn't much of a quest, it certainly did have some potential with this whole dream business.

They talked a lot, laughing and recounting stories of old adventures as they walked onward with the morning mist just beginning to burn off. Both were in good shape, and they covered a fair amount of distance before they stopped for a lunch of bread and cheese. They drank a little water, and were on their way.

For dinner Judith had made a stew, all that was left for Tarthur and Derlin to do was to heat it. It took them a while to find an area that was clear enough for them to build a fire in. The trees had been getting thicker progressively throughout the hike, but eventually they found a small clearing. They thought that maybe they shouldn't make a fire since it could let somebody know where they were, but thought it didn't really matter since there were a few pillars of smoke from various huts billowing up into the sky. The stew was scrumptious, and the boys soon settled into bed after their first uneventful day.

The next day Tarthur and Derlin awoke, their cloaks wet with dew. They struck camp, ate some more bread and cheese for breakfast, and started walking north. Tarthur was skipping happily along when he slipped over the edge of a small ravine.

"Are you okay?" Derlin called out.

"I think I broke something," came the strained reply. Derlin carefully climbed down the crevasse, careful not to fall prey to the same fate as Tarthur. He was so careful in fact that he did not even notice the shadow at the top that blotted out the sun.

"Let's take a look at it," Derlin said upon reaching the bottom. Tarthur was white, but not from the pain. He pointed a shaking finger at the figure. As Derlin whirled around it spoke.

"Hello," it simply said. "My name is Dalin." Derlin looked closely at the man. He was short, but not overly so. He had long flowing black hair, which on first impression made him look like a girl. He was armed with a very handsome long bow and a simple short sword. He was wearing leather armor, which had a dark green stain on it. On his head was a simple green hat with a feather in it. Then Derlin saw the treasure, well almost. This man had a horse. All this went by in a flash of observations.

Dalin, as he must now be called, bounded down the slope with the agility of a deer, to land beside Tarthur. Derlin wanted to stop him but something told him that this man was there to help. Besides, he reasoned, what could he do against someone like this anyway?

"Let me see it," Dalin requested. Tarthur was unsure at first but then let go of his leg and extended it. "Hmm," Dalin frowned as he examined it. "It is a bad sprain, but nothing worse."

"Let me take you boys back to your parents. You shouldn't be out playing around like this." His expression was stern. Obviously, Tarthur thought, this Dalin figured they were boys just playing around in the woods.

"Now where do you live?" Dalin asked his question, and without waiting for an answer he started to deduce one himself. "The nearest village is Krendon, but that is a day's walk from here. You must live in some small woodcutters hut." He paused, "or you are running away from your parents."

"Wrong on all counts," Derlin ventured boldly. "We have been sent to— mrghmrngh." He couldn't finish his sentence—Tarthur was covering his mouth. Derlin quickly remembered that they could afford to trust no one. They were being a little unfair, he knew, but what else could they do? Ironic, he thought, that alone and in this strange world a friend was what they needed most but to trust someone was the one thing they could not afford to do.

"To learn how the mermen make their baubles," Tarthur finished. Everybody knew the childhood stories of the merfolk who played all day with glowing baubles that radiated light. "We have been sent by Zelin."

"What a coincidence," Dalin exclaimed. "I am headed north to talk to the merwizard. I will accompany you for a little while."

Neither Tarthur nor Derlin answered.

"All right," Dalin said, changing the subject. "Let's get you up onto my horse so we can continue our journey."

Dalin was not an overly burly man, but it seemed to Derlin that he had no trouble easily hefting Tarthur onto his waiting horse. The horse was all black and had powerful muscles rippling throughout his body. This Dalin must be a clever fellow, Tarthur reasoned, his ankle already feeling better from the combination of the reduced stress of not having to walk on it anymore and the tight wrapping of cloth that Dalin had applied to it. He knew the location of where we are going and helped me with my ankle. This was certainly not a man in whom to place the full trust of their mission, for that's exactly what Tarthur had come to regard it as.

Why had he agreed to help them go to the merfolk, Dalin wondered silently. They were not going to learn how to make baubles. Zelin knew how to make them; he also knew that only the merfolk could use them. They had probably just heard of Zelin as one of the last of the old gurus still living in the world. Still, it seemed for whatever small reason brooding at the edge of his consciousness, their trip to the mermen might be useful. What then, was their secret? He would find out soon, he promised himself.

It would have taken Dalin the rest of that day to reach the shoals of the merfolk, but now he had to hike, and these two were obviously slower than he was. It was not too bad, however. Dalin, being a man of short stature, was forced to take smaller strides than Derlin, who while he was younger by a good ten years, was also taller.

The day passed much in the way that a day must pass between strangers who appear to be allies but are unwilling to trust each other. Tarthur had to admit that while it was easy enough to tell which way was north, without Dalin's path finding skills they would have had a difficult time finding their way through the tangle of shrub brush and might have fallen into many a ravine. Dalin moved like one who has spent his life in the forest, running with the deer, growing with the trees. Tarthur certainly had no lack of forest experience himself, but even this paled before Dalin's obvious superiority.

That night passed in much the same way as the day, with about the same amount of conversation, even though they were all asleep.

The next morning they woke up early while it was still dark.

"Why do we have to get up so early?" Tarthur bitterly complained. It was well before sunrise. He had been assured by Dalin that it was less than a two-hour hike to the shoals of the merfolk. While getting up early had been part of Tarthur's job back in Krendon (as a matter of principle this does not mean that he did it) he was still sore from the fall the day before which had produced bruises and scrapes, in addition to his sprained ankle.

Dalin looked sadly at Tarthur for a moment, and then turned and began to walk north. Tarthur looked at Derlin, shrugged, and then turned to follow Dalin. They continued in silence for the hike. Although it was only a two-hour hike, by the time they came to the hill Tarthur was sweating profusely. Dalin had pronounced him able to hike, and the horse was to go unburdened. It seemed Dalin had a high respect for his animal, almost as one would regard a peer.

As they reached the top of the hill, Tarthur looked into the valley and saw an endless plain stretching before him. Dalin had lied to him—to cross this plain would take days, even weeks, if it even ended at all. No, Tarthur thought, Zelin himself had said it was only a two-day trip at the most, which meant…It was then that he saw the sun.

The first strands of ambient light came streaking across what Tarthur had thought was the plain, but was now revealed as the ocean. The rays danced and reflected each other nimbly, creating an endless burst of colors streaking out in every direction. In short, it was the most awesome sight he had ever beheld. Soon the sun was shortly above the horizon spilling its sparkling radiance out over the whole sea. The ocean reflected it back, ready to warm the land. Tarthur knew it was worth it, worth a hundred mornings of getting up when he was still so tired, just to see this one morning sunrise. He seemed to remember somewhere at the back of his consciousness that someone had once said that a sunrise on the shoals of the merfolk was the most beautiful sight in the whole world. It was then, unfortunately not before the euphoria faded, that he realized that the ocean was empty.

*   *   *   *

Girn felt sad. He was being disloyal to Tarthur and Derlin. He should've gone with them. But then, whom was his real loyalty to? The king? He had pledged his loyalty to King Garkin when he was old enough to know what he was saying—

everyone in the kingdom had to. His parents? They were both dead, dying when he was an infant. They had both deserted him when he was little, and besides, even if his loyalty was to them, which it wasn't, what could he do? Zelin then? The wizard had befriended him when he was opting for an apprenticeship. He even paid him for his work, a rare quality to find in a master. All Girn did was take care of the outside grounds and run errands. But he had known Tarthur and Derlin before he had known Zelin. Tarthur had befriended him when he had lived in the orphan/servant's quarters. Girn remembered when Tarthur had taught Girn and the younger Derlin how to steal, or as Tarthur used to euphemize it, "permanently borrow." The three had accounted for over ninety percent of the town's crime problem. Of course, it was never major things that they stole, only small items. Girn did not have the heart for the life of crime, and Derlin had only partly so. So in the later escapades they usually convinced Tarthur to do things that, while they were fun, were legal at the same time. So to the boys, now almost men, he thought, must go his loyalty. Nothing was happening in Krendon anyway. Girn sensed that Tarthur would be needing his help soon. What then could he do to help them? They were many miles away. No, in actuality, they were not that far, and they might be in trouble. If only he could find some way to get to them.

Well he could walk, couldn't he? He was the fastest in the village of Krendon, so why not rejoin them? If they were coming back to Krendon, he could even meet them on the way. Then, once they saw that he was valuable, they could take him wherever they were going. Girn didn't really care where, as long as they went somewhere exciting. This plan sounded very good to Girn, who in fact needed no convincing at all. If anybody would have been watching him that night, they would have seen him enter Yrean's shop, and unprofessionally exit with a traveling cloak and a small sum of money, then head off to the North.

✳　　✳　　✳　　✳

Derlin was worried. Where were the mermen? He scanned the endless expanse of the sea, and saw nothing but a few shoals of rock, against which the water constantly lapped.

Then they came. It happened slowly at first. It seemed like the shoals were rising, or the water was descending, or a combination of the two, Derlin did not really know. Derlin had never seen a merperson before; subsequently he was totally awed and inadequately prepared for the spectacle that met his eyes. They rose slowly at first and soon he could differentiate between the males and females.

The mermen had a strong torso constructed almost all of muscles and scales, proceeding downward to an equally muscled fin. This fin had to have incredibly strong muscles in order to keep the top half of the merman above water. Derlin had no doubt that a weak and sickly merman could easily out swim the best human swimmer. The mermen had huge hairy chests, and burly arm muscles. They had long, flowing, golden hair, longer than even Dalin's. The mermaids, on the other hand were much like their counterparts in that they had strong fin muscles, but theirs were slightly smaller, partly because they were slimmer and had not as much weight to carry. They had exposed chests and hair nearly half the length of their bodies, and were very beautiful of face. The first bothered Derlin, (but not Tarthur.) In Krendon women did not go around exposing their chests, it was not proper. Although these ideas were firmly embedded in his head, he knew the mermaids did not care one whit about other people's preconceptions, if they even noticed.

"Hello there, Dalin," one of the mermen called out. He was slightly older than the rest, and his beard was graying. "We welcome you and your companions to our humble shoals."

By the way this man talked he had at least some authority, Tarthur predicted. He had never considered that they would not be able to see the merwizard, or that they might not be well received. In retrospect he probably should have, but now he was glad Dalin had a friend in good standing in the community.

"Truin, my old friend, it is good to see you again after all these years," Dalin replied as he bounded into the water, already beckoning for Tarthur and Derlin to follow. As the trio went into the chill, but rapidly warming water, Tarthur noticed that they only needed to swim a little way, and then they could walk on the shoals.

"Tell me Dalin, what brings you to these parts? I haven't seen you in years." Truin enthusiastically tried to start a conversation with Dalin. Dalin put a finger to his lips. We will talk, he implied, later. Then he said aloud with a wink. "Truin, my good friend, let your wife show these two boys how to make baubles."

With that a brown-haired mermaid took Tarthur and Derlin to a small room in the shoals. As they were being led away, Tarthur glanced up at Dalin, to see for what he thought was the last time, the man that had helped him get there. He would later be proven very wrong.

*   *   *   *

Dalin took a comfortable seat in Truin son of Thruin's shoal. Comfortable seats were at a minimum, (in fact there were only two more in all of the shoals) since only an occasional visitor wandered in. The merfolk were very hospitable when they got the chance, which was not often. Truin Thruinson, Dalin chuckled inwardly at the name, was of high rank in the colony. He was a general and had total control of the wartime forces, which could sort of be called a navy. He was also part of the Council of Elders of the village, which acted as a government. The merwizard himself headed this council. Dalin took off his hat, and pulled back his long hair. This helped reveal who he really was, exposing his slanted brows and pointed ears.

"So," Truin began, "what brings an elven prince like yourself to us in peacetime? I hope it is my wife's cooking and my *kokhor.*"

"I wish it were so, although you know *kokhor* is too strong and bitter for me." *Kokhor* was a potent beer-like drink that mermen made with seaweed and other ingredients. One bottle could make a man comatose for several days, but it just made the stronger mermen drunk. "No," Dalin replied shaking his head. "I am sorry to say it but our outlying villages are being pillaged by small monsters. They come in the night and steal the babies, mutilate children, and rape women, while killing men." Dalin's tone was grave.

"Still," Truin replied, not fully comprehending. "Your father has an army. Why doesn't he take care of it?"

"He has tried and many have been slain. But every time he kills some, more leap up to take their place. Also, there are trolls. We can take care of the situation for now, but I just thought you should know. We at least want you to be alert and ready for a quick mobilization of your troops. We fear the hand of Darhyn." The clouds grew darker, and a chill wind blew through the house.

"Do not say that name in here." Truin reprimanded. "Whenever you say his name he grows stronger, and his greatest weapon is fear. Thank you for coming to tell us this. If the Dark One is planning something, the whole world will be swept up in war and we would do well to begin preparations. The council meets tonight, and you may come make a full report. If they hear it from you, they may be persuaded to begin training of our army, which I must sadly admit has fallen a little bit during this era of peacetime."

Dalin agreed. "My father's army has fallen a little bit also. Yet, training has begun in earnest again. I know that our peoples are friends on the surface, but I was also sent to cement a formal defensive alliance if the Dark One attacks."

"I don't think a defensive alliance will be any problem. We certainly don't plan on starting any attacks, however. If you have sufficient proof that something serious is indeed happening, the council should easily agree to join up. Have you made an alliance with the humans yet?"

"We sent a messenger to them, but he hadn't returned by the time I left. I assume that they will behave likewise, however."

"Let's hope so," Truin mused. "We'll need our combined strength if it turns out to be what you think it is. I pray that it is nothing more than isolated bandits. Or, it is also likely that some overzealous goblin captain is uniting the tribes, and trying for Breshen. That happens every once in a while, and is probably what is happening this time. Still, it is better to be prepared for the worst. In any event, prepare a good speech my friend, and have some yourself some *ghtysa*."

Dalin nodded his agreement and left for the kitchen.

*   *   *   *

Tarthur and Derlin followed the mermaid for a few feet into a small, hollowed out shoal. It seemed to Tarthur that all of the shoals were about seventy-five percent under water, twenty-five above. This allowed them to spend the majority of their time in the water, but still breathe freely. Tarthur and Derlin took uncomfortable seats on some rocks and let their feet dangle in the water.

"Hello," the cheerful mermaid said, emerging from the water. "My name is Wera. I am Truin's wife." Tarthur remembered that Truin was the merman who Dalin had recognized. "I have heard that I am to show you the bauble craft?" She finished questioningly.

"No," Derlin said. Derlin knew it was now time to confide in someone the true reason why they were there. "Zelin has sent us to talk to the merwizard. It is a matter of grave importance."

"I'm afraid not," Wera replied. The shock of this remark cut into Tarthur and Derlin like a knife. They had never expected that this was possible.

"But, but...why?" Tarthur blurted out. After coming all this way to be turned down, they must see him in secret. In this he gained newfound resolve.

Wera's answer shattered his resolve. "Because Tustor, our merwizard, is dead."

"Dead!" The pair shouted at once. Then their whole mission had been a waste. They felt inwardly betrayed. What if Zelin had known all along? No, they conceded, he never would have sent them on this if he had known. Still...

"Who, what, where, when, why, and how?" Derlin immediately rattled off.

"I will tell you all I know," Wera sighed, overwhelmed by emotion. "Three nights ago Tustor retired to his study to sleep. He had a little too much *kokhor*, our strong drink, but he wasn't too drunk, because he is very strong, but also very old. Early two mornings ago, we all heard a shout of joy. When we arrived at his house," at this part in the narrative she paused, trying to ignore the tears that came flowing up. "He...he was dead, with a look of utmost pleasure on his face. I doubt even the Water Orb could raise him now." She finished the last of the narrative with a look of sadness, of great loss on her face.

Tarthur gave a long look to Derlin. They both knew what had happened two mornings ago. "Can you take us to his grave," Tarthur said, breaking the silence. At once he felt stupid for saying this. What good could they do now? They might as well return to Zelin and admit defeat. He almost retracted his question when the last thing Wera had said hit him. If he could read the spell then they might have a chance. A small chance, sure, but a chance nonetheless.

"Well, yes," she said, not fully comprehending. "I will take you there tonight."

The boys spent the day worrying and playing in the water. They had lunch of some kelp-like dish that was tasty. With the afternoon came rain. Derlin looked at Tarthur and knew he was planning something, but he didn't ask and Tarthur didn't tell.

The path to the Merwizard Tustor's shoal was not long. After ten minutes of half walking-half swimming that surely was not made for humans, they emerged on a small island of rock that protruded from the water surrounding it. Tarthur pulled out the scroll and to the equal amazement of Derlin and Wera began to read it aloud...

*   *   *   *

Lithar Lifehater was frustrated, and angry. He, the general of Queen Marhyn's armies, had been assigned to patrol duties. He was a man, a long time ago. He had undergone the black rituals of secrecy that Queen Marhyn demanded, and he had sworn his allegiance to her. In return she had promoted him to general of her armies and given him the power to feel magic, when it happened anywhere in the land. He had served her faithfully for a long time, and now he did not understand being sent on patrol with eight worthless goblins. (There were only seven now, he had killed one for falling behind in the grueling marches he had made them endure.)

In the black expanse of camp behind him, a dinner bell rang. A coarse, guttural, impersonation of the human tongue called out that it was time for their evening meal. Grudgingly he got up and received some slop that these goblins dared call food, and slapped the cook with the back of his hand for making a mockery of an edible substance. Grumbling, he took a couple bites, spat it out, and threw the half-full plate at the cowering cook. He missed, and the metal tin bounced harmlessly on a nearby rock. Lithar looked to the sky. Good, he thought, a storm. The black clouds rolled up, quickly blotting out the sun. Ah, he thought, this is a good sign. It is like when the armies of Marhyn will blot out the sun of Garkin. Lithar would never acknowledge Garkin as rightful king of all the land. As completely and swiftly as the clouds blotted out the sun, so too would Queen Marhyn's forces sweep across the plains to achieve complete and total victory. It began to rain. The sniveling goblins hurried to their tents, but Lithar did not move a muscle. It was then that he felt the Water Orb.

*   *   *   *

Far away, a man more powerful than Lithar, but with a much better disposition, sat and worried. He was too old for this to be happening again. The rain pattered harmlessly against his window. He hadn't been troubled much by the disappearance of Girn. Zelin could guess easily enough where he had gone. He felt a tingling at the edges of his being—something was about to happen. Zelin had seen many years roll by, and he was more sensitive than most to the workings of magic. Then it hit him so hard that he was knocked from his chair and went sliding across the floor. The strain of the magic being used was so powerful he had not experienced anything like it for quite some time. Then abruptly it faded, clearing from his mind, as if it had never been. In that brief moment, he knew. He had seen Tarthur use the Water Orb. Why? Tarthur, as far as Zelin knew, didn't even have control over the Orb. Had Tustor shown him how to use it? Had someone made him use it? And besides, the Water Orb was out of the world. Had Darhyn brought it back already? There were many questions to answer. He would call for Addyean. The knock on the door interrupted his thoughts. Zelin got up and went over to answer it. The flash of lightning illuminated the figure at his door.

"I'm sorry to bother you," Addyean the farmer-spy said as he shook the water off of his cloak. The resounding crack of thunder burst through the walls of the small house. "I'm sure it is nothing, but a minute ago I felt a tingling of something strange." Zelin nodded gravely. If Addyean had felt this then it was powerful indeed. True, the farmer-spy had only felt a tingling, and Zelin had gotten blasted because his magic sense was so much more fine-tuned, more acute. That meant many others had felt it, and the boys were now in great danger.

"What you felt," Zelin explained, "was Tarthur using the Water Orb. I am sure others have felt this also. I must journey now to the Eternal Vale and seek assistance from the Council of Gurus. They must be informed of these events that are happening if they are not already. Have you found any evidence against our Baron Ercrilla or are you going to make a favorable report as I predicted?"

This last sentence revealed the true reason Addyean, advisor to King Garkin and Royal Gardener, was in Krendon. "The only crime I find against him is having a son," Addyean admitted, referring to Mortimer.

"Good," Zelin acknowledged. "We will go to the king and tell him that the Water Orb is back, and advise him of all that has transpired here. Also, we will ask him to prepare his army, because if the Dark One is asleep…we could attack and regain Fire, and we can't let him have control over the Water Orb. I will accompany you to the castle, but then I will take my leave as I have more pressing business to attend to."

"What about the boys?" Addyean questioned. "They could be in trouble, and they might be the keys to this whole business. We can't just leave them to fend for themselves."

Zelin nodded. "You are right, but we both must be off to do our duties, and there is no one else here that I can trust to accompany them. We can trust that Tustor will guard them, though. In the flash of time, I saw them with a strong protector. I wish that we could wait for them to return to Krendon, but I will send a message to Tustor to have them rejoin us later. We need to get the elves involved in this too, since Breshen is so close to the Dark One."

Addyean thought about it for a moment, and then had to acquiesce. "It's settled, then. Let's hope they are safe."

With that the two hopped on their horses and rode off into the rain.

$$* \qquad * \qquad * \qquad *$$

In the northernmost corner of the Savannah plain, a storm always raged. Now was no exception. Nothing real could live here. In the summer the heat beat down, drying and cracking the earth, burning any feeble traveler who was brave enough, or stupid enough to come here. In the winter the cold burnt like dry ice and the snow fell. It was not white snow like that which fell elsewhere, but dirty brown snow, poisoning the earth. In the summer the snow did not melt, it evaporated, robbing the land of any moisture that it might inherit. There was no spring, no autumn. Only the extremes of winter and summer existed. Castle Rathskellar stood as a lone sentinel on this plain where nothing stood. The wind whistled through the all but abandoned fortress. A few black Dwarf sentries nervously paced the battlements. Far away a young boy used the Water Orb, and the Death Lord stirred in his grave.

   *   *   *   *

He was flying. Flying on the clouds far above the earth. He did not know what flying was like, he had never flown before. He could not describe this feeling, indeed he would never try; it was the kind of feeling that transcended explanation. Mere colorful words abruptly paled when used to inadequately describe this feeling. The wind raced past his sleek and powerful body. The cool moisture of the clouds replaced his sweat, flying this way took no energy. Power that was not his flooded through him, making him feel strength like he had not felt for a long time. He was traveling steadily southeast, a journey he had begun a while ago. Up in this euphoria time really didn't matter. He knew where he was going. He passed a small farmer's hut, but the people didn't even glance up at him. If they did, he was sure they would not see him anyway. Then he saw his destination jutting out from the surrounding forests. Higher than any mountains anywhere else in the world the sentinels of the Eternal Vale loomed before him. He knew if he tried to resist going there, he would have no choice. He and this vale were inexplicably bound to collide. It was not, of course that he did not wish to go there. It was the most peaceful place in all of Daranor, where the Creator took his own when their time in the world was up. It was set apart from the world, and no mortal could enter it.

Soon he caught his first glimpse of it. The gentle rolling slopes of the vale were bursting with green. He was glad to be home. Then, slowly, an intrusion came into him, wrapping itself around his body, alien, but soothing. The force became stronger and he recognized it. *Come to me, I need you*, it said. He didn't want to leave the vale, especially after he had gotten a glimpse of it now, but he knew this force was too strong to resist. Reluctantly, Tustor let go, and was dragged back to the earth.

✳   ✳   ✳   ✳

In the council chambers of the merfolk, Dalin waited impatiently, as the rain pattered on the window. Small drizzles flowed down the pane to collide with other small drops to form larger drops. This continued until the drops broke open when they abruptly met the windowsill. Around him sat the higher members of merfolk society. Directly to his left was a gruff, red-haired warrior named Forn. Forn was second in command of the armies of the merfolk, and sat directly to the right of Truin. Out of the thirty or so mermen seated in the chamber, Dalin recognized only these two and Chairman Eor. Chairman Eor was in charge of the council when it met to elect a new merwizard. The current merwizard was usually in charge of the council but whenever the merwizard could not meet, the chairman took over.

Dalin's tired body sunk into his comfortable chair even as his mind sunk deeper into thought. The conversation dragged on and he wished he could inform the council of the events around Breshen. Dalin, however, knew something of politics and he knew that his plea for help would be rejected back in his face before he could finish if he spoke before they chose a new merwizard. So he waited and the storm raged.

Dalin listened on for a few hours while members spoke for or against certain candidates. During the whole time though, he never heard Truin or Forn speak. It appeared this was not a military matter. Time dragged by, Dalin dozed off, and the storm outside raged.

It was the huge boom that caused the rumbling thunder to seem mediocre in comparison that finally jolted him awake awhile later. The merfolk's deliberations abruptly stopped and all heads looked up in confusion. For an instant Dalin thought that they were all under attack, but there was no time to wonder. Chairman Eor quickly dismissed the council and everyone headed out the door, or under it, in the case of the mermen. Truin grabbed a menacing looking pike and motioned for Dalin to arm himself similarly. The pike was too big for him, but fortunately he had brought his short sword. He tucked the leather scabbard into his belt and was off.

The pitter-patter of raindrops and the splash of Dalin's running mingled with the shouts of the excited mermen of the council to create quite a din. Dalin rushed past the inundated shoals of the residential section of the city in a vain effort to keep up with the fast moving mermen.

As he glanced to the side, he caught sight of frightened children and their mothers expectantly poking their heads out of windows, trying to catch a fleeting glimpse of what was happening. They stayed hidden in the recesses of their doorways, and were it not for Dalin's sharpened elven senses he would have not seen them at all. Not that merfolk were a cowardly race, indeed far from it, but the combination of their revered leader's death and these unexpected circumstances had made them cautious.

What Dalin saw as he crested the rise would never leave him. He could never have guessed it would happen, or even could happen. Derlin and Wera stood flanking a figure that Dalin would never have believed to be Tarthur. He was surrounded by an aura of fiercely glowing white light and even floating a few inches off the ground. Dalin could not even begin to describe the exhilaration he saw in the other's eyes. Tarthur seemed only partially in control of himself, he was lashing out in a strange tongue in words, or sounds rather, that transcended understanding. Dalin reached out to stop him, but the touch sent a searing pain through his arm. He tumbled to the ground and the impact forced him to look down.

Deep within Tustor's watery grave the water swirled and lurched. Soon bubbles reached the surface and the water churned more rapidly. Then the middle started to swirl. Faster and faster it swirled, the whirlpool growing increasingly bigger. The whirlpool was now a few feet across, and growing rapidly. It seemed that the water was draining from the pool and joining the whirlpool. A merman appeared in the center of the maelstrom. Beams of light were dancing across the center of the tempest. Dalin saw that this merman was slightly bigger than the rest but was still turned away from the now enlarged crowd of onlookers, so none could discern his identity. The wind whipped Dalin's hair about his head and he felt the cool water strike his face. It was still raining, he thought distantly.

Then with a jerk the merman was brought around to face the crowd and the collective gasp of excitement mingled with amazement reverberated throughout the entire shoals. Tarthur collapsed into the arms of Derlin and Dalin almost fainted as well. Dalin was staring straight into the eyes of Tustor, the now revived merwizard.

Then his arm started to throb and his knees turned to water. This time he did faint. The joyous cries of the mermen were the last sounds he heard as he went spiraling into the void.

CHAPTER 3

▼

A REALLY MEAN GUY

When Tarthur awoke, he was laying in a bed with fresh sheets. A bouquet of sea flowers whose aroma drifted up to his nose reminded him of where he was. Tarthur groaned. He had taken a stupid chance, he realized. (Just how stupid of a chance he would realize soon.) But it had all paid off. Tarthur assumed the merman he had raised was the merwizard. No, he thought, he knew it was the merwizard. The understanding he had seen in those all-knowing eyes had told him this was so.

But he had seen something else in those eyes as well. Power? There certainly was power there, but that was not it. Fear then? It certainly looked like fear, but what would one so obviously loved and empowered as the merwizard have to fear? Then Tarthur realized it was sorrow, sorrow at not being able to depart peacefully. Tarthur had never realized that someone would not like to be resurrected. Being young, he naturally believed that people would want to live forever.

Tarthur looked down and found a tightly wrapped bandage on his arm. It was wrapped maybe a little too tightly, his fingers were turning purple. As he started to slowly unwrap the bandage, the door opened and Dalin walked in. Tarthur could tell he was a little bit angry.

"Well," he said. "Do you have any idea what you just did?"

"Aaa…no?" Tarthur guessed.

"I think you do," Dalin pressed, "and I want to know who you really are." It was not a question.

"I already told you," Tarthur replied, trying to sound as firm and commanding as Dalin, but somehow falling a little short. He didn't owe Dalin anything. Well, that wasn't quite true, Dalin had helped him get there and he seemed like a nice person. But, he had no right to walk in angrily like that. Tarthur sat up.

"Oh, right," Dalin said. "Then Wera taught you how to make baubles?"

"Yes," Tarthur said uneasily.

"So what is the first thing you do?" Dalin asked.

"Um…I'm only supposed to tell that to Zelin," Tarthur stammered out lamely, but defiantly. Dalin's backhand hit him so hard and unexpectedly that he was knocked to the floor.

"You fool!" Dalin lashed out. "Zelin knows how to make baubles. He also knows that only the mermen can use them. I want you to tell me who you are and what you are doing here right now!"

Dalin knew he was taking a big chance. Suppose this young boy sorcerer blasted him to ashes right now for his insult. Surely this was no mere boy. Dalin had seen the look in his eyes when he had used his magic. This boy had power. Could someone else have shifted his form to that of this boy? Perhaps it was someone intent on killing Dalin and preventing him from cementing an alliance with the merfolk? No, he thought. If that were the case, he probably would have killed Dalin already in the forest. Besides, this boy has a distinct personality and seems not to be in control of the magic. That is why Dalin slapped him, but he knew he must be so careful.

"Alright," Tarthur said. He was still in shock. He knew that information was very valuable, and to give some away to someone you didn't trust was dangerous, and stupid. But, Tarthur realized, if he wanted this trust to happen, he needed to tell Dalin at least a little, but he would learn something from him too.

"My name is Tarthur. My friend's name is Derlin. We live in the town of Krendon, in the Hawk Mountains."

"Yes," Dalin said. "I know where it is."

"Before I tell you more," Tarthur probed. "I want you to tell me why you are here, and something about yourself."

"If I tell you about myself, and a secret, and give you proof of this secret, will you tell me who you *really* are?"

"Yes," Tarthur said, this time without hesitation.

"My name is Dalin. I have some standing in my community as a military leader. I came here to visit my old friend Truin." It wasn't a lie, Dalin thought.

"And your secret," Tarthur asked.

Dalin took off his hat and tossed his long hair back. Tarthur noticed that his brows were slightly slanted and his ears seemed rather pointy. "I am an elf," he finished simply.

Tarthur was astonished. He had never seen a real elf before, only in drawings and of course, he had heard all sorts of stories about them, their ability to hide in the woods forever, and their famous archery. The longbow! Dalin had carried a longbow with him. Tarthur knew this was indeed a secret. Neither he nor Derlin would have guessed this, but the more Tarthur looked at him, the more he seemed to fit the profile. He was a military leader also. Tarthur knew from this moment on he would need this person's trust and help.

"Can I ask you a question?" Tarthur asked.

"Yes," Dalin replied.

"Why do you keep it a secret?"

"Usually men and elves live in harmony, but elves have been living in seclusion lately. And of course, you know that there are many human legends about the elves.

"Okay," Tarthur said firmly. "A few days ago I had a dream. In this dream, I did something great, and terrible. I battled monsters out of my worst nightmares, even the Death Lord himself. I copied some strange words onto a scroll. Zelin instructed Derlin and me to come here and talk to the merwizard about this."

"What else did you do in your dream?" Dalin pried, somehow relaxed now.

"When I read the scroll, huge water waves came crashing down on everyone, but I was still dry. I guess because it was water Zelin sent us to come up here and talk to the merwizard."

With that, Tarthur realized that he still hadn't completed his task, and rose and dressed himself to go find Tustor. As they were leaving the room, Dalin couldn't help feeling a little awkward. Tarthur's story sounded farfetched—still though, it could very well be true.

Tarthur blinked as he stepped out into the glistening sun. The day was warm and the autumn rays felt good on his face. The gentle rolling of the tide caressed his ankles as he walked behind Dalin on the route to Tustor's shoal. He seemed to walk a little taller now, and the mermen treated him with a little more respect. He could sense it in the way that they smiled at him, in their gentle "hellos" and their warm pats on the shoulder. He could see that he was not just accepted here, but admired and respected as well.

Tustor the merwizard's shoal had four occupants who rose to greet them when they arrived. Truin shook Tarthur's hand quite firmly and motioned them to the last two comfortable seats in the shoals. (Derlin was occupying the other one.)

The fourth person, a maid pouring *kokhor* for Tustor and Truin, quickly finished and left as Tustor waved toward the door in dismissal.

"Well, Tarthur, it looks like you have stumbled onto something quite big," Tustor said breaking the ice. It was the first time that Tarthur had heard him speak. The voice was strong and manly, but not overly gruff. Instead, it had more of a firm gentleness to it. "I will be honest with you," Tustor said. "You need not worry; this house is safe from prying ears." Tarthur liked the voice. It commanded honesty, but mostly it just commanded. Tarthur was glad Tustor was on his side.

"Well," Derlin said with a hint of pride, and laughter, "Zelin told us to come talk to you and we couldn't let something as small as you being dead interfere with us."

"Ah yes," Tustor said with a chuckle. "But you were very lucky. You see, Tarthur, Derlin explained everything that has happened on your trip so far; yes, everything. I must congratulate you on that pie, nice job. I believe the power you wield is sufficiently less than you believe. The Death Lord has the power to call the spirits of people who do not absolutely reject him and talk to them or use some of his power on them."

"Are you saying that I am one of his own, because he was able to contact me?" Tarthur was incredulous.

"Since the Death Lord has not been around for a long time, the races have all but forgotten about him. In a sense, you have just never been taught better. Then again, perhaps he thought that he could persuade you to become one of his. In any event, we will probably never know. What you have found is just the spell controlling the Water Orb, and nothing else. I am guessing that you were able to use the spell to control the Orb because the Water Orb really is in the Death Lord's possession."

Tarthur's face betrayed puzzlement "But why me? Of all the people in the world, why did he call me?"

Tustor shrugged. "We may never know for sure. It could have just been random. Perhaps we will find out some day."

"I'm sure you could go ask the Death Lord if you wanted to," Dalin broke in with a smile that hinted at his cleverness.

"Good idea," Derlin carried the joke further. "But, why don't you go ask him for us, Dalin. I'm sure he'd answer you. And if he didn't, you could always tickle him until he had no choice but to answer!"

Tustor's hand attempted to silence the four others, who were now rolling with laughter. You know how it is with laughter. Once one person has it, others catch it very easily. Soon everyone is laughing at the stupidest things, whether or not they are funny. The effects, of course, are magnified incredibly when one is drunk, and there had been no lack of festivities the previous night. Derlin and Dalin had each managed to drink a thimbleful of *kokhor,* while Truin had consumed several gallons. The effects of *kokhor* are far reaching and usually last into the next morning, with the hangover occurring sometime that afternoon. Soon, however, Tustor was back in control and the jokes were quickly forgotten.

"Zelin has probably told you this already—the mermen are incredibly close to the water, we know all that happens within it. As their leader, I feel this pull more strongly than the others. I am sure this was the only reason why you were able to resurrect me," Tustor finished, a hint of sadness in his voice.

Dalin looked grave. "My people have long thought the Water Orb to be out of the world, but now if it appears the Death Lord has brought it back, or is about to, then I must bring word to them."

"King Garkin must be warned also," Derlin broke in.

"Right," commented Tustor. "You three will go first to Breshen, and then to King Garkin. Tell them to make sure that their troops are ready to fight. I'm not saying that they need to mobilize quite yet, it would be better if they did, but I fear many will not listen. At least make sure that all soldiers are in training and tell them to start stockpiling food and weapons. Border patrols are also a necessity. We will be ready for him when he comes this time. There is no need for you two to return to Krendon. I have sensed Zelin, and I am sure that he knows of the events transpiring here. In fact, I can feel his life-force already moving towards the capital. That is also why your first priority must be to travel to Breshen."

"Since time will be of the essence, I suggest you leave tomorrow, at first light, or before, if you want to see another sunrise," Truin added. "I will see to it personally that all of the provisions you will need will be packed for you."

"If time is important," questioned Derlin, "why don't we leave now?"

At Derlin's foolish question all the tension left the room, and none laughed harder than Tustor. Slapping Derlin playfully on the back, he simply replied "My friend, you seem to have forgotten that this afternoon you will be feeling the effects of our *kokhor.* I am sure you will be in no condition to travel. Besides, Tarthur needs all the rest he can get." With that, the four left the room, a grin upon the mouth of everyone who knew about a *kokhor* hangover.

That afternoon Tarthur went to look in on Derlin and talk to him about everything that had been happening. A pitiful sight greeted his eyes; Derlin and

Dalin were moaning with such force that Tarthur could have sworn they were dying. (Indeed, Derlin and Dalin did feel like they were dying.) The moaning was interrupted only long enough for one or the other of them to run to the side and vomit in an already filling bucket. Tarthur laughed. Now he could see what was funny about them traveling in such a state.

Wera gracefully swam into the room. "I brought some more herbs for you. Don't worry, the hangover will only last for another hour or so."

"An hour," groaned Derlin. "I'll be dead in an hour."

"Don't worry, my friend. While these hangovers are painful, they are usually not lethal. You see, Tarthur, we have some herbal medicines that can reduce the length of a hangover, but nothing to reduce the severity."

"Let's see," mused Tarthur. "You have a drink that is not lethal but causes severe hangovers, for which there are no cures, but which are still only temporary." His thoughts went instantly to Morty. Now here was going to be a good joke. He could even use this one a few times. "Do you think that perhaps I could have some of that stuff?"

"Certainly," Wera replied. "Truin will give you a bit of his store if you ask him." With this Tarthur left his friends to their plaintive wailing, a smile on his face.

That night, it rained again. It seemed like it rained most nights here. (Tarthur didn't know it, but fall was the rainy season far out to sea, and the shoals of the merfolk received a lot of rain.)

Tarthur knew he should be sleeping. He was in Truin's shoal. As he gazed beside him, he saw Derlin and Dalin sleeping fitfully. His friends bore no resemblance to people who have had a *kokhor* hangover recently.

It was then that he started thinking about Tustor, and what he had seen in his eyes. How could someone as beloved as Tustor want to die? Could Tustor be mad at him? Tarthur knew what he had to do. He got up, laced up his boots, grabbed his cloak, and stepped into the rain. Derlin woke briefly to see Tarthur vanish out the door.

The rain pattered softly on the roof of the dimly lit study. The waves slowly lapped at the base of the house. The waves were growing in strength by the constant infusion of rain into the ocean. Inside, a single oil lamp burned in some vain attempt to keep out the darkness, whose oppressive presence filled the night. The house was dry inside, and a lone figure sat diligently writing on some parchment. The scratching of his quill pen as it made marks of ink on the paper was the only sound to accompany the softly falling rain.

Tustor sighed, he knew it was his job to protect his people, but he could not shake the vision of the Eternal Vale that he had seen. He had seen his family, long since dead and departed, given back to the sea. He had seen heroes of the old tales, and he had felt, in that one instant, a deeper sense of belonging than he had ever felt before in his life. He knew that as long as he lived he would always yearn for that place, yearn to be home.

Tustor felt the draft of cool air blow in and he looked up from the messages he was writing. Tustor knew who the dark figure at his door was. The flash of lightning confirmed his suspicions. Tarthur shook the water from the cloak Yrean had made and slowly hung it on a nail protruding from the wall. Tarthur stood still, unsure about how to proceed. Tustor waited for Tarthur to speak. The only sound was the resounding boom of thunder that echoed throughout the shoals.

Finally Tustor spoke, dropping all pretenses. "Why did you come here tonight?"

Tarthur felt like a child compared to this being of great learning and power. "I came to apologize."

Tustor chuckled, already knowing the answer. "Whatever for?"

"I don't know," Tarthur said. "When I brought you back you just seemed so sad."

Tustor nodded. "I know you can never understand. No one who has not been there can understand. Have you ever heard of the Eternal Vale?"

Tarthur nodded, understanding slowly dawning on his face. "Where the Creator takes all of his own after their time in the world is up?"

"Yes, that is it. No one who enters it can ever come back, save by some great magic. It is a place that transcends understanding. Your heart would burst with pure joy if you had but set foot in it once. The gurus of the Eternal Vale live close to it because it is a place of great joy, and of greater power. It is the very heart of the world."

"When a person's time in this world is up, the Creator separates their soul from their body and starts it on a journey to the Vale, a journey home. When you used the spell the first time I was so overcome with the pure joy of it that my frail old body just could not take it."

Tarthur thought Tustor's body looked a great many things, but frail and old were not two of them. "So, you are saying that I killed you?" Tarthur asked, puzzled.

"No," Tustor chuckled. "It was more from old age than anything. I was almost to the Vale when you called me. In fact, I even saw a little inside it..." Tustor trailed off.

"So," Tarthur said softly, the realization hitting him. "You did not want to come back, but you did anyway because you knew your people would need you in the coming struggle."

"You have great insight for a boy of your limited training and travels. Perhaps you are one of the few given the power to see into people's hearts. It is a great blessing, and a great burden."

Tarthur smiled, admiration in his eyes. "I don't think so."

Tarthur picked up his cloak and started for the door. "I am sure this doesn't mean much coming from a common boy like me to a great wizard like you, but I just want you to know I really appreciate what you gave up, and all of your people, if they could, would love you even more. All of my life I will look up to you and respect you."

Tustor smiled, and nodded. "Thank you."

It was still dark when the door opened, but Derlin was already up and dressed, ready for the day's adventure. "Hello, Dalin," he greeted. "I'll wake Tarthur."

Tarthur moaned as Derlin shook him vigorously. Once awake however, he dressed quickly into his traveling clothes and then all three consumed vast quantities of the kelp-like dish that the merfolk eat with smoked fish for breakfast. Truin was there with Wera to send them off. Tustor was there also with a pile of dispatches he had been writing to various leaders throughout the world. He looked to Tarthur as if he did not get much sleep, if any. Several of the members of the merfolk community who were up at this hour were also there to wish them well in their journeys. They all had warm smiles on their faces and shook hands with the three travelers, admiration in their eyes.

Truin stepped forward and withdrew a small flask of *kokhor*. "Take this, Tarthur. I have only known you for a few days, but I imagine you to be a man of maybe a little too much courage and a great trickster. Be careful with this *kokhor*, and if it is for a joke please use it well."

"I will, Truin. I have a snooty little son of a nobleman in mind for this."

Truin and Dalin embraced each other. "My friend," said the elf prince, "I am sorry this visit was filled with so much commotion. I look to the time when I will be able to make a peaceful visit to enjoy Wera's cooking. I promise you we will be strong. We will destroy the fiend this time."

Truin's nod was stern. "You can count on the support of the merfolk."

Tustor handed Dalin a knapsack of dispatches. "You'd better be going if you don't want to miss the sunrise."

As Tarthur waved to the group of mermen, he suddenly felt sad that he could not stay longer. It was strange, he thought, that they lived this close and nobody ever traveled between the two communities. He made a silent promise to himself that as soon as he had free time he would come and make better relations between them.

Starting up the hill away from the shoals, Tarthur noticed a group of three horses in a small grove of trees. One of them was Dalin's. Tarthur pointed to the spot questioningly.

"You didn't expect them to send us on a trip of this importance on foot, did you?" Dalin asked, frowning.

"Well, not really," Tarthur stammered.

"But where did mermen get horses?" Derlin was confused.

Dalin raised his eyebrows in a knowing smile. "Maybe you will find out some-day."

Tarthur and Derlin were amazed as they walked up to the mounts. In Krendon, it was a great privilege to be able to ride. Only the noblemen and a few of the richer master craftsmen were able to afford a horse. Tarthur looked over his horse. He was pitch black and looked to be very strong. Being the apprentice to the blacksmith, Tarthur naturally looked down to check his shoes. "Look, Derlin. These shoes are an excellent fit." He had, after all, learned at least a few things during his apprenticeship.

"You are right, Tarthur," commented Derlin. "My horse also has good shoes." Derlin's horse was brown and white, and like all of them, had an expensive leather saddle.

The boys mounted up, albeit a little clumsily, and trotted off after Dalin, who had already started up the incline. The clip-clop of the horses' hooves on the hard ground was the only sound that permeated the chill pre-dawn stillness.

After they had been riding for a few minutes, Dalin called a halt and turned his mount. Tarthur looked down and again saw the impassable plain stretching before them. At the end of this plain Tarthur saw a gray area. Soon this gray area started to expand, and the first streaks of light started sparkling over the water. Then more streaks joined them, reflecting light everywhere. Already the first stray rays of light were dancing across the water. Soon the sun had risen fully above the waves, and the sight was a wonder to behold.

"Wow," Derlin said, cutting in on his thoughts. "This truly is amazing, yet I can't seem to shake the feeling that it is not quite as special as the first time."

He is right, Tarthur realized. Maybe it was that there were no merfolk to welcome them, or maybe it was because of the grim things he knew now that he had not before, or maybe the sun was just not as bright today…

"You are very astute, Derlin," Dalin remarked.

Pondering his words, the three rode off into the fog, which was already starting to burn off under the warming sun.

That night they pitched camp in the forest. Without suitable grazing area in the vicinity, the horses were forced to eat a little of the oats that had been provided to them by the merfolk. While the horses enjoyed the oats, Tarthur hoped they didn't eat all the food that was meant for the people. The heavy vegetation had also slowed them considerably, and if it had not been for Dalin's ability to find seemingly invisible trails, Tarthur was sure they would have not progressed very much. After that they had set up the tents and made a fire ring. (Dalin was at least a little impressed that they knew how to camp.) After they had eaten their dinner of dried fish and bread, and washed it down with spring water, Dalin spoke up. "Have you boys heard the story of Tivu, the Cloudwalker?"

Tarthur looked up from a stick he was playing with in the fire and shook his head. Derlin confirmed his answer by shaking his head also, so Dalin decided to begin.

"A very long time ago, in the Rune Mountains, there lived a group of wise sages who dedicated their lives to becoming one with the Power of Air. It is said, when they have been studying for a century, they can change their form to that of an eagle, and they can fly with them. They also studied with the eagles who lived there, who were very wise and could speak the languages of other creatures. At that time the Power of Air was contained in a wing feather of Firewing, who is said to have been the first creature to understand the Power of Air, long before Frehu contained the elements. The sages are also credited with the forging of the Rune Sword, which has some of their magical properties. Now that power is lost to the world. When the sages have been studying for sufficient time to become a grandmaster, they no longer have need of bodies to take them places, as they can simply fuse their minds with the air and use it to carry them where they wish to go.

Now there was a certain boy among them, Tivu was his name. He loved the air. He was wholeheartedly dedicated to his purpose. Indeed, it seemed as if he had more birds as friends than people. When he was six, he was better than students in their early twenties. Young Tivu became somewhat of a favorite of the aging grandmaster. When Tivu was twenty, it seemed to the rest that the old grandmaster had chosen his successor. It was also then that the grandmaster made a fatal mistake. He began taking Tivu on flights with him. He would bind Tivu's soul with his own and fly over the land. One day, as they were flying east, the grandmaster flew a little too far, and they caught sight of the Eternal Vale.

"What is that place of great beauty and power?" Tivu asked his instructor.

"That is the Eternal Vale," the grandmaster replied. "Do you not know of it?"

"Yes," replied Tivu, awestruck. "I just never thought a place of such unspeakable majesty existed."

The grandmaster sadly turned around. "We grandmasters of the air are one of the few allowed to enter and leave relatively freely. All the more reason you should become one," he finished, helping the ambition he knew needed no help.

After that day, Tivu plunged deeper into his studies than before, if such a feat was possible. He frequently forgot to eat, or even sleep, so consumed was he by the vision he saw before him. Three years later, when he was only twenty-three, Tivu received the power to turn into an eagle. It was a good thing too. The old grandmaster was becoming older, and it was said he might die in nearly half a century. But the vision of the vale was haunting him. One day, he devised a plan. He knew he could never go into the Eternal Vale while he was not a grandmaster. He also knew he could not wait that long. So one day, while it was still early, he walked a little down the mountain. He had noticed how the clouds formed there every day. He started to walk on them. A normal person would have fallen right through, but not Tivu. It took all of Tivu's power to control the clouds, and his strength was draining quickly. Fortunately for him, Tivu was stubborn. He used sheer force of will to keep himself afloat. Soon he was in sight of that which no mortal should see, the Eternal Vale. Naturally, the grandmaster sensed what was wrong, and flew with the speed of wind to go get him. But Tivu was already too far. By the time the grandmaster had gotten there, Tivu had lost control, and he fell to the earth. So entranced was he by the vision that he had seen, he could not even think to turn himself into an eagle. As he was about to hit the rocky mountains below him, the grandmaster sent a surge of all of his power to save him. The power caught Tivu as he was dashed against the rocks. Tivu's body died, but the grandmaster's magic prevented his soul from being released. The aging grandmaster had overexerted himself, and there was no one with sufficient healing powers to help him. Thus, the Power of Air was lost to the world, for the grandmaster had died without giving his secrets to anyone."

"But what happened to Tivu?" Tarthur questioned.

"That is the saddest part of all. With his body not able to give up his soul, he is technically still alive, and cannot enter the Eternal Vale, until one from this world goes in before him. It is said that he sleeps by the entrance, until the One is born."

"I thought the only way to get in there was to die," Derlin spoke up, confused.

"There is one more entrance, a wall of glass. One can enter through this wall, and thus pass freely between sides."

The old gleam of adventure lit Tarthur's eyes, as he remembered what Tustor had told him. "I'd like to see if I could enter," he ventured, then amended as Dalin glanced his way, "that is, if we are going there."

"I don't really think you want to try," Dalin said softly. "Those who try to enter, and cannot, face a peril worse than death. They slowly go mad, and are tormented until they die. I had a friend once…but that is a story for another night. We should all be turning in, as we have a long day's journey tomorrow."

That night, Tarthur fell almost immediately asleep. Before doing so, however, he couldn't shake the feeling that there were some very important lessons in the story of Tivu, and he truly felt sorry for him.

Derlin woke the next morning hardly feeling any effects of the hangover. As he stretched and got up, he noticed that Dalin had already made a fire and was cooking some coffee and eggs. Derlin noted with satisfaction that the eggs were the good kind, the ones with cheese and peppers and potatoes and milk in them. Dalin smiled as Derlin met his eye. "Since we will be traveling fast, I didn't want to burden the horses with a lot of food, so I decided we might as well eat it now."

"Excellent idea," Tarthur contributed as he came to stand behind Derlin. Tarthur was one to always enjoy good meals. "Now I know what Morty feels like always getting served every day, instead of having to do the serving all the time like us."

"I'll allow you to cook dinner tonight then," Dalin replied with a smile. "Since you have so much practice, it should be good."

"Derlin will cook lunch then?" Tarthur's question came out even though he hadn't really wanted it to.

"There are many more important things to think of than food," Dalin chided mildly. "But if you must know, we can stop and eat a couple of biscuits as soon as we reach the end of the forest."

Dalin started to pack up camp as Tarthur and Derlin scrubbed the tin dishes. They were now working more efficiently together, and in no time the horses were saddled and ready to go. As they were riding along Derlin started to think that things were going pretty well, and they would be talking with the elves in just a few days. Derlin had never imagined that they would meet elves. With their force alert and ready, the king could be warned, and soon they would be ready for the Death Lord when he came. They would steal the Water Orb, now that Tarthur had the power to control it, and there would be a golden age of peace and prosperity that even the Dark One could not ruin. Right at that instant, however, he was proven very wrong.

Dalin never saw what hit him. The goblin's ill-timed attack, however, cost him his life. Had he waited for the proper signal, all three of the riders could have been subdued without trouble, but as it was, he now lay dying with Tarthur's sword protruding from his chest. Tarthur wrenched the dripping blade free and brought the flat down on another's head, saving Derlin a considerable amount of pain, as the latter was still in shock. Once alerted, however, Derlin sprang into action, as his horse crushed another attacker's skull. Years of being friends had taught Tarthur and Derlin many things, and one of these was how to fight together. Granted, they were not superb warriors, but both had good instincts, and more than a few skills. They were protecting each other's backs as two more goblins fell. There were only two goblins left, and they seemed to be more cautious now, waiting for something.

Their leader stepped out of the brush, catching Tarthur and Derlin off guard. What was a man doing with these goblins? Raising his hand toward the boys, he started to mumble something. Immediately, their limbs started to feel heavy, and time seemed to go in slow motion. Tarthur's sword felt like it weighed about a thousand pounds. The friends toppled from their horses, bags of stones unable to move.

The leader smiled. He knew he had the right one. Cursing something at the goblins, he made a gesture at the boys and another at their horses. The ambush had been good planning, and his queen would be pleased. Grinning, Lithar Lifehater scooped up Dalin's body and shoved it on his horse.

CHAPTER 4

▼

BUREAUCRACY

"Well, I'm sure it is not all that bad," Warren said, attempting to lead the immovable Zelin and Addyean out of the room. "You know his majesty is not feeling well, and he has many pressing matters to attend to." Warren's face lit up as if the brilliant idea had just occurred to him. "Perhaps you could come back tomorrow, his majesty will be more rested and…"

"If we could just see him for a moment," Addyean interjected. "I'm sure he would be well pleased to hear what I have to say. As I've already explained, my position as royal spy warrants certain…"

Warren's tone was bureaucratic. "I have told you there is no record of you being any more than royal gardener, and until I find otherwise, I have no choice but to…"

"You were not even employed here when I left. Just talk to the king and he will admit me. I promise."

"King Garkin is ill today, and he is asleep. But I give you my word of honor as chancellor to the king that I will tell him of you and let him decide whether or not to admit you when he awakes."

"Make sure you do," Zelin spoke for the first time, seriousness in his voice. "Or we may all be very sorry."

Addyean and Zelin got up and walked into the hallway, closing the door behind them. Not until they were very far away did the sound start. It was quiet at first, and hesitant. It slowly gained in frequency and volume, and then it turned hysterical and shrill to the ears. It was the sound of Warren laughing.

Warren's laughter had died down to a chuckle by the time he had walked to his secret basement. Those trusting fools! It had taken all he could do to not explode with laughter when the old man had talked. "Make sure you do, or we may all be very sorry," Warren said with mock seriousness, a parody of the old man's facial expression. He was happy that he had delayed them until tomorrow. Tomorrow, so far away…Warren could devise a million ways to get the ailing king out of the castle by tomorrow. Then the elated man simply lay down on the couch and went to sleep.

The dreams had all started about two years ago. Back then, Warren had been a poor farmer's son, and a farmer himself. Warren, who had always been a little on the selfish side, was feeling sorry for his state of existence one particular day. He was doomed to be a farmer, and a poor one at that, as his father had never been particularly thrifty. Combined with that, his land never was very good in the first place, and there was a drought in the country. While in this state of mind, Warren lay down in a cornfield, and he came to Warren. He always comes to those crying out against their lot in life, and willing to give anything to change it. The Death Lord Darhyn, while his body was in a comatose form, was still able to send out his mind, to choose some who could do his bidding. Darhyn, still in control of the Water Orb, promised to make Warren great. He foresaw that Warren's unrestrained ambition could be a powerful tool, free for Darhyn to mold and temper to use to his own ends. Darhyn had sent the rain then, showing his power over the Water Orb. But the rain had only come to Warren's fields. Warren's now comparatively fertile land produced twenty times as much as farms around it. Soon Warren was in control of the whole region. Through more dreams, the Death Lord had revealed to Warren what to do and say, as he climbed his way through the king's court. And now to be king! Such a thing was greater than…and then the dream started.

Rising through the blackness of Warren's mind, a shapeless shape began to emerge. The formless black spoke:

"*Warren, I am pleased*," the face inside the faceless cowl said. "*You have handled yourself well today.*"

Warren's face twisted into a crude smile. It was not often that his master gave him praise. The dark shape he smiled at was only visible because it seemed to swallow up the light around it. The next time he spoke, Warren was filled with a dread chill. The words were not spoken, they were just felt. It seemed to Warren that every time he met with his terrible master, he learned something new and frightening about him. Warren sometimes thought he was doing it just to remind him who the power was. Ah, but soon, things would change.

"It has come time for there to be a new king over the world. Do you know who that king will be?" The Death Lord's question was ridiculous, yet he asked it anyway.

"I believe it will be me lord," Warren said without flinching.

"Yes. This is how you will accomplish it. Tonight, you will give a vial of poison to the king. This poison will make him deathly ill for three days, and then he will die a rather unpleasant death. Tomorrow morning, early, you will get all of the important and trusted members of the Council and take them with you on your journey. You will travel to the healing spring at Treshin. It is at least a five-day trip if you have to travel slowly because of the ailing king. Since you and all of the other people capable of making decisions will be away, my enemies will not be able to begin a mobilization."

Warren nearly squealed with delight. "That is brilliant, master."

Darhyn continued, annoyed. *"There is more. The poison is made so right before he dies, the last person he sees will seem glorified and absolved of all faults. That person will be you. When he sees you thus, he will proclaim you king. As King Warren, you will not only delay the mobilization, you will stop it entirely. My armies will sweep over the land, and soon you will rule over all other races also. Now, to make that poison, first you take a pinch of fireweed…"*

*   *   *   *

"What are we going to do now?!" Addyean was irate. They had just been told that King Garkin had left and was on important matters of state. The guard who had thus informed them had also said that the king was attending to these matters indefinitely, and might not be back for quite some time. Addyean of course had not believed him until Zelin had used his powers to ascertain that the man was indeed telling the truth.

"I sense some danger," was Zelin's reply. "But as I know neither what is wrong nor how to fix it, I am not exactly sure what I can do."

"Well, one thing is for sure, we can't just do nothing, which is what we are doing now. We need to decide on some course of action. Time is not critical yet, but by waiting, we are losing our advantage."

Zelin nodded. "I agree. I must seek out the gurus that live in the Eternal Vale. I hope they will be able to offer some aid. Meanwhile, you must make contact with King Garkin. I know he is a good man. He will not deny help, but he will have to see the danger it poses to his kingdom."

Addyean's question made Zelin ponder. "But how will I find him?"

"I will probe the guard's mind." Zelin stood still for a minute, his concentration growing. A crimson ray of light that Addyean knew to be Zelin's life-force suddenly streaked from his temples and flew down the hallway. Addyean caught the lifeless body as it slumped to the floor. He waited, scarcely daring to draw a breath. If Zelin lost control of himself, or if the soldier's mind was too strong, Zelin could very easily die. Addyean knew that the risk was much reduced for one of Zelin's abilities, but still, you never knew…and to lose Zelin, one of the last of the old gurus still living in the world…

The crimson streak arced back into the room, and straight to Zelin's forehead. Within seconds, his fingers and limbs started to warm up and regain their color. Zelin coughed, and soon was sitting up by himself. He finally spoke. "The guard actually believes they are on state business. He saw a party of about fifteen or twenty men riding out early this morning. He doesn't recollect seeing the king, but it was still dark, so his vision was probably impaired. They were heading east with a little southward twinge. You should be able to catch up and observe them within a day as they were traveling slowly."

"So it is a parting then?" Addyean said the last with a sad but wistful tone.

"Yes. I will try to meet you after I have secured help. Do not fail."

Addyean's stance was so firm, it could have been chiseled out of pure stone. "I will not."

✳   ✳   ✳   ✳

The captives were not treated badly according to their captor's standards, but to them they were being manhandled. Although, Tarthur reflected, if we are their captives, they probably don't really care what we think. Since the first day, they had been tied to a saddle for the first few hours of each day. After they were fed a barely nourishing lunch, they were made to walk until after sundown. This had been going on for nearly three weeks, and when he could think clearly, which was rare, Tarthur realized they had been making good time going to wherever they were going. And Tarthur was not at all sure that he wanted to go there. All these thoughts passed before Tarthur as he was eating a kind of hard bread for his lunch. He wasn't exactly sure what kind of bread it was, it was filled with raisins and some grains he had never seen before. He assumed that it must be nourishing, because it was all that was keeping him going.

"What is this bread called?" Tarthur hollered to the grim, black clothed man. Tarthur didn't really want to talk to him, but anything was better then this grim monotony he faced every day.

"It is *nishei*. And I told you not to ask any more questions. Don't you remember?"

Actually, Tarthur did not remember. He remembered very little during these past few days.

"So where are we going?" Tarthur liked irritating the evil man. Tarthur could tell he was evil, that much was easy. Tarthur never was one of the more respectful types in normal times, and being dragged about certainly wasn't helping things. Had Tarthur known the atrocities this man was capable of, he might have acted much differently. As it was, the man simply bashed Tarthur on the side of the head with his chain mail fist. Dalin and Derlin looked on helplessly, each bearing their own bruises and cuts from the last time they had tried to help Tarthur.

"Let's go," the evil man said simply, lifting Tarthur onto a horse. He then gestured for Derlin and Dalin to walk. It seemed as if he was a man of very few words. As they began to walk along, Derlin started feeling as if they must reach their destination soon. He knew they must be arriving at the southern edge of the world before too long. Derlin was racking his mind for possible places that they could be traveling to. He remembered a world map he had seen once, but the details were too foggy to recall accurately. Living all of his life on a farm, he never imagined that the world could be so big.

Suddenly, it came into view. Rising above the foothills, rising even above the Rune Mountains at parts, it loomed, dark and impenetrable. The fortress had many towers, all made of some kind of black or dark gray stone. Dark rain clouds circled the tower. Sentries patrolled the area, but one glance told Derlin they were not human, or even close to human. The evil of the place penetrated Derlin, and it even caused Tarthur to stir from his sleep. Derlin wasn't sure, but he believed he could hear faint screams of terror from below the castle. No banners flew from the minarets—Derlin immediately knew that once you saw whom this fortress belonged to, you would never forget. He also knew that the possession of it would never change. He also knew, with grim certainty, that this was their destination.

He could see in Dalin's eyes that he knew this was their destination also. The drawbridge creaked slowly as it opened for their arrival, and swallowed them into the black pit of emptiness.

*   *   *   *

"Steady now," came the ever nasal and annoying, yet firm, voice. "Slow and steady, that's the way to get things done right." Sir Stephen already hated that voice. It was not as if the bearers of the Royal Wagon were being harsh, indeed, far from it. The knights and chancellors were moving King Garkin with meticulous care and attention to detail. They were doing so well, however, that their pace had slowed to a crawl. They had been doing all right for the first part of the morning, until at noon, Warren had decreed that they were moving too fast and jostling His Majesty. Sir Terin, or Ironfist as he was called, tried to argue. After all, old Ironfist had been in many a fight and seen quite a few injuries and sicknesses himself. As a matter of principle Warren had objected, those two always had a fiery hatred for each other. It had all started when Warren had wanted to become a knight; he had tried hard, but in the end, the physical talent just wasn't there. He was smart enough all right, but clumsy and slow. That had all been in his youth. Now Warren could make it, but his pride wouldn't let him ask. Sir Terin knew this, and disliked Warren all the more for his stupid pride, thus the ever-occurring rivalry.

Nobody knew quite how, but Warren managed to know every detail of the illness. He knew when the king would turn purple, what things would make his temperature go up or down, and what would make him feel better momentarily. Since he had such a complete mastery over the disease, no one could really challenge his authority. So, when Warren had pronounced that no cure was possible, all of the king's friends fell into mourning. Warren had let them cry for a while and he had then suggested going to the healing spring at Treshin. Legend had it that it was there the Creator had first sipped water, and it was also there that Frehu had made the Water Orb, and infused it with power. Since then, the abbey at Dun had documented hundreds of cases of miracle healing. It was said the springs would heal anyone who believed...

The scrambling of knights brought Sir Stephen out of his reverie. A tree had fallen across the path and the knights were already hacking away at it. Sir Stephen helped lift the newly cut tree eagerly. Sir Stephen still didn't know why he had been chosen for this mission, which made him proud of the unexpected honor, and anxious to prove himself. Only last year, Stephen had taken his first vows of knighthood, and that was the last time he had seen King Garkin. From that time, Sir Stephen had a blank record. He had done nothing to subtract from the dignity of anyone, he had never spoken harshly to or about his superiors, and he had never been derelict in his duty. Unfortunately, however, he had done nothing to gain himself or the kingdom any honor either. That was why he was trying extra hard in this mission. He was concentrating so much, he didn't even see the shadow following them.

*   *   *   *

Addyean waited quietly behind a rock. It had been too easy to track down the small party. They had left the royal road clean and smooth in their wake. He did not see the king, but he did see quite a few faces that he did recognize, all of whom were friendly. It seemed as if anyone of any import was there. Ah, he thought as he amended his assessment—almost all were friendly. Addyean saw the telltale mop of blond hair emerge from behind the wagon. Addyean had sensed Warren would be here, although, Addyean thought, Warren could be friendly.

When he had told them to leave yesterday, he might've been thinking of the security interests of the kingdom. Addyean's years as a royal spy led him to exercise caution in all things he did. This led him to believe the best course was to wait and see what they were doing. So he waited, and observed the forest. There were mostly aspen trees with a few pine trees dotting the landscape. Since it was autumn, the aspen leaves had turned gold and fallen from their respective trees, resulting in a carpet of gold along the forest floor. A stream trickled down from where Addyean stood, and formed a puddle where the king's party was traveling. The rabbits and other forest creatures scurried about, making their houses ready for winter.

The silence was broken by two conversing knights. Addyean had to lean close, as they were speaking in hushed tones. One of them Addyean recognized as Sir Undbar, a heavyset old knight with a real taste for adventure. The other looked young, and Addyean did not remember seeing him before. The young one seemed to be initiating the conversation, and Sir Undbar just grunted along with him in agreement.

"This whole business is strange, sir," commented the first.

"Hmmgh," grunted Sir Undbar. "Very strange."

"If you don't mind me asking, sir, do you feel as if Warren is accepted here? I mean, I don't know, but it seems like nobody likes him. Like he doesn't belong here."

For the first time Sir Undbar turned and actually seemed to be paying attention to the young one. "You are very perceptive, Sir Stephen. Someday you will make a fine knight, but as for now, we must not speak of anything bad. If the Creator chooses to restore our lord to health, we will see what we can do about Warren. I am not sure we can do anything, for being unlikable is certainly not a crime. I have a sinking feeling he has committed some crime against the crown. Yet without proof…it is best not to talk about these things. You would be wise not to discuss them with anyone. We will know all these things at Treshin."

Sir Stephen seemed to understand a little better, as he nodded and fell silent into his thinking. Addyean pondered these things to himself. He was about to reveal himself, but something was stopping him. Something was not right. And then he knew.

CHAPTER 5

▼

THE QUEEN OF DARKNESS

Girn was lost. Over the last week, he had been trying to find the dwelling of the merfolk. For the first few nights, he had been wandering around the forest looking for Tarthur and Derlin, or at least for their destination. He had seen no signs of any travelers, except for a fire one night. Girn had rushed toward the fire hoping to find his friends, but when he was still a ways off, he had seen that there were three people and three horses, which had made Girn know it was not his friends. In sadness, he had managed to find his way back to Krendon, and he went to apologize to Zelin, and beg Zelin to take him back. But Zelin was not there. Girn had asked around a bit, trying to find any information he could. From what he gathered, Judith was still fuming at Tarthur and Derlin, Zelin and Addyean had left a few days ago, and Morty was telling everyone about how he had single-handedly fought Tarthur and Derlin and given them both bloody noses and now they were afraid to show their cowardly faces anywhere near this town, lest they have to face the wrath of Mortimer.

"So, I stepped to the right, when his ill-timed attack was coming, and then BAM, I smashed my fist right on the bridge of his nose. Of course, the coward called to his friend to come help him out, but I wasn't bothered. Two ruffians of their sort are hardly a match for a gentleman of my caliber. I therefore offered to defer the conflict to some later time so they could round up five or six cronies to attack me simultaneously, because that's really the only way the fight would be fair. But the pugnacious villains persisted, and I whirled with my lightning-quick reflexes and made short work of the pair. It'll probably be some time before their faces heal up enough to come back here again." The young kids listening to Mortimer looked up at their new hero with bright eyes. Girn didn't understand half the words, but by Morty's tone of voice and the way he swung his fists madly around he decided that he was claiming responsibility for driving Tarthur and Derlin from town.

It was funny, Girn reflected, how everyone seemed to have a different story for the boys being absent, yet nobody was bothered about Zelin leaving. It was "normal" for him to do so, but those troublesome boys, stealing away without telling anyone. "I'm just glad he's not my son," and "What those boys need is a good old fashioned whipping into shape" were heard many a time, not to mention an occasional "Too bad they aren't like that Mortimer, now there's a boy with education and class. He's such an angel." (But, mind you, that was only a *very* occasional statement.) Of course, Girn didn't do much talking; he was still shy and he still stuttered. But he listened. He listened for two whole days, sometimes staying in the shadows, sometimes straying into the open. Many times the people conversing did not even notice him. Years of living quietly had taught Girn many things. It had made him a very good listener.

There were no other ways open to him. His master was gone who-knows-where. His friends were swimming with mermaids, and Girn was all alone. In the back of his mind, Girn knew he probably could've stayed with any number of people in the town, but he was too embarrassed to ask. He started to tell himself, as one frequently does, that the people would just laugh at him and send him away, even as he knew it was not true. However, having convinced himself, Girn decided that the best course of action was to try and make it to the shoals of the merfolk and see what he could find there. He had proceeded to procure some food and other supplies from Judith's kitchen when she was not there. When being questioned by Morty and a burly looking guard, he admitted that he wasn't quite sure how all of those things had gotten into his pack. (He must've set his pack down and Judith put them in.) When they failed to believe his obviously true story, he had taken off into the forest. (Tarthur always said, "If all else fails, run until your legs fall off.") Thinking of Tarthur made Girn's spirits rise, and he had set off on his journey. He spent the next few days wandering vaguely northward, entangled in a mess of trees and shrubs.

This brought him up to the present. Girn was sitting and eating a piece of bread and some cheese. He once again thought how lucky he was to have remembered to stock up on food. Yet, always one to plan for the future, Girn was beginning to be worried. While still not critical, his food supply was disappearing, and he did not know where he could get more, since he could not return to Krendon. Worse still, his water was going low, he had not seen a stream since two days ago, and no one had told him that wine only makes you thirstier. He had to find the merfolk in the next few days. Right then, as he stood up to go on his way, a bright flash of light hit him between the eyes. As he walked forward, another flash followed the first. Covering his eyes with his forearm, Girn went up the slope. At the top, he saw what had been causing the light. It was the ocean. And there were mermen in it.

*   *   *   *

The throne room of Queen Marhyn was as enormous as it was chilling. Nearly five hundred meters long and two hundred meters wide, it was made of an eerie dark blue marble. It seemed as if the marble was absorbing the light around it, and as Tarthur found as his hand accidentally strayed across it, it was very cold to the touch. There was not much ornamentation, except for magic objects and symbols arranged neatly about the sides of the room. The chamber angled to the throne against the back wall. Queen Marhyn's throne was solid black onyx, and immense. It was in fact so immense that it was a full fifteen meters tall, with a seat at the top. The cold blue chamber matched the black throne very well, and it gave Tarthur a sense of the deep power that was here. He felt this was an old power, older even than Zelin. Since Zelin and Tustor were the only powers that Tarthur had known in his life, it seemed to him as if they were the only ones that existed. Yet, even with them, he had never felt power like this. The cold chilled him to his very soul, and it made him very, very afraid.

The cold did not seem to bother Lithar Lifehater at all. If anything, he seemed more comfortable here than in the warm, living outside, for indeed he was. The name Lifehater was not his family name; he had earned it long ago. As Tarthur was watching the dark man, he abruptly stopped and saluted. Tarthur turned and he did not have to guess whom it was he was saluting to.

Queen Marhyn was dressed in black robes and all that was uncovered was her face, which was human and vaguely pretty. It had the kind old mother look in it, and it seemed to Tarthur that she was almost kind. She seemed caring enough, and started to speak with warm and amiable words. Tarthur was one to give everyone he met a chance. Suddenly the air was filled with the smell of warm food as a table of hot bread, stew, and meat came forth. The bread was the best kind, steaming out of the oven with butter just melting down the sides.

"I'm so glad you could come," she said. She seemed to be talking more to Tarthur than the others. "I do get very lonely down here. Maybe…wait, I forget myself. Please sit down and eat. I'm sure you must be so hungry."

"Well, yes," stammered Tarthur. "I was just thinking…"

"How good the bread looks," she finished.

This caught Tarthur off guard. He had two thoughts. One was, "and the meat looks good also." This was quickly chased out of his mind by the other—"she can read my mind! She knows what I am thinking!"

This made Tarthur really scared. He was so scared, he could not walk, move, or even think, and for a while he forgot to breathe. Tarthur was the kind of person who normally was not frightened easily. He would try anything, scale any cliff, cross any river, jump over any rock, and tell anyone he was ugly to his face, all without being afraid. Oh, he had been a tad worried he would be caught at this or that, and one time he was concerned that his master the blacksmith would disown him, and now and then he thought he was going to die, but nothing like this, ever.

He glanced at the table wonderingly and then back at the cold object of his terror. Instead, he saw Dalin. The elf had positioned himself between Tarthur and Queen Marhyn. In his eyes, Tarthur could see the shining clear message. *Don't touch the food!* Tarthur was glad for the break Dalin had made between him and the Dark Lady, especially because Dalin had to put his back to her. In a time like this Tarthur looked for the most adult person around.

Then Dalin was out of the way again, and Tarthur was facing the Dark Lady once more. Her soothing voice flowed out through the room. "Why don't you sit down and eat. You must be just famished."

"Well, actually, I'm fine." Tarthur's hastily stammered reply wasn't fooling anyone.

She continued. "I had my close personal friend try not to overfeed you as he helped you come here for your vacation." Close personal friend, more like fiend, Tarthur thought. And this a vacation? Either I learned the meaning of the word wrong (which had happened at least a few times) or this is no vacation. Tarthur cursed himself for thinking. It was hard to get used to the idea that your thoughts weren't even yours anymore. He looked up quickly to see Queen Marhyn's reaction.

Her face had not changed.

This made Tarthur wonder. Could she really read his thoughts? He decided to try something. In his mind, Morty ran up the steps on the throne and grabbed Queen Marhyn. This wasn't what the real Morty was like, because in Tarthur's mind Morty seemed uglier, stupider, and fatter than he really was. In fact, all of Morty's good traits were overlooked, and his bad ones were magnified. This bad impersonation of Morty then immediately proceeded to give Queen Marhyn a big full kiss, right smack on the lips. Queen Marhyn turned into a frog, grew wings, and flew away. Soon she hit the ceiling and fell, landing on her head on the throne. Tarthur had to bite his cheek hard to keep from laughing. He looked up again.

Her face still had not changed.

So, he thought. She either is incapable of laughter or fear at being kissed by Morty, or she cannot always read my mind. Although, as he thought later, both were probably true, at the time he concluded that she could not always read his mind. After deciding this, he felt a wave of relief sweep over him. He resolved to still be careful though.

"Well," she said disappointedly. "If you aren't hungry now perhaps we could talk. It isn't every day that I get to talk to someone who is as young as you who has so much power. Actually, I have never seen someone with so much power who was not old and past his prime."

As she talked, she seemed to become much younger, although, was it just a trick of the light? Suddenly Tarthur found her very desirable, and he wanted to do anything to have her.

"Maybe you could come to my quarters so I could give you some more personal attention. I am looking for a man such as yourself to share my rule over the world. What do you say?"

"No!" It was Derlin who replied. Almost forgotten in the conversation until now, he had boldly stepped forward to voice his objections. "Tarthur, she's evil. Can't you see? She wants to use you to get what you have."

Hearing Derlin speak seemed to return Tarthur to his senses. When Queen Marhyn saw that she had lost her hold over them, she sighed, as if she was being done a great injustice. "Well, until you change your mind…"

Suddenly a black and blue clad soldier came and took them away, down the hall and into their room.

*   *   *   *

"Truly disgusting, my queen." In one of the secret and dark rooms of Queen Marhyn's castle, (the fortress was literally full of them) Lithar Lifehater and Queen Marhyn were holding a secret council. Also present was Tyven Scarface, Admiral of Marhyn's newly formed navy. In a way, Tyven was the opposite of

Lithar. While Lithar had been born a man, and converted part way to darker things, while still keeping the appearance, so that anyone one who didn't see him from very close, or didn't look under his clothes, would believe him to be human, Tyven had began as a hideously deformed creature created by Marhyn's magic as an "experiment." Later in life, he expressed a desire to be human, so to command more respect in this world of men. Because he had been such a faithful servant, and because he was somewhat of a favorite of Queen Marhyn's, she had summoned all her magicians and they had all worked together to do what they could. The result was a creature not unlike a man, but whose face was still a tangled mass of scars. Tyven said very little, because talking was hard for him and it strained his jaw muscles, which were very weak. Just a few months ago, Marhyn had sensed something, and said the time was right for war. They had then set to vigorous work building shipyards and turning out ships and captains and their crews as fast as they could. Tyven was the natural choice for the leader, both because of his ruthless nature, and because when he was "created" he had fins instead of hands and he was always in the ocean. There were always those willing to join the crew for some gold. Partly because of this and partly to build new prison space, Marhyn had begun a vast excavation project deep into the Rune Mountains. Only two other people were anywhere close to the trio, and they were both servants who once hadn't been productive. (Tarthur was lucky that he was not born as one of Marhyn's servants, a similar fate would've certainly awaited him.) Queen Marhyn had heard that they were fond of idle talk on the job. In order to help them past this difficulty, and to give the other workers more incentive, she had cut off their ears and ripped out their tongues. Now they were used for special councils and other things that required absolute secrecy. Still, they weren't even allowed in the same room.

"Nothing necessary is wrong, Lithar." Marhyn often used this saying; it was one of her favorites. "I tried to persuade him with an old mother appearance that I cared for him, but his mind is too strong, and it was already set against me."

"Could you not enter his thoughts?" The question was from Tyven. After all, he had heard about the encounter and he wondered why his queen did not simply enter his mind and destroy his thought, like she did to so many. This burning curiosity had been enough to prompt him to ask his halting question.

"That is very strange," she answered. "While I was able to observe him closely and see certain things about him, I was blocked from his inner thoughts. Still, some things came through to me. I even felt he was mocking me once."

"What was so strong that it blocked you?" This time the question was Lithar's.

"I don't know it. I have never felt it before. Who were they in contact with recently?" Marhyn thought and then answered her own question. "The only two powers they could have been with are that wizard named Zelin and the merwizard." She looked at Lithar. "What did you feel when you felt the Water Orb being used?"

"I just felt its use, nothing more."

Marhyn nodded. "When he used it, I felt that he used it to bring the merwizard back to life. If he would have had help from the Council of Gurus, Tustor could've placed that spell on Tarthur. Still, I think I would've been able to recognize their shield. Besides, you know how isolationist they are. They don't usually interfere in the affairs of men."

"It is also strange that he was able to use the Water Orb, without possessing it. My brother still has it out of the world. How can this mere boy use something that is out of the world? Unless, has Darhyn brought it back? The construction must be hastened—the time is rapidly drawing near."

"It seemed as if you almost had a hold over him when his companion broke it. Why don't we break that hold by destroying the free thought of his companions?" When someone talked to Marhyn, they always said we instead of you. To suggest that the queen was at fault or should try something new wasn't usually a good idea. Being ranked as he was, Lithar took some liberty over the normal rules, still it was always better to be safe than sorry.

"That is another unusual thing. The shield seemed to be protecting the other two also. The source of this magic puzzles me immensely."

Tyven, by his usual method of communication, slid a piece of paper over to Marhyn. It said: "Doesn't the Water Orb have the power to control things?"

Marhyn thought a moment, and then replied. "The Orb does have a life of its own. But I think my brother has enough control over it to stop it from doing anything important. Unless, perhaps Darhyn himself placed the protective spell over them, maybe this boy can use things that don't exist and Darhyn wants to use him for his own ends. It is an interesting possibility, and one well worth looking into. Tyven, that will be your job."

"Since I can't probe their minds, the prisoners are useless to me. They may, however become very valuable later, especially the boy Tarthur. Lithar, put them in solitary confinement in the newly constructed prison cells. That will break their spirits the fastest. Meanwhile, I want the mountains to be excavated and the tunnels extended. Let's keep that gold coming. More gold is the way to keep the loyalty of our mercenaries. Admiral Tyven, I want a navy trained and ready to sail in a month. They don't have to know how to fight yet. We will take them to our secret base and train them there. For now they just need to know how to sail. Lithar, you will stay here with part of the troops who will be the diversion. When Tyven and I leave you will, of course, be in charge."

This plan was agreeable to the trio, so they relaxed, had the servants prepare some food, and talked for a few more hours until they had made a very, very good plan for taking over the world involving a mass slaughter of their own troops, treachery, violence, and a volcano.

✳   ✳   ✳   ✳

The grieving knights knelt in the meadow at dawn. The sun was at the point where it has not quite risen yet, but where it still gives some light to the world below. It was October, so there was usually a chill in the early morning air. Sir Stephen knelt with the rest, who were arranged in a circle around their ailing monarch. He thought, "I'm glad it's not the middle of winter yet. It would be freezing out here," and then immediately, "why did I think that? The king is dying and I'm thinking about winter! I'll never make a good knight if I keep thinking about myself. There I go again!"

In spite of his inner turmoil, Sir Stephen's exterior was unmoving. He wanted to look for a friendly face, to combat the sense of utter loneliness that he was feeling, but then he stopped himself. He would be a man this time. In the pre-dawn hours, Warren had summoned all of the knights and counselors, saying that it was urgent and that King Garkin's condition was worsening. Warren had said that King Garkin could no longer travel, and was at the very brink of death. They selected two knights, put them on horseback, and told them to gallop as fast as they could to Treshin and try to bring back some water. Even if they rode the horses to exhaustion, it would still be a good day to go there and back. By that time, the king would probably not be alive anymore. Still—it was their only hope.

That is how all the knights got to be kneeling in the grass around their dying king. For now, all they could do was to wait, and pray. It was the morning of the third day after they had set out from the capital.

Suddenly, King Garkin sat up. "I will die soon, but I see him," he uttered in a trance-like state. "The one who will be king after me." King Garkin pointed a shaky finger out from his body. To the horror, and amazement of everyone present (except one,) the king was pointing to Warren.

His heart leaping with excitement (his plan had worked!) Warren was compelled to speak. "Your Majesty, I am sure I am not worthy, still if you think it is best for the kingdom…"

Warren would never have believed what happened next if he had been told about it. King Garkin said, in a perfectly coherent voice, "No, not you, the person behind you!"

The knights turned as one man. As Sir Stephen looked into the rising sun, part of the sun was obscured by a black shadow. The shadow walked deliberately, and steadily. As he came closer, Sir Stephen saw the shadow turn gradually into a man. As the man approached the king, Sir Stephen wanted to do something, but a restraining hand on his shoulder checked him. It seemed this man was well known here.

The man walked to the king, and dropped to one knee. He reached inside his jacket and brought forth a flask of something clear. He opened the flask, and gave it to the king. As King Garkin drank the contents, color started to return to his cheeks and he visibly seemed to gain strength. Soon he was well enough to stand. Suddenly he collapsed into the arms of the mysterious man. Sir Stephen was stepping forward to help when suddenly he realized it was not a fall. It was an embrace. King Garkin's whisper was heard by only one person. "Thank you, Addyean."

CHAPTER 6

▼

A NEW FRIEND

The last time Tarthur had seen his friends had been two days ago. That was when some gruff-looking goblins had separated them in their rooms and sent them each to a separate prison deep within the mountain. Before going, the trio had made plans that if any one of them should escape, they would immediately proceed to the king and tell him of all that had happened. Breshen was too far away, Dalin said, and they might be able to meet up with Zelin at the capital. They had also reaffirmed that no matter what Marhyn said, they were to remain her sworn enemy. Being reminded of their capture and ordeal just to make it there certainly helped Tarthur forget her apparent kindness to him and listen a little closer to the screams of absolute terror that periodically radiated from the darker parts of the citadel. The friends had said what they hoped weren't last goodbyes and proceeded to follow the goblins. The goblin that brought Tarthur to his cell wasn't like the two he had dealt with before. This one was rude and uneducated, certainly of the rougher sort. It definitely seemed as if Tarthur's red carpet treatment was now over.

Actually, in the last two days it seemed as if his captors had forgotten about him. Each day, he received food from a slot in the wall, but he had seen no other sign of any life. Worse yet, he had tapped on all of the walls, to no avail. The cell itself seemed to be both poorly and newly constructed. The walls were not all that thick, and the dirt was still fresh. From his limited knowledge of these things, Tarthur guessed that these cells had been made in the last month.

In his cell, thoughts began to go through Tarthur's mind. In all he had heard about the famous adventures, he had never bargained for this. He began for the first time to wonder, what happened to the vanquished? Why did he not hear their side of the story? Tarthur had never dreamed that in his life he would be anything other than a conquering hero. With the beginning of this quest, his spirits had risen. Now was his chance! But some things he had not bargained for. Tarthur assumed they would go to the merfolk and become instant legends, conquering all obstacles. But now here he was, rotting away in some jail far from home, without a chance of getting out. The thought that he might never see his best friend again was almost more than he could bear. The usually overconfident Tarthur was now depressed and alone. He and Derlin had grown up together; they had been in every scam imaginable together, and now they might never do anything together again. He wished he could just go to sleep and wake up in Krendon, and have it all be a dream. He promised that if that happened, he would never again be ungrateful. Heck, he'd even kiss Morty if only he could be back there. It seemed to Tarthur that these cold, uninviting, catacombs would be his tomb. Feeling alone and afraid, Tarthur slumped down, buried his face in his hands, and cried.

In the days that followed, Tarthur's spirits rose slightly. He had managed to use the heel of his boot (which, fortunately for him, his captors had not taken away) to clear a small hole in the wall. The diameter was a good foot by now, and it was nearly ten inches deep. Having no other plans of escape, and being observed by his captors only infrequently, he was able to spend all of his time with this project. The food, while not what one would call nourishing, certainly gave him strength enough for his task. Thinking of the consequences of not succeeding made Tarthur pound at the weakest part of the cell with a vengeance. So it was that on the eighth day of his incarceration that something quite extraordinary happened. Tarthur fell through the floor and landed on someone.

Tarthur's constant digging had weakened the structure of the cells that Marhyn's goblins had so carelessly built. When it could stand no more stress without the support of the wall, the floor collapsed. Brushing himself off and checking for injuries, (there were none, fortunately only part of the floor had collapsed) Tarthur heard a loud groaning sound. Startled, and a great bit disappointed, Tarthur realized that he had not broken free as he had intended to, but rather, simply fallen into another person's cell. At least this was better than being alone. As he helped the man to his feet, Tarthur wondered just how much help this man could be to him.

As he looked at the old man uneasily, Tarthur decided to begin rather frankly. "My name is Tarthur. I'm sorry I fell on you."

"Yes, yes, I'm sure you are now," the stranger said, looking around. "But where are my spectacles?"

"Well, they are on your head," Tarthur said, confused.

"What are?"

"Your spectacles."

"Why," he exclaimed with surprise. "So they are! Dratted things are always trying to hide from me. I'll have to apologize, I'm a bit forgetful."

Tarthur replied good-naturedly, "I'm sure you are."

"Are what?"

"Forgetful."

"Who is?"

"You are!" Tarthur, never a patient one in any case was beginning to get angry.

"Whoa," he replied. "You must not get too angry. I have to tell you that I am a little forgetful."

Tarthur decided not to get into that again, but rather to start completely over. "I'm sorry I fell on you. My name is Tarthur"

"Me too," he added, still referring to Tarthur's first statement.

"So what is your name?" Tarthur pushed further.

"Tarthur. I just told you."

Tarthur let his head sink into his hands once more. Getting anything useful from this man would prove a long, difficult, and frustrating task. Tarthur took a deep breath and started.

Over the next few days, Tarthur learned that the man's name was not Tarthur, but in fact Yan. Yan didn't remember much concerning how or why he was imprisoned, or how long he had been there. Tarthur wondered if Marhyn had done something to his mind to inhibit his thinking. Talking to Tarthur seemed to improve Yan's mind, for soon he became much more aware of his surroundings. On the third day since their meeting, Tarthur decided that he needed to tell Yan about his problems and see if they could escape. At first, Yan was against the idea.

"They'll kill you," the old man said plainly and without emotion. "I know."

"The guards will notice the hole in the cell soon enough. What do you think they'll do then? Serve us a roast beef dinner? Invite us to tea? No, they will punish us for trying to escape, even if that is not our intention. The walls are probably weakened by the fall. Besides, I am important to the world outside."

When Tarthur had told Yan of their quest, and the "world outside," Yan had seemed skeptical that such a place existed. It seemed to Tarthur that Yan had spent all or most of his life here in Marhyn's prison. He had only faint memories of sunlight and bright colors. Animals and happiness were beyond him. Tarthur felt sad for Yan, and vowed to get even with Marhyn and do what he could to stop this, if he got out. When he got out.

"The world outside needs me," Tarthur continued, unsure if it was true or not. If it wasn't, Tarthur didn't mind lying. "I have control over a thing that is very powerful. It is called a Water Orb." Yan stirred faintly at the words, as if trying to recall something hidden. "There are powerful armies out there. They can defeat Marhyn." Tarthur wasn't even sure they were at war with Marhyn.

"Oppose the Dark Lady? Impossible! And defeat her!" Yan broke off into a sort of quiet hysterical laugh.

In the end, Tarthur's constant talk of the world outside convinced Yan to try to escape. They made their plans for right after the next ration of food, and settled down for some rest. Tarthur wondered if it would be the last time he fell asleep and woke up.

Tarthur awoke just in time to see the goblin put the stale bread and putrid water into the slot that served as the only means of interaction with the outside world. He saved the bread and drank the water hurriedly so as not to gag on the rotten smell. He then took a piece of bread from his store and consumed it. Tarthur kept five days worth of bread at a time, and when a new one came, he ate the oldest and saved the newest. He realized this gesture was largely symbolic— the bread was stale and moldy in any case, but Tarthur wanted to do everything possible to attempt freshness. Tucking the bread away in his vest, Tarthur hopped down into Yan's cell. The old man was receiving his bread and water also, and he too put it away for later. Tarthur waited in silence until he heard the footsteps of the retreating goblin fade into the darkness. He turned to Yan.

"It is time." Yan merely nodded in agreement.

With their combined strength, Tarthur and Yan kicked at the wall. The first kick sent up a cloud of dust, but the wall showed no visible sign of giving way. They were at the part of the wall where Tarthur had judged it to be the weakest, right below the hole in the ceiling. Tarthur and Yan kicked in earnest, and soon there was a small crack. Yan began to dig this crack out as Tarthur picked up a good-sized boulder that had once been part of the roof. He motioned to Yan, and the duo picked it up and hurled it at the poorly constructed wall. The first hit made quite a sound, but didn't do much in the way of destroying anything. So

Tarthur and Yan picked it up again and tossed it violently at the wall one more time. This time it knocked a large chunk off of the wall. Progress was certainly being made. "Wait," called Yan. "If we keep using that big rock someone is bound to hear us. Let's use these smaller ones. I need to rest for a while."

Yan did look tired, and it was a good idea. Tarthur had noticed an improvement in Yan lately, and he seemed more rational and thinking now. Tarthur was glad for the change, but anxiety over Derlin and Dalin kept him nervous. He called the rest break short and started once more to pound the wall mercilessly.

In time, Tarthur and Yan managed to make a big enough hole for them to crawl through. Deciding that now was as good a time as any, Tarthur squeezed through and helped Yan through after him. He stared into the darkness of the corridor both ways, but he saw nothing and heard only the sound of Yan's ragged breathing.

Tarthur weighed his decision carefully once again in his mind. He knew that he must get out at all costs. Before parting, the three friends had agreed that if any one of them were to get out, they would immediately proceed to the king. Tarthur also knew that this was especially important for him; he was the one who controlled the Orb. So he knew what he was about to do was crazy, yet he still could not leave his friends in this horrible place. Especially not after what he had seen had been done to Yan. So he resolved to look for them for an hour, no longer, and then continue along his way.

Tarthur and Yan crept through the silence. It seemed to them to be too quiet, almost as if the whole of Marhyn's army had already left. But this fantasy was checked when they were forced to press against the wall twice while goblins passed by.

By searching the cells close by, and calling his companions' names softly, Tarthur soon ascertained that finding them would be no easy task. The cells were constructed in such a manner to have many cells close by, yet all of the cells close to Tarthur's were unoccupied. It seemed that only by mere chance Tarthur had been close to Yan. Once Tarthur and Yan had searched all of the cells in their area, they decided to move into another area. Tarthur assumed that there could be no more than a few areas, and with any luck, Derlin and Dalin might be incarcerated in the same place. But the cold realism of the uninviting stone caused Tarthur to curse himself for his foolishness. They were probably dead. Who could even be sure of anything in this cold, dark, place anyway?

When Tarthur and Yan had searched three separate sections of the jail, and still found all of the cells unoccupied, Tarthur knew that it was time to go. (He hadn't found a way out yet, though.) As he was rounding a corner, Yan placed a comforting hand on his shoulder and spoke. "I know they were your friends. We may never find them again, but you know you tried."

"Maybe just one more hour," Tarthur purposed, knowing the hard facts as well as Yan. "We couldn't have checked all of those cells." As Tarthur turned to go, Yan tightened his grip on Tarthur's shoulder.

He didn't speak, but as he looked at Tarthur, his eyes said, "You know what you have to do."

Tarthur just nodded once and started to go.

The attack came from on top of them. A dark figure jumped down from a previously unseen hole in the ceiling and kicked Tarthur into Yan. The force of his kick sent both the old man and the boy sprawling.

Within seconds, Tarthur was on his feet and flying into his assailant. He was relieved to see only one, but fighting was not the time for thinking. Before the shadowy figure knew what was happening, Tarthur had buried his left fist in the creatures gut, and come down across his cheek with the right one.

The creature, however, was not without defenses of its own. As Tarthur sent him sprawling with the punch, it swung its leg around and hit Tarthur so hard with its heal that he almost dislocated his jaw. "Tarthur!" Yan reached out and saved Tarthur a considerable amount of pain by grabbing him before he collided with the wall.

The creature hunched in the shadows, tasting its own blood in its mouth. "Tarthur?" The voice was familiar. "It's me, Derlin."

Tarthur stared at the figure in the shadow. Now that he saw him in this light, Tarthur didn't see how he had failed to recognize his lifelong companion. "I thought you were goblins," Derlin began. "This place, it does things to you. Tarthur, can you ever forgive me?"

"Forgive you? Of course. You don't ever need to ask again. Still, it seems as though you should forgive me. I did get the better of the fight."

"What? I am doubly surprised that you say that. Firstly, because you know I'm faster, and secondly, because I gave you such a shot in your jaw, I'm surprised that you can talk at all."

The two went on arguing in this manner for a short time, until Yan finally cut them off, suggesting that they wait and see whose injuries healed more slowly, the other person being the winner of the fight, to which they both readily assented.

Derlin told a most remarkable story. He had been in a section of the jail like Tarthur's, but with all of the cells surrounding his empty. He told the others about how he had tested the door every day. On only the second day of his confinement, Derlin had escaped and was looking for Tarthur when a pair of guards jumped him and nearly beat him senseless. So it was that Derlin had spent most of his time in a kind of half-conscious state, before he rested and was nourished (barely) by the food he was brought.

"A few hours ago," he continued, "I found the door once again unlocked. I tried to look for you all over, and of course we all know how I found you."

By putting together all that they had learned by experience in their captivity, along with reason and logic (which Tarthur rarely used) they were able to deduce that there were ten sets of prison cells. Tarthur and Yan had searched through three, plus the one they were in, and Derlin had searched through two, plus the one he was in. This left only three areas of cells left, and gave the boyhood friends a good hope of finding Dalin. Tarthur had come to miss Dalin in the weeks that they had been separated, and now he was wishing for his old friend again. Still, their hopes rose now that they had a plan, and it seemed to Derlin that they would soon be enjoying the company of their old companion.

This time, however, a real attack cut short their fabulous rescue. Figures, who had apparently overheard the trio planning in hushed tones now rushed into the corridor, and Tarthur was willing to bet that Dalin wasn't one of them. Tarthur motioned to Derlin, with a vague gesticulation in the direction of the old man, who was both surprised and lost at this new turn of events. Derlin, understanding immediately, pulled Yan to the back and out of harm's way. Simultaneously, the boys went to draw their swords, which they had grown accustomed to wearing at their sides ever since they had met the merfolk. Groping about uncertainly, both were rather dismayed to find that they weren't wearing any. At this point, they both rushed forward as if they were one person, and flew into their attackers with a vengeance. Fists and feet were flying haphazardly, and soon the pursuing goblins were forced to wait and think twice before proceeding. It is no small wonder that Tarthur and Derlin had not hit each other with their furious attacks, many battles in Krendon had taught them to fight well together. It had also taught them something else. Once you start to attack, you don't stop. The only way to stop the wild attack is if one or the other combatants becomes unconscious, or if someone, particularly an adult, stops the fighting for you.

So it was that Tarthur and Derlin were chasing after the goblins, ready to pummel them once more. At this point, however, the captain of the goblin troop was astute enough to remember that the members of his group had weapons, and were therefore at an advantage. Summarily, he turned his troop around with one course command in his guttural language as the goblins drew their short swords. This caused Tarthur and Derlin to stop immediately, for although this was not one of the two acceptable reasons for ceasing to beat your enemy, it was certainly a good reason to run away. The two turned back in the direction of Yan, and began to hurry toward him, all the while calling ahead for him to run.

While Tarthur and Derlin were good at fighting, they were also very good at running away. They had been in enough misunderstandings caused by their liberal interpretations of morals and rules to know how to run away when it needed to be done. Yan, whether motivated by this knowledge and experience, or just sheer terror, was also doing quite well. The companions were also aided by the shortness of the goblins' legs, which made them take many more steps to cover the same distance.

Soon, however, the goblins began to catch up with them. They were more sure-footed and accustomed to the dark and damp surface. Tarthur, who was by this time half carrying Yan, looked up as the old man pointed. He was pointing to a hollow tunnel that was leading out from the main tunnel. It was smaller and looked as if only one person, if any, could fit through at a time. If they could make it there, they would have a more reasonable chance of safety.

As the heroes finally approached the tunnel, the goblins caught up to them. One swung his blade in a blatant attempt to decapitate Derlin. Derlin ducked just in time, reached into the goblin's belt, and pulled out his dagger. This he immediately plunged into the creature's heart, before it could swing its sword back around. Derlin grabbed the sword from the staggering creature, and turned to face the next one, who was surprised to now be facing an armed foe rather than an unarmed one. Derlin didn't need to think twice about this advantage, he quickly dispatched the creature.

He tossed the sword in his hand to Tarthur, who formed a protective shield around Derlin, who was taking the dead goblin's weapons, and Yan, who was frantically looking for a way out. The death of their companions had made these monsters wary, and now Tarthur had a much more difficult time dealing with them. One, dressed differently than the rest and seeming to have some authority, was issuing a strange call from a bugle-like instrument. Tarthur listened with horror; it seemed to him as if the call was the call of death itself. As he was parrying a well aimed blow from his assailant, Tarthur felt a dagger whiz by his head, and even take off a lock of his now shoulder-length hair. Tarthur whirled to look for another attacker behind him, but all he saw was a big smile on Derlin's face.

"I couldn't resist," he said with a shrug of his shoulders. "Besides, we can't have them bringing reinforcements." Tarthur turned once more to see the leader with the hideous instrument fall to the ground, one of his own men's daggers embedded in his neck. This gave Tarthur great hope, since there were only half a dozen or so monsters left. It also appeared as if the call for help had been in vain.

Fighting side by side now, Tarthur and Derlin were able to have the better of the fight. The narrowness of the tunnels allowed only two people to be standing side by side at any rate, so the superior numbers of the enemy didn't hamper them. Also, being taller, they were allowed unobstructed opportunities to rain down blows on their opponents' heads. Within a few minutes, however, the boys began to tire, and it soon became apparent that either the call for reinforcements had been heard, or their clamor in the first encounter had been noticed. In any event, new goblins and other monsters, even a few men, were beginning to appear at the end of the tunnel. This new force was also better equipped to fight in these conditions; they had spears and other long thrusting weapons. The boys looked into each other's eyes while both were blocking a pair of thrusting spears. The message was simple and stunningly clear. They knew it was only a matter of a few minutes before this crypt indeed became their burial place. The only thing working for them was that as of yet the monsters had only come at them from one side of the tunnel, and so they only had to fight in one direction. It would be all over if the monsters snuck up on them from the back as well.

In all this commotion we have quite forgotten Yan, who, as I mentioned before, was seeking an exit. He motioned excitedly to Tarthur, who immediately hurried over, leaving Derlin to defend their position solo. Yan excitedly pointed to a crevasse in the wall that led to another chamber and another tunnel. Yan had been digging at it vigorously until his fingers became raw and bleeding, but he had succeeded in making it just wide enough for them to fit through. Tarthur squeezed Yan through, nearly breaking the fragile old man.

By this time, Derlin had noticed this plan for escape, and was intensely trying to concentrate and find a way to buy enough time to get through. He yelled for Tarthur to get through first, so he would be able to pull Derlin through quickly. Tarthur immediately saw the sense of this plan and he started to go through the crevasse. With only Yan, who had been much weakened by the ordeal, and who wouldn't have been too much help even if he was in prime physical condition, to pull on him, Tarthur found it a long and difficult struggle.

While Tarthur was so occupied, Derlin began to pile up the bodies of the slain goblins to use as a rampart. He was exhausted as he finished the wall, which nearly reached up to the short ceiling. The creatures on the other side furiously hacked apart their friends' bodies, in an effort to escape a similar fate, which would certainly await them if the Dark Lady found out that her prisoners had escaped. In their fury, many times the goblins accidentally mistook a live body for a dead one, adding another corpse to the pile.

The wall of death held out well enough, however. As the first ones were making their way through, Derlin noticed with satisfaction that Tarthur was on the other side of the hole. The boy immediately followed. Since he was a bit skinnier than Tarthur, Derlin knew that he would have an easier time. Derlin stuck his arm through the crevasse and was reassured when he felt his friend's arm grasp his own.

"Pull!" The muffled shout came from the other side. Derlin felt a searing pain in his right arm, and then everything went black.

Tarthur, on the other hand, was both worried and relieved when he pulled his friend through. He was worried because he had almost pulled Derlin's arm off, yet relieved because he now saw that the pursuing goblins were too fat to come through the hole. Derlin was unconscious.

Still, there was no time for rest just yet for the weary trio. Carrying Derlin between them the three tried to move as fast as they could, which certainly was not very fast, down the tunnel and away from the nightmares that were behind them.

When they had gone nearly a hundred yards down the tunnel, Tarthur turned, and he saw the torch light glint off what must be a goblin sword. Tarthur realized that they were trying to use the swords to pry open the narrow fissure. All of a sudden, Tarthur heard a loud rumbling, and felt the walls begin to shake. In trying to widen the slot, the goblins had moved boulders that had for countless centuries stood as the only support for the ceiling. Too late, the overzealous captain realized this, but as he ordered his men to turn around, their world came crashing down upon them. Tarthur continued to look as the screams of agony echoed throughout the catacombs. Tarthur now knew that there was a great possibility of escape. Their pursuers effectively sealed behind a wall of granite, Tarthur and Yan slumped down to rest.

When he awoke, Tarthur immediately cursed himself for sleeping so long, but was somewhat relieved to see that Derlin was at least the first part of alive and well, and moving about in a vain effort to combat the soreness in his limbs.

"Hello, Tarthur," Yan greeted. "While you were asleep I had to pop Derlin's shoulder back into place. It seems that you dislocated it when you pulled on it."

"Yes, Tarthur," Derlin added. "Do you remember what happened to Morty quite accidentally two summers ago?"

Tarthur's face seemed confused, as if he was lost in thought, trying vainly to remember. And then he did. And he started to laugh, for two summers ago Morty had begun riding lessons. The great majority of people in Krendon certainly did not have their own horses, but of course the Baron Ercrilla had four and Tarthur and Derlin had none. So it was that one day, by pure coincidence the jealous Tarthur had wandered over by the stables and when no one was paying particularly close attention, helped the strap on the bottom of Morty's horse untie itself. That day, merely by chance, Tarthur, Derlin, and Girn had happened to be there when Morty rode by to insult them, saying that if they liked to see a gentleman ride why didn't they come more often, to which Tarthur replied the absolute truth that they were just passing through on their way to do more chores and support their town. As Morty rode off, the saddle (which was probably of inferior quality in the first place) fell off, and Morty was left to be dragged off by the horse. This wasn't helped when some anonymous person, who Morty claimed was Tarthur, had slapped the horse on the rear. Although, Morty was under strain and couldn't have been thinking clearly. (If Tarthur ever found the real culprit, he would make sure he was punished heavily.) In the impact, Morty had had his shoulder dislocated. The best physician in Krendon, who happened to be a barber most of the time, promptly fixed his arm. The boys had laughed so hard as they were running away that they fell down, but luckily there were no witnesses and the baron just scolded his son for riding without checking his equipment first. At times when Tarthur was melancholy and sad, all he had to do was to remember this incident and he would soon burst out laughing.

Now was the time for many things, however, laughing was not one of them. So the ragtag band of companions once again started their journey through the catacombs. They journeyed down what seemed like endless tunnels, always being careful to deposit a scrap of their clothes whenever they made a turn. In this manner they saved themselves from becoming endlessly lost, and they were able to make progress rather rapidly.

When they had been traveling for only a few hours, it became readily apparent that they weren't in the new section of the remains anymore. There was a thick carpet of dust lining the floor, and the walls seemed very, very old. A couple of times Tarthur even noticed strange carvings in them. Since neither Tarthur nor Derlin could read or write more than their name and a few other words that they needed to know, they asked Yan if he knew what they meant. Yan, although thinking that he did, could not in fact read them, so the heroes could only stare at the strange symbols. Using reason and logic again, (this was twice in two days now for Tarthur) the group concluded that they must have escaped Marhyn, their most immediate enemy, at least for the time being. They decided that they had escaped into an older network of tunnels, and that they were now somewhere deep within the Rune Mountains.

CHAPTER 7

▼

A CITY REJOICES

Addyean didn't have much chance for the prophecy to bother him, with all of the rejoicing over the king's good health. In the recent days, there had been many parties, especially since the commotion had occurred just two days before King Garkin's 37th birthday. King Garkin was a wise ruler, and he knew that a people who work all year long are depressed and moody. So it was that thirteen years ago he had proclaimed that every year, the day of the king's birth was to be celebrated with partying and feasting. The common people adored him all the more for this magnanimous act, and the rich merchants didn't mind either, because the huge quantities of food and other supplies that must be bought for a party were all exempted from tax on that day. In this way the king lost a little revenue and gained something many times more valuable, the admiration of his people.

As Addyean strolled through the brightly decorated palace hall, his thoughts again turned to Warren. Addyean knew that he should give the king's counselor a chance. Still, something did not seem right. Addyean had not learned anything new about Warren when he had gone to Treshin. It seemed that if Warren were evil he certainly would have. After all, what an experience that had been! He still almost couldn't believe it himself, and if he told people what had happened, he was sure they wouldn't believe him either. Addyean weighed his decision again in his mind. He wondered if his resolution to ask King Garkin to exclude Warren from their secret counsels was right. On the one hand, with a good possibility of war, Addyean could not let personal troubles stand in the way of their command.

Since he had risen in such a short time to be the Royal Counselor, he probably could offer good advice. We must be unified, if we are to defeat the Evil One! But, suppose Warren was not here to help the kingdom? What then? The potential risks of having Warren far outweighed the potential gains. So he decided to use his refined observation skills on the blond pest and see if he could come up with anything incriminating.

Addyean started wondering about the boys. Addyean had been so caught up in all of the things that had been happening lately that he had quite forgotten about them. Zelin didn't explain why Tarthur had used the Water Orb, and Addyean had not asked. Maybe Zelin didn't know. Addyean wondered where the boys were now. They are probably safe and sound with the merfolk, he thought, or maybe they were on their way to Tealsburg. This thought made Addyean feel better, for while the court parties were fun in a way, Addyean was bored and longed to be outdoors, or at least doing something else, anything else, than being hailed as the hero he knew he wasn't. He was sure that if Tarthur were here, there would be some lively tricks played. Years of being a spy and sharpening his senses caused Addyean to turn as he felt the life-force of the figure behind him.

"Didn't mean to startle you," Sir Terin said politely. "Are you on your way to the council meeting?"

"Yes, as a matter of fact I am," Addyean replied, sheathing the dagger that he had hastily drawn. "Your silence has much improved since I saw you last. Then, you could not sneak up on old Master Werd, and he was near deaf."

The companions laughed at the day when they were both pupils of the gruff, but kindly Master Werd. What Addyean wouldn't give to have those carefree days back.

"If you don't mind me asking, you know Baron Ercrilla is a good friend of mine, and I was hoping..." Sir Terin haltingly broke the silence.

"You don't need to worry," the farmer-spy assured him. "Baron Ercrilla has been cleared of all wrongdoing. If the truth be known, King Garkin sent me just as much because I was tired of court life and wanted to get back to soil."

Sir Terin was certainly glad to hear this, and left Addyean to his thoughts for the rest of the journey. It was funny, Addyean thought to himself, that Baron Ercrilla didn't recognize him when he went back, since they had in fact met many times over the years. But Addyean was careful to spend his time in the shadows, and when he did meet people he always seemed so ordinary that they soon forgot him. Baron Ercrilla would never look a poor farmer in the eye and see who he really was.

Addyean and Sir Terin soon arrived at the king's private council chamber. Finally, it was time to talk of war.

Upon entering, Addyean noted with small dissatisfaction that Warren had indeed been invited. Apparently the king trusted him enough; Addyean would have to talk to the king in private later. Also present was General Cilio, a master strategist, a man Addyean both admired greatly and feared. His pure intelligence made most people, Addyean included, very uneasy. Yet, whenever a battle was to be fought, his schemes so beguiled the enemy that his battles were legendary. There were songs sung about him in taverns that said he could defeat thousands with an army of three. Addyean was sure there was a measure of hyperbole, but not very much. They would certainly need him to counter the master strategies of the Dark One and his sister. Those beings had a completely different way of thinking, and they didn't mind sacrificing their own armies to gain an advantage. That made them very difficult to fight against.

There was another that Addyean did not know standing in the corner, his face hidden by a cloak drawn tightly over his head.

King Garkin was enthusiastic as he surveyed those assembled in the council chamber. "Welcome, friends! Since everyone is here, we can begin."

The servants, who had been pouring wine and waiting on the dignitaries, didn't need to be told twice to leave and join the festivities in another part of the city. When they had left, six solemn people remained in the room.

"Since we have much to accomplish here today," began the king. "I trust we can dispense with the formalities. Does everyone know everyone else here?"

"All but one, my lord." Sir Terin would always be formal.

"There is no need for formalities, Ironfist. I had forgotten that many of you don't have the pleasure of knowing this most distinguished warrior. May I present to you, Hano of the elves. He has come to us from Breshen. It seems the Elder One is having quite a problem with isolated border infringements from the East."

With this the cowled figure removed his hood and stepped from his corner to join the rest of the council. General Cilio, always one to be thinking of military matters, was the first to speak. "We are indeed very fortunate to have allies so close to the Dark One."

"Too bad all humans don't feel that way." Hano's statement was colder than he meant it. He did not really like humans in the first place, and being in this confined city where the humans were partying when they should be preparing irked him. Plus, with Dalin still missing, Valena was more nervous than usual.

Hano knew that Dalin could take care of himself, but to see his beloved worrying night and day over her vanished brother was almost more than he could bear…

"I apologize." Hano's deeply ingrained elven manners surged to the front immediately. "Please forgive me for my rudeness. I have had a lot on my mind lately."

"As have we all," King Garkin commented gravely. "Except me, actually. I have had nothing on my mind, and I would be in the eternal sleep of death if it had not been for Addyean here. Tell us one more time about your trip to Treshin. I saw in your eyes, the first things that I saw when I was revived, that something wonderful happened to you there. You changed more than a few years of hard farm work could have done."

Addyean, it is fair to say, felt a little intimidated. He was among the most powerful men in the world, and they were all staring at him, ready to listen to his fabulous story. Addyean wasn't even sure why he was at this meeting in the first place. Everyone here, with the exception of Warren and himself were great military leaders. Addyean, not for the first time, wished Zelin were present to help them. How Addyean wished for Zelin's wisdom, to help him explain the events of the last few weeks, but Addyean knew that he was not there, and that Addyean himself must give the narrative. Still, there were three here that Addyean did not fully trust, his years spying having made him perhaps a little too cautious. So he decided to lie.

"When I saw that you were ill, I hurried to Treshin, the holiest place that I could think of. When I got there, I explained the situation to a priest, who immediately got a vial and drew water out of the spring. I came back to you as fast as I could and gave it to you."

Everyone present except Hano burst into applause. When Addyean turned to look at him, the elf muttered under his breath, so only Addyean heard him. "Perhaps we'll get to hear the truth someday."

Addyean focused his startled gaze on Hano, unsure if he had heard him right. Addyean could adopt a new identity easily, and he was never caught lying. One look in Hano's eyes told him that he had indeed heard right, but also that Hano was going to leave it at that. Hano knew that Addyean had his own motives for lying, and he would not pry.

With his statement finished, the king abruptly drew his sword. He commanded Addyean to kneel, and promptly bestowed upon him nearly every honor possible in the kingdom. King Garkin explained that he would much rather have given the honors at the festival in public, but the less the public knew about his spies, the better. Someday, when King Garkin no longer needed him, Addyean would receive a rich retirement indeed.

All of the formalities out of the way, the council turned to the task at hand. General Cilio brought a huge map of all of the known Lands of Daranor, and spread it out on a table that had been constructed for just such a purpose. "Let's begin with all that we know," he began matter-of-factly, as he stuck colored pins over areas of concentration of certain forces. "Darhyn, shown by red, presumably has an army positioned here, at Castle Rathskellar."

"Do not say that name," Terin reprimanded.

"He lives on your fear," Cilio replied, unmoving. "If you do not fear him, he cannot touch you." General Cilio, at that moment did indeed look like he did not fear anything. It was not the kind of courage Sir Terin knew of, however. To Ironfist, courage was when you did your job on a battlefield even though you were afraid. To Cilio, on the other hand, fear was unnecessary, and indeed debilitating. This absolute unshaken confidence was what made Cilio a very good general, and what made a good many others fear him considerably, and at the same time be glad to be on his side.

"Put red dots around Breshen," Hano added sadly. "He has been sending small parties of goblins and black dwarves into our outer villages, raping and pillaging." Cilio placed the red dots accordingly.

"Will you be joining us in this struggle?" Cilio asked Hano. "Can we count on your army?"

"Certainly," Hano replied, a little taken aback. "We are the ones asking for your help in the first place. You can always assume that the elves will defend our beloved forest to our last breath."

"I expected as much," Cilio replied icily, putting green pins in the area around Breshen. "But in war you *never* assume anything. Assumption leads to all mistakes. If you remember in the last great war, nearly three hundred years ago, Darhyn *assumed* that Marhyn was there to help him. He could have won the battle so easily, such was his advantage in strength. But when he left his flank open for her to join, she had her troops slaughter his army. That is really the only reason we 'won' that war."

"Speaking of Marhyn," the king cut in hastily. "Will she be in this conflict? If so, what will be her plan?"

"If this turns into a full war, the Dark Lady will certainly be involved." Cilio's answer left no doubt. "As to how, your majesty can bet it will be a crafty plan. We should send spies to ascertain more specific details." Sir Terin put a black pin in Marhyn's fortress, and King Garkin made a mental note to get some people over there.

"What about the mermen?" Sir Terin asked his question as he looked about the room. "They would be valuable aid indeed if we need to engage in any water battles."

"My friend Prince Dalin went to ask them for aid," Hano replied. "He has fairly powerful friends there." Hano said it, condescendingly, almost as if having friends of other races wasn't the best thing to do. "He had not yet returned when I left. Perhaps he has returned since I have been here."

"As I see things now," the king began slowly, "there is not sufficient reason for war. I will not order the troops to attack if there has not been any provocation. The Death Lord may be the embodiment of evil, but I can't put the entire world on hold to go attack a fortress just out of the blue. This place has just remained there abandoned for the last three hundred years. Half of my kingdom probably doesn't even believe it exists." King Garkin held up a hand as Hano tried to reply. "We can aid your people in their border clashes. But there is a big difference between some border clashes and mobilizing the whole country to attack an abandoned fortress. I just don't see what we can really stand to gain from it."

"Very good plan, my lord," Warren added, speaking for the first time. "The people of Daranor are enjoying peace. There is no reason to start this slaughter. You have been in battles before, all of you. You know in war everybody loses."

"There is just one other thing," Addyean broke the silence. "There is a boy named Tarthur who lives in Krendon, the village I was working in. The reason that I came here, other than completing my assignment, is that a few weeks ago he had a dream. It is said that the Death Lord can communicate to some by his thoughts. In this dream, he killed the Dark One and found a spell hidden in his castle. Tarthur copied the words down while he was still asleep, on a scroll his friend gave him. When he showed this scroll to Zelin and I neither of us could read it. Zelin believes that Tarthur may have found the spell that controls the Water Orb. Zelin also believes that the Death Lord was sufficiently weakened by this defeat. If we muster all of our forces and attack now, we may be able to capture the Water Orb. With both it and the Power of Earth that you possess, we could have almost unchallenged dominion."

"Where is this Zelin now?" questioned Hano.

"He went to seek aid from the Council of Gurus," Addyean replied. "I hope he will return soon. If the council will help us, he will obtain their aid."

"The Water Orb is the key to success." King Garkin mused silently. "This changes everything. If we could regain the Water Orb, the kingdom would increase in prosperity and we would be secure from virtually all enemies. So I will order the troops to begin training and I will make sure all of my fortresses are stockpiled with weapons and armor. Hano, return to your people and continue to try to defeat these bandits. I hope dearly that they are nothing more. Cilio, I want you to go and help the elves in these frontier conflicts. With your guidance, I am sure they will be promptly routed. Addyean, wait for Zelin, and when he comes, we will have another meeting, where we can hopefully achieve more than we have achieved here. At that time, we will finalize a plan of attack. I must say that we will need some time, though. We haven't fought a war in many years, and our army is out of training. So we better get started right away."

The counselors all agreed that this was the best course of action, at least for the time being, and all set about their tasks. Hano agreed to return with Cilio in a month, for by then they might have crushed the goblins. After all, as Warren pointed out, goblin uprisings were fairly common, happening every generation or so when a relatively pugnacious goblin chieftain would take control of the tribes and attempt to wreak havoc throughout the kingdom. They were usually repelled without much trouble, and there was no real reason to believe that these goblins were linked with Darhyn. Hano hoped this would be the case here as well. Although his pride was hurt at taking this human which he felt unnecessary, Hano had to be at least outwardly friendly with the king. He knew even the elves would need help if there was a war. Besides, he could have been stuck with a much worse companion.

There were a few pats on the back, and the companions emerged from the council chamber of King Garkin, ready to join in the festivities, at least for the time being.

A priest gave him the water! Warren could not believe that was all that prevented him from becoming king. He made a mental note to kill this Addyean. No! Not just kill him! He would torture him and make him pay for ruining their scheming. Actually, as he would learn in a dream later that night, Darhyn had anticipated the turn of events, and had already modified his plan.

*   *   *   *

It was fully two days after escaping Marhyn's forces in the landslide that Tarthur, Derlin, and Yan found the treasure. Tarthur had been going on ahead to scout out the way when he came to a massive door. The door seemed old and mystical, full of power. Tarthur had excitedly called in a hushed voice to his friends—it seemed to use regular talk was to somehow desecrate this sacred site.

When all three had reverently examined it, Yan pronounced that it gave him a feeling of good, something that he had not felt in a long time, imprisoned in the cold, uncaring stone that was the prison of the Queen of Darkness. There was something written on the door. Again, Yan thought he could read it, but after trying very hard, had to finally admit that he could not. So the boys had slowly pushed open the door, the feeling of the place making them both excited at some wondrous possibility and anxious from the chance that what was inside would turn out to be evil.

For the first time in nearly three weeks for the boys, and many, many years for Yan, light met their eyes. Having eyes that had long been accustomed to the darkness, the trio was forced to squint and cover their eyes in pain. Soon, however, Tarthur was able to see. Too soon for the duration of time that they had been without bright light, Tarthur's pupils adjusted. Wondering why, he noticed that the light was not the harsh glaring light of the sun on a midsummer's day, but rather a soft, caressing light, enveloping him and making him feel safe and secure, like he was back in his mother's womb, the mother that had given him his name and little else. He could see in his companions' eyes that they felt this too, and for the first time, Tarthur saw Yan smile.

As they looked for the source of the light, the eyes of all three were drawn to an altar in the middle of the room. This altar was raised up upon a rectangular pyramid, and there was a sword and scabbard resting on it. The light was coming from the sword.

Filled with awe at this object of beauty and power, the companions ascended the stairs in a trance-like state, hardly daring to breathe, lest they disturb the majesty of the place. As they climbed closer, the light began to dim, so as to center on the sword, and have a radius of the length that the companions were away from it. In this way, the light showed the heroes what they needed to see, and nothing extraneous. When they had drawn close enough, Tarthur observed that there were strange, old letters traced all along the blade and a newer set of letters along the altar.

"I feel…at peace here," Yan slowly said in a hushed voice.

"Yes," Derlin said, "it is like I am in a field, on a sunny day, lying down with the wind blowing through my hair and no one to bother me."

"I…I can read this," Yan startled the boys, pointing to the inscription on the altar. "It says:"

> *Hail, all who come here in peace*
> *This is the Rune Sword, crafted by the masters of Air*
> *Take it, you who the Light of Truth burns deep within.*

In normal times, Tarthur was not one who could be described as having the Light of Truth burning deep within—some days Tarthur told more lies than truths. Yet, staring into the sword, Tarthur somehow knew that this was not the truth the inscription was talking about, it was the truth that was deep inside. For all the boyish pranks that Tarthur loved to play, he knew when to tell the truth, and he did. Tarthur was always honest with himself, and he would never lie in a situation that he knew was serious.

Uncertain of how to proceed, Tarthur looked at Yan, who nodded slowly. In that moment, Tarthur knew what he must do.

His trembling hand reached out, and Tarthur grabbed hold of the handle of the sword. In that instant, Tarthur knew he had made the right decision. The sword seemed to fit, to be made for his hand; it seemed to talk to Tarthur: *Take me*, it said. *Take me away from here and I will guide you with the Light of Truth.*

As Tarthur examined the sword more closely, he saw more strange runes carved deeply into the blade and traced on the scabbard, which he was now buckling around his waist.

"Are you sure we should, Tarthur," Derlin said, facing away from Tarthur. "I mean, I'm sure it won't be of use to anyone else down here, and it is so wonderful, but Tarthur, we don't know anything about this power. It's so strong..."

Tarthur turned to face Derlin. When Derlin looked into his face, he knew it was the right thing to do. He knew that this sword was meant for Tarthur.

"We must take it," Yan said, suddenly becoming knowledgeable. "The Rune Sword is an object of great power. Besides, Marhyn has been digging deep within these mountains. If we leave it here she might find it, and that would be disastrous." This last point firmly convinced the three, who in fact needed no convincing anyway. The heroes backed away from the altar reverently, bowing as they silently exited. Tarthur and Derlin closed the massive oak door, and the three resumed their journey looking for a way out of the mountains.

The journey was much improved, for the sword still provided light, and at each fork in the tunnels, the sword spoke to Tarthur softly, beckoning him onward. The sword never spoke more than one word, only "*right*" or "*left*." It spoke plainly, never joking, only one true word. Tarthur never had to doubt that it was right.

Assisted in this way, they could tell that they were making real progress. After a few more hours, however, the sword began to dim. At first, Tarthur was worried that he had broken it, but soon Derlin called out that he saw real light up ahead. It seemed that the sword could tell when it was not needed anymore. They rushed excitedly forward to the light, and soon Tarthur was once again breathing fresh air, the same air that he had so recently wondered if he would ever breathe again. Gratefully he sank to his knees, consumed the last of his moldy bread rations, and sank into the best sleep of his young life. As he quickly lost consciousness, he had a vague impression of Derlin and Yan following his actions; the actions of one who has been through so many emotional and physical trials, and who just realizes that he has survived.

When Tarthur awoke the next morning, he was almost unbearably stiff, and cold. As he got up and tried to move around to combat these two forces, he was suddenly struck by a third, thirst. He looked around, and soon he heard Derlin calling him from a short distance away.

Tarthur went over to his friend, who was also accompanied by Yan, the old man looking more fit than ever. Derlin had discovered a small mountain stream, which danced and glistened in the early morning light as it wound its way through the rocks and shrubs. As Tarthur bent over to drink the cool, pure water, he was abruptly reminded, more than by the cold in his joints, of the time of year. The water tasted good, almost sweet to someone who has drunk the untainted water of the mountain streams from his youth, but who has been recently deprived of it for some time. Tarthur took a large gulp of the water, and immediately realized his folly, for the water was so cold, it took his breath away. From this point on, he was required to take small sips, so as not to drink too much at once.

Once they had all drunk their fill, they decided to start moving. Derlin reminded them that they should move rather quickly, if any of Marhyn's forces were still in pursuit. (None were, thanks in a large part to Dalin.) They also knew that without food and warm clothes in this strange land with winter approaching, the cold would finish the job for the Queen of Darkness. They didn't have much of a plan, Derlin only recalling (he thought) that the castle of King Garkin was somewhere to the North. Not that they had much choice in the matter, they weren't about to go back south toward Marhyn's fortress. They then agreed to travel north until they came to some small village, where they could get some supplies and ask for directions.

So they followed the stream, which fortunately for them happened to be going north, having its origin somewhere in the tops of the Rune Mountains. By noon, they had arrived at the base of the Rune Mountains, and here they paused for a midday rest. (In normal times it would be called a lunch, but having no food, the companions didn't feel it was fair to call it that.)

As they journeyed on, once Derlin stopped and glanced back at Marhyn's citadel. All three turned and stared at it, although it was very far away. It seemed that they had traveled more than they thought. None of the companions wanted to sleep with that monstrosity looming over them, invading their sleep with nightmares and leaving them frightened, so they traveled a little further and made camp, if it could be called that with no tents or fire ring, in a grove of aspen trees where the shadow was not so ominous.

When Tarthur and Derlin awoke the next morning, Yan was gone.

There was no note, no sign, no footprints that announced his absconding. Tarthur's stiffness and chill were quickly forgotten as this new problem arose. They searched for Yan the better part of the morning, then gave up when it became apparent that the search was futile. Tarthur was genuinely worried about Yan. Yan was so alone, so frightened in this new world. Tarthur and Derlin were his only friends. Where could he have gone? It was supposed to be the grownups worrying about the kids, not the other way around. With a sigh, Tarthur and Derlin, feeling alone once more, started their day's journey. This was not the first companion that they had lost, Derlin reflected sadly, and he knew it would not be the last.

There were not many words said that day, a sharp contrast between the usual habits of the boys when they were alone. Back in Krendon, there was many a joke shared by the two at another's expense, and there was never a dull moment, never a time when neither of them had anything to say. This day, however, was different. The boys were beginning to grow up, to know that there are times when words are not the best way to communicate feelings.

As the shadows were beginning to lengthen and the early winter chill was beginning to come into the air, they finally caught sight of a small village. This village was at the first outward appearance much like Krendon, only a little smaller. Judging from the lights that were already lit in the windows, this town consisted of about fifteen or twenty houses. Both were glad for the size of the town, they knew small town people and how they acted.

As they approached the center of the town, they saw that there was a huge bonfire, and around it several townspeople were laughing and joking merrily. Tarthur and Derlin were happy for the apparent disposition of the revelers, for they seemed hospitable enough. Oddly conscious of how torn and bedraggled they must look after their ordeal in the mountains, Tarthur approached the group.

"Excuse me," he began as the startled townspeople looked up, "but my friend and I are travelers, and we were wondering if you have a barn or somewhere we could sleep, and perhaps some food. I'm sorry, we have no money to pay you."

"There will be nothing of the sort," A tall and heavily muscled man stood up from his drumstick. "Imagine that! Of all of the…"

"I'm sorry we offended you," Derlin hastily cut in. "Let's go," he whispered to Tarthur.

"Guests sleeping in a barn! And on the King's Birthday, nonetheless. You, sirs, will have the finest house in the village! We don't get many visitors here, you know. So when we do, we must take every chance we get to show our hospitality. But, I forget myself. You two look hungry. Have some food first." He finished his magnanimous words by offering Tarthur his own drumstick.

An extremely startled Tarthur and Derlin turned, looked at each other to make sure they had heard the man right, and then began to dig into the feast with a vengeance. The townspeople always gave the boys anything they wanted, even if the townspeople themselves happened to be eating it at that moment. The experience of being treated as one privileged was new to Tarthur and Derlin. As Tarthur reflected later, they probably had taken advantage of the townspeople's hospitality. Back then, Tarthur, although he was improving quickly, was not one to take the feelings of others into account very often. The generous hosts never complained, and soon they had put Tarthur and Derlin into a room in what was truly the finest house (although there was not much competition) in the vicinity. That night, the last thought Tarthur had as he gently slipped into oblivion, was how he wished more towns were like this one.

$$* \qquad * \qquad * \qquad *$$

"I say we kill it now." The voice was coming from one figure, as he hunched over the sleeping body. "We have revealed ourselves to it. When he awakes, it will be too late."

"You are crazy, Og!" The hushed whisper came from a misshapen form in the other side of the room. "You are assuming we could even kill him. We must let him awake and treat him respectfully."

"Og is right," said a third form, conversing with the other two. "And if there ever was a time, it is now."

These three had been planning what to do with the slumbering figure that had so abruptly come into their care. There were two in favor of killing him right off, to obtain the sword that he wore at his side and thus obtain some of his power.

The sword that he was wearing was a banner to many races, whoever carried it would have the support of vast armies in the war that they were bringing on. Yet, something about the slumbering one kept them at bay, making it seem as if he would awake and crush them before this deed was done. After discussing the matter a short while longer, they finally agreed that they had come this far, they might as well finish what they had began. There were no moral questions clouding the decision. Ones such as these would kill in the thought of a moment, barely even remembering who they had killed a second later. Sometimes they even killed for fun. After receiving a nod from his companions, Og raised his knife…and plunged it into the heart of the sleeping figure.

The figure's eyes opened. Og dropped his killing blade, paralyzed in fear. The Death Lord Darhyn, now fully awake and regaining power, stared into Og's eyes. Neither figure moved a muscle; the Death Lord out of relaxation, Og out of pure, terrorizing fear. Darhyn entered Og's mind, destroying rational thought; calm, joyous memories of Og's boyhood, and wonderful, happy memories of his wife, and systematically replacing them with cold, black terror. This terror is by its very nature indescribable, anyone who has experienced but the smallest portion of it will be utterly lost; plagued forever by nightmares so real he can feel them, taste them, and smell them, even when he is awake. As Og ran screaming out of the room, Darhyn added a piece of his life-force to the poor creature, making him endure this sentence until his death, which would not occur for many, many, years.

Turning to face the other cowering goblins that had tried to defeat him and take his power, Darhyn decided to be lenient in his punishment. He had been watching with his mind all of the discussions, and he knew that these two had been mainly prodded on by Og. Using this generosity, he calmly drew the black Sword of Darkness that hung at his side. Darhyn could feel the sword come to life, eager to taste blood once again. The Sword of Darkness had been made by Frehu, and it still had much of his power. Darhyn had destroyed Frehu's intellect that had been in the blade, leaving now only a desire to kill present in the talisman.

The first monster, upon seeing the black blade gleam red where there was no light, immediately fell on his knees and began to beg the Dark One to spare his life. Without listening, the Death Lord sliced through his body. The goblin screamed as the blade touched his skin. A unnatural chill, a thousand times colder than the chill of the worst winter night, coursed through his body, leaving red frost, made from freezing blood along where the blade had touched his now severed in half body.

Turning to face the last conspirator, now frozen not from the icy blade, but rather from pure terror, Darhyn decided to be merciful. Since this one had been against the futile attempt on his life, Darhyn simply spoke one word in his raspy, unemotional voice. "*Die.*"

The unfortunate soul burst into flames, which quickly consumed him. Annoyed, Darhyn pulled the knife from his breast and cast it down at the flaming goblin. His screams were still faintly echoing in the corridor when Darhyn felt the sword speak to him. It was questioning. It felt the pain of the last goblin to die, yet it wondered why it had not done the killing. It knew that the pain of the last was significantly less than the other two. The Sword of Darkness wanted more killing, more pain. Darhyn understood. Putting it back into its sheath, he promised it that soon there would be a great slaughter, and they would all be drunk with blood.

CHAPTER 8

▼

AND IT ALL CAME FROM A HUG

Girn was frustrated. After this long trip to come see his friends, they had already come to the shoals and gone again. He didn't have the means to go to Breshen or King Garkin's castle. Why, he had gotten lost and nearly killed himself from lack of food just trying to get here, and the king's castle was certainly many times farther away than the short distance between Krendon and the shoals. Plus, stealing those supplies had pretty much cut off any hope of his of returning to Krendon. It was stupid, he realized, looking through the unclouded lens of retrospect, to have cut off his retreat, but he had not been thinking then. And the mermen, while hospitable and generous, were rather worried about him living with them, both out of genuine concern for the people he had left in Krendon who should know he was safe, and out of a sort of incompatibility between their lifestyles.

"Well, I really can't go back," a dejected Girn was telling Truin, a stern merman whom he was getting to know rather well these last few days. "I had a most unfortunate misunderstanding with a person there. He is a snooty son of Baron Ercrilla, who is the leader of our town, and he has a large deal of influence." This was more than Girn usually said, but upon arriving in the shoals, Girn had decided that at least for the beginning of what he hoped to be a long stay here, he must speak up, even though forming the words was still difficult for him.

"Ah, yes," Truin said with a smile. "He must be the one for whom Tarthur wanted the *kokhor*."

Talking of his old friends made Girn sad, and he wished for the good old times again. Actually, he mused, there really hadn't been that many good times. Girn was younger than both of the boys, and even though Tarthur and Derlin accepted him the way he was, Girn often felt awkward with his stammer. So it was that many times Girn had declined invitations to participate in the boys' schemes, on grounds of some real or imagined task for Zelin. Zelin thought, and he was probably right, that the way to keep young boys out of trouble was to keep them busy. Even though Zelin personally disliked cleanliness, (he professed that if his things were strewn about the floor, he could find them much easier) he purposefully ordered Girn to keep the outside clean, mainly to give him something to do. Girn had always lived in Tarthur and Derlin's shadows, looking up to them but never quite equaling them. With the great things that were happening now, Girn had felt that he would finally have a chance to be with Tarthur and Derlin, and now everything was ruined. All he could do was stay and wait, since Truin had already told him that the mermen would play a great role in the struggle that he said was fast approaching.

Girn looked up from his position in the comfortable seat, one of the three in the whole shoals, to see a person who he had never seen before, yet knew from just one glance to be Tustor, the merwizard. Tustor nodded politely, and began with a simple greeting. "Hello, I understand that you are a friend of Tarthur and Derlin. I owe much to them."

Girn wasn't sure how to proceed, or even if it was his turn to talk. Too late, he thought of offering the merwizard his chair, and then of the stupidity of thinking this. What could Tustor do with a chair? At times like this when Girn became nervous, his stammer came back.

"Y…Yes. Th…Thank you. I w…w…was also Zelin's a…a…a…pren…" Girn collapsed on the difficult word. Fortunately for him, Tustor rescued him with a hand on his shoulder and a warm smile of reassurance.

"Yes, I see that you are. You have no power yourself, but you bear the mark of one who has been around someone with great power for a long while. I am very glad of this fact, because it makes what I am about to do easier. You, see, Girn, the Death Lord is, or rather was, a human. As you may or may not know, a very long time ago, his master, who also used to be human, took something that belonged to us. He came to us one day, professing to want to know more about the wonder of Water. We believed him, and showed him our secrets. To repay our kindness, he cast a powerful spell, containing the wonder of Water in a single

Orb. My people were closely tied to this thing, and when he took it, many perished over the sheer sadness of living without our most precious treasure. That was a very long time ago, but still my people are loath to let humans into our deepest secrets. Oh, we are friends with humans and are much interested in their welfare. On the status of nation to nation, we are allies and very friendly. But as individuals, our hospitality dictates that we should let them visit for a few days, and then we must send them on their way. But just recently, something has happened to change all this. Your friend Tarthur arrived."

"Before he came, the Water Orb, which is still in the Death Lord's possession, was kept out of the world. This means," he continued, simplifying the complex magical terminology so Girn could understand it, "that it was kind of like something that does not exist because you cannot see it or touch it. Yet, it still exists. There was also a spell that can call the Water Orb to the aid of the person that has it. A few weeks ago, the Death Lord began to bring the Water Orb back into the world. He sent his mind out of his body, and attacked Tarthur in a dream. We are not sure how, but Tarthur managed to defeat him and steal the spell that controls the Water Orb. Zelin sent him here to learn more about it from us. That is when we sent Tarthur and Derlin and another named Dalin to talk to the king to tell him to be ready for war. My people have a great hope that we can attack the Death Lord before he can awake and gather his powers. If we can do this, while gaining back the Water Orb, the balance will be thrown onto the king's side and my people will have a joy and feeling of fulfillment like we have not felt since our beloved treasure was stolen from us."

"There is one thing the revered one of the sea has forgotten to mention," interrupted Truin, just as Girn was beginning to digest all that he was being told. "He has humbly left out that when the Orb first came back into his consciousness, Tustor, out of love for the sea, died of pure joy upon learning that the Water Orb was back in the world. Using his spell, Tarthur was able to resurrect him, and now Tarthur and his friend Derlin are owed in these shoals."

A brief shadow, imperceptible to the others, passed over Tustor's face. He wished it were out of humility that he had omitted this last part, but it was because he had, at least for the day, forgotten. He had been trying to forget it, trying to throw it from the depths of his soul, erase it from his memory as completely as if it had never been. Yet each time he found himself thinking of the wonder, the indescribable feeling of power and grace and belonging that he had felt there. At times, he even got mad at himself, for the merwizard was one who had a superbly strong mind. He was used to bending all things to his iron will, but still he could not forget it. He constantly reminded himself of Tivu, and of the inescapable sorrow that always stalks those who have seen It, and yet always It comes, like a wolf in the night, to attack Its victim and tear his mind to pieces. He had thought many times of sharing his secret with the rest of the mermen, but he knew at the same time it would be futile. No one could understand.

At the same time, Girn was feeling more awe and awkwardness at being Tarthur's friend. Tarthur and Derlin, before set up to be heroes in the impressionable mind of young Girn, were now made to be giants. Imagine, defeating the Death Lord and raising a figure of power from the dead! Girn was impressed when the boys played a trick on Morty or stole something under heavy guard. But now, Girn was sure that they would be included in some great tale, passed down from generation to generation, read by the firesides of countless old men and young boys who would one day say to their mothers, "Look at me, mommy! I'm Derlin, the hero. I'm gonna kill this dragon," as he viciously attacked a cow with a stick. Girn sighed wistfully, sad that he would never be in this tale. (He was, of course wrong. No mother who had ever paid any attention whatsoever to the dubious characters of Tarthur and Derlin would want her son exposed to the scandalous morals of the boys. Oh, yes. He was also wrong about the other thing. This is that story, if you have been wondering.)

"There is a certain feeling that I have," Tustor started, hastily regaining his composure, "that since our treasure was lost through a man, it must be regained through a man also. As you have said, you cannot return home, and you certainly cannot travel abroad in the world. You are young and you are still marked with a twinge of magic. There are some who would seek to use you for their own ends, which would not be pleasant for you."

Girn felt calmed, and reassured by the soothing voice of the merwizard. It seemed to say the way things are, and the way they will be. There was no doubt or room for questioning. Still, Girn wondered why the merfolk had let Tarthur and Derlin go, while they kept him here. The two boys were certainly nothing close to responsible. What was the big difference? He haltingly inquired his questions to the two mermen.

"I have already given a few reasons. You are marked as the apprentice of a great one. I don't honestly think Tarthur and Derlin could make it by themselves in the outside world, but fortunately for us they are not alone. An excellent guide named Dalin is accompanying them. He will take them to Breshen and King Garkin and then we will hopefully be able to transfer the spell to someone more powerful, and Tarthur and Derlin will stay in the capital or return home. It really won't be that momentous a trip for them," the aged merwizard said, trying to pacify both Girn and himself. "Besides," he added, using sound reason and logic, but unfortunately his remark was to be an ever constant thorn in Girn's heart. "You are just too young and small."

Girn nodded forlornly and left the room, holding back the tear that was beginning to form in his eye. He was completely alone and could do nothing about it.

✳   ✳   ✳   ✳

Tarthur stretched and yawned, rubbing the last bits of sleep from his eyes. He was stiff from resting, for the first time in a long while, in a comfortable bed, but the soreness was disappearing rapidly as he put on his clothes. He noticed that the townspeople had given him a new set, which was freshly pressed and while not elegant, was of fairly good quality. Tarthur was glad for the change; the cloak that Yrean had woven him was ripped to shreds. Tarthur was surprised that it didn't simply fall off. Tarthur glanced at Derlin who was busy polishing his sword. (He still had the one he had taken from the goblin before the wall collapsed.)

Noticing the close scrutiny of his friend, Derlin glanced up. The Rune Sword was also polished, lying upright on the table. It still had a faint glow, but nothing like it had in the cave. "When I woke up before you, as I usually do, I felt bad. These townsfolk have really been helpful to us, so I decided to get up and see if I could help them with their chores."

Tarthur was a little startled. Why would anyone want to do chores when he does not have to? Tarthur could not figure it out. In his later years, his mind would stray back to the merwizard. Sometimes things needed to be done regardless of how unpleasant they were. And there were many more unpleasant things than everyday chores. Recognizing this was a step toward growing up that Tarthur was not ready to take yet.

"But you know what happened?" Derlin continued his narrative. "They would not let me help them in the least bit. They just told me to go to sleep, and even brought some breakfast up. These people do not look like hearty and over-prosperous people. I think that they are giving to us out of their sustenance. That is why I told them we would leave soon today."

Tarthur nodded. While he would not have objected very loudly if someone had asked him to stay, at the same time he knew their mission was of vital importance, and to tarry further could prove disastrous. Tarthur finished dressing himself, and reverently fastened the Rune Sword at his side. The boys had made no formal decision about who was to carry the sword—back in Krendon they would have argued over it and maybe even gotten into a small scuffle (what would be termed among the more refined members of society a "vicious brawl") but afterward they would have come to a decision. Now, however, the sword just happened to be with Tarthur. And even these boys weren't about to fight over something so sacred.

The boys painstakingly made the beds and cleaned up their little room, something that was not a habit for them. Being treated so courteously by the people of the town had changed them into people who wanted to help others. Tarthur thought, "We have news which is incredibly important to the king, and here we are making beds!"

Walking down the stairs and into the small antechamber that was also the kitchen and main room of the house, Tarthur caught sight of the heavily muscled man that had offered him his drumstick the day before. "Hello," he called out heartily. "I trust you slept well?"

"Yes, thank you. Better than I have slept in quite some while," Tarthur replied good naturedly.

The man nodded in approval and smiled. "My name is Yonathan. My friend told me you were leaving, but perhaps I could trouble you to stay just a few more days. If I may say so, you two do look like you could use a little rest and food. Besides, the king has declared a feast for his birthday and the three days following it. That includes today and tomorrow, and tonight we are having roast antelope. And it is bad luck to be traveling on the King's Birthday."

Derlin raised a restraining hand before Tarthur could weigh the good points of the argument, which were numerous. "Thank you, Yonathan, for all of your hospitality. But I am afraid that we really must be going. I assure you that if we are ever in this part of the world again we will visit."

Tarthur proceeded to inquire about a map of the roads leading to the king's palace, which turned out to be to the Northeast, through a large tract of grassland. Before setting out, Tarthur saw a pretty girl, and since he was not one to let a good opportunity go by to offer his thanks, he embraced her, to thank her for their hospitality. Derlin likewise hugged Yonathan.

A shriek that brought back memories of their imprisonment in Marhyn's fortress tore through the early morning light. The townspeople seemed frozen by the terror, unable to move. Derlin whirled to see the source of the sound, and found that it was coming from the girl. Wondering what Tarthur had done to her, he looked angrily at his friend, who was as puzzled as Derlin.

"No…NO…Anything but that! Please…" She was starting ahead, blankly. Then she seemed to realize what was going on and turned to look at Tarthur and Derlin. Her voice had now lost its wildness, but was pleading and afraid. She spoke in a whisper, as if to prevent anyone else from hearing. "Help us. He's got us all. Underground. Terrible things. You must help. Quickly."

"Who?" Tarthur asked immediately

"Shh," she said putting a finger to her lips. "He'll hear you, he'll…" With that, she let out a scream like a caged animal that knows it will be killed and can do nothing to fight back, yet a hundred times worse, and collapsed to the ground. Tarthur rushed forward and felt for a pulse, which was beating faintly. He turned to look at the townspeople, who were still frozen in a state of suspended animation. The girl was breathing, but still motionless. Soon, however, her fingers and toes began to disintegrate, leaving nothing where they were formerly. This process continued up her arms and legs until there was nothing left of her body. The boys stared in a mixture of disbelief and horror at the vanishing girl.

"What was that?" Derlin spoke the question that was on both of their minds. The two stared at each other, neither knowing the answer.

"A few girls have rejected me before, but nothing like that." Tarthur was puzzled. Derlin waved the absurdity away. Then, it hit him.

"The sword, Tarthur. It brushed against her when you hugged her."

"But why would this sword cause something like this? I felt it, before in the vault. This sword is good, I know it. Why would it do this to an innocent girl? And who is this 'he?' What is he doing to her?" Derlin could not respond to Tarthur's barrage of questions, but fortunately he didn't have to; the townspeople were slowly coming out of their shock.

Yonathan was the first to speak. "Well I certainly hope we have a chance to take you up on your offer," he continued as if nothing had happened.

"What was that shriek?" Tarthur addressed his question in the general direction of the crowd.

"Oh," a young man, whom Tarthur had seen before, came forward to answer. "I didn't hear anything, but you must have heard a *walerer*. That's a bird that lives 'round these parts. His mating cry could raise the dead."

It soon became apparent to Tarthur that these people had neither heard the sound, nor witnessed the girl's disappearance. Tarthur looked at Derlin and motioned with his head toward the trees. It was a signal that Tarthur and Derlin had used many times before back in Krendon. We will talk, it implied, in the forest. Having made this plan, they thanked their hosts once again and started to take their leave into the forest.

All of a sudden, Tarthur felt a burning pain at his side, coming from the Rune Sword. Thinking only of relieving himself of the pain, Tarthur flung the sword from his body. It flew through the air, and landed blade down in a pile of brown earth and pine needles in front of the townspeople. Light began radiating from the blade, encompassing a few of the townsfolk. Those affected began to scream in pain, falling to their knees in agony.

At that moment, Tarthur wanted nothing more than to run away. To run away and leave this dangerous sword that at one moment seemed good and at the next evil, and to leave these matters for people like Zelin who knew what they were doing. At the same time, he knew he could not. So, he did the only thing he could think of, he ran towards the Rune Sword, intending to hurl the cursed weapon into the forest where it could not hurt these people any longer. He rushed forward into the light, but as his hand closed around the handle, a searing pain shot through his arm, knocking him down. Not being what one would consider bright, he came forward to try again, but this time a voice interrupted his progress.

"Stop!" Yonathan called out to Tarthur. At this moment, the sword became again lifeless and clattered harmlessly to the ground.

Tarthur whirled to face him, and then began to apologize profusely. Yonathan, however, held up a restraining hand. "We…we have been under a spell for a long time now. There is a terrible wizard who lives in a small cavern underneath this town. During the day he works on his magic and during the night he makes us…well, it is better not to say what he makes us do. It is not fit to be told in the world of daylight."

"Why didn't someone in your town ask for help?" Derlin asked, puzzled.

"The spell was such that even our bodies were not under our own control. His magic has 'programmed' us to act certain ways, but always our souls have cried out. There has never been anyone to hear us."

"Why would anyone want to do something like this?" Tarthur wondered out loud.

An older man, whom Derlin remembered was named Uris, answered. "He wants to become like the great ones. Like Frehu and the Dark One and his sister. Thirty tears ago, he came into this town and enslaved the people by his magic. He made us lead false lives outside. He gave us something to do for every situation. In this our minds and our bodies have said and done whatever was normal. But our souls cried out in hidden anguish!"

A woman stepped forward. "Let me explain. It is as if I have no control over my body. Every morning I wake up at the same time. I walk down the stairs, left foot first, and then into the kitchen. I reach down with my right hand and pick up a pot. I go to the yard, grab a piece of firewood, and then go back and start the fire. I make the same oatmeal every day, with two cups of oats and one cup of milk. I always put it in with the same hand. I always stir the oatmeal thirteen times counterclockwise, and then let it cook for thirty seven minutes. I don't will any of this to happen. Every day, over and over it happens. The wizard wants our town to appear normal on the outside. His magic makes us respond in a certain way to every possible situation. That way anyone who doesn't stay here for more than a week or so will think our village is perfectly normal, but in the night he tortures us and steals our life."

"Why would it end now?" Another townsperson stepped forward and asked his question. "I felt something in that sword, but I…I don't know what it was."

At this the people of the town turned expectantly at the boys, as if asking them for the answer. Tarthur didn't have the heart to tell them he didn't know.

"Tarthur," Derlin said slowly, as if getting an idea. "Didn't the sword say something about truth? It may be that this sword made them tell the truth."

Uris nodded gravely. "I have heard of such a thing. Truly, we were leading false lives. The light of truth has revealed what was hidden inside."

"A sword that compels truth?" Tarthur wasn't sure he liked the idea. In fact, he could not think of anything that might be worse, so he decided to try an experiment. "Derlin," he called out. "Take the Rune Sword and touch it to me." When his friend had done so, he decided to try the biggest lie of his life. "I wish Morty was here and he kicked me in the nose." Nothing happened.

"I guess the sword does not compel truth, or at least all truth," Tarthur said with a shrug of his shoulders.

"Whatever the case may be," Uris interrupted, "we must deliberate it later, for now there is work to be done. The magician will be sleeping now, but I fear that the unraveling of his spell will wake him. We must proceed immediately to his cavern and destroy him now while he is weak!" This last cry was met with rounds of enthusiastic cheers on the part of the townspeople, now freed of the spell that had so long tortured them. They were hungry for vengeance.

Tarthur and Derlin naturally began to follow the commotion, but Yonathan turned sternly to face them. "We thank you for all you have done to help us, but this is not your fight. If you are determined to help us, however, we certainly could use you." The choice thus made clear for them, the boys followed Yonathan, who seemed to be something of a leader in the town, and soon they arrived at a large boulder imbedded in the side of a cliff. The people found a nearly imperceptible crack, and rolled the boulder away to reveal an opening. It was easy to see that the townspeople had done this many times before. As they were descending into the gaping maw, Derlin glanced over at Tarthur. He didn't need to speak, the message was crystal clear. "Not again!"

Yonathan promptly lit a lantern, more for Tarthur and Derlin than for anyone else. Everyone else knew this passage. They knew every stone, every turn, every crevasse, for they had tread this way many times before, with the stark terror and repetition that makes for a clear knowledge.

The passage was not long, and soon they came to a chamber, inside of which was a floating bed containing a slumbering figure. The figure lay peacefully on his back, an aura of green mist floating about his body. Tarthur and Derlin didn't have time to take in further observations; as soon as they entered the chamber, some of the stronger townspeople led by Yonathan rushed forward and began to viciously hack apart the still figure. At the same time another group of the rest of the people, this time led by Uris, fell to in the laboratory, smashing wooden racks of glass vials and ripping books of ancient knowledge to shreds. In this manner, they quickly destroyed everything of value in the chamber. The people destroyed with a vengeance and hatred that the boys had never before witnessed. They viciously attacked everything in sight, as if, in this one moment of extreme violence, they could atone for years of suffering. There were even a few times when the usually courageous and unconcerned Tarthur was scared of their fury, and had to remind himself that they were on his side.

When the men had almost finished hacking the wizard's body to minuscule pieces, a small fire started, which is nearly inevitable in a place with no ventilation where many chemicals that are meant to be separate are mixed into one mess along the floor. At first Tarthur fancied that the fire had been kindled from the heat of anger and reckless destruction that the townspeople participated in. Soon the flames began to spread and the people were forced to evacuate. They hurried quickly out of the small tunnel. Once they were a safe distance away all turned to see the spectacle.

A thick cloud of black smoke rose from the small chimney. Intertwined with the rising black Tarthur thought he caught a glimpse of a small pillar of green, but it could've just been a trick of the light. With a crack that was to be heard many miles away, even as far as the palace of Queen Marhyn, the small cavern exploded. Soot blackening their faces, and many leg hairs and eyebrows singed by the searing heat, the townspeople erupted into a victorious shout.

CHAPTER 9

▼

ANOTHER SWORD OF POWER AND AN OLD FRIEND

After cleaning their faces and many warm congratulations all around, the people of the town sat down to have lunch. This may seem like a rather ordinary thing to do, after having just defeated an evil wizard, but this was no ordinary lunch, for this was a feast. Their last feast, which seemed like centuries ago (although it was only the night before) had been artificial, they were merely doing the work of the wizard. Now, it was their first chance to use free will in a long time. They weren't about to let the opportunity for a feast escape them. They also weren't about to let the reason for it leave either. After the evil being who had held the town so long in bondage was destroyed, Tarthur and Derlin had tried to leave, citing that they had pressing business to attend to with the king. Yonathan politely told them that if they tried to leave, they would have a whole town chasing after them, and while they could destroy monsters and such, they might not defeat the determined townsmen. He also had to remind them that they needed a guide and a map if they were to make it much farther, neither of which they possessed, and both of which Yonathan could provide, after which the boys had to grudgingly agree to stay.

Even though they were forced to stay, and Tarthur had a principle of never enjoying anything he was forced to do, soon the boys were reveling with the best of them. The girl that Tarthur had hugged was still missing, and presumed dead. Others had lost loved ones as well. Still, there were no loud cries of mourning. The people kept their grief in silent agony, or else forgot about it, for now was not the time for such things.

As the celebration continued on, Uris came forward to make a presentation. The people abruptly quieted, expectant to see what was about to happen. "First and foremost," he called out in a loud voice. "The results of the vote are in. From now on, this village will be Freeton, since we are at last free to do what we wish." This remark was greeted with enthusiastic cheers, since most of the people had voted for it. Uris raised his hands again for quiet, which was soon given to him. "And, by a much closer margin, the new mayor of Freeton is Kandan Ironsmith, with Yonathan as his assistant." More ecstatic cheers came from the public, for Kandan and Yonathan were known by all to be honest and trustworthy men. The people had been allowed free rein of their bodies for a few minutes every night, and it was then that the townspeople had gotten to know each other. The residents felt confident with Kandan and Yonathan in control of their town.

The crowd had begun to disperse, sensing the conclusion of the announcements, but Uris called them back. "There is just one thing more." At this remark, Yonathan came to stand beside him, carrying a large bundle, wrapped in purple silk. "Yesterday we were lost, living in hidden terror. But two came from the South, breaking the spell and setting us free. They asked for no reward for their help, only wanting to go on and help others."

At this point in the speech, Tarthur looked at Derlin to see which two from the South they were talking about going around and trying to save everyone. Uris was mistaken; Tarthur and Derlin were just trying to stay alive. Derlin was a little confused too, but eventually the boys decided that they were talking about them. Tarthur realized that the speech was now drawing to a close, and decided to pay attention again.

"And so, this town has decided to give them this sword which was found in the lair of the fiend before we destroyed him. Unfortunately, the scabbard was lost in the fire. Nonetheless, let me present to you, Tarthur and Derlin, the Light Sword."

Once again thunderous applause burst from the assembled townsmen, as Derlin went forward to receive the weapon. The hilt was of pure silver, beautifully crafted, with the blade coming out from the mouth of a dragon and his tail making the grip. Two silver wings branched out to form the hand guard. The blade, for lack of a better color, was the color of bright yellow light. Derlin rotated the blade in his hand, truly awed at its beauty.

As he lifted it, he noticed that it seemed to weigh too little for its size. "It certainly is a light sword," Derlin said as he looked questioningly at Uris, who inwardly chuckled.

"No," he said, smiling. "While it does weigh little, it is *the* Light Sword, not just a light sword. The blade is made of pure light. I am sure it has many magical properties, but I am of but humble skill and I cannot find them. You said that you are traveling north to see King Garkin. I am giving this sword to you because I am sure there will be someone there who has sufficient knowledge in the arts of magic to unlock its secrets. And I know you will use this sword for good."

Feeling a little embarrassed, Derlin nodded and turned to collect Tarthur so to continue on their journey.

When the three were at last ready to leave Freeton, the people were on hand to see them off. Yonathan had insisted on accompanying Tarthur and Derlin. They had declined at first, and then realized the obvious advantages of having a strong adult along, especially one with a map and money. Having Yonathan accompany them really made Tarthur miss Dalin. He hadn't thought of his friend much lately, but it made Tarthur wonder where he was. Tarthur hoped he would see him when they got to the king's castle, but something made him wonder. He also thought about Yan. Exactly where did he go? Again, Tarthur hoped for the better, but deep inside, Tarthur was afraid that the senile old man had gotten lost and was now hopelessly confused in this strange new world, or else dead. When he told the people of Freeton they offered to set up search parties for the next few days and send them around the vicinity to see if they could pick up any traces of Yan. Tarthur thought it was a long shot, but definitely worth trying.

Outfitted in completely new gear that the people had so generously provided, Tarthur, Derlin and Yonathan finally made it into the surrounding woods amidst hearty cheers of "Come again soon! You'll always be welcome in Freeton," and "Your friends will always be welcome here also," and a "Heck, anyone that's even ever heard of you can stay as long as he likes for free!" (Although, Tarthur was sure the last was an overstatement.) Yonathan led them on an old deer trail for what was left of the day, which was not much, but at least they covered a few miles before sunset. It felt good to Derlin and Tarthur to be traveling again. There was something about the forest. The smell of pine needles mingled with sweat made hiking called out to their spirit of adventure, which, though dampened by their many trials, was beginning to burn anew. Having an adult guide and new clothes and food in their stomachs and packs helped considerably, but even had they not had these necessities, nothing could have quenched the spirit of adventure that burned within them that night. In fact they were so excited that Tarthur proposed traveling at night, to which Derlin readily assented, but they were vetoed by Yonathan, on account of his not being able to find the trail.

The new morning sunlight brought the boys once again refreshed and reenergized out to eat breakfast and start. It was a sharp contrast from the Tarthur who had complained bitterly at being forced to rise at five in the morning to see a sunrise. How long ago had that been? It seemed to Tarthur like months, even years, but the biting chill of the early morning air reminded him that it was just nearly winter. He had only left Krendon in the middle of fall. Their renewed spirit of adventure coupled with their need to get moving to combat the chill forced them to travel at a strenuous pace for the rest of the day, stopping only once to admire the scenery while they ate lunch. Because of their rapid progress, they soon reached the junction to the king's highway, where Yonathan advised them to stop for the evening and camp. Although wanting to travel on at least until it became dark, the boys saw the logic in this plan and settled down to cook dinner. Tarthur and Yonathan gathered sticks for the fire, which was mostly Tarthur pointing to good sticks and Yonathan using his bear-like strength to break them off, while Derlin took some rabbit meat, carrots, and vegetables and began to make a stew.

After the excellent dinner, (nothing tastes better than a hot meal you have cooked after a long day of hard work) Derlin began to put a stick in the fire and carve it with a knife one of the townsmen had given him. As he was chipping off the charred part of the stick, he could not help but gaze up at the setting sun. The sun was completing its day-long journey across the sky from west to east with a background of orange, with streaks of crimson and deep purple striking out from the sides. While nothing like the sunrise on the shoals of the merfolk, this was truly a wonder to behold.

Suddenly, instead of gradually becoming dark as usual, a shadow fell over the campsite. All three looked into where the brightness of the sun should be, then immediately wished they hadn't. Coming from the East was something monstrous; they could not see the figure, but only its shadow as it blocked out part of the setting sun. They did not need to, for although it was not very clear, all three could immediately recognize it for what it was. It was a dragon. It was huge. And it was coming straight for them.

*   *   *   *

"Here it is, sir!" The soldier snapped to attention as his commanding officer stooped to examine his work. He gave a tug on the rope, saw that it was secure and adroitly made, and frowned his displeasure. "That's horrible, sailor. Way too slow. How is the empress going to take over the world with this slop? I want you to make a hundred more knots like this one and then report back to me." The sailor's face was crestfallen, and his eyes showed his disappointment. "What!" The officer said, again displeased. "You should have more pride in your work. I'll teach you confidence, if it's the last thing I do. Report to kitchen duty for a month!"

"Yes, sir!" This soldier knew better than to argue with this officer, even though he was burning inside with shame.

Captain Nilad, officer in command of twenty five troops of Her Highness, Empress and Ruler of the Lands of Daranor (or soon to be) Queen Marhyn, had a reputation for a slightly bad temperament, along with a quick hand at the sword. A few weeks ago, one of the men called him a traitor. Before he could finish, Captain Nilad's sword was dripping with blood that used to belong to the deceased man's neck. No one really cared, they were all a bunch of drifters anyway, social misfits who were along just for the money, and maybe a few women once they started taking over the land. The pay was good, and gold. In fact, it was rumored that the Dark Lady had an endless supply stemming from the tunnels underneath her fortress.

Captain Nilad looked over at a bunch of soldiers of his command who were drinking freely from a flask of ale that was being passed around while they were supposed to be practicing to ready their ship to leave port in just one week. "Keep up the good work, guys," he said while patting one of them on the shoulder in a comradish sort of way.

Retiring into his quarters, Dalin couldn't help but smile. He knew it was a risk he probably shouldn't have taken, but as long as he was leaving today he had to have a little fun. All along, he had covertly been draining Marhyn's strength from within by busying the adept and skillful members of the army with bothersome and endless menial tasks, while allowing slobbery to be permitted ever so slightly. In this way he was draining minuscule amounts of Marhyn's strength, while much more importantly, keeping his eyes and ears wide open for any details about what the Dark Lady was planning. So far, he had discovered that Marhyn was using a fair number of men who were being trained in sailing but not fighting, except the very fundamentals of raping and pillaging, of which most were familiar with anyway. It was easy to see that she was planning a naval foray, and from the orders he had glimpsed of his commanding officer, they were planning to travel west. He wanted to stay and find out more, but a nagging suspicion told him that he might soon be caught. He had come very close once, a man of his group had been coming in to talk to Dalin about some unrelated matter, when he had glimpsed Dalin take off his hat and run his fingers through his hair. His pointed ears had thus been revealed, and Dalin's startled look had betrayed him further. He might have talked his way out of it, for while elves were known for their hatred of killing, and were very uncommon in mercenary armies, they were not absolutely unheard of. Instead, he decided to do the safe thing. When the man opened his mouth to call him a traitor, Dalin was ready with his sword, and that was that.

Dalin hated killing any man, but he knew that he had no other choice if he wanted to remain and learn more to help the king and his father. Ah, yes, and his friends Tarthur and Derlin. Dalin thought back on all of the events that had transpired since the last time he had seen them. Dalin hoped they had escaped, but he was also worried that they were buried in the many tons of granite that had fallen as they tried to flee. He thought about Tarthur, and knew in his heart that he had made it somewhere. Dalin just hoped Tarthur had enough sense to proceed directly to the king and tell him what happened. Dalin sighed; he hoped he would see his old friends when he went to Tealsburg.

He smiled fondly as he remembered his escape. Shortly after he was put into the low class cell, he had withdrawn the straw and a needle that he kept in his boot for just such an occasion. The needle was tipped with a virulent mixture of herbs and tree sap from his home in Breshen, and while it was not lethal, it would leave whomever it came into contact with in a stupefying daze for a few minutes, and then relax them into a natural slumber. Only needing one shot, Dalin had infected the guard, and then kindly asked him to unlock the door, which he did. Dalin had respect for all life, and that is why he used this dart instead of killing his jailer, but he harbored no illusions. He knew what would happen to this unfortunate creature when Marhyn learned of his escape. So Dalin told him to flee the castle, and he agreed. Dalin hoped the fleeing creature would make it, and also help to draw off any pursuit.

Dalin decided to make a quick sweep of the area to see if he could find Tarthur or Derlin, because Tarthur and the Water Orb were very valuable to the cause, and they were also his friends. He was cut off, however, by a rather large group of men who were traveling into a larger cavern. Dalin was trapped! Frantically he looked around for exits, but none were to be found. So, he did the only thing he could think of. He joined them. Fortunately for Dalin, they were all dressed in various garb, and all were mangy and scraggly, though not as bad as other mercenaries. Dalin fell right in step and contented himself to rudely joke with the rest while looking for a side tunnel that he could slip into. Unfortunately, there were none to be found, and soon they reached their destination.

The men filed in slowly, and what Dalin saw on a raised platform made him gasp in shock. Lithar Lifehater stood, ready to address his troops. Dalin pulled his hair a little closer into his face. He hated always having to hide his elven features, but knew in this, as always, he had no choice. Dalin fitted in behind a bigger man and hoped the darkness would hide him from Lithar's remembrance.

"You have all been called here on account of the Dark Lady's extreme generosity and kindness." Lithar didn't seem to see Dalin, who if he would have thought about it, was so bruised and dirty that even his mother might have failed to recognize him. This made Dalin relax ever so slightly, but remain cautious. "There have been many who have flocked to the banner of the empress, Queen Marhyn. They have come from all lands and peoples. In her mercy, she has allowed you to be chosen to hold positions of responsibility and service to her. You have all proven in your tests to be competent enough to become captains in her imperial army. Prove your worth, and you will be rewarded heavily. Flout our orders and, well…" Lithar nodded. Everyone understood.

The speech was small; Lithar did not feel the need to talk with the lower officers much. After that, they all filed out, leaving their name with a recorder who proceeded to give each a black overtunic with crimson sides that would serve as a crude but sufficient uniform for the captains. They were also issued a long sword, a steel dagger, a pouch of tobacco and a bottle of brandy, both of which Dalin had used to befriend his own commanding officer, before taking a look at his orders from up top. They also received an advance sum of gold. The captains were extremely lucky. Regular soldiers got none of the above, except a sword if they had none. Tobacco and brandy were of high value in the camp, since they were in such short supply.

When it was Dalin's turn with the reporter, he quickly reversed the letters in his name and received his supplies. He had wanted to escape, and now was a perfect chance, since he had new supplies and could follow the others and find a way out. However, soon the situation he was placed in began to lure him. He was in a position of command among Marhyn's troops, and he could use this to a valuable advantage. He might even find out where Tarthur and Derlin were and help them.

As he reflected on the ease of which he had been promoted, Dalin thought about the move by Marhyn, and concluded that it was a smart one. She had given a test to all new recruits, and helped out some of the brighter ones. In this way she appeared generous and giving in the eyes of her troops, and Dalin knew this was vital. The biggest problem with mercenaries was lack of a will to fight, lack of a cause. By spending just a little money, she was taking a step to promote loyalty. It made Dalin once again remind himself not to underestimate Marhyn's forces, and to begin to fear not only her evil, but also her intelligence.

So Dalin had taken the commission, and become Captain Nilad. He had not had time to search for the boys, but he had aided their escape. By pure chance, Dalin had been commanding his men when he had received word that there was a attempted prisoner escape in the third quadrant of the new area, and that he was to send two of his men for aid and bring the rest to help immediately. By taking the proper route to the third quadrant, Dalin could attack the escapees exposed back. So Dalin had promptly brought his men into the seventh quadrant, and given orders to his two others to relay the word. So instead of coming upon his friends unexpectedly with a group of men, in a few minutes nearly two hundred men and goblins were making sure no one escaped from the seventh quadrant, which happened to be empty anyway. The commanders were absolutely furious, but fortunately for Dalin the messenger had died in the fight so he simply told them that he had received the wrong information. The whole affair was a commotion, since the army was not properly organized yet and the escape was so unexpected, along with the fact that many had died in the collapsing of the wall. Not wanting to lose the goodwill of her soldiers that she had paid to gain, Marhyn contented herself with torturing just a few of those who were proved to be truly responsible.

But now, Dalin needed to escape. He had collected a substantial amount of information, and he truly believed he could not safely collect more without being captured. He also needed to get back to his father if his information about the mermen and Queen Marhyn was to be useful. So he had made the decision to leave, and now he got ready to implement his plan.

Gathering all of his possessions and stepping out of his door, Dalin roughly commanded some of his soldiers to lower a lifeboat so he could proceed to go on land and to Marhyn's castle for a meeting for the captains of the army. He had a soldier named Biorf and another named Jog accompany him for the fifteen or twenty meters to shore, and then Biorf rudely joked to his remaining compatriot about going into the woods and taking a piss, while Jog stayed with the boat. So Biorf and Dalin walked together until they came to the edge of a grove of trees, where they said their goodbyes, Dalin giving what remained of his supplies to the other.

Their plan was simple, both went alone into the woods, and Dalin would then flee. Biorf, returning with his goods, would tell how Captain Nilad had given him one insult to many, and tempers had flared. Biorf had thrown a rock and killed Captain Nilad, thus deserving to take over his post. No one would know the truth. No one would care. Mercenaries couldn't afford to make friends, soon they were dead or gone. It was a sad way of life, but it fit for the restless soul who thrived on adventure and didn't mind killing others. They both got something out of the deal. Biorf got to become Captain Biorf rather easily, and he got to help out Captain Nilad, for he understood that sometimes people miss their wife and children and wish to give up the military way of life. And Dalin got his way out.

Walking alone that night, Dalin wished there were more trees along his path to King Garkin's castle. In the trees he was raised, and they made him feel comfortable and secure. No one could find him if he wished to remain hidden. But trees were not in most of his path, and as Dalin snuck by Marhyn's impregnable fortress, he wished the moon were not so bright so it could hide him better.

Dalin heard a snap of a twig behind him, and he turned just in time to see the knuckles of a fist come slamming into his face. That was the last thing he saw before everything went black.

*   *   *   *

Dousing the fire in hopes that the dragon had not seen them yet (it was in vain, for they didn't know that dragons have very sharp eyesight) Derlin, Tarthur and Yonathan began to ready themselves for some kind of fight. Tarthur remembered babbling incoherently, "What are we doing?! This is a dragon! We can't fight a dragon! It will tear us apart without stirring," and then thinking, "Wait, he is attacking us. We don't have any choice." It was unfair, and it made Tarthur recall with shame some times when he had picked on smaller boys. It really was wrong for the strong to terrorize the weak, and Tarthur made a promise never to do it again. He laughed bitterly as he remembered their situation and the nearly inevitable fact that he never would have a chance to implement his promise. Well, at least he made it, he thought in case the Creator was listening.

"We should all run in different directions," Derlin suggested, "that way he will only be able to get one of us, and the others can meet up later."

Yonathan held up his hand to avoid further contemplation on this plan. "He would catch us all. He can fly, remember? No, our only hope is those magic swords. Do whatever you can to use them, for if they cannot save us, I will try to attack, but I am afraid he would be more in danger of forgetting how to fly and landing on a pointy mountain than of sustaining a wound of any size from me."

While they might have wanted to say more, caution dictated that they be quiet and hide behind some rocks, which served as meager and inadequate protection indeed. As they could think of nothing else to do, they hoped the crimson beast would continue on its way without noticing them.

It did not work. Tarthur had always heard of tales of these beasts, and knew they were real and extremely rare. Not all humans believed this, however. In fact, the blacksmith whom Tarthur had been apprenticed to had said that elves and dragons were creatures of legend, and not real. One day he had even beaten Tarthur, who had insisted that they were. Tarthur had hoped a dragon would swoop down on Krendon and devour the blacksmith at that very moment, but none had. Now he inwardly cursed himself for ever wishing to see one. He also regretted that he would never get to talk to the skeptical and practical blacksmith, now that he had met a dragon and had an elf for a friend. It is amazing, he thought, what people could find once they went beyond their narrow mindedness and looked for wonder in their world. This dragon, who Tarthur now saw to be quite huge, was covered with red scales thicker than the king's own armor, and had a long skinny neck which ended in a flat head, much like that of a crocodile, only with much sharper teeth. Its belly was enormous, and it had two wings protruding from its sides, the span of which seemed to be near fifty feet. Still, he looked almost transparent, as if he was only an apparition, and not real. As it landed near the rocks, Tarthur could be sure of one thing. The paralyzing fear was real.

Before the dragon had time to attack, Derlin burst from his cover and raced toward the beast. Derlin hastily drew the Light Sword and as the dragon was turning to look at him, brought it down in a sweeping arc on its narrow neck. Tarthur expected the sword to bounce harmlessly off the thick plating, but instead it cut right through his neck, never even encountering enough resistance to break the arc. The next thing surprised Tarthur and Derlin more, however. The dragon's head did not fall off, but he turned to face them as if nothing at all had happened. Tarthur valiantly tried to call the Rune Sword to his aid, but alas, it just stood there, dull and very ordinary, with not even a hint of the light that once burned so deeply within it.

Then the dragon spoke in a raspy voice that alone would have filled Tarthur with terror, without even hearing the words. "Whoa, sorry there, I guess I gave you a little scare. I am just getting used to this thing you know. Can't expect me to get it right on the very first time. I forgot you wouldn't recognize me."

These last words confused Tarthur and Derlin immensely, and they looked at each other just to make sure they had heard him right. Now they had seen quite a few people in their lives, and if one of them cut his hair and grew a beard or was wearing a disguise, they could see how they might fail to recognize him. But Tarthur was pretty sure he hadn't known any dragons, and if he had, he was certain he would be able to recognize one in a crowded marketplace. Lithar must have hit him on the head a lot harder than he thought if he was forgetting things like knowing dragons. Tarthur turned to ask the dragon for more details. If his friend was leaving things like this out, he needed to have a serious talk with Derlin about it later. When he looked, however, the dragon was gone, and in his place, was Yan.

Tarthur was speechless. He just stood there, awed and confused. For a moment, he even thought his brain was failing to work. Morty's tutor told him that if you don't use your brain, it would become weaker and eventually stop.

"Wait a minute here," Tarthur said calmly, and completely confused. "I think I just saw a dragon turn into Yan. Will someone tell me what really happened?"

"Yan," Derlin exclaimed excitedly, "we all thought you were dead!"

"Certainly," Yan said, replying to Tarthur's question and coming to stand by the confused heroes, of which Yonathan was the most confused, having never seen this man in his life. "But it's getting dark, and we better sit down."

So they all went to sit around the fire, Yonathan pulling up his own log so he would not have to sit by this dragon who wore the guise of humans, and Yan began his narrative.

"First of all," he started calmly, "I must apologize for leaving you so abruptly, after we had escaped the Dark Queen. Well, let me start at the beginning. I am very old, I knew Zelin when he was just beginning to learn the ways of magic. In fact, he taught me many things."

"Wow!" Tarthur exclaimed excitedly. "You knew Zelin?"

"Shh," Derlin reprimanded him harshly with a swift poke of his elbow in Tarthur's gut. "Of course he did. Now don't interrupt!"

"A very long time ago," Yan continued, unmindful of the interruption, "There was a great war upon the lands of this continent. Zelin and I were strong back then, but the forces of the Dark One and his sister were stronger. By luck, we managed to win that war, but I was captured by Marhyn and my mind was destroyed. My friends all searched for me, but since my spirit was gone, none could find me, and all assumed I was dead. So I have been in her prison ever since."

At this pause in the story, another question came to Tarthur, who this time politely raised his hand in the normal manner of asking to be recognized. Yan nodded his frail head in his direction, and Tarthur asked quietly, "How long ago was the war?"

Yan's face showed no emotion. "Nearly three hundred years ago. Yes, I have rotted in her prison for nearly three hundred years, not even knowing who I am."

"But then you came along, and freed me. I am sorry you found me in such a state of incoherence, but you must understand the pain I also feel. I was an intelligent man before. I was wise beyond my years; people always sought me out for advice in the workings of the world, even though I was younger than they. When you appeared, I started to regain parts of my consciousness, but slowly. Very slowly. When we found the Rune Sword, it started to come back much more quickly. Also, when we escaped her prison, and came out into the fresh air, I once again knew most of who I was. The second night after we escaped, I felt a call, coming from the East, for a special meeting was being held. I was not invited, but I would have been, had they known I was alive. Who called this meeting? Have you ever heard of the Council of Gurus?"

Both boys shook their heads no, but Yonathan spoke up. "I have heard Uris mention such a thing before, is it where the wise of the world hold discussion near the Eternal Vale?"

Yan nodded. "You are much closer to the truth than most people. Some people are even ignorant to our existence. The Eternal Vale is a place of tremendous power. It is even the very residence of the Creator, though he freely goes where he chooses. The council is a group of the wisest...no, not the wisest," he said with an angry face, then amended, "the people with the greatest knowledge of magic, who meet to decide how to use our power to benefit humanity. Or at least that is what we profess, if in words only."

Yan's body seemed to sag, and he uttered a sigh of frustration. "I am sorry. I am just angry, and very frustrated. You see, I went there, and there was a great meeting. There were even a few people there who knew you, Tarthur." Tarthur's eyebrows revealed his skepticism, but then he shrugged his shoulders; if Yan could turn into a dragon, anything was possible. Still, who would he know?

Seeing his disbelief, Yan smiled. "I am sure you have not forgotten your friends Zelin and Tustor? They both spoke quite highly of you. In fact, you are a great part of the reason that this meeting was even called. You see, Tarthur, you have put us into a great quandary. You have an item of great power, the Water Orb spell, but you can't use it and don't know how you got it. Some of the brightest minds in Daranor have spent endless hours pondering over what to do with you. It has caused quite a stir in the council."

Tarthur nodded, understanding most of what Yan said. "Did Tustor really swim all the way to the other side of the world?"

Yan chuckled—he still had a lot to explain about the council and its methods. "No, of course not. In fact, his body wasn't even there. We just communicated by sending the collective mind of our council out to him. It is a rather complicated process, and not one to go into detail with here. Perhaps some other time."

Tarthur was about to ask Yan to explain, you did not just tell Tarthur something about removing your mind from your body and then tell him to wait to learn the rest. He would probably try it and hurt himself in the meantime. Before he could ask, however, Derlin began to talk.

With an anxious mixture of excitement over the hordes of wizards that he imagined would be aiding them and of apprehension for his friend, Derlin asked the question. "So what did they decide?"

Yan looked down, then took a deep breath. "There were many signs that the Death Lord and Marhyn are about to attack. Tustor, Zelin, and I and a few others suggested joining with King Garkin and using our might to defeat him before he can gain enough power to put up a fight. But there are others, many of whom have since passed into the world of spirits, who would be content to isolate themselves and let the world take care of itself. They are selfish, and they are idiots!" Yan's voice rose until he was almost shouting then sank into a low, pain-filled state, his frail body trembling with every word. "They have ruined our chances, and now there will be war. Many people will die. Young men with bright futures ahead of them will be forced to join with the king to defend ourselves and many will be killed by horrors out of their darkest dreams. I have seen his army before! Women and screaming children they will trample without a thought. They will lay the land bare, and destroy all life wherever they tread. I have seen it happen."

"This is not the first time that there has been a resolution to go and destroy Darhyn while he sleeps. Some tried it as soon as he was defeated, and every fifty years or so someone suggests we go to his palace and destroy him while he slumbers. None of the other expeditions have been successful, and so the gurus tire of the plan. But this time is different, because now we have the spell that controls the Orb. We could steal the Orb this time, and this time there are signs that he is about to awaken. This time it's serious, but we were unable to persuade the others to come back and help us defeat him."

"He is strong, but we are not without hope. Reluctantly, the council has agreed to give some small help to those who would stay and try to prevent this. We have given Zelin strength in his old body, and he will now be able to use difficult spells without tiring as much. The same they have done for Tustor. And for me, I am now a shapeshifter. I can transform into any shape I wish." Yan finished this off by becoming like a silver liquid, and emerging as a new figure.

The Yan that stood before them now was completely different than what they were used to. He was slightly shorter, and dressed all in black cloth that wrapped loosely about his body. His face looked young, and Tarthur knew that this man was about thirty years old. His jet-black hair was barely visible, because of the dark veil that left only part of his face exposed. This formidable figure was shocking enough, but what astounded Tarthur and Derlin more, and made the still cautious Yonathan draw his sword, was the presence of a miniature dragon, crimson red, and perching docilely on his shoulder.

"You must understand," Yan said as though nothing had happened, "that while I appear to have tremendous power, there are some limitations. When I transform into something else, I assume all of the strengths and intelligence of that object. That is why I prefer this form. I can keep my mind but my body is no longer plagued by weakness and age. You don't know what it is like, to be able to run and jump and feel good again after so long…" Yan trailed off slowly.

Tarthur was still awestruck by these new developments. "You mean you can transform into anything, even this rock if you wanted to?" Tarthur pointed at a rock that was lying by Yan's feet.

Yan nodded. "But remember. Were I to transform into that rock, my mind would think like a rock, which I imagine is not very well. I would be trapped in that form until I willed myself to become something else. And if I could not think…I would remain a rock forever." Yan paused, then began again. "That is why I will usually be either a dragon, or a person, or both as I am now."

The Ninja Yan closed his mouth, and the minidrake began to speak. "Another limitation is that I can only transform into things as much as myself. It is hard to explain without detailed study into the workings of the universe, but know that if I wish to transform into something big, I will be less solid, and if I wish to transform into something smaller than myself, I will be more dense. I can split my being also. This person and I are both Yan, but we are each not quite fully him. That is why I seemed somewhat transparent when I was the big dragon."

The other Yan spoke now. "One of the small things the council has done for me is to give me a little leniency in this rule, by making my original self denser. It will help a little, but the rule still applies."

"How far are we away from the king's castle?" It was Tarthur's turn to talk.

"If we continue at the pace we are going now, a little more than a week and a half," Yan answered. "We will have to try to walk fast if we want to be of maximum help to King Garkin, so I suggest we all try to get some sleep." Yan turned to Yonathan. "I wish to thank you for all of your help, but you can return to wherever you came from now, I will be able to protect Tarthur and Derlin from here until the castle."

"Good idea," Tarthur agreed. "Yonathan, I wish to thank you again for all the help you have given us by coming with us, especially when you have lots of work to do as the assistant mayor of Freeton."

Yonathan's iron form placed a hand on Tarthur's shoulder. "Kandan can take care of things while I am gone, but I must insist. I told the people I would accompany you and that is just what I plan to do." He turned to Yan, the big man watching the dragon almost fearfully. "Now, I mean no disrespect, but what if he's not on our side? What I mean is, well, if he can transform into anything, who's to say he's not an evil one who just transformed into your friend to fool you, and then will kill you when I'm gone? Even if he is on our side, it's always been known that I'm a good man to have around when it comes to ruffians."

Yan, who wore a scowl of displeasure, and also a look that if killing Tarthur and Derlin was his intention, he would have already accomplished it without so much as a minor interference from Yonathan, nodded his head. "If you wish, you may come with us. Now," he said with the authority that closed the matter, "we leave at first light, so everyone try to get some sleep."

Had he known Tarthur and Derlin better, he would have known the folly of this command. They were so excited, with their renewed spirit of adventure and after finally meeting a dragon, telling them to sleep was like trying to persuade the king to find a penny in a hill of mud. "Wow," Tarthur said, voicing his excitement. "I'd like to see someone try to mess with us now."

Yan overheard him, and turned to look at the startled Tarthur. "No you don't. If someone does, may the Creator have mercy on his soul."

CHAPTER 10

▼

MORE BAD GUYS

When he awoke, the prisoner let out a groan of frustration and hopelessness. As his vision came into focus, he saw something that vaguely resembled a man surrounded by two or three tough looking mercenaries. He was lying on a crude table, which was bobbing up and down with the rest of the room. As he turned his head to get a better view of his surroundings, Dalin felt something run down his cheek, and into his mouth. It tasted salty—Dalin realized what it was and spat out his own blood.

One of the guards noticed his stirrings, and came over to examine him. "Admiral Tyven, the bugger's awake. What shoult we do wit'im?"

The creature that resembled a man came to stand by Dalin, and the elf soon saw that there were many things about him that Dalin would not consider to be human. He had flippers where both his feet and hands should be. Tyven Scarface, Admiral of the Dark Queen's navies, simply stared at Dalin. Dalin tried to stare back, but soon had to look away from the cold and horrible face. Dalin felt himself wishing the monster would talk, condemn him, anything. But Tyven just stood there, silent, radiating evil from his very being. With a gesture of his flippered hand, the mercenaries lifted Dalin again and took him into an iron cell.

The floor never stopped moving. Dalin thought he had been hit on the head very hard to cause this unusual sensation, but soon he found out that others were feeling it too. He was not crazy, but on a ship in the middle of the ocean. His jailer was a gruff looking black dwarf, and Dalin was indeed surprised to see him. Black dwarfs, while an unimportant and minuscule race of no more than a few hundred creatures that lived in mines in the Tabletop Plateau, were known for their hatred and distrust of outsiders, and it was fairly uncommon to see one roaming about the world. When Dalin asked him his name, the creature simply grunted and went back to consuming his ration of food.

In fact, Dalin didn't receive any new information about his surroundings until he was visited, rather unexpectedly, by his old commanding officer, Commander Erda. Erda was a tall, muscular man whom Dalin had given his tobacco and brandy to in order to get him drunk enough to take a quick glimpse at his orders. That is where Dalin had learned that they were to sail west. Dalin smiled when he remembered his clever ploy.

"Smiling, Dalin?" Commander Erda's remark caught Dalin off guard. "One such as you has little to smile about, no?"

Dalin quickly set his face into a defiant look, and with a calmness that did not match his expression, Dalin made his reply. "I can smile when I look to the day when our forces will wipe Marhyn and her piddling army from the face of Daranor."

Erda shook his head sadly. "Dalin, Dalin, Dalin, when will you see? You should have stayed with us when you had the chance. Not everyone can be a captain in her majesty's army. She will win, Dalin, I know. You haven't seen it yet, but I know. Did you really think you could escape from us? Nobody escapes from us, Dalin."

"Two boys did," Dalin spat his answer. "Two unarmed boys!"

"They had magic!" Commander Erda's face twisted into a state of uncontrollable rage, and then he forcibly calmed himself. "And yet, you could not. Two boys did and you could not."

"Who gave me up?" Dalin was desperate to find this answer, to find his mistake. He had purposely led the conversation in this direction, and then asked his question hoping Erda would gloat in the answer and rub it in Dalin's face.

Had he been a man of lesser intelligence, it might have worked, but Commander Erda was too smart. "You don't really expect us to tell you that, do you? It could have been a million ways. Was it Biorf? Did the great one, Lithar Lifehater, remember you? Or was it the Dark Lady herself? Or I? You may never know. But, I will let you think about it until you go crazy."

Dalin tried again, this time nearly pleading. "Just tell me. What will it hurt you?"

Erda shook his head and smiled an evil smile. "We're not taking any chances. Knowledge is power, Dalin. The less you know, the better. We will win this war,

Dalin, and you will help us." When Dalin's face showed that he had no intention of helping them, Erda let out a rolling laugh. "Of course not like that, boy. Your father will be very happy to see you, and we can find a use for his gold."

Dalin was about to protest that his father was just a poor farmer, when suddenly his words caught in his throat. Until this time, he hadn't realized that Commander Erda was calling him Dalin. Used to forgetting about his real identity ever since he had left Breshen to seek out Truin, he hadn't noticed his real name. Now he knew the situation was hopeless; his father, adoring all life, would pay every cent his people owned to get him back. And for them to be broke going into a war...

The echo of Commander Erda's laugh was all that Dalin heard in his mind for the next few days.

*   *   *   *

The warm liqueur refreshed him, and helped wipe the sleep from his eyes even as he glanced at his candle and saw that it was nearly burnt out. They put a special drug from the *kafen* plant into his cider, and it helped him keep awake and alert late into the night. It wasn't that King Garkin didn't trust his bureaucracy, on the contrary he knew he had some excellent and competent ministers. It was just that with matters of the safety of the realm, he preferred to handle things himself. It had always been like that, and the demands of being king were already beginning to show themselves in his body. Well, being king did have some advantages for his health. He had the finest doctors, plenty of exercise, and excellent food. But the emotional strain of being responsible for the safety and well being of thousands of people was enormous, and it always weighed down on his consciousness. While it was only midnight, King Garkin looked at the stack of letters he had already written, and compared them to the stack of reminders for letters he had yet to write. The latter, unfortunately, was much higher. It was going to be a long night.

The servant's knock on his door startled the king out of his reverie. "A man is here to see you, majesty. I told him to return tomorrow but he says it could be urgent and should be handled without delay."

King Garkin nodded with anticipation. "Send him in."

Addyean walked calmly into the room and took a seat in a chair on the opposite side of the king's desk. "I am sorry to bother you so late, your majesty, but I have been busy all day and I must return to Krendon to gather supplies in the morning."

"Think nothing of it," The king replied jovially. "You just saved my life a few days ago, remember? You could wake me up in the middle of the night, and I wouldn't mind one bit. What is on your mind?"

"Your majesty has always known me to be a rational, down-to-earth man, have you not?" Addyean questioned.

The king nodded his head. "Certainly, why?"

Addyean took a deep breath and continued. "Because, what I am about to tell you may seem impossible, and unbelievable. I want to tell you what happened at Treshin."

"Oh yes," The king replied. "You said something about a priest giving you the holy water that saved me."

Addyean nodded. "Yes, but that is not what really happened. When I got there, the spring was deserted. I knew priests usually tend to it, so I was a bit worried when none came out to greet me. I walked in to the outer spring, but no one was there either. I was about to fill up the flask there, when something stopped me. The door leading to the inside spring, the Holy of Holies, was ajar. I walked inside, and there…"

King Garkin motioned for him to go on. "And there…?"

"And there I saw Him—the Creator himself in the form of a cloud of light. I fell to my knees, but he told me to rise. Actually, I didn't hear the words, or even feel them, I just knew them. Whenever he talked, I just knew what he was saying already in my mind. That place was filled with such beauty. There was an incredible aura of serenity that permeated the room. I have never felt more power or more peace at the same time. He gave me the flask of water, and told me to take it to you, for your leadership would be needed soon. I wanted to ask him more, but something kept me from doing so. We talked for a while, and he showed me memories from my boyhood that I had forgotten."

King Garkin stared at him in amazement. The Creator never came out from the Eternal Vale—half his people didn't even believe the Creator existed. He could see why Addyean kept it to himself. "I…I feel unworthy. Why me? This has never happened to any other in my family, at least not in any recorded history."

"He said you were needed. I guess this means that there will be a war. Great things are happening now. Perhaps this means that we will win, and finally destroy Darhyn."

King Garkin shrugged. "Perhaps. But I have a feeling that the future is not yet determined."

"I don't think it's determined either, at least not in full. This is why I have a potentially important question to ask you. Tell me everything you know about Warren."

The king sat back in his chair and began. "Well, he came to us a few years back. Always was a rather annoying fellow. In the beginning, he wanted to be a knight, but he was just too clumsy. I think he had a falling out with old Ironfist then too. Those two have always hated each other. Anyway, we were in a drought then, and I put him in charge of rationing the grain. He did a good job of it, and when the drought was over I let him handle some of the economic issues of the realm. He's done so well that we've actually been able to cut taxes each of the last three years. After his economic success, I made him my general advisor, and he has offered me only good advice from then until now. Why?"

Addyean replied, "When Zelin and I first came to see you, he told us that you were ill, and then snuck out. Now, I imagine that he was thinking of the safety of the realm. But something in his voice and his manner led me to believe he might not have the best interests of the kingdom in mind. In my years as a spy, I've always prided myself on being an excellent judge of character. Something just is not right about him."

King Garkin thought about it for a minute. "You are not the first person to tell me this. Yet, for all of the complaints, he has never been found to be guilty. I even fully investigated him six months ago. We found nothing. He has only brought good things to the realm. And I wonder about one thing. If the Creator wants to protect me, why would he let Warren into my confidence?"

Addyean had wondered the same thing. "If Warren was allied with the Evil One, I think the Creator would have warned me of it at Treshin. But still, something is not right."

"I have an idea," King Garkin began. "In consideration of your skills in judging people, I will not tell Warren everything. He still is my advisor, however, and he can offer me very valuable advice. In the meantime, I will keep my eyes open. You too, I will allow you to personally check up on him."

The king had spoken, and Addyean decided it was for the better. "Very well, your majesty. I will see to it at once. In the meantime, I will let you get back to your work. May I help you in the writing of any of these letters?"

King Garkin smiled and shook his head no. "Thank you, Addyean, but I can take care of it myself. It is nothing, really. I will have these finished soon and then I will get some sleep."

Addyean stood up, excused himself, and then left King Garkin to his duties.

*   *   *   *

The burning sensation at his side woke Tarthur that night. It was the darkest part of the night, only a few hours had passed since they had started to sleep. Groggily, Tarthur tried to rub the sleep from his eyes and find what had prematurely awaken him. It was in vain, for he had slept for long enough to turn off his body, but not long enough to restore the energy needed to operate it. As he groped about himself uncertainly, a bright but soothing light wrapped around him. His eyes drawn to the source, Tarthur saw the Rune Sword, its handle pointing toward the back of the tent. That's odd, he recalled. He thought he had left it by his side when he slept. Following the point of the blade, Tarthur pulled aside the tent flap and peered outside.

In a dreamlike trance, he glanced about the forest. A black cloud passed over the moon, as if to rob the land of every meager ray of light that it might provide. Hesitantly Tarthur surveyed his surroundings. A thick fog wrapped itself through the trees and around the rocks, creating images so real and terrible that Tarthur had to force himself not to think about them. The sensation made him shiver— no, it was only the cold. The forest was oddly quiet, not even so much as the sound of a cricket penetrated the night. The chill fog created intangible wraiths, which vanished as if they had never been with the slightest puff of wind. Staring ahead, Tarthur caught sight of something that made him indeed wish it was a dream. Burning through the fog, too far away to reveal their origin, but close enough so that there could be no mistake about their purpose, were two fiery red eyes. Tarthur felt like they were boring straight into his heart.

Hurriedly he ducked back into the tent, and vividly shook Derlin to wake him. Much too slowly, Derlin came out of his slumber and started to mumble. Tarthur quickly put a finger to his lips. Derlin, now more fully awake, immediately understood and followed the direction Tarthur's shaky hand pointed, out of the tent.

He only needed one word. "Eyes."

Derlin strained to find them, but he could see naught in the darkness that enveloped the camp. "I don't see them, Tarthur, but I feel it. It is evil, and I'm scared."

Tarthur could only nod, the fear creeping into him and beginning to paralyze him also. While independent and stubborn about asking others for help, Tarthur didn't even need to think about this decision, which was a good thing since his sleepy mind wasn't working too well. "Let's wake Yan."

Derlin could only nod, and they hurriedly walked the fifteen yards to Yan's tent. To Tarthur, it seemed like fifteen miles, and it might as well have been. They never made it.

Surrounded by an aura of decay and fear, the black robed humanoid laughed shrilly. Paralyzed, Tarthur and Derlin could only watch as he raised his scythe and prepared to cut them down.

From the side, a streak of crimson flew into the terror. Ripping with his claws and razor teeth Minidragon Yan began to tear at their assailant. His battle cry filling the night air, Minidragon Yan ripped off the flesh of its cheek, and exhaled fire hot enough to boil blood, had the creature possessed any. Tearing out chunks of flesh from its chest and following it up with fire to char the tissue, the minidrake was about to make short work of this horror.

The spell of fear for Tarthur and Derlin was broken. They were about to rush forward and help Yan, when Tarthur pointed to something emerging from another grove of trees. Apparently, this fight was just beginning.

The new creatures all wore armor, but it was so ragtag and mismatched that Tarthur wondered if it served any real purpose. It seemed to all be centuries old, covered with rust and the blood of valiant men who had long since passed to dust. Derlin stared in horror at the advancing troop. Although he was not sure, he thought he saw that they were little more than skeletons with rotted flesh randomly clinging to parts of their bodies. There were only three of them, but they moved in a slow and evilly confident manner. Before they reached the boys, a huge bear-like form charged out from behind them. "Stay back," Yonathan yelled. "I'll handle these!" Screaming his battle cry of "Freeton Forever!" Yonathan stabbed his sword into the chest of one of the attackers. When he seemed unaffected, Yonathan pulled the blade out and brought it slicing down across the creature's neck before it could react. Yonathan happily watched his head roll in the dust.

The creature calmly went over, picked it up, replaced it, and continued as if that were an everyday occurrence. As Yonathan stared at him, aghast, the second and third creatures began to mercilessly rain down blows on his body.

That was enough for Tarthur and Derlin. Even though Yonathan had told them to stay there, they didn't even take time to rationalize away his orders. Drawing their mystical swords, they rushed forward to help Yonathan with all the speed they could muster.

Yan reached them first. His jet-black form streaked into view and entered with a flying kick to knock away the second attacker. The third, alerted to this new enemy, turned and raised his sword to cut Yan in two, but before he did, Yan's sword hacked twice into his opposite arm, then Yan whirled and cut off his leg at the hip. One legged, the creature began to topple over, but before he hit the ground Yan struck again twice, slicing the sword arm into three sections.

Tarthur saw Dragon Yan still in battle with the other creature, and wondered who this new fighter was, before he remembered that Yan could split his person. This was confusing! While Tarthur paused for just this brief thought, Derlin was already racing toward the third attacker, and Yan had turned to face the first skeletal knight. Again, the slow confidence of the monster was no match for the reflexes of Ninja Yan—within seconds his dismembered body was lying in pieces on the ground. Yan hacked at the pieces for a minute, grabbed what might have been an arm and flung it away from where the pieces were already beginning to reform.

Derlin rushed forward to meet the third terror, his heart racing so wildly he thought it would explode. As Derlin stared into the creature's eyes, what he saw made him almost drop his sword. The eyes were cold and lifeless, yet full of hate and malice. They were single-minded in purpose; Derlin knew they would follow him wherever he went. They would follow him around the world and not stop until they had killed him. The creature swung his sword at Derlin's neck, and Derlin hastily flung up the Light Sword to defend himself. The resounding clang that filled the chill night air and the fact that he was still alive convinced him that he had succeeded. His confidence rising, Derlin began to take the offensive, raising his weapon and bringing it down on his opponent's head. The deathless creature raised his sword to block Derlin's blow, but the Light Sword passed right through it and through his body, slicing him in two lengthwise.

Unsure of what had happened, Derlin stepped back, confused. He looked around and saw his friends beckoning him to come join them a few yards away, so he hurried over. A quick glance around him told him that all the monsters were not moving, or else just hiding.

"Are you alright?" Derlin called out to Yonathan. It was a stupid question, but one that was often asked anyway. A doctor wasn't needed to tell that Yonathan was not all right. He was a mess of hair, sweat, and blood. The assistant mayor of Freeton was bleeding badly from several cuts, the worst of which was a nasty laceration nearly an inch deep in his side.

Tarthur interrupted frantically. "Who...no, what are those things? Why us? Can we stop them?"

Yan quickly silenced him, and Derlin noticed that the dragon was perched upon his shoulder, looking well, but with a few wounds of his own. It appeared that he had not had such an easy fight after all. "We must hurry, we don't have much time. They are called the Order of the Skull, and they cannot be killed, because they are already dead. They will reattach dead limbs and continue steadily until they have killed all of us."

"Then we're gone? I don't want to die here. Let's run!" Tarthur started to hastily pack up his provisions and flee, and Yan almost had to hit him to quiet him.

"We're not going to die. Tarthur, you stay here with him. Derlin, you and I will hack them to pieces, while my other self will fly them away and scatter the pieces as far away as I can. Tarthur, get ready to leave. We can't stop them, but we can delay them enough to let us get to King Garkin. Zelin is sending an advance party to welcome us, but we won't meet them until tomorrow night, even if we hurry." Yan spoke rapidly in a breathless voice, for already the attackers were regrouped and beginning their assault anew.

Derlin was still nervous, but Yan's reassuring presence at his side quieted him somewhat. Yet, he had no time to think about it, for soon he was engaged. Born by the defeat of the first skull knight, his confidence rose with every mounting second. He hacked away at the intruders, as if by doing so he could hack away at his own fears and doubts of himself. Their armor and weapons offered no resistance to the Light Sword. It sliced through shields and swords vainly raised in an attempt to parry an unparryable blow as if it were light, yet when it struck, it was hard as forged iron.

With each blow that Ninja Yan and Derlin struck, Minidragon Yan came and snatched up the dismembered body part and flew away, where he deposited the part behind a shrub, under a rock, or down the side of a steep ravine. He then flew back to receive others. He spaced them as far apart as possible to lengthen the time it would take to get them back together.

When the gruesome yet bloodless struggle concluded, the weary fighters came to see how Tarthur and Yonathan fared. Tarthur had calmed down, and was back to himself, or an even better version of himself, for he had made a stretcher for Yonathan and had washed and dressed most of his wounds.

Yan nodded his approval, and then spoke. "We have bought ourselves a few hours at the most. Even though it is still night, we will have to leave immediately and head north. Once we start to travel, we should be okay, since we can move faster then they can. Nevertheless, I will send part of myself ahead to tell the advance party to hurry."

With these words, the minidrake lifted off Yan's shoulder and began to fly northward.

A groan from Yonathan broke through the night. "Save your strength," Yan admonished, but Yonathan seemed determined to talk. Though wheezing and coughing up blood, Yonathan spoke. "I...I know you must travel fa...fast. Your mission...too important...I...I'll just slow you down...must...leave me here."

Tarthur was aghast. "We can't do that! I made you a stretcher, we can make it."

"Too...heavy...now go..."

Both Derlin and Tarthur looked to Yan for his leadership. The black cloaked figure sadly nodded. "What he says is true, but his wounds are not so serious as they won't heal. I think we can make it with or without him, though it will certainly be much harder if we have to carry a stretcher. After all, he is a big man."

"So what are we doing?" Tarthur asked Yan.

"Leave me!" Yonathan's voice was gaining in volume.

"That is a decision you must make. If they attack again, we may be able to defeat them, but it will be difficult. In the morning their powers are weakened, but still strong.

Yonathan was shouting now. "LEAVE ME! I'll be in the folklore of Freeton forever! Do you wish to save my life and lose your own?! Your life is not just yours anymore, don't you see? Listen! You must take the swords to the king, and live!"

Tarthur made up his mind. "Yonathan, walk with us. That way you will not slow us down, and you can save your life."

Yonathan pondered the compromise, and then nodded slowly. "But you m...must agree to leave me i...if I slow you down, and leave me at any...h...hut or cottage."

This was an agreeable plan to all, and Yan smiled under his mask.

A million questions filled Tarthur's mind as he stumbled on in the pre-dawn darkness. To a boy who used to love adventure, to cherish stories of old heroes so that he could recite them word for word yet still forget nearly half of his chores on any given morning, things certainly weren't turning out like they were supposed to. They were happening so fast! It seemed not too long ago that they had been playing in Krendon, then setting off on a grand adventure with Dalin, who was now who knows where, if he was even alive. They had befriended a senile old man, who left just as suddenly as he came and reappeared again, some powerful creature who he didn't even understand. He started to think of what would have happened if Yan hadn't appeared when he did, then pushed the thought into the back of his mind, dreading the certain answer. Yan had moved so fast, so confidently, as if he knew he didn't have to be afraid of anything. He had made ten, no twelve strikes into his attacker for each one feeble attempt the other vainly tried. And the dragon! He had torn into that fear creature viciously, with a fury that would have even scared the bravest Royal Knight.

With Dalin, Tarthur had never been scared, never worried until Lithar Life-hater had ambushed them. Yan had faced much tougher enemies, and won. A single tear, unbidden, came from Tarthur's eye. He cried for Dalin, already lost, and for the many more who would die if there was a war. Again, he thought, why me? What had he done to deserve being thrown into the middle of this conflict? All he did was have a dream. He had been used to causing trouble before in his life, but nothing like this! He didn't realize that it was just the way of the world, cold and unfeeling, that had positioned him thus; others were merely prodding him on. He was just some pawn in a huge chess game being played by the powerful forces in the world. The stakes were very high; to the one winner, the world. To the other players, death. And there were no takebacks.

Wiping the tear off his face in hopes of seeing Dalin at the castle of the king, Tarthur turned to look at Yonathan, and quickly looked away. He was a mess, the bandages that Tarthur had carefully applied already soaking with half-clotted blood. Tarthur didn't want Yonathan to know that he was looking at him; it would break the big man's heart if he knew he was slowing them down. No, he already knew it, although they were making relatively good time. He could see that the exercise was forcing more blood to be circulated and lost from the many wounds. Yonathan's body had failed him. He was running on spirit now. Pure will forced him to continue, driving him mercilessly onward, never relenting until they reached the advance party. He looked into Derlin's eyes and he knew that he saw it too. They were both glad that they would have Yonathan's strength to lean on in the future, if they made it. When they made it.

The first rays of daylight were beginning to shine through the morning mist when Yan called a halt for the frozen and exhausted party. Yan, while usually strong, was showing the effects of being without half of his person.

"No, I can go...go on." Yonathan's raged voice was barely audible. "Not...not tired."

Yan shook his head at the big man with admiration. "Come on now, we all need to rest. Tarthur, Derlin and I are exhausted."

Yonathan seemed adamant in his plea that he was not tired, despite overwhelming evidence to the contrary. He seemed to think the rest was his fault. "Go...on...ahead...you...catch up...I'll...later."

"Oh, there is really no need," Yan interrupted, and then when he saw the confusion in the others' eyes replied with a wry smile. "They're here."

*   *   *   *

Sir Stephen exhorted his horse onward, but soon relented when he saw that the poor creature was giving all he could. The magnificent animal had been foaming at the sides for the last hour; Sir Stephen had been driving him like mad ever since the little dragon had appeared early in the morning. Sir Stephen wondered at this creature, but he had seen a king raised to life by water, and he had a feeling he would see many more strange things in his career as a knight, which had so far been uneventful and uninspiring. But all that was about to change. Who knows? Someday someone might even write about his adventures. How foolish, he thought and dismissed the absurdity from his mind.

Eager to prove himself again, Sir Stephen had ridden to the forefront of the mad chase through the early dawn, only the leathery dragon outdistancing him. Soon, ahead, he caught sight of some figures, and to his surprise the dragon flew and landed on the shoulder of a black clad one. Reigning in his horse, Sir Stephen thought that if these were the heroes that they had been sent to find, heroes must be sorely lacking in this world.

One of them, a big and burly man, was so covered with a tangle of hair and blood and sweat as to be almost indiscernible. Two more were only young boys, a few years younger even than Sir Stephen himself. Their clothes were torn and raggedy, little more than strips of cloth that hung in places from their bodies. Yet, both carried something that made Sir Stephen lose any doubt he had in their identities, for both carried mud-spattered swords, but ones that seemed mystical and powerful, or at least would seem that way when they were washed. The last was the only one who had any real bearing of one of power, although it was marred by a black cloak tightly drawn around his person. Of course, appearances weren't everything…or indeed, anything.

"Don't just stand there, get this man some help!" The black figure's harsh command made Sir Stephen inwardly curse himself for his lack of promptness, and outwardly blush furiously. By now the others had arrived, and Sir Stephen busied himself with caring for the man's wounds while others gave the man and the two boys some food and drink.

The party was successful, and soon the physicians took over the injured man and propped him into a stretcher. A few of the armed men set up a patrol around the perimeter, and the weary travelers slipped into a much-needed rest.

During the day, which was spent mostly in slumber by the party who had slept only a few hours in the last two days, and in nervous conversation among the knights, one of the lookouts reported seeing three death knights in the distance. But the creatures, who normally would have had no trouble crushing thirty or forty men, stayed at a distance, and eventually vanished completely, probably out of fear for the boy with the sword that cut like light and the dragon-man. Yan assured the knights that they were gone for good, but that night many a fearless warrior cast a fearful glance over his shoulder, to assure himself it was just the shadows.

The next morning brought all in good spirits and ready to travel, except for Yonathan, who was dangerously ill, but on a stretcher and ready at least to be carried. He had severely overspent himself, and all were hoping for his recovery, but fearing the worst. Having rested the day before, the column awoke early and began to travel the one-and-a-half week journey to the castle of King Garkin. Yan, who had taken over the position of leader from Sir Terin with a swiftness and completeness that astounded many of the younger knights, hoped to travel both early and late and to sleep in a bed before the week was out.

The group was ready to go in an unusually small amount of time for their number, and soon was trotting briskly along the king's highway. Sir Stephen could not help but feel wonder and curiosity for these heroes. He was forced to admit that his first assessment had been untrue, he could now see that behind the dirt and tattered rags that covered them, there was a nobleness of character, a strong spirit, and in their eyes there was a fiery will, that he had never seen in such intensity before, and would have never thought it could be present in one so young. Plucking up his courage with curiosity, Sir Stephen drew his horse near to the blond headed one.

He rode alongside him for an eternal moment, took a deep breath, and began the conversation.

"Hello, my name is Sir Stephen. It appears you have had quite extraordinary travels." He knew it was a very lame thing to say, but he could not think of anything better. The boy seemed almost not to hear him; his head was down as if he was thinking. Then he looked up.

"My name is Tarthur. Are you a real Royal Knight?" Sir Stephen replied that he was, and Tarthur took a deep look at him. In all of his life Tarthur had longed to be a Royal Knight, to have a horse, and a sword and shiny armor, and respect. He and Derlin would ride off on magical adventures, (complete with saving a few damsels, of course) and return home to sneer at Morty, who had spent the day in school. Now that he had his own version of it, complete with magic swords and powers he didn't understand, (except for the girls, for which he silently thanked the Creator for not confusing him more) he was not so sure he wanted to be the hero anymore.

"I am a Royal Knight," he answered, "but you look to be the one who should be in my place. I haven't gotten any chances to serve my king yet, although, I have a feeling that soon I will get my chance, and then, I won't hesitate, I'll...I'm sorry, I guess I'm just excited."

Tarthur, knowing the feeling well, nodded and smiled. Yet, when he looked in Sir Stephen's face, with his youthful innocence and determination, he could see only one thing. He saw the young knight's body, rotting in a battlefield for the slain. All around him, the dying called out for aid, but no one heard them. The earth was charred and barren—only two forms of life inhabited it. A little girl cried for her father. "*Daddy, daddy get up, the bad things are gone now daddy. Let's go play now, like you promised. Remember, you promised me and mommy...when they're gone you'll come home, and we'll play all day long like before...*" Her uncomprehending voice was drowned out by the other form of life, the harsh wail of the vultures, circling and waiting. Waiting...yet they were full, for as Tarthur looked over the countryside, there were battlefields everywhere...

"You know," Tarthur said seriously, looking in the young knight's eyes. "Many people are going to die. There will be a war."

"And we will win." Sir Stephen finished, but did not see the same confidence in Tarthur, who looked at him as if to ask "What have you seen of the enemy? If you knew them you would not be sure. In fact, you'd be insane..."

Tarthur looked away. "I'm sorry, I just have a lot on my mind. My friends are scattered all over the world, if they aren't dead. I have a sword that burns me sometimes yet is regular metal when I need it, and I'm supposed to have a great spell but I don't even know how to use it! There is about to be a war and a lot of people are going to die, and what if it's my fault!?? Not to mention, I've been trying to reach the king for about two months, and every two days I see something that most people don't even believe exists!" He exhaled and then apologized again. "I'm sorry. I just need to go to the council meeting, and find some things out. If they have the answers..." Tarthur trailed off into silence. He knew he shouldn't be this way. The young knight had done nothing to him. He was just in a volatile mood, and had never been able to control his temper very well.

Sir Stephen rode off ahead, inwardly cursing himself. He had blown another chance with his itinerant babble. Feeling despair, he wondered when he was going to learn and start acting like a knight.

CHAPTER 11

▼

MORE QUESTIONS

Tarthur nudged Derlin uneasily, as more and more figures came to be seated in the council chamber of King Garkin. There were so many unanswered questions, things he normally would have pondered over for days, but that he had not even thought about lately. Larger, more important questions crowded the smaller ones out of his consciousness. They were in a chamber that was rich with ornamentation and luxury, with servants coming periodically to fill their cups with hot spicy cider, the aroma and heat of which did much to dispel the cold.

They had come into the city late the night before under the cover of darkness, and consequently had not gotten to see the wonders and majesty of the city that they had always heard tales of. But as exciting as it might be, sightseeing would have to wait.

"He should be here by now, if he was coming." Tarthur put out his statement, pleading for Derlin to contradict him, to tell him that Dalin would walk through the door any time now, or sneak up on them from behind, or anything, to stave off the feeling of the inevitable that was slowly creeping over them. Dalin was not here. And Derlin said nothing.

The servants soon filled everyone's cup and then left, shutting the doors behind them. Dalin was not in the room. A hush descended on the members present, and then King Garkin entered. Tarthur had never seen King Garkin (or any other king for that matter) nor even heard his physical attributes described, but he knew immediately who he was. He was dressed in a robe of royal purple, which would have made Tarthur laugh if not for the solemness of the moment and the king's face, purple having always been a girl's color. King Garkin was of middle age, with black hair and beard, and strong of body and spirit. Next to him walked none other than Zelin, who started Tarthur on this whole business in the first place. Tarthur wanted to run to him and ask him for the answers, and Derlin almost had to place a restraining hand on his shoulder to stop him from doing so.

All of the members took their seats, which were arranged in a circle with a raised place for the king and a map of Daranor with colored pins stuck in it in the middle. Dalin still was not there.

The king stood up and formally started the meeting. "Welcome, and thank you for coming so early this fine morn. I realize it is not the usual time for councils, but we have pressing questions which must be attended to without delay." Tarthur and Derlin both thought it was quite absurd for the king to be apologizing for the early hour of the council. He was the king, didn't he just command? The country boys had a lot to learn about court formalities—and court power.

After this waste of time, the king introduced all of the people in the room. There was Warren, his advisor, General Cilio, and an elf named Hano who had just returned from fighting on the border. Tarthur wanted to ask Hano about Dalin, but he kept silent. King Garkin introduced them next, and then his royal spy Addyean. Neither of the boys could believe it, but it was the very same Addyean with whom they plowed the fields. A royal spy! This was almost too much for Derlin, who remembered Addyean as a hardworking and honest farmer. What a strange world this was!

There was the captain of the advance party that had rescued them, and who also seemed to be in control of all of the Royal Knights, Sir Terin. And of course Yan was also present, in the form of human and small dragon, as if to intimidate help from this council where he had failed in the Council of Gurus.

So there were ten of them, about to decide the fate of the world. The king asked Tarthur and Derlin to tell their story first, everything since the dream, omitting nothing. (Tarthur thought about omitting that part about the pie, but then he decided that he had better obey the king, and it probably wouldn't get back to Judith anyway.)

Tarthur was about to begin his story, but Derlin interrupted. "I'm sorry, your highness, but we had a friend named Dalin who was supposed to meet us here, and we were wondering if he has made it here yet."

Hano's surprise got the better of him. "You know Prince Dalin?!!"

At this reply Tarthur's heart sank. He knew Dalin was not there. Hano continued to tell him that the last time Dalin had been seen or heard from was when he went out in search of Tustor, the merwizard. Prince Dalin? Well…if Addyean could be a spy, anything was possible. What would he find out next, that Derlin was an earl?

So with heavy hearts, they began their story. They told about Tarthur's dream, about Zelin's decision to send them north to see the merwizard, about their meeting with Dalin, about how Tarthur had used the Water Orb to raise Tustor, and how they were on their way to Breshen, and then the king to tell him all this when they had been ambushed by Lithar and brought to Marhyn's dungeon. They told how they had been separated from Dalin, and how Tarthur had fallen through the floor and found the senile old Yan. They recounted their harrowing escape through the tunnels, and the majestic Rune Sword that they had found. They told how Yan disappeared unexpectedly, and what happened in Freeton, culminating with the citizens giving the Light Sword as a weapon to fight evil. They told of Yan's equally unexpected return as a dragon, and about the ambush by the things that didn't die. Finally, they told of Yonathan's wounding and the search party finding them and giving them aid. Addyean, Yan, and Zelin nodded in agreement at various parts of the narrative.

When they had finished, Zelin calmly walked over and began to examine their swords. "We have been truly fortunate, for these swords are things out of legend. The Rune Sword, which was crafted long ago by the masters of Air, does indeed compel truth."

Tarthur stood up. "That's what we thought, but then I told a lie and it didn't do anything, it didn't even glow."

Zelin nodded. "It is not that kind of truth that it compels. It searches out the truth of your being, what you really are. It may be that your true nature is to tell lies."

"We prefer to call them unique interpretations," Tarthur interrupted, and then blushed, sorry that he had.

Zelin seemed irked at first, and then smiled. "Yes, whatever you call them. Yet, they are not serious lies. They are not lies against your inner self, merely outer, superficial untruths. That is why it reacted the way it did to those people under the influence and control of the wizard."

Tarthur didn't understand half of the words, but he was beginning to get the idea. "At times I felt like the sword had a mind of its own, like it was trying to talk to me."

This time Yan spoke. "Many objects of power are alive. They can sense and feel things and they can communicate with others. They don't have a life like you or me, however. They can't feel emotions except fear and good, and a few other basic ones."

"What about the Light Sword?" This discussion was intriguing to Derlin also. He wondered what strange power his weapon held.

"It is also more than just a sword," explained Zelin. "It has no special magical properties, other than the ones used in a battle. When it encounters something like an enemy blade or armor, it turns itself into light and passes through it with ease. When the sword strikes flesh, however, it becomes once again as hard as iron and slices straight through. That is why you were able to defeat those skull knights with so much ease. Unless he hits you first, no one stands a chance against you while you possess that sword."

"That is also why the sword passed through me the first time I met you," Yan added. "It knew I had no ill will toward you so it didn't hurt me. That is also why it is an excellent training sword. If you are fighting your friend and accidentally strike him, there will be no harm done."

The one that Tarthur remembered was named General Cilio stepped forward. "This is all the more reason that we need this sword in the front lines when the war begins. It will increase the morale of the troops! When they see their hero destroying the enemy right and left, they will get courage and rally to him that holds the sword. This person will be able to break through the toughest lines of the enemy and maybe destroy their leadership."

Old Ironfist was incredulous. "You can't just take his sword away! The people of Freeton gave it to him, and he should be the one who uses it. Besides, it may not answer the call of another."

"Who wields it is not important, if the boy proves able, he can be the one, but we will likely need a warrior who can take punishment and probably death on account of the whole enemy trying to kill him and steal it." General Cilio's icy voice was unfeeling—it accepted death as if it were nothing to him. Maybe it was.

Sir Terin was about to argue back, but Derlin cut him off. "Stop! Everybody stop! We will all need to work together here. I am willing to give my sword to someone else to use in the war. It is not really even my sword in the first place. The people of Freeton gave it to me so I could bring it and use it to help our cause. Any way that we can use it to win this war is fine with me."

That having been settled, Warren brought up the next issue. "Everyone is talking of the war, preparing for it as if it were inevitable. Do we really need to endanger the lives of all of our simple, hardworking citizens? And for what? As far as I know, we don't even have any enemy!"

King Garkin cast a sideways glance at Hano and Cilio, and they rose to proceed. "We have a report from the northern border," Cilio began. "His majesty sent us there to control fighting between black dwarves and goblins and other things that were attacking there."

"As for your reports of no enemy," Hano's temper was once again getting the better of him. He had had enough with these humans, especially that Warren one. Something about him just wasn't right. "Tell that to my people whose homes have been burned. Tell that to my friend Geriyo. His three beautiful daughters were raped, his son was killed! Tell them that we have no enemy!"

General Cilio once again took over the dialog. In the weeks that they had fought together, Hano had been forced to gain a grudging admiration and respect for Cilio. "My friend Hano is excited, yet he has every right to be! We found the enemy, and they were weak and disorganized. We routed them and sent them back into the desert with fear! Now an elf doesn't see a goblin but he sees his backside!"

"The enemy is real. The Death Lord Darhyn is preparing for war, and he sent out these parties to catch us off guard and capture Breshen, so as to give him an ample supply base for his army, which is growing stronger by the day, deep within Castle Rathskellar. Tarthur mentioned hundreds of empty prison cells that Marhyn has freshly dug. Do you think they are for her cattle?!! The evil ones are preparing, they have been for some time. Each day, each day that we stand waiting, they grow stronger and we sit idle. We must attack now, while we still have a slight advantage. We must be in action, and it must be two words instead of one!"

King Garkin reached down and removed a piece of rolled parchment from his cloak. It looked much like the one Tarthur had seen before, in the Death Lord's castle. It seemed ancient, and was yellowed and cracking around the edges, but seemed to be in good shape overall. "This is the spell that controls the Power of Earth. It has been handed down in my family for hundreds of years, and we have always kept it for the time when we may need it again. From what I hear, it indeed seems as if you, Tarthur, control the spell that has power over the Water Orb. Unfortunately, one of my ancestors was growing old and he had a fiery son who had no respect for laws or moral decency. My ancestor was afraid his son would use the Power of Earth for evil, so he cast a lock spell on the Earth Grain so that it can only be used in self-defense. Thus, I will not be able to use it until Darhyn attacks me directly."

The spell! He had forgotten all about that. He groped around uncertainly in his pockets, afraid that he had lost it in the mad flight from Queen Marhyn, and then remembered that it had been incinerated when he had used it to free Tustor. Zelin reached out a fresh scroll to Tarthur. "Of course I made a copy before you left Krendon. Do you think I would let you have the only copy in the world?"

That was obviously a stupid question. Tarthur thought for a minute, and then handed the scroll back to Zelin. It was time for wiser and stronger people than him to handle these things. "I'm afraid not," said the old wizard. "Even if I wanted to, I can't read it. (Derlin was surprised to see that the wisest man he knew was illiterate.) You are the only one, because you have read it before. So you must be the bearer of this power, at least until we recover the Water Orb." Zelin turned to look at King Garkin, who nodded.

Tarthur felt trapped.

General Cilio came forward and placed a bit of earth next to the king's castle on the world map, and a red tongue of fire and a blue wave next to Castle Raths-kellar. "We must not forget the armies of Queen Marhyn, though we have no reasonable estimate of her size or strength yet. What I wouldn't give to know more! I take it that none of our spies have returned yet?"

King Garkin nodded sadly. "We have confirmation that two have been killed, but nothing on the others."

Yan spoke up, "If your majesty will excuse my boldness, we need to establish an elaborate and powerful network of spies like there was in my time, so long ago. This will help us both now and in the future."

King Garkin assented to this, saying, "That is a good idea, but remember, no titles of rank and respect here. If we went about sir-ing and your majesty-ing, we wouldn't get anything done."

General Cilio took it from there. "Actually, we do have a network of spies, and the head intelligence officer is here now." A few of the men looked surprised, including the officer himself. Cilio saw their looks of dismay, and then chuckled. "You all know that his name is never revealed, even to this group here. There may yet be a traitor among us."

The room was silent for a moment, and then Cilio, who seemed to be some-what in command, turned his icy glare to Tarthur, and part way to Zelin. Tarthur didn't like this man, in fact, he made him feel uneasy. "If we were to gain possession of the Water Orb, could you use it quickly to our advantage? The combined power of Water and Earth would be sufficient to destroy the Death Lord, would it not?"

Cilio's unflinching gaze was beginning to eat at him. It was picking him apart, analyzing him, slowly, methodically, until he arrived at the center of his being.

"I...I'm not sure," Tarthur managed to stammer. He looked at Zelin, as if hoping the wizard would rescue him.

"Yes, I think that Tarthur will be able to use the Water Orb, especially if we give him more training in its use and history, and the fundamentals of magic. As to the other question, yes. As long as he is not at the peak of his power or if his army does not have an insurmountable advantage, it will at least defeat him, and likely destroy him. But remember, the king can only use the Power of Earth in self-defense. It may not end up being much good to us."

Cilio seized the moment to carry his point. "Since we are agreed that this impending war is inevitable, we should seize the opportunity and attack first. It may be that we can capture this Water Orb and destroy Darhyn and be done with it."

Sir Terin was not quite sure that he liked this idea. "We don't want to be the aggressors. How will you all feel when the blood starts flowing, and you know that you caused it?"

"A war is never avoided, Sir Terin, but only deferred to one's disadvantage." Cilio was speaking in his tone of teacher to pupil, the tone he frequently used when speaking to those whom he considered to have lower intelligence than himself, which of course was everyone.

Sir Terin was not finished. "How many people will join us if we start this? They see no threat to themselves, and we really don't know what is going on up there in Castle Rathskellar. We will need a full army if we are to defeat him."

Cilio shrugged his shoulders. "So we will wait until their homes are being attacked and burned? We won't have any enlistments until it is too late. Don't forget, we can order mandatory conscription."

Hano finally joined in the discussion. "We will have more troops than we need, if things go the way that they have. The elves are ready to fight to a man, and we would need but a handful if the Death Lord's other troops fight like his first ones have. General Cilio and I have sent them scattering! They are nothing to us!"

"Then you have seen nothing," Yan interjected. "He has terrors you cannot dream about. To even think on them would be to destroy yourself. Do you think he uses only humans? No, soon you will see creatures of evil from out of legend. They are monsters of horror and power."

"Yet they still bleed," Hano interrupted, pushing his point. "They still feel steel and they still die."

"Oh, no," said Yan with a bitter chuckle of mixed sorrow and mirth. "Unfortunately for us, they don't die."

This unnerved and hushed the room and the silence hung heavy over each member, the thoughts of what was to come eating away their bravado. Tarthur felt the chill of the winter outside fill him. Finally someone spoke; it was General Cilio, only his unfeeling nature was undisturbed.

"Are we in possession of enough power of our own to neutralize the magic creatures that Darhyn is sure to create if he has not done so already?" Cilio was always considering the military aspects of any point.

Zelin looked at Yan, took a deep breath, and began. "We do have a considerable amount of learning and power on our side, and Yan and I will be able to make a strong impact in the battle in any case. Yet, without knowing what minions he is making or summoning from other worlds...well I can only surmise. Yet it is imperative that we retrieve the Water Orb. With its power, we could win, unless he has something up his sleeve, such as an alliance with Marhyn, which I would not discount. One thing is for sure, the more time he has the more powerful the evil we will be faced with."

Cilio nodded, satisfied it seemed. "So then our present course of action would be to ready for an attack on Darhyn." He raised his hand to ward off Sir Terin as he tried to make his point. "Your elementary concern is true, yet can be dealt with easily. We need the support of the people, that much is obvious. We must simply use the intelligence network to spread our propaganda. Whoever here is the leader must have his workers spread posters and announcements, we must set up plays and shows to help get the minds of the people into this fight."

Tarthur raised his hand, and asked Cilio to explain this "propaganda." Cilio seemed slightly annoyed at the interruption at first, but then started explaining it to him.

"You see, Tarthur, it is very important for the heart of all the people to be with us in this struggle. We are going to send people to every village, every street corner, and have them make up stories about our army and the Death Lord. We'll be the valiant defenders of truth and justice and they will be all that is evil and loathsome. We'll make stage productions of the old stories of his defeat, polish them up, and add some stories where common citizens have a stroke of good luck and suddenly become heroes. Of course, we'll leave out all the true parts of war, like the dying and blood and pain and losing, and all that. We'll send people to start talking, and start rumors (there's a mountain of gold beneath his palace, you know.) We'll do all these things and the people will be crawling over each other just to get a chance to enlist."

Derlin was a little bit confused. "We're going to lie to them? What if they get killed because they think they are fighting for gold and fame and glory? That is wrong to the people."

King Garkin, a ruler who was removed by rank and stature from the common people, yet still felt for their lives and happiness, nodded gravely, yet said nothing.

General Cilio still perceived King Garkin's discomfort at these lies that he was about to perpetrate, and he got angry at these troublesome morals and ideals that the others held. They would be the downfall of the army if he didn't do something quick. "Nothing is wrong if we win! The end justifies the means. Don't you see that following these high-minded ideas will get us in trouble? If it helps you any, think of it as stretching the truth rather than lying. Darhyn is, after all, evil, and we are the good guys." Cilio took a deep breath, focused intently on the king, and began to speak again, this time in a more calmed tone. "You hired me to lead your armies and to give us victory. That is my job and I will do it. Your job is to protect your people, and you better start doing it too!"

If the whole land of Daranor, outside of the regions belonging to the Death Lord and his sister was searched up and down, not another soul could be found who would dare address the king in that tone of voice or manner of words. Yet King Garkin did not reprimand him. He simply muttered, "Yes, I see now that it must be done. Please forgive me." So the matter was settled, but Tarthur could not help notice a shimmer on the king's eye, as if moisture were slowly departing from it.

After a brief pause, Yan changed the subject. "If that is settled, then I would recommend that Tarthur begin training in the Arts of Magic immediately. We must teach him all that we possibly can about this power that he possesses."

The rest nodded in agreement, and Sir Terin rose, saying "That is a good idea, and may I suggest that you and Zelin take him under your personal care? It seems as if you two are at the peak of your profession."

"Thank you, Sir Terin, but no. Yan and I will help Tarthur and oversee his education, but we have other pressing business to attend to. We will, of course, stop by periodically and check on his progress, but I am sure there are others qualified to help him in the beginning."

Warren tried, though unsuccessfully, to phrase his question with guile and cunning. "Just what exactly is this pressing business?"

"For one thing we are going to visit the merfolk and see exactly how they can help us in the coming struggle," Zelin answered seriously, then "oh yes! And then we are going to try to make the whole army fly." The unseen tensions between the rest of the group and Warren were revealed as the company burst into a mirthful laughter, and Warren's embarrassed face wore a scowl.

King Garkin rose again. "It appears that things are settled then. We will gather an army, train it and be ready to leave with spring. I know that is some three months from now, but making a good army takes time, and we could not attack him in the winter anyway, his power is stronger then. And Tarthur will learn about magic. I am sure I don't need to remind any of you, but what is said in this room stays here. This is very secret information, and it could be the doom of our country if any of it got out. Is that clear?" Everyone nodded, so the king continued. "Well, then, if no one has anything else?"

No one did, and so the meeting was adjourned. Tarthur and Derlin were led to their chambers by a male servant, and soon they were reclining on a bed made of goose down. The bed had rich, thick, comforters, and enormous fluffy pillows. The room also had a huge fireplace, which Tarthur deemed unnecessary, seeing as how that bed alone could keep him warm in just about any temperature. It felt so different for the boys, who were used to sleeping in a wooden cot with maybe one woolen blanket, or even sleeping outside with nothing but a thin tattered cloak. It was almost uncomfortable to have a servant lead them around and call them sir and provide whatever they needed. It made them feel out of their place. They had always made fun of Morty at home for his luxuries and schooling, but now they were in a much more luxurious room then there ever was in Krendon, and Tarthur was going to have to go to school for a few whole months!

Despite not sleeping the night before, Tarthur and Derlin were ready to get out and see the city. Before they could, however, a tailor came in and started to measure them for new clothes. Tarthur and Derlin were dying to get away, but he informed them that they were to stay with him for the remainder of that day, and that the next day they might visit the city, but after that they were to study every day, with only Sundays to do with as they pleased. Tarthur gasped at this, but Derlin only nodded.

They should have paid more attention to the tour that the tailor took them on, for he showed them the dining area, the latrine, the other people's quarters, the study, and other places of interest in the castle. In the study, Tarthur met a somewhat tiresome middle-aged man, whom the tailor introduced as Akin. Akin was one of the principal magicians, and to him was entrusted Tarthur's learning. From the very outset, Tarthur knew that he would dislike him, and while he seemed perfectly nice, something in his manner and voice irked him. The voice was thin and dull, and by the look of him Tarthur guessed that he had little or no experience having fun, or doing anything that was not horrendously boring.

When the tour was completed, the tailor brought them back into the dining area where he took his leave of them. He informed them that servants would be around if they had any special needs, but otherwise they were to fend for themselves. The three meals would be served in the dining hall daily at the seventh, twelfth, and sixth chimes, respectively. They were to report to their places of education (Akin's study for Tarthur and the knights' training courtyard for Derlin, who was learning swordsmanship so he could take part in the fighting) as soon as they finished eating breakfast, or by the ninth chime at least.

The meal was of average quality, but to one who rarely eats meat or any hot meal at all, it was more than satisfactory. The food in their stomachs, coupled with not sleeping much the night before began to take its toll shortly after dinner was finished. There was a roaming bard who went by the name of Wendel Grayleaf singing songs of yesteryear and telling about old stories that had been all but forgotten. Tarthur wanted to hear him, but it soon became obvious that he would have to wait until tomorrow, when he fell asleep during the very first song.

"Let's go to bed," said Derlin with a yawn, as he shook Tarthur in an attempt to rouse him. Fortunately it worked, and the two soon were walking through the halls, in search of their quarters. By some miracle of chance they found them, and as soon as they hit the pillows they were fast asleep.

*   *   *   *

After falling asleep, he began to dream again. It was like that other dream, awhile ago, back when he was living in the small village that had been his home for his whole life. The dream carried him across a barren wasteland. He floated effortlessly over the decay that was an eternal reality in this place where no living thing dared to disturb the stillness. But this was not a calm stillness, not a place for a troubled soul to find solace and peace. It was an electric stillness, a kind of perverted calm before the storm, where the land knows of the coming tempest, and eagerly anticipates it with a charged energy that makes skin crawl and hair stand on edge.

He looked up and saw the reason for the anticipation, and the only monument that broke the endless stillness of the Savannah Plain. It was Castle Rathskellar, and the darkness where it cast its shadow was just a little darker than the surrounding countryside. It was here that he floated on the dream currents, or rather to the one inside that he knew he was bound. He continued to float on, past sentries, through walls, over a regiment of the evil army training for battle. He saw by their startled looks that some saw him, even recognized him from when he had been there before, yet he was not afraid. He could tell by the way the monsters quickly turned away from his gaze, as if his look was death, that they would not hinder him. They did not seem particularly afraid of him, yet they remembered what had happened the last time the floating one with the golden hair had come, even though they cared not to.

Soon he was before the last doors, and halted. Runes of protection and seals of destruction too numerous to mention wrapped about the doors as if they were strands of ivy around a crumbling marble column in some ancient house. Even without his body as he now was, the potent spells would destroy him, so the dream current stopped and he waited. Soon the door swung open by itself, and the current resumed once more. It carried him in this way past ten more identical doors. The last one was much larger, and even he, who as of yet had no learning in the ways and powers of magic, felt it. Soon the twelfth door opened, and he floated inside.

Standing over a map of the world was a formless figure in a black cowl. As he looked up, a plain skull was all that could be made of his face. He had no heart-beat, and the only rhythmic sound in the room was the pulsating of evil from the Sword of Darkness that was at his side. It sent out waves of malevolence, unseen and unheard, but nonetheless felt. Being here sent such a chill down the sleeper's spine that he tried to will himself awake. It didn't work. He had come here to do something, and now he would do it.

The two fiery red eyes burning inside the otherwise vacant sockets began to eat away at his resolve, and the dreamer had to remind himself that he was not going to be hurt. He had promised that when they had first made their pact. Thinking of the pact made him wonder again why he was making it. Why was he selling out his own country, his people? It was like Sir Terin had said, people were going to die. And it was going to all be his fault. No, he thought again, that's not quite correct. I'm just helping along the inevitable. He thought back to that other time he had come here in a dream, and of the horrors he had seen. I guess deep down inside I want the king to win, but I *know*. I know what He can do, I've seen it. I'm just being smart, survival of the fittest, the strong and smart, that's what it's all about.

"They are amassing an army to attack you, my lord." Warren usually refrained from addressing anyone with that title, but this was not anyone. It was Him. "They believe that you are still asleep and that they can destroy you before you awake." Warren looked into the Death Lord's face, to gauge his reaction, but he did not move, almost as if he had not heard. He could have been stone were it not for the dancing tongues of flame that were his eyes. "They plan to attack with the spring, as if it will help them any!" With this Warren burst into a sort of laughter which quickly died out as Warren remembered what had happened the last time someone tried to joke with Him. The Death Lord did not joke. Although Warren saw no reaction from Darhyn, he felt his malevolence increase, if indeed that was possible, and inwardly cursed himself for his foolishness.

"*It is as I had hoped.*" The words resounded in Warren's head, and with that he knew the interview was over. He had no sign from the Evil One whether he was pleased, but as the dream currents wrapped around his body and began to lift him from the room, he thought he felt the evil pulse of the Sword of Darkness quicken slightly in anticipation…

*   *   *   *

The one who had been asleep arose slowly at first, trying to shake off the last efforts of sleep to drag him back bodily to its own domain, and at the same time trying to remember where he was and how he had gotten there. When the remembrance hit him though, Tarthur shot out of bed and flew to wake Derlin. After a few hurried words, the pair quickly dressed in the clothes that had been laid out on a small table in the middle of the room. If they would have taken the time to notice, they would have remembered that these were the clothes that the tailor had made for them the night before. In their excitement, Derlin had put on Tarthur's pants, and had to exchange them for his own when it became apparent that if he walked around in them he would most certainly trip before he had gone ten feet. In their excitement, they nearly neglected two small leather bags. When Tarthur looked at the contents, he saw that they each carried an enormous and incredible amount of pure golden coins! (Actually it was a very modest sum, but to the boys, who had never seen more than a few pennies at a time, it was quite a fortune.) They both foolishly deposited the whole of their allowances in a hidden pocket which appeared to be made for just this purpose, and hurried down to eat breakfast, for they had not a moment to lose.

Today was the day they got to see the city.

Walking quickly, or rather running just slowly enough so anyone not looking closely would assume they were walking in a dignified manner, but still going fast enough to obtain minimum travel time, Tarthur and Derlin talked about what they might see in the city. Baron Ercrilla and a few people from Krendon had been there before, and the stories (which were usually made up of half-truths and some of them even of quarter-truths) told of wonders and sights amazing to behold. They told of streets, where people sold things from the far corners of the world. They told of new animals, and street shows, complete with magicians and acrobats, and other things you wouldn't believe even if you saw them. They told of awe inspiring wonders from the biggest gathering of people in any single place in all of Daranor…and now the boys were about to see for themselves. They walked past the guard at the door that led from the inner keep of the king's castle and stepped out into the city…

…And they saw filth. Buildings and houses crowded against each other, creating narrow alleys filled with refuse and stray dogs. They saw trash over nearly every possible space. But what amazed them the most was the feeling of enclosure. To Tarthur and Derlin, it seemed as if they were still inside. They began to walk among the shadows that were cast by the tall buildings that monopolized the landscape.

"I don't see any fair," Derlin stated grimly. "Maybe we are just in the wrong section of the city."

Tarthur nodded, unconvinced. The two began to walk through the alley. They had never been in anything more than a small village before, and not knowing where to go was puzzling to them. In the places they had visited or lived in, one could see the entire town from wherever he looked. Mountains or forests or places where no one lived were places to get lost in, but cities?

As it turned out, they were indeed in the wrong section of the city if one wants to see a fair, and within a few minutes their alley came out onto one of the city's major thoroughfares. They followed this one for some time, and soon they came upon the fair.

This fair was truly like nothing they had ever seen. Tarthur and Derlin would have been intimidated, if they were the kind of boys that got intimidated easily, which they were not, by the sheer numbers of people. They were accustomed to towns where everyone knew everyone else by name mostly and at least by face. Their travels in the world had numbed them somewhat, however, and as Derlin looked at the many wonders from all around the world, he couldn't help realizing how big the world was, and how small he felt in comparison.

The boys spent the before noon looking at the wonders from exotic and faraway lands (not to mention the ones from close and boring lands) and almost forgot that they had money to buy something if they wished. They also talked to many people about whatever the others wanted to talk about. If the conversation ever got too boring, the boys would all of a sudden remember some commitment, and quickly walk away. At one point, Tarthur decided to buy a rather high quality sword, and Derlin had to stop him. He explained that this money was all that they had, and they might not get more for quite a long time, and besides Tarthur already had a sword. Tarthur was forced to acquiesce on the last point, and so the pair decided to buy dinner instead. In their excitement to try and see everything, they had quite forgotten about lunch, and now evening was fast approaching.

They stopped at one particularly nice looking vendor, and Tarthur opened his money sac to hand the man a coin. To his surprise, one coin was enough for both his and Derlin's meals, which consisted of roast turkey legs and warm apples covered with something called caramel. The caramel was a sweet, brownish thick liquid that tasted sugary and left one's hands very sticky. Their hands being thus in their present state of stickiness, the pair was forced to search for a well, or some other suitable means of cleansing themselves. What they found was an enormous and beautiful fountain, erected in the center of the town square.

Derlin was musing about the outhouses that a jovial old man had told him about earlier in the day. He had explained that they had some mystical and amazing apparatus called plumbing, of which neither of the boys had ever heard. It was rumored that some secret magical force called suction coupled with water carried their refuse away from the toilet and through the sewer system. This was then mixed with the old parts of the wheat that was unused, to form fertilizer for the coming planting season. Derlin was more than a little skeptical. He had always been interested in the mechanical things, plus he had quite a powerful urge to go, so he went to check if these things were really true. Tarthur, for his part, was left standing by the fountain. Having nothing better with which to occupy his time, Tarthur began to study the center.

The figures in the center were beautifully carved in much detail, and they seemed to be of some ancient battle. Tarthur was bending over to get a drink, when he saw a reflection of a beautiful girl's face next to his own. Startled, he turned around slowly, afraid to lose the girl's image if he spun too fast, afraid the girl's face would only be a trick of the light, or some new magic. It was not.

"It's beautiful, isn't it?" She spoke in a soft, musical voice, yet one that hid a strength of character so formidable that it would have startled Tarthur, had he seen it. "I always like to come here in the evenings, when you can see the colors of the setting sun reflect off Hana-Chan's forehead."

Tarthur felt like staying there all day, watching her. He didn't know why, maybe it was something in the way she carried herself, or maybe it was in the twinkle in her eye when she smiled, or maybe it was the gentle sigh she gave when she finished talking. Whatever it was, curiosity and the need to say something prevailed, so he asked, "Hana-Chan?" Tarthur wondered why he couldn't think of anything better to say, and after he had said it a million things came into his mind. Too late.

The girl seemed puzzled. "The king who defeated the Evil One. Everyone around here knows Hana-Chan. You must be new in town?" Her question left a scent of possibility in the air.

"Yeah…uh, yes, I'm new in town," Tarthur stammered, a little embarrassed. He felt inferior next to this girl standing before him. She was tall, but not overly, and a little heavy, but not fat. It seemed as if most of her body was made of muscle. She had flowing blond hair, which caught the rays of setting sunlight and danced with them before throwing them back into the fountain, there to dance again. Tarthur wanted to show her that he knew things too. "Oh, three hundred years ago, he was the one who defeated Darhyn?"

"Don't say that name," she chastised him, and then Tarthur felt her body press slightly closer to his and her hand inadvertently slip into his own. "I mean, you must be very brave to say that name. I'm glad you're not afraid." Tarthur was about to tell her the truth, but her last statement checked him. How he yearned to tell her of his meeting with the Death Lord, how he had stabbed him, how he had traveled the world and found objects and friends of power! But he didn't, because he was afraid. He had been afraid then, and he would be afraid when the war came. So he said nothing.

Tarthur turned and instead let his smile do the talking. "No, I'm not very brave." He tried to make it sound like he knew he was brave but was just trying to act modest but she should still think he was brave. Or something like that.

She flashed him a smile back, hesitated for a moment, and then said, "My name is Yvonne."

"And I'm Tarthur," he finished simply.

The two stood there silently for a moment, the gentle night breeze wafting the girl's perfume into Tarthur's nose. It was a fiery scent, but it also felt cool and clean, and it made Tarthur oddly conscious of how he must smell, filthy and sweaty. When was the last time he had taken a bath? He usually took one every other spring, whether he needed it or not. One and a half years ago? Tarthur resolved to take one immediately upon returning to the servants' quarters. It made him embarrassed, and he felt like he had to say something quick. "This sculpture is very beautiful."

She nodded for a moment, and Tarthur wondered if she had heard him. Then she tuned and looked into his eyes and said, "Sometimes we find beauty in some very unexpected places." They stood looking into each other's eyes for a moment, and Tarthur was worrying, "What if she kisses me, I don't know what to do!" Then a voice from somewhere inside said, "kiss her back, stupid!" He never got the chance, because she suddenly seemed to think better of it, almost as if she received some hidden signal from somewhere. In any event, she turned away sadly. "I've got to go home now." The way she said it left no room for discussion.

"I would like to see you again," Tarthur wasn't sure what to say, but he had a feeling she was going to slip away from him if he didn't do something.

"I would like to see you again too. How about tomorrow night, here by this well? You are very handsome, you know." Tarthur returned the compliment, and said tomorrow would be just fine. Too late he thought about Akin and his school, but even if he had remembered in time he would have still promised Yvonne that he would be there. And he would.

As she waved goodbye, Tarthur in a state of wonder and amazement watched her walk down to the end of the street, where then she turned and faced him again. "Oh, and Tarthur, it is Tarthur, isn't it? Don't ever carry all of your money like that. Well, as if you had that problem now." She finished this statement and blew him a kiss, and before it reached the dreamy Tarthur, the meaning of her words hit him. The money! It was gone. She had robbed him of all of his money. Horrendously embarrassed and furious he charged after her, but she had gotten the jump on him. As Tarthur raced through the streets that she had grown up in and he had just seen for the first time, he realized just how foolish he was. He was mad, but more at himself than her. He, the master thief in Krendon, had been outsmarted and robbed, and worst of all it was by a girl! A girl! She had played his emotions, and now all he knew was that he wanted to catch her. He must catch her.

Tarthur had on his side a naturally stronger body and a deep desire to catch this girl and make her pay. Yvonne had on her side a head start and knowledge of the many twists and turns of the city streets. Tarthur's pure desire and force of will proved to be the deciding factor. Soon she was within ten feet, and he was closing rapidly. Just as he was on the verge of catching her, she disappeared into a side tunnel in one of the buildings. Tarthur turned to look for her, but as he was examining the hole, he heard a voice call out from behind him. Tarthur spun around, and at first couldn't tell where the voice was coming from.

"Hey cutie! Looking for someone?" The voice was coming from the roof of a building. As Tarthur looked at it, he could see Yvonne on top taunting him. How had she gotten there so fast? She must know a secret way. Losing no time, Tarthur started to climb the side of the building, Yvonne still at the top taunting him. As he started to climb, Tarthur reached for an unsafe handhold and as it crumbled away, was sent sprawling onto the street below.

Yvonne let out a burst of laughter, which only increased Tarthur's desire to catch her and harm her. It wasn't even about money now. It was personal.

Tarthur was incredulous that only a few minutes ago he was thinking about kissing her. Now he just wanted to hit her. This time up the building Tarthur was careful, and chose his holds accordingly. Yvonne was still taunting him, but as he got closer and closer to the top, her taunts died off and she began to run away again. It appeared as if this country boy could climb buildings.

Upon reaching the roof, Tarthur was just able to see the top of her blond hair disappear as she leaped onto another building. Tarthur was hot in pursuit and he saw her glance back just once to see if he was still chasing. He was. After leaping from rooftop to rooftop in this way, Yvonne suddenly opened a trapdoor in the roof of one of the buildings and slid gracefully in. Tarthur was quick to follow and if he had thought about it, he would have wondered why she did not lock the door after herself. But he was in too much of a hurry to notice such things.

Light from a dozen or so lanterns and a fire greeted Tarthur as he stepped into the room. The voices of many men, relaxing from a day's hard work over a mug of ale and a pot of stew, surrounded him. The men were gruff looking and unshaven, but on the whole seemed congenial and friendly. Tarthur realized that he was in a tavern. If he was not so single-minded of purpose, he might have stopped for a glass of ale, but of course he couldn't because he had no money. At least not until he found that girl and took it back!

The prospects for finding her in here were rather bleak, however. There were plenty of places for her to hide, and a cloak covering her blond hair could make her hard to recognize. It was just then that he saw a man walking a little too gracefully out the door, and he saw a wisp of gold come ever so slightly out of the hood. Stealthily, Tarthur followed her, out the door and into the streets, where she started to run. Tarthur ran after her, and soon she shed her cloak so as to run unhindered.

When Tarthur had almost caught up with her again, she disappeared once more and reappeared behind him some fifty feet. Puzzled, he charged after her again, but this time she disappeared once more and appeared back where he had almost caught her. Instead of running again, she called out to Tarthur, "Hey! You're not as bad as you look! Anyway, I've had fun with you tonight, stealing your gold and leading you on all over the city and all, but you're really no challenge for me, and frankly, I'm bored. So I'll stop giving you hints and slowing myself up so you can catch me! Well, save up some more gold so I can take it again. See ya 'round."

With this she disappeared again, and this time Tarthur could not pick up her trail, but it was probably just as well that he didn't, because he was so furious that he couldn't think straight. All of his life, Tarthur had been playing con games and pilfering small things. Now, he had gotten beaten easily by a girl! And not only that, he never stole when it would really hurt someone, but now he had the added problem of not having any of the money that he might really need. It hadn't occurred to him that he could ask the king for more, seeing as how he was now quite important, but his mind was not thinking correctly, and he didn't even know how important he was to the security of the realm. But the worst part of all was that she said he didn't even challenge her! Tarthur vowed right then and there, that sometime, somewhere, that girl would pay.

Tarthur returned to the fountain to find a mildly worried Derlin, who had since returned from the outhouse to find his companion gone. "Where were you?" Derlin called out in a slightly exasperated tone. He was not really mad, only a little scared that something had happened to Tarthur, or as was more frequently the case, Tarthur had happened to something. Upon seeing the look on his boyhood friend's face, however, Derlin quickly softened his tone. It appeared that this disappearance was a case of the former.

Derlin's slightly harsh rebuke did not bother Tarthur, for in fact he never even heard it. Derlin just heard him repeating something over and over. When he got closer, he heard him saying, "That tramp! I'll kill her! Not a challenge indeed! I'll show her a challenge!"

"What is it, what happened?" It was not too often that Tarthur swore, but now he looked really angry.

So Tarthur took a deep breath and began his story, beginning from when Derlin left up until Yvonne was saying goodbye. At this part he stalled, unwilling to tell it to his confidant to whom he revealed everything. "Then she...well, you know."

"What? She kissed you?"

"No, she...uh...shestolmymonynleft." Tarthur mumbled his answer, embarrassment preventing him from saying it outright. Lifelong friends, Derlin still caught his meaning, and burst out laughing. To think, here he was worried about Tarthur all this time and his friend had only been off planning a joke. This was a pretty good one too! And it was so realistic that Derlin would have almost believed it if it weren't for the absurdity of the whole situation. Imagine! His friend Tarthur getting tricked like that! Derlin continued to laugh out loud, but Tarthur wasn't amused. "Good joke! You almost had me for a second there, except, next time make up something more believable, I mean, come on even Morty isn't stupid enough to get fooled like that!"

Something in Tarthur's face told him that this was not a joke.

Derlin decided this was one of those times when it was better to say nothing, so the two friends walked back to their quarters in silence. The city was beautiful at this time, with all of the people beginning to turn on their lights. The lights were new to the boys. It almost seemed like it wasn't night at all, but only dusk with the light of the lanterns sweeping out across the streets like foamy waves on a beach, yet staying in place instead of rushing back to join the surf as a wave would. Derlin's breathing was slow and regular, keeping perfect time with the soft patter of his footsteps on the worn cobblestone pathway. Derlin's relaxed, easy manner contrasted heavily with that of his companion. Tarthur's shoulders were tight, and he breathed haggardly, not at all in rhythm with his steps. Derlin could see by the deep lines of concentration on his companion's face that he was hatching a plan.

"What are you going to do?" Tarthur knew that Derlin had guessed what he was thinking, but he made his friend ask the question.

"I'm going to go back tomorrow and find her."

"And what then? Beat her up? Tarthur, you can't get your money back even if you find her. All she has to do is yell 'rape' and then you'll be in trouble."

Tarthur thought about it for a moment in and then spoke: "I…! I, that's strange. I feel as if I would like to see her again, even if I don't get the money. In her eyes, it was like…" Tarthur trailed off and took a deep breath. "No, she may have seemed like she was a nice girl, but after what she did to me, I'll slap her if I ever see her again. And then I'll take back my money."

"We can't go back until next Sunday, anyway. Remember, we have to be busy studying."

Tarthur looked at Derlin incredulously. "It's just for one night, and we'll be finished with all of our classes for the day before I go to look for her."

Derlin looked sternly back at Tarthur. "We've got to study hard and learn as much as we can, remember? Besides, I'm sure she won't be there. It was just a ploy to get you so wrapped up in your emotions that you would forget to watch your wallet. Tarthur, I want you to promise me that you won't go back there tomorrow."

Tarthur was about to retort angrily, he was not in the sort of mood for someone to tell him what to do and what not to do. But when he saw Derlin's concerned face, he softened somewhat. He knew that his friend would not stop until he won, and he was not in the mood for a protracted argument either. Suddenly Tarthur felt tired, tired of running, tired of losing, tired of having other forces control his life, tired of other people taking advantage of him. If he had had more energy, he would have felt like fighting back, but now he just felt like sleeping. So he promised his friend, and they returned to their rooms to sleep in a nice warm bed, for tomorrow their schooling would begin.

*   *   *   *

Yvonne brushed aside the moth-infested canvas and walked through the three pieces of splintered wood held together by a handful of rusty nails that pretended to be a door. She was greeted by the light of a robust fire that glimmered off the walls and made dark shadows that danced on her face and then sauntered off. The smell of roasted turkey slowly turning on a spit lured her nose, and as she turned, she saw the unbelievable. It was true. So Yvette must have been back with the money already. Two small children rushed up and jumped on her legs, laughing and squeezing until Yvonne thought her legs might fall off. Failing to pry them off, she playfully started to walk with them on. The children laughed for a while, but soon grew tired of it and found some new diversion.

Yvonne walked through the room and found Yvette sitting in her chair, munching on a turkey leg. Yvonne looked through the air heavy with smoke at her twin. "I know we have reason to celebrate, but do you think it is wise to have spent the money so soon?"

"Of course, you haven't heard yet," Yvette said, walking to greet her sister and put her arm around her. "You got quite a fine catch this time. That boy's pocket had twelve gold pieces in it. This has got to be one of our finer operations in quite some time."

Yvonne nodded, and smiled. "Yes, it was, wasn't it? We sure fooled him good. I bet he probably wants to kill me right now. I wonder who he is…I mean, I've never seen him around here before."

"Probably some son of a country nobleman, with the way he got fooled and the amount of money he was carrying, all in one place too. He certainly hasn't grown up on the streets if he was that careless." Yvette saw Yvonne nod slowly, and she could immediately see what her twin was thinking. All of their lives, the twins had known each other like they were one person. At times they could even feel what the other was feeling, even though they were miles apart. So Yvette asked her question, not to learn the answer, but rather to make her sister say it. "What's wrong?"

Yvonne knew her sister already knew the answer, but she spoke it anyway. "I just wish we didn't have to do this. I mean, I felt bad taking that boy's money so easily. We took it without any problems, but I can't help feeling that that boy is more than some stupid gentleman's son. I don't know…"

Since Yvette had already known the answer, she had had time to prepare her response. It had always been this way. In contrast to ordinary ladies at court and elsewhere, neither girl would be described as "soft" or "ladylike." They were stronger and better at running and jumping and climbing than most men. Yet between the twins, Yvonne had always been the emotional one. She sometimes felt with her heart and not her head, and Yvette had to work hard to correct this. One did not maintain her position as head of the Guild of Thieves by feeling sorry for others.

Yvette pointed into the next room. "Tell me, Yvonne, what do you see there?"

"I see young children, abandoned by their parents, getting a hot meal and some clothes to wear. I see old men and women, warming themselves by the fire so they will not freeze to death. I see the outcasts of society who have found a home here." Yvonne turned angrily toward Yvette. "You don't have to remind me of the good we do here. I know we help out many people who have no other way and that Tarthur boy is probably sitting with his dad and his dad is probably telling him to be more careful next time and just giving him some more money. I know that I enjoyed working and I will do it again, and again. I know that this is the only way and it is the way we must go. Just because I wish that there was another way doesn't mean I won't do it again in a second if I get the chance." Yvonne turned and went to the fire, picked up a piece of turkey, and then went to sit with the children.

∗   ∗   ∗   ∗

Bong, Bong, Bong, Bong, Bong, Bong, Bong. The deep clear tones of the castle bell woke Tarthur the next morning. He counted the bongs over again in his mind. There were seven, and that meant it was time for breakfast. He woke Derlin and the two dressed themselves and went down to eat. This morning they were served oat cakes and the juice of what one of the serving boys said was an orange. He seemed surprised that the boys had never had one before; at the castle they ate them nearly every day for breakfast. After that, the boys parted and Derlin went off to see Sir Terin and Tarthur went to Akin's study.

Sir Terin was busy with preparations for the war, so Derlin was met instead by Sir Undbar, a gruff old knight who believed in basics and fundamentals. All Derlin ever heard him preach was "basics and fundamentals" and the good sense and reliability of a sword. After Derlin got to know him better, he would say that Sir Undbar distrusted magic, and while he knew that it was a powerful force that would sway many battles, Derlin couldn't shake the feeling that the gruff old knight would like a world without it better. Of course, Sir Undbar would never admit it to anyone, but as Derlin got to know him better and better he began to see that it was true. He wanted a world where a man's strength and courage were the deciding factors. They should meet and let the one who was the real man win the contest of strength and wills. Sir Undbar was not a very intelligent man, he disliked battlefield trickeries like general Cilio's; he preferred the armies to simply charge each other and see who emerged bloody, sweaty and victorious. Still, he was congenial and serious about his work, and while he wished the world to be otherwise, he saw the necessity of such techniques.

That first day, Sir Undbar told Derlin to practice hacking at a wooded replica of a human being. Taking his chance, Derlin had jumped in the air, spun around, and sent the head of the figure flying, in a near perfect imitation of a move he had seen the lightning-quick Yan perform. Derlin had always been agile and quick, and the move proved both effective and powerful. Sir Undbar, however, had yelled at Derlin for his fanciness. He seemed to ignore the fact that the move was well performed and gave Derlin a long speech extolling the benefits of basics and fundamentals, after which Derlin was sentenced to perform one thousand each of various blocks and strikes, while the gruff old knight looked on, frowning.

If Tarthur would have looked out of his window, which he didn't, he might have seen Derlin at his misery. But as it was, Tarthur had neither time nor space for thought left in his brain. He had no time because of the vigorous schedule Akin was holding Tarthur and another pupil named Pol to. He had no space for thought because Yvonne was crowding into his brain, occupying nearly every free thought. And on top of all this, Akin was even succeeding in interjecting a few comments about the origin and fabric of the universe, although because of the relative unimportance of the matter, this number was very few indeed.

Ever since he had met the blond girl, Tarthur had not been able to shake her from his mind. The funny thing was that he had actually tried. He had tried to push her away, tried to listen to the dull and monotonous voice of Akin, yet every time some thought of her would come back to him. He would see her face exactly as he had seen it for the first time, the beautiful shimmering reflection in the fountain. When he saw her like this he was captivated by her majesty, but then he would see her taunting—yet still beautiful—face, and want nothing more than to slap it.

The day passed thus in drudgery for the companions, and while Tarthur's interest in most magical subjects was not raised by Akin as it should have been, Tarthur did find one phenomenon that he was interested in. For some strange magical reason, time slowed down in Akin's classroom. Tarthur would listen to his lectures for at least three hours, then turn and look through the window at the tower clock, only to find that it had not advanced five minutes! Tarthur wondered if Zelin used this so he could live for hundreds of years while appearing to be only eighty or so. Maybe they were casting this spell on him so that he could pack years of study into just a few weeks, and Tarthur resented that. He would have made a mental note to himself to look into it later, except at that very moment he was caught up in a thought of Yvonne again.

So it was that a sore pair of boys, Derlin's upper body sore from performing thousands of sword techniques, and Tarthur's sore from sitting in a desk nearly all day, returned tiredly from the evening meal to their beds. Tarthur seemed preoccupied with something, but Derlin was too exhausted to care. They slipped off their clothes and slid gratefully to bed, both dreading the next day, although both also glad that they were at least alive and well and not being chased by monsters anymore. Derlin was already asleep when Tarthur rose, dressed himself, and silently exited the room.

CHAPTER 12

▼

ESCAPE

Girn was tired. After a long day of helping the strong mermen harvest their kelp that they used as their staple food supply, he had eaten a meal of *ghtysa* and was now ready to retire to bed. He was not alone in being tired, however. All of the members of the merfolk community were busy harvesting extra food so they could be ready to fight as soon as they were needed. Their remote location had isolated them and kept them uninformed of the rest of the world. They could send no overland messenger except Girn and for Tustor to send out his mind to communicate with others like him would be much too risky, especially for the beginning of a war that they all felt ominously approaching. Girn would always feel inadequate and small, but the calm and gracious demeanor of the mermen was beginning to win over his heart. As he became more comfortable with them and their way of life, he talked more and stuttered less. He had just slipped off his clothes and slid into bed when he heard a shout from up above. Girn's residence was in a submerged cell that was nevertheless airtight, so he was always dry and comfortable. The shout sounded urgent so Girn hurriedly redressed and climbed above. What he saw was ten ominous black ships, heading straight for them.

The already fatigued mermen had only enough time to jump up from bed and hastily arm themselves before the gigantic and well-armed battleships of Queen Marhyn were upon them. The twilight attack had taken the community completely by surprise. The men from the ships hurled boulders and hot oil and shot flaming arrows that were quickly extinguished by the damp sea. Small boats, piloted by a dozen or so men, charged furiously at the mermen. They leaped from their boats and into the shoals, stabbing and cutting their way through the surprised and unarmed mermen. A group of them ran for Chairman Eor, who looked up in surprise. He reached for a pike in the corner of his shoal, but the man sliced off his arm even as Chairman Eor grasped it. The arm that held the pike spurted blood all over the floor. Clutching his stump in a vain attempt to stop the bleeding, the chairman called out to his wife and children to swim away. Only the scream of his daughter answered him, and then nothing. Eor turned to face his attacker, and got a sword through his chest. The man pulled it out and went to find his next victim.

At first, the scattered defenders could do little but defend their own homes with their wives and children, but soon Tustor had organized a retreat of those unable to fight, which included Girn. While this task was being completed, Truin organized those left into a fighting force, who regrouped behind a large rock.

Truin surveyed the remains of his scattered army. Nearly seven of every ten had been killed in the first onslaught. He cursed and hit his fist against a rock, drawing blood that quickly mingled with sweat and water. The attack had been so sudden! As he looked into the brave yet fearful eyes of his companions, he knew that they were thinking the same thing as he was. Their race was going to be eradicated as a force that night, but they would exact heavy losses before they were done! Organized and relatively rested now, the mermen were ready to launch their counterattack. Truin divided the party of about forty into two prongs, one lead by himself and the other lead by Forn, who thankfully was still alive.

Truin's hastily constructed battle plan called for the two parties to separate and attack the ships that had come in from both sides. They would smash as many ships as they could and hope that the men aboard were weak swimmers, so the current could finish them off when there were no more mermen alive to do it. Truin was about to launch his counterattack when Tustor appeared looking tired and old all over again, but with a fierce determination burning in his eyes. Truin was about to ask him to go back to safety, Tustor was too valuable to their cause and they could not afford the possibility of him dying. But when Truin saw the fire that flared at the end of Tustor's fingertips and the water around it sizzle from the heat, he knew that Tustor was ready to fight; to tell him to go back would be both futile and stupid.

Truin turned to Forn and nodded. Forn nodded sternly, lifted his head back, paused, and then thrust his fist in the air and screamed the battle cry of the mermen. The rest followed, letting their yells take out all of their frustration and anger and fear. The attack was begun. Fortunately for the mermen, at the point where most of their people lived the waters were shallow, and the first attacking ship had been foolish enough to strike there, splintering the bottom of its hull as it had done so. The smaller lifeboats that had been launched in the main attack were being drawn back into the safety of the larger vessels. The men killed and then ran. It was toward the men that had been on the splintered ship of death that that the mermen turned their fury. The men were helpless in the three foot deep water. As they sluggishly tried to fight or flee, they were quickly set upon by the mermen, lightning quick bodies that shot through the water and into their prey. Bolting through the water with pikes and swords held before them, the mermen easily decimated the unorganized force. Within minutes the bodies of hundreds of men who had made up the original strike force lay floating in the multicolored water, made yellow and orange by the setting sun, and red by their blood mixed with that of the sleeping victims they had slaughtered.

The relentless mermen now turned on the second ship, which had already turned its enormous stern and was beginning to make straight for them. Before it did, however, two bolts of lightning lit up the sky and converged on Tustor. The merwizard was floating a little behind the rest, and had not yet used his magic; he had been building his strength. While Tustor had been surveying the battle, he knew that barring a miracle, his race would lose. The army that opposed them had chosen their attack too well, and they were just too many. Tustor knew that his people had just one chance, he must destroy whoever was the leader of this force, and he must do it quickly. Tustor had noticed two ships hanging back a little from the rest, as if they were merely watching the confrontation and not really taking part. The leader of this force must be on one of the two ships, but which one? Tustor had guessed left, the one farthest from the battle and had begun his spell. Now, as the bolts of lightning struck him and filled him with power, he felt the wild exhilaration surge through him just like it did every time he used powerful magic. He turned to the ship on the left and sent the magic with every ounce of force in his body.

The mermen looked up at Tustor as their leader was struck with twin bolts of lightning, gasped in amazement when he lowered his hands, and then cheered when he sent the fire lancing into the side of the ship, tearing a hole in it and forcing it to sink. Two down, Truin thought, eight to go.

Now they were at the next ship, and Truin led his group around the starboard flank to draw the enemy's fire, while Forn and his command dove under and started to destroy the hull of the ship by attacking it with their pitchforks and other mean looking harvesting implements that also served as weapons in war-time. The kelp-like plant that they harvested was tough; if you could cut its stalk, you could cut a man's bone in half easily. The men on this ship didn't realize what was happening until it was too late, but even if they had they would have been able to devise no counterattack, for they had no weapons that could attack under the water below them. The men screamed in panic as the ship started to go down, watching the dark shapes of the mermen darting about through the water, knowing what their fate would be as soon as they were forced to fight in the now fairly deep ocean.

Truin shoved his great three-pronged triton through the trunk of a black clad man who was flailing about wildly with his sword in an absurd attempt to strike him, and then turned to survey the scene. Mermen were finishing off the last of the attackers on the third ship, and he was relieved to see that nearly thirty mer-men were still alive and in fighting condition. If they could keep up their plan, they might have a chance. The sea was also becoming more turbulent—waves were hungrily splashing against the sides of the attacking boats. It was almost as if the sea itself was coming to their aid. Truin paused for a moment, regrouped his force, and started toward the next ship.

*   *   *   *

The bolt of lightning rocked Dalin's cell and sent him flying to the floor. Only a few minutes earlier he had been awakened by sounds of combat, and a tear came to his eye as he saw the destruction of the peaceful shoals of the merfolk. He had seen Tustor raise his hands, double bolts of lightning strike him simulta-neously, and then watched as he had lowered his hands and sent the bolts flying into his ship. Dalin struggled to get up, dizzy and groggy from the power of the blast. As he looked around, the elf realized that he would have to act quickly or he would be lost, for the ship was already beginning to sink. He had to get clear of the wreckage soon or he would risk getting tangled and caught in it and dragged to his death at the bottom of the sea. Dalin grabbed a piece of still smoldering wood that had been blown loose by the blow that had destroyed the ship and jumped into the turbulent waters below.

There was a sharp hiss from the hot wood and Dalin was under. The cold of the winter water sent a shock into his heart, and almost stopped his breath. Yet the buoyant piece of wood bobbed him back to the top, and once above water again Dalin gasped for air. The air brought much needed relief and he began to think clearly for the first time. He must rejoin the mermen, but how could he do so without being mistaken for the enemy? Just as a plan was beginning to take shape in his mind, a piece from his makeshift life raft broke off. Dalin reached down, trying to hold his unseaworthy craft together just long enough to reach land, but in doing so he slipped on the wet wood and went down into the sea. Catching a last breath before he went under, Dalin thought of how to get back up. When this failed him, the fatigued elf thought about his friends, his sister Valena and Hano, her fiancé, and his home back in Breshen. After this, he thought no more as he slipped into the inviting blackness.

∗   ∗   ∗   ∗

"That's enough." Queen Marhyn spoke softly, yet everyone listened. She turned to Tyven Scarface. "Send them." The attack on the shoals of the merfolk was proving to be more costly than she had anticipated, yet far less costly then it could have been. The surprise attack on the merfolk that evening had been part of her brilliant plan from the very beginning, and she smiled inwardly at the success that it was achieving. Yes, it was an excellent idea, yet the truly brilliant part of her plan was still to come. When that was enacted, she would stand alone as a power in Daranor and the lands beyond. She had watched her ill-trained soldiers struggle and die, yet it was not out of any foolish pity or goodwill that she had ordered the withdrawal of her men. It was not out of any misplaced concern for their lives, but rather the fact that if the men died now they would not be around to serve her and worship her as a goddess later. That attack by the merwizard had almost hit her ship, just missing and hitting the prisoner ship to her right. Besides, she had always assumed that it would be necessary to send in the second wave. Her plan required that no one escape to tell who had devastated these people and wiped out their race.

Marhyn watched as her dark hordes of monsters and things conjured from nightmares swept over the battlefield, and smiled.

∗   ∗   ∗   ∗

Truin and his ragtag force were descending on the next ship when it suddenly turned around and retreated. The mermen gave a cheer, hoping the rest of the ships would follow suit and retreat also. It seemed as if they had finally stung their enemy enough to cause it to go back to wherever it had come from. They were wrong. The first ship retreated, but in its place a new ship surged forward. This ship was not like the others, it was darker and had spikes jutting out from every imaginable position, and it was teeming with dark life that hung in the shadows.

The ship headed straight for Truin and his mermen warriors, and still no clear definition of any shapes was possible. Then, suddenly a huge winged monster, looking like some deformed dragon with beady red eyes and razor sharp claws burst from the deck. It shot upward, hovered in the air for just a second, then with one beat of its leathery wings propelled itself downward and into the closest merman. The creature dug his claws into the merman's muscular chest and then ripped out his still beating heart. As the dead merman slumped into the water, the creature let out a screech of pure rage. The sound hurt Truin's ears, but what he saw hurt his eyes even more. At the creature's battle cry, Truin saw hundreds more creatures of every shape and size emerge from the dark recesses of the ship and start forward. Their queen had told them to attack, and these monsters did not need to be told twice.

Unlike the confused and untrained men the mermen had earlier encountered, this new enemy did not cower and sink but swam and viciously attacked, a whirlwind of knives and claws and teeth. The mermen were not without defenses of their own, however. Truin lead his half of the men straight into some hairy eight-armed beast, bearing down on it, cutting limbs off, and stabbing its trunk, but the monster would not fall. Truin watched it grab his friend Urhdi and tear him in half. It threw Urhdi's upper body at Truin, but Truin dodged out of the way and struck the blow that finally finished the nightmare.

As he glanced to his right, Truin saw Forn engaged with a gigantic serpent. The creature darted in to bite him but Forn smashed his three-pronged pitchfork down on its head before he had the chance. Stung, the creature brought his head back, weaving about, waiting for his next opportunity. The snake cautiously circled Forn, waiting…

Tustor sensed movement on his left, whirled, and sent fire lancing from his fingertips into the creature. The creature screamed in pain, then became quiet as Tustor sent the fire into its throat and burned out its heart. Lifeless, it floated on the water for a minute until Tustor gave it one final blast, turning it to ash. Now a new creature attacked Tustor from the front. Tustor looked at him, made a gesture, and then nodded his head. The molecules in the air about the creature exploded with such force that pieces of the creature were splattered for ten meters. A piece of greenish black ooze landed on Tustor but he quickly brushed it off. What was that monster anyway? It was like nothing Tustor knew of. It was a mass of teeth and claws and muscle and sinew unlike anything Tustor had ever seen before. And Tustor had traveled over most of the natural world…

Tustor stumbled and caught hold of a rock to steady himself. His use of the magic was further draining the already weakened merwizard. No one used magic without consequences. When the Creator had first made the world, he had arranged it this way. To have power, one must sacrifice. That is what the Death Lord and his sister did not realize. They took the power, but they ignored the consequences. Dark forces absorbed the pain for them, dark souls whispered that they were the exceptions…so they used their power recklessly, but it would catch up to them in time.

Once again, the vision of the Eternal Vale shined forth for Tustor. He saw the peace, the serenity, and the joy that awaited him as soon as he died. How easy it would be for him to die this day! He had just to gather up his magic, make one final blow, and then let himself quietly slip into oblivion. As soon as he had thought this, he banished it from his mind. His place was here, with his people! His people needed him in this world. But again, another vision shined forth for Tustor. He saw his friends, the mermen who he had ruled over and loved all of his life, flying through the air and into the Vale. Who was he kidding? His race was no more! They would all be killed this night and he would be a leader without a people—his people didn't need him here, he had no people! But what about the survivors, a voice whispered in the back of his head. Some of the mer-folk had made it to safety in the caverns, and the boy Girn was with them also. Tustor let out a sigh and with it let out his hope for reaching the Vale anytime soon. He would be needed if the Water Orb was to be of any use to the forces of the king and his alliance. And if it was ever to be of any use to the mermen again. If there were any mermen to use it.

So in that moment Tustor made the decision that was tearing at his soul. He longed to lie down and die and leave the pain of the world behind, but he knew that he could not be that selfish. If he was not there to help Tarthur use the Water Orb, the knowledge could be lost forever, and probably the Orb along with it. The boy Tarthur was the key to his people regaining their beloved treasure. Tustor used his magic to make a lifeless replica of his body and sent it to attack the nearest monster. The monster howled in delight at being able to face the one that his queen said must be destroyed at all costs. He heedlessly tore into the body and decapitated it, then swam back to show his master the prize he had gotten her. Tustor nodded in satisfaction, then quietly slipped away to go join the survivors.

A creature that was half fish and half demon and fully grotesque charged at Truin. Truin answered the charge and swam forward, bringing his huge triton smashing down on the creature's head. As he did so, the tail of the creature whipped around and knocked into Truin's side. The tail was sharp, barbed, and equipped with spikes and wires that drew blood. Truin glanced down at the nasty wound in his side, and saw he was not only bleeding red, but green and purple and black also. Poison! Truin dove under, hoping the stinging salt water would wash the wound clean and dispel enough of the poison to render it ineffective, or at least slow down the spread long enough for him to finish this battle and seek help. Truin was not planning on losing. Truin hit the bottom and then shot back up, burying his three-pronged triton into the soft underbelly of this thing that had come from some nightmare, and then tore it free, sending small chunks of flesh throughout the water, which was already beginning to turn black from the dark creature's blood. As Truin surfaced, the beast shot forward and tore a chunk out of Truin's forearm with his razor sharp teeth. Truin dodged away just in time to avoid being devoured whole, and then looked down in horror as he saw the white of his bone exposed. Oddly, it didn't hurt. Truin was so numbed from seeing his children and friends and countrymen slaughtered and from fighting this battle, he didn't feel anything anymore. Now his head was beginning to pound and Truin was beginning to become a little dizzy. The poison is working, he realized, and with it the grim certainty of his own death. He had failed to wash out enough of the toxin and now it was inside him.

At that moment, Truin became mad. He wanted nothing more in the world than to kill this thing that attacked him. It became for him the symbol for all the bad that had happened in his life, for all of his failings and shortfalls and everything that he had not done as he should have. It became the symbol for the things that had attacked them this night, as if by destroying this one thing he could win the battle.

Golden hair flying in the wind, Truin turned to face his adversary.

The monster swung his huge and dangerous tail at the enraged Truin once more, but this time he brought up his triton to block it, then reversed his direction and stabbed his fearsome weapon into the thrashing tail. Truin pulled it out and black blood spurted out from three holes, but Truin did not notice. He was already attacking the head. The creature opened its jaws wide in anticipation of this foolish merman who was swimming straight for his mouth. Truin used his powerful hind fin one last time to propel him into the mouth of the beast. Raising his pitchfork, he rammed it down its throat and into its heart. In rage, the creature bit down once and then was still. Truin felt a searing pain in a dozen places on his back as the monster's teeth ripped through his flesh, and then nothing.

*　　　*　　　*　　　*

The night had faded into morning, and Marhyn stood alone on the hull of her personal ship studying the smoldering remains of what history books would record as the place that once was the dwelling of the merfolk, from the beginning of time until their destruction by Queen Marhyn in the first battle of the war in which she took control of the Lands of Daranor. Their attack had accomplished their purpose entirely, there were no survivors. Most importantly, one of her dark ones had brought her the head of Tustor; his death was one of the principal reasons they had made this attack. To destroy Tustor with no successor was to severely hamper or even stop any plans the king had for finding and using the Water Orb. And without that to aid them, King Garkin and her brother would be at a perfect balance…

Marhyn ordered the ships to set sail west in the direction of home just in case anyone had survived, it was always better to leave nothing to chance. The captains would change the course in about an hour, and Marhyn's killing force moved on.

CHAPTER 13

▼

SOMEONE'S IN LOVE...

He didn't even really know why he had come. He kept asking himself that question over and over in his mind as he was walking through the empty and silent city streets. The whole idea was rather perplexing. Tarthur had no rational reason to believe that Yvonne would be there, and although back in Krendon Tarthur frequently did things when he had no rational reason, this time it was different. It was probably useless, even stupid, to come out here just to see this girl again, to try and get his money back. Although, somewhere deep inside him, Tarthur knew it wasn't just the money. But what did it matter anyway? She wouldn't even be there.

Tarthur lay back on a bench and just stared into the fountain. The statue of Hana-Chan had already faded into darkness, and Tarthur looked down into the swirling water and let his tired gaze flow with the clear liquid over and around the fountain. Tarthur sensed a presence in the darkness and looked up. A figure stood tentatively in the shadows on the other side of the fountain.

"Tarthur?" The voice was a mix of shock and pleasant surprise, mingled with fear. Stern faced with a hard and unmoving exterior, Tarthur got up and walked slowly to meet the figure. He realized he didn't have the first clue about what to do, if the figure was even who he hoped it was. It was Yvonne.

"Tarthur, what are you doing here?"

Tarthur stood still for a moment and then answered. "I uh, I was just walking through this part of town when I got tired and so I decided to rest on that bench.

No, I mean I was coming to remember what Hana-Chan's sword looked like. I had forgotten. Yeah."

Yvonne just looked at him and laughed. It was not a mean-spirited laugh, but it put Tarthur on the defensive. "Well, what did you come here for? You better have come to give back my money or I'll lick you, even if you are a girl!"

Tarthur's remark cut into Yvonne only as much as her defenses would allow, yet it still irked her. "Well you can go ahead and 'lick me' 'cause I'm not giving you the money. I don't even have it anymore. Go ahead you big brave man, hit a girl. Hit me!" Yvonne stood with her arms out only inches in front of Tarthur, waiting for the blow that Tarthur knew he could never give. She stood there, vulnerable to attack, and Tarthur could feel the heat of her body drifting toward him in the chill winter night.

Yvonne realized she had won, at least for now, and continued to taunt Tarthur. "Why won't you hit me, huh? You stupid little rich boy, with your morals and ethics, you think you're too good for me? Well, you're an idiot, that's what you are! If you took a moment to see how the world really works you wouldn't be so naive as to get your money stolen. In fact I'm glad I stole it, you deserved it!" Tarthur just stared ahead blankly. Rich boy, with morals and ethics? What was she talking about? Tarthur looked down at the ground in confusion. Yvonne, however, mistook his confused look for shame as if she had not discovered the real reason Tarthur did not hit her. "So that's not even it, is it?" Yvonne probed and cut deeper with her words and twisted them around as if in an open wound. "You're afraid of losing, aren't you? You know that I can really beat you and then you'll go home crying to your daddy; some poor, bloody, pathetic, nothing that got whooped by a street girl!"

Tarthur had been furious before in his life. He had wished he could kill Marhyn for the evil she did to Yan, and for the lives of so many that she wasted. He had wanted to punch Morty in the nose so hard it would come out the other side on numerous occasions, and he had always wished he could get back at some authority figure in Krendon who had punished him (usually rightfully) for something he had done. But he had never, in his entire life, felt like this. With reckless abandon he charged into Yvonne, trying to hurl her to the ground. The surprised girl spun just in time to hit the ground with Tarthur on the bottom and herself on the top. Tarthur felt a thud as his back hit the ground and a whoosh as his air was knocked out. Heedless of the pain that was burning his stomach and lungs, Tarthur rolled and pressed his weight against Yvonne.

On top now, Tarthur seized his opportunity and swung for her jaw with his right fist. Yvonne deftly blocked the blow, then Tarthur brought his left straight down onto her nose. The blow struck with a little more power than Tarthur had intended, and he hesitated as he saw a stream of red emerge from her nose and trickle down her cheek. Tarthur felt so bad that he would have been inclined to stop the fight right then and there, although this wasn't one of the acceptable reasons to cease fighting, except that at that moment Yvonne launched a flurry of blows in Tarthur's gut with her right hand. The unexpected nature of the attack gave Tarthur no time to tighten his stomach, and soon he rolled over in pain. It appeared this fight was not over yet.

As Tarthur grabbed Yvonne while the two rolled around on the floor by the fountain, he couldn't stop thinking. Tarthur had always subscribed to the doctrine that thinking was usually a bad thing when one is trying to pummel an enemy, especially if it is not even about the fight. But try as he might, he couldn't escape the heat that came from her body. He couldn't ignore the feeling of touching her. He could've regained his feet after the last pass, but his instincts told him to grab her.

Tarthur was trying to gain the top again and was succeeding with a whirlwind of strength, before which Yvonne had no choice but to succumb. Tarthur got ready to punch Yvonne again, but before he could Yvonne felt her hand up his leg, then grabbed where it counts, and squeezed as hard as she could. Tarthur yelled out in pain and then rolled away. Exhausted, Yvonne did not pursue.

The two stared at each other in the darkness, each recovering from their wounds and catching their breath. It was a long moment before either one spoke.

"I told you I could lick you," Yvonne said, wiping a stream of blood from her nose.

Tarthur was about to charge in and begin the fight anew, but then thought better of it. "You are so stupid. You don't know who won the fight; you don't even know anything about me!"

Yvonne spat into the dust. "I know you're a used-to-be rich boy who doesn't know anything of the streets and the way the world works!"

"Have you ever been out of this town?" Tarthur's question caught Yvonne off guard.

"I have taken many trips around it and met many people from far places who come here and…"

"Just answer the question." Tarthur's words were harsher than he had intended them to be. Yvonne shook her head no. "You say I need to know how the world works?! You think I'm some gentleman?! Well, I've got news for you. I've been around the world. I know how it works! How dare you talk to me like that!! I have seen things in real life that you wouldn't even dare to see in nightmares!"

"Oh, is that so," Yvonne retorted, trying to sound doubting but at the same time believing him herself. "Do you know what pain is? Do you know what it's like to live in fear? Have you ever seen your friend dying, right before your eyes?"

"Yes." In that moment, when Tarthur had uttered this one word, he looked into Yvonne's eyes, and she met his gaze directly. He felt all his preconceptions of her melt away, and saw her as a young girl with pain, a girl way too young to have felt all of the problems in her young life. And she saw the same thing in his eyes. In that moment they both realized how little they knew and how much they had to learn.

By the light of the silver moon, they sat on a bench and began to talk.

$$* \qquad * \qquad * \qquad *$$

"And so, the power of magic is really all around us at every moment in time, and it remains only for the individual, that being the magician to act upon it and to capture a part of it for his own use. The currents being extremely potent to the right user, as a matter of course, one must only try to harness a small amount, or you all know what will happen, namely, the destruction of balance and equilibrium; and to tear at the fabric of the universe is to invite disaster. For example, to summon the forces of fire, one need only imagine a fire burning to the correct destination and say the three words of *Derse, Yreds*, and lastly..."

"Tarthur, Tarthur wake up! This is the third time today that you've fallen asleep in the midst of a very important...I'll not tolerate this and it shows a complete lack of respect for both Pol and me, for me because I'm your teacher and when you fall asleep it severely limits, yes severely limits the amount of attention I am able to give to Pol and furthermore..." Akin droned on for a few more minutes, and then finished off his words by wrapping Tarthur smartly on the head several times with a pointer that he had been using to point out certain things on various charts and posters throughout the room. It wasn't that Tarthur wasn't trying to pay attention, (although, Akin was without a doubt the most boring person he had yet encountered on the face of Daranor, and sleeping helped the hours to creep by) but rather the fact that Tarthur had been up until five o'clock talking with Yvonne on the park bench. The two still had their differences, but Tarthur knew that the meeting had ended with the two on a friendship, or maybe even something more. Tarthur had even given Yvonne his coat at the end of the night (after checking the pockets first, of course) and this time she even promised to return it later. There had been no mention of the money.

So Tarthur heard the words Akin was saying without listening to them, and stared blankly ahead. He had learned a lot about Yvonne last night, or this morning rather. He had learned that she was a poor street girl who had no father or mother, although whenever she talked of her father she talked with contempt and almost spat the words, yet when she spoke of her mother she talked with a loving sadness. Tarthur could see that she didn't offer any further information on the subject, and he didn't ask for any. Yvonne had also mentioned that she had a twin sister named Yvette, and this was how they had tricked Tarthur into believing that he was chasing only one thief. Tarthur laughed at this cheap trick, with admiration for Yvonne for thinking of it and foolishness for himself for falling for it. He resolved in his mind that just because they had a wary friendship didn't mean that he still didn't owe her for the money trick. He would never forget to repay her.

Yvonne had also said that she and her sister were the heads of the Guild of Thieves, an organization that most respectable people spat on but that Yvonne made pains to point out did much good. It was a loosely knit organization of thieves from all ages and backgrounds who were united by their poverty. The guild clothed and fed and housed all who were in need, and also trained them to commit acts of larceny from the richer members of the town. Tarthur liked the way Yvonne created her own euphemisms. He felt as if she would fit in very well with his friends back in Krendon. By way of softer words, she turned the act of blatant stealing into "helping the rich give to charity," thereby "much improving their standing with the Creator." And (as she pointed out, Tarthur could personally attest to this fact) they were very good at what they did.

"So then the forces are really only manifestations of inner desires, which can be summed up by the magical term…Tarthur?"

"Huh?"

"No, Tarthur," Akin sighed tiredly. He was getting nowhere with this student. He wanted to throw his magic at the boy and teach him a lesson, but Zelin himself had told him not to use any magic on this boy, under any circumstances. Ah, well, at least he was trying his best to impart knowledge to Tarthur, but the boy would just not listen. "No, Tarthur the term for the forces of your inner desires is not 'huh?' It is *Loi*. Please try to pay attention, Tarthur."

The day passed much in this way, Tarthur trying weakly to listen and learn and then failing miserably with interludes of Akin exhorting him to at least try, followed by more times of Tarthur falling asleep. When the classes finished for the day, Tarthur gratefully went through the castle halls and went to sleep.

He was awakened a few hours later by Derlin, who was returning from the evening meal that Tarthur had missed. "Akin must be working you hard if you're so tired already. You missed the evening meal you know." Tarthur just groaned and rolled over in his bed to escape the light that had followed Derlin in. Derlin was not daunted by his friend and knew he would be up and about shortly. "Come on, Tarthur, show me something Akin taught you. Look at this—this is what I've learned." Derlin finished off his words with a flourish of different techniques, which Tarthur, now sitting up in his bed, had to admit looked crisp and effective.

"We haven't learned anything specific yet," Tarthur sleepily replied. "Just a few general things about magic and stuff."

"I see," said Derlin, obviously disappointed. He nodded for a moment, and then brightened. "Tarthur, guess who I saw today?" Then he replied before Tarthur could guess. "Yonathan. After my training, I went to see him in the infirmary. He's just beginning to sit up and eat well again. Isn't that wonderful?"

Tarthur nodded. It was indeed good to hear that Yonathan was doing better. It seemed so long ago that they had come to the castle with the wounded assistant mayor of Freeton. Things seemed to be so different now, and he knew that the biggest difference was Yvonne.

"Tarthur," Derlin continued, "when I first started these classes, I was miserable. But now I know that Sir Terin has so much to teach me! I thought I knew everything back in Krendon, but now I realize I didn't know a thing back then." Derlin paused a minute to shake Tarthur awake again and then pressed his friend one more time. "So at least tell me something you learned. I am excited to know about magic myself."

Tarthur looked at his friend sleepily. "Nothing. We learn nothing. In fact, it's just a waste of time. I sit there all day and listen to some boring old man talk about things that make no sense."

Derlin frowned, worried. "You mean, you're not learning anything? Tarthur, that's not good." Derlin paused for a moment while he mulled over the dilemma, then an idea suddenly hit him. "If you're not working hard, why are you so tired today?"

"I was up until five talking with that girl Yvonne on a park bench last night," Tarthur mumbled with marked disinterest.

Derlin was aghast. "Tarthur, you lied to me! You told me that you would wait to see her! Why did you do that?"

Tarthur was unfazed by his friend's expression. "Oh, I'm sorry. I didn't mean to lie but I really just didn't think about my promise. It just didn't ever cross my mind. Besides, what's the big deal anyway? Just take care of yourself and I'll take care of myself."

At this point, for the very first time in his life towards his friend, Derlin exploded. "What's the big deal?!! The fate of the world is the big deal! Don't you understand, Tarthur? We always play tricks and have fun at home, but there are times for games and there are times to be serious. Now is the time to be serious! This is not one of your games!"

"So just because I met a girl now you want to become so righteous all of a sudden?" Tarthur was fully awake now, and his retort was full of bite. "Now that I have something special you don't want me to have it!"

Derlin was shouting now, his harsh words drowning out any feeble protests that Tarthur would attempt. "You fool, that's not it! I don't care at all about that girl. But you are right, you do have something special—your life. And you have been chosen to have power. Don't you see? Your life is not just yours anymore! It's not yours! You have a responsibility to use it for the whole world! Yes, a responsibility! Do you know that word? Maybe the Death Lord chose you because you can't do anything with your power! He knew you would lose." Derlin held up his hand as Tarthur tried to protest. "Maybe not, but that doesn't matter now. Think of Yonathan, Tarthur. He was ready to die for you. To give up his life just for you and you treat it like it is nothing!"

"I know what he did," countered Tarthur. "I felt his blood running warm through my hands. I saw his pain! I know just as well as you that there will be a war, and other people will bleed like him!"

"Then why don't you do something about it!" With this statement, Derlin turned, walked through the door and slammed it shut, and Tarthur was left alone to think. He sat alone for a long while, slowly nodded his head, and began to cry.

*   *   *   *

In the weeks that followed, the boys never again talked of their conversation. Derlin returned to his studies, and achieved the first order of Royal Knighthood in record time. He ate and grew strong, and soon was a rival for students who had been practicing many years. Tarthur, for his part, continued to see Yvonne, but only during the recesses of his studies. He gave himself over to the learning of magic as his first priority, and in so doing learned many useful things. Tarthur realized that Akin was different in style and manner from himself, and while he would never allow anyone to suggest that he was imitating Akin, Tarthur did gain an admiration for the man and all that he knew of the secret world of magic. Tarthur and Yvonne grew closer and Tarthur began to feel things that he had never felt before.

Tarthur visited Yvonne in almost all of his free time, and he would have liked Derlin to come with him, but Derlin got very few chances indeed because he didn't have any free time. He was always needed by Sir Terin and Sir Undbar for various war preparations. There was so much to do that Derlin seriously doubted that they would have it all ready in time for spring. One of these visits was a day that Tarthur would always remember. Tarthur walked through the door and was greeted by warm smiles of children and adults alike. The members of the Guild of Thieves often joked with Tarthur since Yvonne had revealed him to the thieves as their mysterious benefactor. Tarthur chuckled with them outwardly, but inside he laughed at something else; this was the day that he would get them back.

Tarthur had been searching and searching for a way to get back at Yvonne since the original incident had occurred, but he had been able to come up with nothing. Then last week he had been sitting out on the castle wall when he had seen a cloaked and hooded figure walk cautiously through the gates and into a tunnel. Tarthur had recognized the figure at once as Yvonne. He could tell her by her gait and the smooth yet rugged way that she walked. But what was she doing here? Without hesitation, Tarthur had followed her into the tunnel, just before the entrance had swung shut. Tarthur had a vain hope that she was here to do something for him, but then chased it away as she went deep into the fortress. She obviously knew where she was going.

Careful not to be seen, Tarthur followed her until she stopped and entered a room lit by torch light. Tarthur waited until she had shut the door and then cautiously peeked through the keyhole. What he saw inside made him gasp. Yvonne was having a conference with Sir Terin and one other who Tarthur thought he recognized, but was not sure of. Listening at the door, Tarthur had heard enough to realize that the Guild of Thieves was linked with the crown! When the meeting had concluded, Tarthur had hurriedly left and remained unseen. It was not until a few days later when he had spoken with Sir Terin that he had finally ascertained the truth.

Upon first being confronted alone in his study, Sir Terin denied and pretended not to have the slightest clue what Tarthur was talking about. But when he realized that Tarthur had seen too much, he knew that he must tell him at least part of the story. Tarthur took a seat and then Sir Terin began.

"You see, Tarthur," the knight began, "there is a lot more to court policies than just the rule of the king. The king must have money for his programs, and most of the money is hoarded by rich nobles. In order for the king to govern, he may use money from the royal treasury, but he must also ask the nobles for money. Ask, Tarthur, not order. Oh, the nobles will soon enough help in a time of war, but in peace, they are very stingy with their money."

"About seven years ago, the situation in our city was desperate. There were homeless people in nearly every street and there were robberies and beatings and murders. King Garkin saw this and made a welfare plan to try to combat it. He wanted to set up houses for the homeless and places where they could receive food and rest; he wanted to find jobs for them also. His majesty was so excited about his ideas, and when the nobles refused to fund the plan, he was furious. Fortunately, our king is a wise man. He told me, secretly of course, to organize a so-called Guild of Thieves. The original leader was a man named Qeunten, and when he disappeared two years ago, the girl Yvette and her sister Yvonne naturally assumed leadership. They provide care for the needy, and we give them jobs in whatever area of government is open. They also are a high class bunch of thieves. They only steal from the rich, and they give us information about any real criminals in the city so we can arrest them. In return, the guild is not touched and we supply them with information about the movements of some of the nobles who are particularly opposed to the king, and unfortunately those very same nobles often watch the sun set with a much lighter purse than they watched it rise."

"They also serve as a part of the intelligence agency that you heard mentioned at the council meeting. They are an incredible help to the kingdom, and they only take gold from people who don't deserve to have it in the first place."

Tarthur was struck by the cleverness of the plan, it was brilliant. It made him wonder how many hidden things and secret alliances were right under his nose. There were probably quite a few. Tarthur felt privileged to know this. "So how many other people know this?"

Sir Terin thought for a moment and then released the information. "You, me, Yvonne, Yvette, the king, and of course the head of the intelligence agency."

Tarthur nodded. He would have liked Sir Terin to tell him who the head was; he remembered that it was someone who had been in the council room. But it was such a heavily guarded secret, Tarthur was sure that he would never know. "So why was Yvonne coming to talk to you?"

Sir Terin frowned. "Recently, it seems that there has been an increase in calls for an end to guild activity. We have shrunk the membership drastically by recruiting many of them for the army, but there are still others who could not serve. The nobles are feeling the money that is stolen more deeply now that they also have to give large amounts to the war effort. Officially, there is no such thing as the Guild of Thieves, but many nobles still know about it and are calling for a crackdown on crime. Yvonne and I were meeting to discuss possible solutions to the problem."

"Why not arrest them?" Tarthur questioned, a bright idea coming into his head.

Sir Terin looked at Tarthur tiredly. "I have already told you that they have full immunity."

"No," Tarthur said. "Arrest them and then let them go after a couple of days. The nobles will think that the guild is destroyed and they will thank you for a job well done. Then they can continue on the streets and no one will be the wiser."

Sir Terin thought about it a moment, then nodded his assent, for it was a good plan. Now Tarthur waited in the guild, for it was time to put the plan into action, with his own variations, of course.

Yvonne and Yvette walked through the door and smiled. Everyone smiled with them, and cheered for them, for this was their birthday. Tarthur couldn't think of anything better; his plan was good enough, but doing it on Yvonne's birthday just poured salt in the wound and rubbed it around. "Happy birthday," the guild cried in unison. Tarthur was walking up to Yvonne to congratulate her personally when he was interrupted by a loud crash.

Simultaneously royal soldiers splintered through the walls and converged on the unsuspecting thieves. Big burly men closed in from all sides and swiftly arrested the elderly and young thieves before they could even think to run. Only a couple of the thieves really had any chance of escape, and these were soon overwhelmed. A muscular and quick guard darted forward for Yvette, but she side-stepped him and grabbed a piece of the broken wall, then swung it down on his head. The man slumped unconscious to the floor. Another man charged forward for her and she swung the wood into his side. The man doubled over in pain, but Yvette's wood broke in half. She threw the useless half at an officer, who moved his head easily out of the way. Three men ran forward and overwhelmed her.

Tarthur was the only one to escape. He had used his foreknowledge of the attack to hide under a bench where he knew the guards would not look. He felt sorry for the guards that had been injured, but it did make the attack more believable. As he surveyed the remains, he noticed that all of the thieves had been captured. Yvonne had been grabbed and was yelling and screaming, demanding that they take her to Sir Terin the leader for an explanation of their gross mistreatment. "Sir Terin's not in charge anymore," growled the officer, just as Tarthur had asked him to. After that, Yvonne shut up, and Tarthur smiled as the soldiers led the members of the Guild of Thieves into the castle.

The same night, Tarthur visited Yvonne in the prison. He told her how sorry he was that she had gotten caught, and that he was just lucky to have escaped. (Either that or he had incredible maneuvering skills and superior senses of danger. Tarthur wasn't sure, it was probably the latter.) He also told her of the one chance that they had. Yvonne had noticed a tunnel leading out of their particular prison cell that was hidden and barred by a locked door. If she could just get out and open it from the other side, they might have a chance for escape.

"I have been talking to a guard," Tarthur began, "and I can persuade him to look the other way to your escape. It will take a little gold, however."

"How much?" Yvonne had some gold with her, but by no means wished to spend any of it.

"At first he said thirty gold pieces, but in the end I got him down to twenty four."

Yvonne was incredulous. "Twenty four gold pieces! Why, that's exactly twice as much as I stole from you!"

Tarthur turned his face away so Yvonne would not see the twinkle in his eye nor the grin that came to his lips. "I know."

First Yvonne had been adamant in her denial, but Tarthur informed her that this guard was leaving the next day on a supply mission to Breshen and this would be her only chance. When he pointed to the elderly who were sick and might not live too long in the damp cell she finally agreed and slammed the money into Tarthur's waiting palm. Tarthur smiled at her anger. "Hey, you should thank me. I'm doing you a favor."

The next day Yvonne easily escaped, and when she had made it past the castle walls Tarthur told the guards to bring the key to the tunnel door, give it to Yvette, and instruct her to release three people each day. In the meantime, the rest were given good food and had the time of their lives.

The next time Tarthur met Yvonne, after the whole affair was concluded, he did not mention his plan. He had a burning desire to do so, to rub it in her face that would be made crimson by blushing, but stopped himself. Yvonne also said nothing, but Tarthur could tell that she knew. And that was all that mattered.

The days turned to weeks, and the weeks to months, and soon the bulk of the army was ready to set out for Breshen in the first leg of its journey that would lead to the abode of the Death Lord. It was late in the month of February, and

General Cilio had determined it best to attack in early April at the latest. Tarthur was dreading the day when he would have to take his leave of Yvonne, but a few days before they were scheduled to leave Yvonne had abruptly told him that she was going with him. Not asked to accompany him, but told him she would journey also. Tarthur tried to protest that it was too dangerous, but she laughed at that, saying that she could handle herself and would stay at Breshen if she was in any real danger. Tarthur didn't believe that she would stay, but his feeble protests were soon drowned out. Besides, inside he really wanted her to come anyway.

CHAPTER 14

▼

THE SURVIVOR

Girn was glad, for their work was almost completed. The merfolk who had escaped Marhyn's deadly attack had hidden themselves in the caverns, and Girn was told that he was the first human ever to be admitted since the time of Frehu. Oddly, while he was grateful, Girn didn't feel especially special. There were only eighteen of the merfolk left alive, and only three of them were men. They had not been able to fight, so they had escaped with Girn by taking secret tunnels that led deep below the ocean floor.

The caverns were amazing, though. They had holes above ground to admit light, which was magnified and reflected by various lenses and mirrors so it appeared as if it was daylight inside. The caverns were nearly thirty feet tall, and had canals crisscrossing them in all directions so the mermen could traverse them easily. Surprisingly, grass was growing down there, and Girn even saw that they had a few horses grazing.

In normal times if there was a shipwreck, the mermen would take the wood that washed up and use it to construct the houses underwater, but this time was different. Tustor had said that all the wood and bodies must be collected and burned together. The mermens' bodies were to be thrown out to sea to their grave where the tides would take them, but the invaders were all to be burned in one heap together with their ships. Since Girn was the only one able to reach many inland areas, he had the almost monumental task of retrieving everything that the merfolk could not reach.

Girn had never touched a dead person before, but almost surprisingly they seemed just like normal people, except that they were so cold. Girn felt the chill as he hefted them onto the pyres that were being built in the center of the shoals. Girn was making one last sweep through the beach when he saw a body that he had missed. He went over to pick him up, but something seemed different. As he approached closely, the body moved.

Girn jumped back in shock, unsure if he had seen it or just imagined it. He reached down to feel for a pulse. The man had one, but it was feeble and irregular. The young boy turned around in shock. He didn't know what to do. He knew that he should kill this invader right then and there. Girn knew first hand the damage these people had caused. He had friends that had been killed. Girn's hand tightened around his dagger in his belt.

His arm tensed up. He couldn't do this. This was actually killing another person. Girn was only a young boy. He couldn't kill someone. What if this man had a family? What if he had a son like Girn himself? And now, to just kill him, even though he was already almost dead, it just wouldn't be right.

Tarthur would kill him, the back of his mind told him. And Derlin too, that's why they're great heroes and you're not, because they're not chicken like you, you weak little boy. And, the man would probably die anyway…

Yet, still Girn could not plunge his dagger into the exposed man. He realized with embarrassment that he didn't even know how to kill someone. Oh, he was sure he could manage it, but where should he stab him? Suddenly, the man on the ground gave a groan.

"Tarthur…" Girn started at the name.

"What did you say?"

The man only groaned incoherently again. Had he heard his friend's name? Or, had he just imagined it so he would not have to kill this man whom he wanted to kill but knew he couldn't? He wished a merman would swim up and finish it for him. That gave Girn an idea. He would go to Tustor and ask what to do, reminding him that he had uttered his friend's name.

Girn rushed away, and soon came back with Tustor. At first, the merwizard had only casually suggested killing him; he was still in much pain after seeing his people blown away. But, when he had heard Tarthur's name, the merwizard had become curious. So he had accompanied Girn. What he saw made him gasp. "Prince Dalin!!! Quick, Girn, go get that man some help! Bring him to me and I'll carry him down. Be careful not to move his neck if you can avoid it."

Girn, being always ready to help, went over and carefully lifted the man. It made him worried, though. Tustor had said that Tarthur and Derlin's guide was named Dalin. Tustor had said that Tarthur and Derlin were okay, but that their guide had become captured by Queen Marhyn. So this must be the Dalin who they were speaking about.

Tustor cradled the elf prince in his arms, and swam away to get help.

In the next few days, Dalin recovered, although his recovery was very slow. He had been beaten, and nearly drowned. But he had not sustained any wounds of considerable size, and this was probably the only reason he made it. He had babbled whenever he had the chance trying to tell as much as he could, and it wasn't until Tustor used some magic to calm him and tell him that Tarthur and Derlin had escaped and were well, and that other things were known, that he finally rested easier. Three days after the initial attack, Dalin was still in bed, but the mermen decided to hold the fire.

Girn gazed out northeast over the endless expanse of the sea. What would it be like to traverse it? It seemed as if it would never end. It made Girn wonder, what could possibly be on the other side of that? Was there another land, with people like those in Daranor? Or was it just an endless ocean of water, going on forever? Well, something had to be there, it couldn't go on forever, because no matter how many miles he sailed, he could always sail another. Girn resolved someday to try to find out.

The sun hit the shoals and gave off a brilliant mix of purple, red, and orange. All the enemy corpses were piled up on a rocky island, along with whatever wreckage of their ships was left. Girn saw Tustor swim up to it and light it with a torch. It caught slowly at first, and then started to burn quicker until the heat from the roaring flames made Girn take a step back to avoid burning his skin and singeing his hair. The extreme heat bent the air, something Girn had never seen before. It caused wrinkles in the air and caused the sunset to be all the more stunning. Yet, this was not like the dazzling radiance of a sunrise, which laughed and danced and sung out for joy. No one said a word. This was an ending, and it had such a bittersweet sadness that Girn almost thought his heart would burst. It was soft, and the feeling flooded through him. The colors of the sunset mingled with the reds and oranges of the flame, so Girn couldn't tell what was being burned by the sun and what was being burned by the fire. He looked over and saw the mermen crying freely for what seemed like an eternal moment, and then turned back quickly and began to cry himself. Girn stood motionless for many hours into the night, until the remains had been turned to nothing but a pile of smoldering ashes. Tustor came up and put a hand on his shoulder, and the two silently left.

It was a week later when Dalin was ready to travel. Girn had gotten to like the elf rather well, and was feeling extremely lucky that he had not killed him. Now that he was near full strength, Girn began to doubt whether he had even actually had the chance or not, Dalin seemed so strong and in control of everything.

For a moment, Girn thought he was finally going to rejoin his friends at the capital, but Dalin was only going home to Breshen. All the lines of communication had already been established, and Dalin was needed by his people. Tarthur and Derlin themselves were going to embark with the army to attack Darhyn anyway, and Girn desperately wanted to join them, but he realized that he'd just be slowing up Dalin. Also, Tustor had convinced him that he really was needed in the shoals to help rebuild. Zelin was nice, sure, but for the first time Girn felt like he had a family. He loved the shoals, and the sea constantly called out to him. Before the attack, he had even learned how to swim. So when the others had asked him to stay, he really had no choice, but he was not bothered. He liked it here. He told Dalin to give his regards to Tarthur and Derlin, and watched him ride off into the mist.

*   *   *   *

The company set out from Tealsburg on a fine morning, and all were in good spirits. Flags were flying high and the knights were resplendent in their brightest apparel and newly polished boots. General Cilio had wished they could leave secretly and give his adversary less time to prepare for their coming, but since this was obviously not possible, he made a full show of the exit. Neither Tarthur nor Derlin had ever seen so many people in one place before. The parade was announced, and the citizens turned out by the thousands cheering and waving flags. It was an emotional spectacle, and before it was over and the last soldier had marched from the city, dry eyes were rare indeed.

Tarthur and Derlin had never had the experience of traveling with an army before and while it was exciting and there was always something to do and someone interesting to talk to, their progress was exhaustingly slow. They were traveling through open grasslands, yet they barely covered ten miles on the first day. The horses, endless lines of supply trains, and sheer time it took to do everything that should be done quicker slowed their pace considerably. It was enough to make the boys think that they might never make it to Breshen.

At the beginning of only their third day of travel, a messenger came from the spy network and held a hurried council with the leaders of the army. General Cilio looked relieved, and then announced that they finally had word that Marhyn's army was beginning final preparations to leave her base, and that it was moving to attack northward in an attempt to destroy towns and crops in that area. General Cilio explained that their idea was probably to destroy the king's supplies, let the two armies in the North destroy each other, and then attack the weakened victor, who would have no food and submit easily. The army was only three thousand strong and Cilio would take four thousand out of their present force of ten thousand and go back to meet them. This he believed would effectively foil their plan. The Duke of Walis also accompanied him, as that was his land. The rest of the six thousand troops would continue in to Breshen and wait for Cilio and his group before attacking the Death Lord.

Tarthur and Derlin weren't sure where they were to go, but Zelin assured them that they were to travel with him to Breshen. If the Death Lord made any surprise attacks, Tarthur and the Water Orb spell would be needed in the front lines. Yan would go with the force under the command of General Cilio to deal with magical monsters that were sure to be a part of her force, and to counteract the magic of Queen Marhyn herself. King Garkin went ahead to Breshen, to fulfill the necessary diplomatic duties, and so that he could stay with the bulk of his troops. As for the weapons, the Rune Sword went to Breshen and the Light Sword went with Cilio. Neither yet had bearers.

It had been nearly two weeks since the separation of the forces, and Tarthur and Derlin were finding that the army travel wasn't as bad as they had first thought. Many of the initial quirks that had plagued them on the first day had been worked out, and with the separation of the army they had been able to travel much faster.

Traveling with the army was an incredible experience for the two small town boys. Six months ago, it would have been a normal and commonplace experience for them, being conquering heroes traveling with their army to destroy the Death Lord personally and banish him from the face of the world. Only this time they were not pretending. It seemed so easy back then, only the bad guys died. People who had no other wish than to be left alone just stepped to the side. Now, it seemed as if the whirlwind was encompassing them all, drawing everything into a chaotic mess, and Tarthur had to wonder at the outcome. Their side had many strengths, he realized. They had lightning-quick Yan, whom it seemed no one could ever touch. They had Zelin; they had magic swords, and almost two elements of power, not to mention thousands of hard working people willing to die for their cause. But who could really understand a monster such as Darhyn? He had the power of fear and he would love for the people to die, for any cause.

So it was that on the thirteenth day since they had set out from the capital city they came in sight of Breshen. It was a thick forest, full of trees taller than any Tarthur or Derlin had ever seen. The trunks reached forty to fifty feet into the air, and the branches spread out over huge areas. Derlin was stunned with their majesty, but Tarthur just wanted to climb one. Derlin and Tarthur dismounted with the advance party of the army; obviously it would be impossible to use horses in the dense foliage.

"A wise decision, my friends," came a familiar voice. "It is always better to let an animal go unburdened if possible."

"Dalin!" Both boys cried at once, running into the arms of their friend. They both well remembered how Dalin had made Tarthur walk on the day of his sprained ankle rather than burden Dalin's horse. Ever since they had received a letter saying that Dalin was alive and well, they had been waiting for his story. He had not sent it with the letter; he preferred to share stories personally. So without further ado, they left the rest of the main party and proceeded to Dalin's personal rooms to exchange stories.

Dalin's tree was a large one in the middle of dense foliage. It was at least twenty feet wide at the trunk and seemed impossible to climb, were it not for a small door opening in the base. The boys ducked under the door and soon found themselves in a small but comfortable room. From there they climbed a winding staircase that brought them to the top, some thirty feet above the forest floor. There were many more rooms here, some built into the tree and some attached onto the side of the tree nestled in between the humongous leafy branches. The boys followed Dalin out onto a roped-in balcony that seemed to be made of some combination of bark and solid wood and green vines. They had a seat on a pair of leafy and extremely comfortable chairs, and Dalin began his story.

Dalin told them of his escape with the poison needle, joining Marhyn's army, his failed escape and capture, the journey on her ships to the shoals of the merfolk, and their sad annihilation. Tarthur and Derlin had been told of the defeat of the merfolk and that Marhyn had returned to her base, but it hadn't really struck them yet. Hearing Dalin tell it made it so much more real. He told of the fight, of Tustor's attack on the boat that had freed him, and what he had heard of Truin's death. Tarthur shed a tear for his friend, he remembered his promise to go back and help the people of Krendon and the merfolk understand and befriend each other, but now it was for nothing. There would not be a merfolk race of any size for quite some time.

The only bright part that Dalin had to relate besides his own survival was the fact that Girn and Tustor were still alive. Tarthur knew that Tustor was valuable to their cause; he knew more about the Water Orb than any other being now living. And more importantly, Tarthur knew that Tustor would not only be there and ready, but also able to help him when the time came to test the skills Akin had taught him.

Tarthur and Derlin then proceeded to tell Dalin their story from the time the three became separated, much of which Dalin had already heard from General Cilio and Hano. But there was also much that he had not heard, and he thought strange, such as the business with Yan and the town that was under the wizard's control. When the boys were finished, they could tell that Dalin thought they had been extremely lucky. They could also see in his face that he had gained a great deal of admiration for them since they had last met.

Soon after they had finished their stories and were enjoying a cold tea made from roots and berries, a servant came in and told them that it was time. Tarthur and Derlin didn't know what time it was, but it certainly seemed important to the servant and to Dalin also. Dalin explained to them that it was an elven custom whenever foreign heads of state or dignitaries came that they must all bow to each other in the sacred lawn. Foreign heads of state? Didn't they all live in the same world? Tarthur shrugged his shoulders and followed.

Dalin explained that as they were members of King Garkin's entourage they must be on his side for the bow in, so they left him and went to look for their best clothes, found that they were already wearing them, and then hastened to join the procession.

Tarthur and Derlin took up a place behind Zelin, which they guessed was appropriate and followed the king. Twenty or so of his officers and advisors did the same. They walked in a thin mist that wrapped the trees and floated through the branches. Soon, they left the trees entirely and began walking into a clearing. The king walked to the center, bent down, and kneeled. It seemed that he was familiar with this ritual. Zelin and Warren kneeled down on the right and left of King Garkin respectively, and the rest of the knights and commanders followed. When they were all kneeled, they waited, and watched.

Directly opposite them in the field, the fog began to lift. As it rose, Derlin could discern shapes, and soon, he saw them to be an equal number of kneeling elves. In the direct center was a gnarled old elf, looking himself almost like a tree. His beard fell to the ground. All of the other elves were clean-shaven. On the right of the elf king was Dalin, who looked somehow older and more noble than he had looked five minutes earlier, and as Derlin turned his gaze, he caught his breath. On the left of the elf king was the most beautiful girl he had ever seen in his life.

She was dressed in a long black dress that seemed tight to her body as she knelt. Her hair was jet black and done up formally above her head in a way that let one strand curve down along the line of her cheek. All of this was stunning to derlin (who was so enthralled that he forgot to capitalize his name,) but what was most astonishing and beautiful were her eyes. They were black, matched her hair and dress exactly, and went well with her light golden skin. Those eyes called to Derlin, they wrapped around him, dragged him in, and held him with a tenderness that made his heart ache. The voice of the elven caller who called out the names of those present was doubly lost on Derlin, firstly he was speaking in the ancient elven tongue that has fallen out of common use and is used today only for ceremonies, and more importantly he was captured by the beauty of the girl. When the caller had finished, the elves bowed in unison. Derlin saw the girl lift a delicate hand to her cheek, brush away the strand of hair, and then put both of her hands on the ground and bow with the rest of the elven envoys. He had never seen anything so graceful.

The king's side then returned the bow, albeit with quite a bit more clumsiness and disharmony. Derlin waited to see what would happen next, and saw that both sides rose to their feet. They then walked around and entered into normal conversation, and Derlin saw that all of the tension that he had earlier felt was gone. King Garkin went forward and greeted the elven king, and the two began to talk like the old friends that they were.

Tarthur and Derlin for their part began to talk to Dalin. Derlin told himself that he would go and talk to that girl, but as soon as he said so he knew that he wouldn't. He looked over and saw her talking with some other girls, and embarrassed, resorted to speaking with Dalin.

Tarthur was going over their story again and filling in details that he had forgotten to tell Dalin in their first recollection at his tree. Derlin wasn't interested much in the talk, and he was ashamed to find his gaze meandering over to the girl. He couldn't help himself. He just let her beauty take him and amaze him.

Once the girl looked over. Derlin quickly averted his gaze, but he had a feeling that she saw the crimson rush to his cheeks. It was just a look, but it made Derlin feel like a desperate criminal, made him feel guilty for stealing it, as if his gaze might profane her perfection. All of a sudden, she started walking to where the three friends were in conversation. Derlin couldn't have wished for anything more in the world, but he felt embarrassed, trapped, and looked for a place to hide. Too late, she was upon them.

"Oh, hi," Dalin said casually, noticing the girl for the first time. "I'm sorry, I forgot that you don't know each other. This is Tarthur, and this is Derlin. They were a big help on my trip, and are very powerful and wise men." While doubting its veracity somewhat, Derlin secretly rejoiced over the introduction. And he was infinitely thankful to Dalin for saying men, not boys. Dalin continued the half of the introduction that Derlin most wanted to know. "And this is Valena, Princess of the Elves, my sister."

CHAPTER 15

▼

FREETON FOREVER

Yonathan looked up from his desk and the paperwork that he was busily filling out to see the messenger who arrived at his door. The big man nodded, and the messenger relayed his message. "General Cilio and his army will arrive within three days' time. They hope to find as much food and water as you can spare, and you are asked to plant your seed as soon as possible, as an early harvest may be needed to combat food shortages on the northern front." Yonathan nodded again. He had expected as much. After healing, he had decided to travel north with the army to Breshen to assist Tarthur and Derlin in their cause. The whole town owed their lives to those two boys, and after getting to know them, Yonathan believed any cause they were willing to support he was willing to die for. But when the army had split, he had come south with General Cilio to assist in the defense of his hometown. He had hurried ahead of the slower moving army and had been back in Freeton one night. It felt good to take up his job as assistant mayor. He only hoped that the war with the Death Lord would end soon and he could come back to take up his position permanently. Freeton was growing in population and prosperity since he had left. The people were happy, and they were beginning to prosper. They had been slaves before, and a freed slave is the last one to lack incentive.

As Yonathan got up from his desk to survey the grounds, he was struck and overwhelmed again by the optimism of the people. He would not have thought that a people so deeply scarred and so burned by their past would be so quick to recover, but everywhere they were playing and working with unbounded joy. Kandan Ironsmith was a favorite and a good choice for mayor. All of the people of Freeton loved him dearly, and since the time of his election they had been building new houses and business as people moved in from neighboring towns and the countryside.

A shout abruptly brought Yonathan out of his delightful reverie. The watchman was screaming something, and as Yonathan turned his gaze southward, he saw. On the southern horizon, a sprawling mass of Marhyn's troops was coming toward them across the plain.

Yonathan rushed to Kandan's office, where many of the men were already gathered. Kandan rose to greet him when he came. "Thank you for coming, Yonathan. It is up to us to decide what to do and how to combat this menace."

Yonathan nodded. "I have just received word from General Cilio. He and his army will be here in three days traveling at a normal pace. I recommend that we immediately send the fastest messenger to alert them and to beg them to hurry."

Kandan nodded at the obvious wisdom of the idea and pointed to a young man who had been preparing for just such an incident. The young man ran to get his horse and be on his way. "I have received reports that the enemy is nearly two hundred strong, so this must mean that it is just an advance party and the bulk of the army is situated elsewhere."

Yonathan pondered a moment and then suggested, "Why don't we leave? No man wants to lose his home, but it is at least better than his life."

Kandan shook his head no. "This town means too much to us. We have just rebuilt it. We have all suffered here. We will stand. Besides, our main grain fields are located just north of the town. They are vital to the war effort. We can't take the chance that they will be destroyed, or worse yet fall into enemy hands."

Yonathan sighed and then nodded. "Two days. We can hope that they will not reach us until tomorrow, and then we will have to repulse them for two days. How many men can we count on in fighting condition?"

"Sixty or seventy. The women and children will also be able to help out."

Yonathan was almost afraid to ask the next question. "Weapons?"

Kandan sighed. "Twenty or thirty swords, a few spears, pikes, and the rest will have to make do with captured weapons or farming instruments."

It was as bad as he thought. He wanted to suggest that they at least evacuate the women and children, but he knew it would be futile. They would all stand together. Yonathan tried to lighten things up with a half joke. "They have just about every advantage, don't they?"

Kandan was stone serious. "They're not fighting for their homes. We will be ready. We will drive these monstrous invaders back to the sea. We will win."

Dawn broke on the following day, bright and clear. A hint of spring was in the air, a hint of freshness and beginnings, of a chance to start anew. How ironic, Yonathan thought. He was hiding in the bushes with his group of fifteen men, eagerly awaiting the attack he knew was sure to come at any time. Kandan had divided their force into two groups of fifteen men each and one big group of the thirty or so who remained. Kandan had stayed with the big group who were stationed in the town center. Yonathan and Uris, who commanded the two groups of fifteen, had taken their respective commands and had hidden in the trees to either side of the town. Their plan was to draw the attacking enemy into the town center. The group in the center of the town would try to draw the enemy forward and into a line, then Kandan and Uris would bring their groups simultaneously into the exposed sides of the army. There was a group of houses that blocked off the center of the town. They hoped to use these to cut the opposing force in half and then destroy the half that they had surrounded. Yonathan had a flint that he could use to ignite the houses into a huge conflagration, and they had already been soaked with kerosene. If these were ignited, the extreme heat could push the rest of the army back and let the defenders face better odds inside of the town center. If they fought well, and didn't lose too many men, then they might be able to repulse the rest and face better odds on the next day. If…

The ugly and guttural sound of the goblin trumpets broke through the early morning stillness and shattered the peace. It was time for war.

Yonathan watched stoically as the first ranks of the advancing army came forward. It alternated rows of ten men with rows of ten goblins. They all wore black tunics and had an array of different swords. It appeared that at least the army was not standardized, and that gave Yonathan a faint glimmer of hope that they were undisciplined and would be easily defeated. But even this faint ray of hope went out when he saw how well synchronized they looked when they marched.

On the order of the commander, the first group broke ranks and charged into the town center looking for money and possessions and women. Yonathan gripped his sword tighter in furious anticipation when he thought of the latter. None of these foul beasts would touch the women of Freeton. Soon they reached Kandan, and the brave blacksmith-mayor screamed their battle cry, "Freeton Forever!" When he heard those words, Yonathan and the rest of his group felt a tingling down their spines. Yonathan was so proud he got goose bumps. They would win this day!

Kandan charged into the first rank of the enemy who was surprised to see any resistance. Kandan sliced his huge broadsword down on a goblin's neck, sending his head rolling. Then he charged forward and plunged his sword into the next attacker, ripped the dripping blade free, and charged after the closest enemy. By this time, the enemy had recovered from its initial shock, and they were now starting to use their superior numbers by massing together so they could protect each other. Still there were confrontations all about as fighters from Freeton infiltrated their ranks. A mercenary soldier swung his blade at the head of a boy of no more than ten or twelve. The boy ducked and then reached forward, grabbed the soldier's own dagger and then plunged it into his heart. A goblin charged at the boy from his right, and the boy pulled free the dagger and sent it flying into the goblin's chest. The goblin screamed in pain, then toppled over. Another goblin came at the boy from behind, swinging a huge spiked mace into his skull, crushing it. The boy slumped lifeless to the ground.

Eleven. That is how many columns Yonathan finally decided to let through before he ordered his and Uris's forces to move in and seal off the retreat of the larger army, surrounding them and then attacking them from their back. He was debating, as the original plan had been to allow nine columns, but now he felt that they would be able to handle it and give them a better chance to hold out the next day or even win the battle this day. "Freeton Forever!" Yonathan screamed as the eleventh column began to join the attack. He heard the cry repeated two hundred yards in front of him and saw Uris and his group charge into the flanks of the enemy.

Yonathan rushed forward and hit the flint. It took a while to give a spark, but when it finally did, the houses ignited quickly. The other ninety troops of Marhyn's army were cut off and useless to their companions.

Superior knowledge of the terrain and what houses could give cover gave the fighters from Freeton the advantage. Soon Yonathan and his men, including a few on horseback, were slicing through the sides of the enemy. A goblin tried to attack him with his short sword, but the big man smashed his shield down on the unfortunate creature's arm, breaking it. The burly Yonathan picked up the goblin in his hairy, muscular arms, and threw him full force into another attacker who was charging forward with a drawn sword.

The goblin landed on the blade, bowled the attacker over, and lay howling on the ground. Before Yonathan could blink, Kandan was there to finish them both off.

Uris's group was having a harder time as the battle shifted. A group of the frightened enemy had broken off from the first thrust and were attempting to rejoin the main group who had not attacked yet as they were separated and waiting until the fires died down. Uris and his group were trying to prevent them from doing so by killing as many as they could and driving the rest toward the other Freeton forces. They were having moderate success.

"Oh dear," mumbled the often forgetful Uris as he fumbled through his leather purse while two goblins charged straight at him. "I know it was in here somewhere. Ah yes, here it is. *Derse, Yreds, fewtersd*, and POW!"

One thing about Uris's spells was that they rarely turned out the way he planned them. The spell did not produce the intended effect of sending a ball of flame into the monsters, but it did at least singe their eyebrows. The goblins fell back in pain, and did not break through the line.

As the day wore on, the inexperience and lack of a heart to fight in Marhyn's army caused the defenders to win and destroy over half of the invading force before the day was through. It was not as if they had no will to fight, for it was plain that they fought for gold, and with the Dark Lady as their commander, they knew that they were probably better off to give their life on the field than to fail. But the heart of fighters like Yonathan and Kandan prevailed in the end. As they settled into an uneasy sleep by the fire at the end of that day when they were once again sleeping in their own beds that they had worked for and made, they were grateful that now only ninety of the enemy force remained, and now everyone in Freeton had weapons including bows and arrows which they had taken from the slain invaders. But now there were only thirty men in Freeton alive who could do any kind of fighting. They had fought a brilliant battle that day to reduce the odds from one to four to one to three. They had fought to keep alive for one more day, after which Cilio and his army would arrive and crush Marhyn's piddling expedition force. Yonathan stayed up late thinking of just how to give them that one more chance that they needed.

The people of Freeton increased their numbers the next day by stationing those unable to fight in the upper rooms of the houses. Armed with the captured bows and arrows, they could wait and pick off targets at their leisure. Ninety men and goblins was a lot to kill, Yonathan realized grimly, but it was still possible. The men of Freeton had slept in watches that night, and exhausted though they were, they had not slept idly. There would be enough time for rest later. That night they had built fortifications along the edge of the town where the enemy would have to attack first. They also moved any valuables they had into the rear houses. Yonathan knew that it was inevitable that some more of the houses would be sacked and looted. There were just too many of the enemy to do anything about it, but they would fight bitterly and give nothing away. The enemy would purchase every inch of territory with blood.

The attack began the next day in much the same way as the first. The men of Freeton wearily manned the battlements, and then came to life as they heard the battle cries breaking the early morning stillness. While their physical strength and endurance had waned from the day before, their determination still burned strong. Soon the attackers were at the first battlements. The hastily constructed barricades were never really intended to stop the enemy, one could easily tell as much by their ragged appearance. Their only purpose was to attempt to slow their advance, and give General Cilio enough time to get his army there. Yonathan knew that Cilio would get his army there quickly, but how much time would they need to hold off the attackers? Probably until the end of the day.

Yonathan was jostled out of his reverie by the first onslaught of the enemy. A black clad man was attempting to climb his barricade, which was nearly five feet tall. The barricades were like an interconnected fence that the people of Freeton had made from timber on hand in the village. The prosperity of the village had induced many people from the surrounding countryside to move in, and therefore there was much timber that was being used to construct their houses free to use in the barricades. That had been a stroke of good luck indeed.

Yonathan brought his sword swinging down towards the man, who quickly rolled out of the way. Yonathan's huge broadsword dug into the barricade, almost knocking it down. He pulled it free, and then hopped down to combat the man on foot. The man swung his own sword, but Yonathan parried it to the side and then swung his huge fist into the man's nose. Yonathan stepped forward and with a wide downward slice that glittered in the sun, finished the job.

The barricade held two hours. The attacking force seemed stronger and more prepared than they had the day before. This time they brought not only goblins and men, but some fierce ogres and trolls as well. Though only about ten in number, they were big and heavily armed. They also took a lot of punishment to fell. On his right, Kandan Ironsmith was engaged with one of the monsters. Kandan rushed forward, slicing his sword into the ogre's thigh. The ogre swung a menacing-looking club at Kandan's shoulder, but the nimble blacksmith quickly ducked out of the way. Kandan came up, stabbing his sword directly into the creature's bowels. This time the fierce ogre screamed in pain as it doubled over. Still it was not finished. Kandan swung his broadsword to decapitate the creature, but it flung up its left arm in a last ditch attempt to save itself. Kandan's blade bit into the tough skin of the monster's armored forearm, but at the same time the monster swung his clawed hand down on Kandan's right arm. Kandan screamed as the heavy claw with its grotesque and putrid yellow nails cut deeply into his heavily muscled arm. His right was his blacksmith arm. Undaunted, and grimacing in pain, Kandan brought his sword straight down and sliced open the monster's skull. A black and green slime oozed from the wound and over the creature's lifeless face.

That day Kandan and Yonathan fought as men possessed. Shaking from a mixture of pain from many wounds and rage, the two relentlessly dispatched fighter after fighter of the opposing army. They were merciless and unfeeling. The years of pain from the wizard and the fresh attack on their town had taken all feeling from their souls, leaving them numbed and empty, with only anger to fill the void. They sliced through the enemy, in a cloud of unfeeling. The screams of the men they killed did not even pierce their bubble, so aloof were they. They mowed men down like wheat, maiming, cutting off heads, legs, arms, whatever presented itself, and they always finished the job.

The battle was wearing on past noon, and into the afternoon hours. With each passing moment, it became more and more likely that Cilio and his army would reach them in time and save the town. Already a few houses on the fringe had been destroyed, but the people of the town were making good use of their knowledge of the terrain. Kandan rushed forward and confronted a troll that was using his heavy mace to smash apart a house. The troll swung his mace for Kandan and Kandan reached up his sword to block it. The mace had a spiked ball at the end of a chain by which it was connected to the main shaft. Kandan blocked the shaft, but the ball wrapped around and slammed into Kandan's right arm. Oh well, he thought, only dimly aware, at least it's the same arm. Full of rage, Kandan jumped forward, kicking the troll's knee with his heavy boot, shattering it. Kandan rushed forward as the creature fell to the ground, viciously hacking at it with his sword. Kandan screamed unintelligible words, as he kept hacking and slicing at the creature. Fueled by anger, killing it wasn't enough. He hacked at its body until it was no longer anything even vaguely recognizable, a tangled mass of broken bones, torn flesh and green blood. Through tears, he turned to the next enemy.

A black clad soldier of Queen Marhyn sliced his sword through the chest of a man of Freeton, and Yonathan cut the man down from behind. Yonathan glanced up to the plain north of the city. Through tears of joy, he saw what he was waiting for. It was as if his eyes had been made for no other purpose in life than to witness this moment. Coming from the North with the speed of air was a sprawling mass of the king's troops. Yonathan saw thousands of bright weapons and pieces of armor glinting in the light. They were galloping as fast as they could with Yan as a red dragon flying at the head. Yonathan began to cry, he was so happy. Freeton would be saved! His city would be saved! Yonathan had never been prouder in his life to raise his voice and yell the battle cry of his victorious town. "Freeton Forever!" He screamed at the top of his lungs, thrusting his blood-stained sword high into the air.

No one answered him. Yonathan turned and surveyed the remains of the town with horror. Everywhere Marhyn's servants were setting fire to buildings, and the fire was quickly spreading from rooftop to rooftop. Yonathan did not see a single man from Freeton up to stop them. Even Kandan had disappeared somewhere in the inferno. In that moment, that moment where elation had turned so quickly to despair, Yonathan ran. Freeton was lost—it was useless to stay any longer. To do so would only be to lose his life in some hopeless cause. Yonathan thought about staying. He should fight to his death and stay with his town. Every man who did this that he could kill would help ease him into death; he would even embrace it with open arms. No, that was the easy way out. To die here and now would not benefit his town any. The ones in charge who did this must pay. And Yonathan swore on his soul that it would be he that made them pay, with their lives.

As evening approached, Yonathan watched the smoldering town from the edge of General Cilio's camp. The army had come and routed the rest of Marhyn's force, but the damage was done. Yonathan was the only survivor. A young knight came up to offer the big man a blanket to ward off the evening chill. Yonathan pushed it away. The people of Freeton had no blankets on the cold nights that the wizard abused them! The town had been through so much together, and now it all ended like this.

The emptiness that Yonathan felt to the bottom of his soul consumed him. It felt as though he would never conquer it, as though the void was swallowing him and eating him up. The loss of his town would never be replaced. Yonathan thought of the bright future that the town had had. It would have grown and prospered. It could have become a great city even. He also thought of his friends, the people of Freeton with whom he had shared so much and who were now dead. They could have been anything in life. They were such good people, so undeserving of their end. Only a few months ago they had been freed from the wizard's spell, and now they were all dead. Their whole lives had been wasted and they had only a few months' time to show for it. Lapsing into melancholy, Yonathan stared at the ashes for the rest of the night and early into the morning.

*   *   *   *

On the other side of the world, or at least very far away, Derlin was sitting that night and talking with Valena. Tarthur had gone off with Yvonne (they were uh, talking, I think in some abandoned corner of the elven forest) and Derlin had stayed in Dalin's house with nothing much to do. All of a sudden, she had walked into the room. Derlin gave a start at seeing so beautiful a creature here in this room, but then he had remembered that as she was Dalin's sister, she probably lived there. Derlin had blushed furiously at first, and then started talking.

Derlin was terribly embarrassed and nervous when he began the conversation, stumbling over his own words, which only increased his anxiety all the more, further causing him to blurt out something wholly unintelligible. He thought that they would never understand each other, but Valena had an easy way about her, and while he couldn't exactly put his finger on what it was, it was something that made Derlin feel relaxed and comfortable. While at first he had been totally at a loss for any subject that he could talk about that could possibly have any interest for her, soon he found out that she was indeed mortal and ate food and drank water and did just about all of the other normal things that other mortals, including Derlin, did.

Words seemed to flow from Valena like honey, her golden sweet voice made Derlin wish that he could capture her voice in a jar and listen to it for hours when he was by himself. They talked of his boyhood, his travels, and his friends. They talked about her also, but she seemed more closely guarded when it came to revealing things about herself.

Derlin was just telling Valena about the time that Morty had started a fight with Tarthur in the town center, back in Krendon. Tarthur had of course been up since well before daybreak attending to all of his chores or he would have been more attentive when Morty jumped on him from behind and knocking him to the ground, started to attack him with all of his meager strength. This totally unprovoked attack (Tarthur had done something inconsequential to Morty the day before, but it really had nothing to do with the attack) was quickly repelled by Tarthur and Derlin's supreme battle tactics and ended in Morty receiving several bloody noses and three fat lips. Not a hair on Tarthur nor Derlin was put out of place, of course. The head of Krendon, Baron Ercrilla, witnessed the fight and the unlawful attack on Tarthur and Derlin and sentenced all parties involved to a day without food. Tarthur and Derlin felt that their pure innocence was violated, so assuming the philosophy of civil disobedience set forth in our world by Thoreau, decided to eat anyway.

Now, although Thoreau advocated nonviolently breaking an unjust law and taking the blame rather than submitting to evil, the boys decided it would be better if they broke the law but Morty got the blame. If they stole food, it would be inevitable that someone would be blamed and beaten, and by a unanimous vote the two boys decided it would be better it were Mortimer than them. The boys weren't that hungry at dinnertime, as their frequent escapades often left them without at least one meal, but by morning they were ravenous. Derlin couldn't remember exactly, he thought that they were already up and started on their chores, but he was sure he saw two figures sneak in to Judith's kitchen and steal the magnificent eggs that were to be served for breakfast. These two shadowy figures actually had the audacity to cook the meal there, and then devour it as if they had been sent to bed the night before without dinner.

Well, the boys made sure to stay away from such shadowy characters, but one of them ran by and deposited a small piece of the omelet in Tarthur's pocket. Now that morning Tarthur had gone over to Morty to apologize for the previous day's beating and see if any of Morty's five black eyes had healed yet. Tarthur genuinely meant to reconcile the situation right then and there, but Morty was so crabby that Tarthur was forced to leave without making the amends that he wanted so badly to make. Now at that very moment the piece of omelet miraculously jumped out of Tarthur's pocket where it had been deposited by the shadowy creature who had really committed the crime. The omelet leaped from containment and actually landed on Morty's table! Tarthur and Derlin hurriedly left as they didn't want to lose one precious second that they could be working.

When they left the room Morty hungrily gobbled the omelet, but who should appear at that time but none other than Baron Ercrilla and Judith, who were jointly investigating the disappearance of such a succulent morsel which was to have formed breakfast for the baron himself. Now the passing by of these two stern angels of justice was purely coincidental, and Tarthur and Derlin's visit had had absolutely no reason for occurring at the time it did save by pure chance.

Tarthur and Derlin often meditated on the real culprits, for Morty was forced to take the blame by his father on account of such overwhelming circumstantial evidence, but they had absolutely no idea who could have committed the heinous and dastardly crime. And all that was the truth, and nothing but the truth, exactly as they had told it to the town authority figures. (Derlin remembered the story with some slight variations, but they really weren't worth telling especially since it could implicate him and Tarthur. He was pretty sure none of this would get back to Judith, but he couldn't be too sure. Besides, Baron Ercrilla was in Breshen with the army.)

When Derlin was telling her about Morty's injuries, Valena laughed. When she laughed it made Derlin's heart stop. The sound was so pure, so clean, so full of life. Her laughter not only radiated joy, it filled the room with it. It filled up Derlin, until he thought his heart was going to burst. When Derlin stole a glance at her face, he saw the joy reflected in her face also. Her laughter made Derlin feel alive, more alive than he had ever felt before. It made her perfect.

As Derlin continued his story, he wanted to make her laugh again and again. The more he heard her laughter, the more he wanted to hear it, the more he yearned for it. He tried to embellish parts, not that their stories needed embellishing. Valena helped him out. She laughed. And it made Derlin's world brighter.

Derlin regretted when he finished. Precisely three minutes had passed since Valena had entered the room, yet he glanced outside, and by the same phenomenon that Tarthur had observed in Akin's classroom, or the reverse of it rather, it was already dark! Derlin assumed it was solely a trick of the tree branches, but then he saw Valena stretch and yawn. It appeared someone had cast a spell that transported them four or five hours into the future, for it was indeed late.

"I really have enjoyed talking to you today, Derlin." Valena's soft words made Derlin's heart beat so quickly that he almost fainted. "Good night." With her gentle goodbye, she gracefully floated along the floor and into the darkness. Derlin was left in the room in silent wonder. *She* had enjoyed talking to *him*. The fact that it was just formality never even occurred to him. Derlin sat in his chair for a few more hours contemplating Valena, her hair, her face, her eyes, her words, her personality, too stunned to move. It was past midnight when he got up, left the room, and went to find Tarthur.

"But how will I know, Tarthur? When did you first find out that Yvonne was the one for you?"

Tarthur contemplated the question for a while and then responded. "I think it was right after I gave her the bloody nose. Yes, that was definitely it."

Derlin shook his head in disgust. "Tarthur, that's not very helpful to me. I certainly don't plan to sock her in the nose. Can you imagine, to mar such beauty? To destroy such perfection? The world would be a sadder place for the loss of one of her eyelashes."

"Although, a happier place for the loss of one of her ear-hairs," Tarthur joked. Derlin looked at him angrily and was about to leave. It appeared that his friend would rather make jokes than give advice.

Tarthur saw that it was now time to be serious. "Wait. I know it is a big deal to you. Who is she?"

"The elven girl. Dalin's sister."

Tarthur nodded. "Yeah, she's pretty." Tarthur looked around quickly, hoping Yvonne had not sneaked into the room. The last time she had heard him call another girl pretty, she had decked him in the ear, and it still smarted. (The funny part about the incident was that that girl was Yvonne's identical twin sister Yvette, and Tarthur was only trying to give an indirect complement.)

"Look, Derlin, you'll know. When she walks by, do you feel it? Do you get the awe, do you say, 'Wow?'"

"No," Derlin said. "It's more than that. I don't get a 'wow', I get a 'BOOM!!!!!!' My body turns to lukewarm water and I feel it in my heart like a shot from a cannon. It knocks me over. I wish I could tell you how it feels, but words, they seem so dry, so uncolorful compared to the real feeling! It just..." Realizing the futility of explaining such a thing, Derlin trailed off helplessly.

Tarthur nodded. "I know how it is. Now, all we need is a way to impress her so that she'll like you too. I can use some magic, and we'll get Yvonne to help also..."

And with that the boys began to plan...

The next day brought a few ideas, and a note that Valena was to be in charge of teaching elven customs and manners to Tarthur and Derlin. It seemed very important to the elves that everyone learn their culture and follow it. In any event, the invitation couldn't have pleased Tarthur and Derlin more, especially the latter, and soon they were off on horseback through the woods, Valena leading, Tarthur and Derlin following behind. Valena had blushed when Derlin had helped her onto her horse. It appeared these men weren't as uncivilized as others.

As they rode along, Valena would identify a flower or herb, and the boys would vainly try to remember each one. In the interludes between flowers that the boys were required to learn, she lectured them on elven history. As the forest was thick with life, however, these interludes were few and far between. Valena was showing them one flower, a beautiful blue one that gave off a cool and delicious aroma. "This one is called in the ancient tongue *Poeloe*. Our people use it for love. It is my favorite flower and I just love the way it smells." Derlin remembered that.

The night before they hadn't been able to come up with too many ideas. Actually, ideas were not the problem, but rather the fact that Derlin didn't know enough about Valena and what she would like. The boys agreed to halt further planning until they could find out enough to make something successful.

After their ride, Derlin and Tarthur went back to where the bulk of the army was encamped. There they trained and ate some heavy food for the first time since coming to Breshen. It tasted good, but Derlin missed Valena already.

In the days that followed, the boys stayed in Breshen, training, eating, resting, learning, and of course, planning.

*   *   *   *

It had been three days since General Cilio and his forces had turned away Queen Marhyn's army at the Goblin caves in the Tabletop Plateau. After the fall of Freeton, the rest of Queen Marhyn's army caught up with the expeditionary force and then they had veered sharply east. This was an apparent attempt to out-maneuver General Cilio's army and attack King Garkin's castle while there were no troops in it. They were attempting to pass along the Tabletop Plateau so they could use the goblins there as a help and with the rough terrain slip by Cilio and attack the soft underbelly of the capital.

General Cilio, however, had by some unknown means become aware of their plan, and had moved his army to the Tabletop Plateau to prevent Marhyn from passing through. For three days her dark armies had come, and for three days General Cilio's impressive battle tactics had stopped them. Then Marhyn had withdrawn south, seemingly content to attack the lowland villages of Synthy, Ruf, and Shen. Those cities were valuable producers of grain and meat for King Garkin, and Cilio rushed after Marhyn's armies to defend them.

Two more things: Cilio was becoming concerned with the conduct of Marhyn's army. So far, he had not seen the Dark Lady herself, and while destroying their grain would definitely harm and weaken the king's army, it would never defeat them. So far, except for the aborted attempt on the capital, Marhyn seemed content to burn and pillage. Beings like Marhyn were almost immortal. He knew that she would never attack if she didn't think that she could win. Cilio began to fear that she was lulling them into a false sense of security, only to explode later. It was either that, or alliance between Marhyn and her hated brother. The latter was beginning to seem more and more likely. If Marhyn could tie up a sizable part of the king's forces in the South, Darhyn would probably be able to take Breshen. Cilio was worried that Marhyn's army was just acting as a diversion, but reports from Breshen indicated that no forces had been sighted outside of the Dark One's fortress, and he was likely still asleep. So Cilio knew he had at least a little time to defeat Marhyn. Also: Yonathan was wrong. There had been one other survivor at Freeton. Early the next morning they had found Kandan Ironsmith, burned and injured, yet still barely alive, in the charred ruins of his town. Two knights had made a stretcher and carried him immediately to Treshin. His right arm had to be amputated.

Marhyn's army had a good two-day lead on Cilio, and they veered for the village of Ruf first. General Cilio had expected as much, for while the village at Synthy was closer, it was smaller by a good five hundred inhabitants and was barely worth destroying. If Marhyn could only destroy one, it would be Ruf. The only problem was that Ruf's cornfields were to the North of the town. They grew a special type of corn that could be harvested all year round, and produced much of the food for the king's army.

General Cilio and his army caught sight of Marhyn's forces on the third day near sunset, when they were only a day or so out of Ruf. That night, they lost them in the darkness. The next morning, they awakened to smoke. It was billowing out southward, huge black clouds that rolled up from the ground and rose to obscure the sky. It appeared they were already too late.

*   *   *   *

Garseon crouched motionless in the branches of the pine tree, the heat of the fires from the burning grain fields hot on his face. The Guard raised his reed to his lips, took careful aim, and fired. The goblin that was at the base of the tree slumped over dead and Garseon moved forward.

Floating effortlessly through the tall grasslands out of sight of Marhyn's army, Garseon soon caught sight of what he was looking for. It was good, he thought, that Cilio had sent a member of the Guard rather than an ordinary scout for this mission. It ensured success. The Guard was the best in the realm, even if only twelve people even knew of its existence, and ten of them were members. General Cilio and King Garkin, however, were the two people who made the differences in this world.

Marhyn's army had only burned the cornfields to the North, they had not actually attacked the town itself yet, and this was a blessing indeed. Now, Cilio's forces had Marhyn trapped between a weak force and a strong force. Garseon was soon at the perimeter of the town, and from that he quickly found the building he was looking for. It was an easy task for one who was required to know every building in Daranor, who built it, with what materials, secret exits, location, and purpose. Garseon opened the door to the iron forge and then quickly descended the steps to the basement. It was here that he found Baron Koy's son, Verg. Verg was busy presiding over plans for the city's defense when the invading hordes came.

The Guard noiselessly descended the steps to the basement, silently going over everything in his head to make sure he got it right the first time. Baron Koy was with General Cilio's army, and so Garseon would have to take over from Koy's son. As he entered the fire-lit room, he cleared his throat. This was a necessary step, no one had seen, heard, or felt him enter. Four figures whom Garseon immediately recognized turned to look at him. There was not a little bit of surprise on their faces, most town business was conducted in the town hall, and the blacksmith's office was only used for matters of great importance and secrecy. Garseon nodded, and then greeted each one by name. There was Verg, of course, and then Gwerth, Baron Koy's chief advisor. Next, he shook hands with Kevin, the blacksmith who was leader of one of the most powerful industries in Ruf, and Jeq, the leader of the farmers, the other important member of the town council. All were bewildered at this new stranger, whom none knew. The Guard were, of course, required to learn by face the most influential people in the realm, their histories and any hidden sympathies. Garseon knew from their records that these were all good men.

Garseon lost no time in beginning. "Hello," he greeted, "my name is Johnston, and I'm a military scout with King Garkin's army. I have been sent to help coordinate the defense of this city, as we have no time to lose. Where have you ordered those not willing or able to fight to go?"

"As a matter of fact," Verg broke in, "We were just discussing that very point. They have been ordered to get ready, and should be ready shortly. We were thinking about sending them west."

"You will send them west," Garseon replied, with a little too much authority. He should let the others make the decisions, as long as they chose correctly. A Guard was never allowed to betray his position. "Send them to Synthy. General Cilio has observed that there are no enemy forces in that area and the people of Synthy have been preparing for an influx of refugees since he sent them a messenger. They will have plenty of extra food and shelter available."

Verg nodded. Garseon had to be careful, he knew, because Verg was a little impatient. Eighteen years, that age of fire and yearnings to be a man, that was Verg's age. He was hungry for power, and Garseon didn't want to spoil his turn at command.

The meeting proceeded for another half hour, and Garseon revealed that two hundred men from Cilio's command would join them later that evening, if they managed to elude Marhyn's army. Then they made plans to defend the city only as long as possible without losing the superior position, and then the men should fall back into hiding and let Cilio's larger and better trained army take over and win, thus sparing their lives. This much said, they went to work designing barricades, ramparts, and positioning men for the battle they knew was coming with the dawn.

The day dawned calm, not a voice shattered the solemn silence. Garseon had been awake for a few hours, going over the final preparations for the defense of the town. The reinforcements from General Cilio's army had arrived shortly after midnight, and had been trying furtively to secure whatever sleep they could before the long day they had in front of them. Baron Koy had come back with the reinforcements, and had taken control of the force defending the town. He had been up with Garseon, making sure everything would work out right. As he looked over the smoldering remains of the once immense grain fields that he had worked his entire life to build up, the elder noble looked ragged, yet ready.

They hoped that Marhyn's force would ignore their little town and instead concentrate their strength on Cilio's much larger force. That way the town would be saved and the Koy's force could attack the back of Marhyn's army. Their hope was a faint one, however, and soon was shattered, just as the evil guttural sounds of the goblin battle horns shattered the early morning stillness.

Marhyn's force opened the day by striking southward into Ruf. They apparently hoped to wipe the baron's force off the map as soon as possible so that they would not have to fight long on two fronts. Cilio for his part quickly attacked Marhyn's rear. The back half of her army then turned to face him.

The hordes of goblins and mercenary men that streamed into the town soon met the first barricade. Perched atop it were archers and men who hurled boulders and hot oil down upon the goblins. Their sheer numbers soon overcame the heroic efforts of the defenders, who then fell back and set fire to the hastily constructed barricade. The heat of the flames stalled Marhyn's army, who were forced to wait until they died down before continuing. The men of Ruf had no scruples about destroying their property. Not a man among them had any illusions about what this day would bring; their town would be annihilated. That much had been certain as soon as Marhyn had decided to attack. The only question was how long they could hold out for and force Marhyn to fight on two fronts.

The next charge into the town brought men on horseback. Marhyn now wanted to take the town as quickly as possible. These mounted riders were just what Garseon had hoped for, however. When they charged into the town center, he released the second defense; with the cutting of a rope, hundreds of spiked logs rose from the ground diagonally right in front of the horsemen. Screaming as they saw the certainty of their own death, the riders and their beasts could not stop before slamming into the spikes and impaling themselves.

The confusion in the town had wiped out the organization of the defenders, however, and now it was just a free for all. Bodies were flying everywhere, and Garseon knew it was only a short time before Baron Koy gave the ultimate retreat order. Until then, he held his ground. A goblin swung a long broadsword at him, and Garseon ducked under the blade, then came up and threw a cloud of dust into the goblin's face. The dust sparkled for a moment, and then exploded into a vicious ball of fire.

Garseon saw Verg on his right, insanely battling three goblins and two men. He was fighting like a madman, and enemies kept falling around him. Behind him, a burly man lifted his sword...

"Tat tat tat" Garseon fired three quick shots from his blowgun and that man and two others died standing up. Verg didn't even notice, he just kept on fighting.

Garseon was wondering why Baron Koy did not sound his horn and give the order to retreat. It was obviously past time. Garseon engaged two more goblins and a troll, who had now come forward to join the fray. Soon all three were dead.

Garseon heard a feeble voice call his name. "Johnston..." He whirled and saw Baron Koy, lying in a pool of his own blood. He had lost a leg and had a gaping wound in his chest. Even the Guard had no medical skills to combat something like this. Garseon hurried over and took the dying baron in his arms. Koy looked right into his eyes, and at that moment of death his eyes unnerved Garseon more that anything he had ever seen. The hardened Guard took a step back in shock. When he looked again, the baron was dead. Garseon picked up the horn and falteringly blew it. The horn cracked at first, but soon gave forth a clear, strong note.

The overdue order for retreat being called, the men of the town lost no time carrying it out. They hurried away and massed in the grassland outside of the town.

"Wait," Verg cried to Garseon. "I have to go back for my father. I can't just leave him in there..."

"Your father is dead," the Guard responded. "I saw it."

"I know he is dead," the boy spat back, grabbing onto his arm. "I need the body! It is our honor that has been taken."

"It's all over now," Garseon said quietly, ripping free his arm and setting off the third defense. He flicked the edge of his flint with his dagger, sending a spark into the kerosene soaked wick that led into the town that had been soaked with fuel and sprinkled with Garseon's exploding powder. Verg had tears in his eyes as the town exploded, incinerating those from Marhyn's army who were still inside, sending waves of heat onto the faces of the surviving defenders, and burning away his memories.

The battle raged on past midday and into the afternoon without much changing of positions by either side. Cilio had observed Lithar Lifehater on his horse behind the lines of Marhyn's army. Indeed, if she was not commanding it, as now looked to be the case, Cilio was sure that he must be the leader. Although, the fact that he still did not see the Dark Lady disturbed him immensely.

General Lifehater had been playing it rather conservatively, and since Cilio had the superior numbers, he was willing to let him play that game. Cilio knew that he probably could send his army in one huge rush and decimate Marhyn's force, but instead he bided his time. A straight charge would lose him men, since Marhyn would only have to defend her position. So he contented himself with waiting and slowly destroying their army with tit for tat tactics. Cilio had about three times as many men as Lithar and with luck the battle would be over by a few hours after dark. He preferred to fight in the light, Cilio didn't want any surprises. Besides, his men were tired from a long day of battle. So he decided that if he saw a break, then he would go for it. If not, then he would order the men to withdraw for the day and attack again the next morning. That way, if Lithar wanted to pursue, Cilio would be on the defensive and Lithar would be at a disadvantage.

Atop his horse, Cilio's eagle eyes scanned the battlefield, looking for any sign of the break in Marhyn's lines that would allow him to send his army in and separate her line in half. A surrounded army is as good as destroyed if it does not break free. And Cilio had enough men to easily surround Marhyn if he could only split her line into two.

Suddenly a great ogre that had been holding a particularly stubborn section of her line fell, with swords sticking out all over his body. That was all Cilio needed to see. Lightning quick, he dug his heels into his horse and galloped forward, calling for the men to charge in the direction he was pointing his sword. The weary army was a little surprised at the suddenness of the order, after hours of waiting for it, but they quickly regained composure and rushed forward into the gap.

General Lithar's army was also surprised at the suddenness of the charge. In that second, all their iron determination and fear of the Dark Lady melted away, and they broke and ran like cowards. Cilio's army cheered loudly and rushed into the void. Cilio reigned in his horse and let the soldiers rush past him.

As the original confusion died down, Cilio surveyed the scene. In what appeared to be an anarchical retreat, Cilio now saw that some had run backward and formed a new line two hundred yards away, and some had instead ran to the left or right. Cilio saw it now. They had been lured into a pinchers move and now Marhyn's army was forming a V and Cilio was trapped inside. Marhyn's army could now attack both of their exposed sides. Cilio whirled his horse and began to call for his army to get out of there. They still had time before the trap closed.

The cry for retreat died in his throat. Coming at them from the North was a hideous army of beasts from nightmares. There was every kind of terror: black serpents, ogres, trolls, fish with legs, things too horrible to mention and impossible to describe. They effectively sealed off the mouth of the V and enclosed General Cilio and his army in a triangle. At their head, perched upon a massive black dragon, was Queen Marhyn herself.

CHAPTER 16

▼

A BATTLE AT NIGHT

General Cilio lost no time wondering neither how he had been lured into check nor how Marhyn had concealed her army from him in the goblin caves of the Tabletop Plateau. Those things had already happened, it was not important how, only that they did. Now was the time for action, there was no time to lose. "Right! All men veer to the right and charge! We must break through!" Cilio screamed as he thrust his sword in to the air at the right. He knew that one of the sides of the V would be the weakest, since the mouth that had just appeared was fresh and filled with formidable monsters and Queen Marhyn herself. Right was better than left because it was also west, and if they controlled the West they could send their wounded back to the refugee camp in Synthy.

Cilio did not anticipate any problems breaking through Marhyn's force. Once his commanders had reorganized his force and he had sent his best units to the front, it was only a short matter of time before he broke through. Cilio also sent his wild cards, Yan and Yonathan. Since the destruction of his hometown, Yonathan had grown more eager than ever to repay the enemy who had done it. Cilio usually did not trust fanatics with his most valuable possessions, but his gut feeling told him to go with this one. So he decided to arm Yonathan with the Light Sword. Now that they must break through the lines with all speed, Cilio was at least glad that somebody had it.

Breaking through took more time than Cilio would have wanted. Marhyn had anticipated that he would turn right, and she had stacked her line. But the line had never been intended to stop him, only to hold him long enough so she could attack from all sides long enough to cause serious and irreversible damage. It did not work. Cilio brought his army onto the plain with only minimal losses.

As Cilio turned his army to face Marhyn's, which had now massed together, he saw that he was only slightly outnumbered, by about five thousand for her to his three thousand five hundred. But many of her force were monsters and this rendered his estimation meaningless, because he didn't know how many monsters would be equal to one man. Cilio turned and saw Yan, Yonathan and the Duke of Walis come up to stand by him. At least all his commanders were here to help him decide what to do next. "Are our chains of command still intact?" Cilio asked the first question, and nods greeted him from all three leaders. He feared the answer to the next question more, however. "What is the condition of the men?"

"Their morale is high, but they are fatigued and have not eaten all day," Walis replied. "We need to rest, but can fight if there is no other way. They hope that the next developments will wait until morning." Yan and Yonathan nodded that their men were in much the same condition, although Yonathan himself had a look that said he was eagerly anticipating the next rush.

Cilio made his decision quickly. "Send one third of the force into the front with orders to wait and repulse the enemy if they attack. Of course, we will much prefer if they wait to attack, but I seriously doubt it. She knows that we are fatigued. The other two thirds should be sent to the back and given food and rest for one hour. After that, they will switch for one more hour. When they have both had their rest, we will see about attacking. During the first two hours, we must feel out her army and see what these beasts can do. Go, quickly." With these words, the three commanders went to carry out his orders.

The line held for the first hour without much incident. It appeared Marhyn was trying to let Cilio think that she had finished for the day, only to explode when he let his guard down and set up camp for the night. Either that or she was planning something. Cilio vainly hoped the Dark Lady herself and her massive dragon would not be able to make a large difference in the fight.

The second hour was much the same, with Marhyn sending out small thrusts and charges that included both monsters and men, but they were all repulsed by Cilio and his men. It was at the beginning of the third hour that Marhyn realized that she must send a powerful attack or her advantage of night and fatigue would soon dissolve.

Cilio had ordered the lesser magicians to light balls of fire that hovered over the army, thus giving them just enough light to see by. He had to be cautious, however, or they would expend themselves, and they might need magic in this coming battle.

Cilio wished Zelin and the rest of the army were still with him. Then he would be able to easily rout Marhyn's force. He inwardly cursed himself for not bringing more men.

Marhyn and Cilio had positioned their armies in lines that went roughly north-south, with Marhyn's army on the east side and Cilio's on the west. At the south side of Cilio's line was a small grassy knoll, which rose to less then thirty feet in height, but was nevertheless the highest ground on the otherwise flat battlefield. It was on this small hill that Marhyn first attacked.

It wasn't a particularly strong thrust, only about two thousand men or so, but it was the largest so far. Cilio sent Walis's and Yonathan's thirds to deal with it. The two sides flew into each other, a mass of swords and men and monsters and blood. Using his trained eye, Cilio could tell the fight was going about even. Marhyn and her minions were more rested, and they had the use of horrible monsters, but the men of the kingdom had superior numbers and organization. After a tense fifteen minutes, Cilio could tell that they were about to repulse the attack, but before they could, Marhyn sent about another thousand into Cilio's left side. Cilio was about to rush troops there, but he had the feeling that it was just a diversion. So he left Yan and his third to handle it.

Soon he saw that he was right. The remaining two thousand of Marhyn's army charged into the original attack point on his right. He left Yan to handle the left side and spurred his horse on to the knoll, which was luckily still controlled by his men, although, they were losing ground every minute.

The battles on the front lines were fierce. But that night, the king's men fought as men possessed. They hammered and hacked at all sorts of monsters, making Marhyn earn every inch of territory she got. By the end of the hour, it was about three thousand to four thousand. The odds had closed. If the king's men lost the hill, however, the battle could shift. The forces were evenly matched; Lithar Lifehater was a skilled commander as well. Cilio's army could not match the magic of the Dark Lady's minions.

The battle was approaching its critical point, Cilio knew. He could feel it. In some battles there was one point, often one confrontation, one break in a line, which would decide the entire fate of both armies. Cilio wondered what it would be this time.

General Lithar Lifehater saw the weakness in his enemy's line, and knew it was time to attack personally. If they could break through there, they would be able to capture the hill and gain the upper hand. He nodded to two huge ogres to follow him and dug his spurs into his gigantic armored horse. The horse was jet black and covered with armored spikes that protruded from every possible place. Lithar himself was armed with massive silver and black armor. His helmet had blades attached to it, and his shoulders, elbows and knees had razor sharp edges. The massive sword he wore at his side looked as if it could decapitate ten men with a blow; although, the most he had ever killed at one blow before was seven.

Cilio saw the weakness and sent twenty men to fill it. The ogres rained down blows with their cruel maces, destroying ten before one of them was killed and the other wounded slightly. Lithar rode into the gap, literally riding straight into the men. His massive sword and armor killed most, while his horse wounded countless others. Already the rest of Lithar's troops were beginning to follow him through the hole. It seemed as if Lithar would break through…

Standing in his path was Yonathan.

"So you are the leader," he called out, and Lithar reigned in his horse. Why was this fool talking to him? "You are the one who is responsible for this murder, this slaughter of innocents. You are the one who destroys so much hope! You are the one who destroyed my town!!!" Lithar shrugged at the accusations. This man was too kind; he didn't deserve all of the credit.

"Their souls cry out to me day and night! Their blood demands justice!" Yonathan was almost crying now, his anger, rage, and emotion filling him up and spilling out into his words. Lithar shrugged, unaffected. He was tired of this petty man. The remaining ogre rushed forward to take him out of the way.

Yonathan sliced down through the ogre, cutting him in half diagonally. Lithar raised his eyebrows in surprise. Maybe this man was worth destroying personally after all. Charging his horse forward, Lithar hurriedly mumbled some words and drew his sword, sending a fireball from the tip. Yonathan flung up the Light Sword and the fireball exploded, leaving the big man unhurt. Lithar charged his horse at him, and when he got near, his horse reared up on its hind legs while Lithar rained down two blows on Yonathan's head. Yonathan blocked both with the Light Sword, and then sliced through the horse's armored rear leg, diving out of the way just before horse and rider fell in a tattered heap of armor. Lithar barely had time to roll out of the way before his horse's armor accidentally pierced him, and stood to face Yonathan on foot.

Cilio sent an extra column of men to be ready to finish Lithar if Yonathan died before he could do it. The hole was closed up for now, but if Lithar won and was able to get some support from his army…

The defenders on the north side weren't doing as well. Although Yan's force had the numerical advantage, some of Marhyn's deadliest monsters had been placed there. Cilio realized that if Marhyn were able to break through there, she would be able to surround the hill that had the bulk of Cilio's force. And if she could surround them in such a small area, she would be able to thicken her lines and give them little chance of breaking out. Then she could deliver the killing stroke. But it looked as if both of Cilio's lines were holding, at least for the time being.

Right then Marhyn delivered her knockout punch. On the north side of the line, her huge black dragon rose from the battlefield and got ready to attack Yan's force. Cilio knew if it was not stopped immediately his line would collapse. So that had been her plan. To put her men into battle in the South, but to concentrate her strength in the North and thus break through. Now that he saw it too late, he had only one hope left.

Yan quickly dispatched a monster that he had been fighting with, turned into a liquid silver, and rose. Their one hope flew up and faced the Dark Lady, who was perched high atop her dragon. "So, we meet again," began Dragon Yan, in the ancient tongue of dragons. "Although, I would venture to say the circumstances are much different from last time."

Queen Marhyn nodded as if she still recognized him, and then raised her hand and brought it down quickly. Her black dragon did not need to be told twice to attack…

Cilio watched the twin battles taking place above him and in front of him. Above, Queen Marhyn and her dragon circled, taking every chance to dart in and strike Yan, who held his space, hanging motionless in the air, moving only to counter the other dragon's strikes. Before him, he saw Yonathan and Lithar, cautiously circling. The rest of both armies did not need to be told that these battles would decide their fate. The opposing forces had almost stopped fighting, watching alternatively the air or the sky. Both forces were loosening their armor. When these fights were over, they knew they would have to run. The losers would run away from the victor, and the winners would chase after them. Cilio could feel the tension mounting in the air, and felt small and helpless for the first time in his life. Now the battle was out of his hands.

Lithar raised his sword above his head and charged, bringing it down in an arc that glittered eerily in the artificial fire of the magicians. Yonathan brought up the Light Sword to block it, and then sliced down diagonally. Lithar instinctively spun out of the way, sending one of his protruding blades across Yonathan's side. A slow trickle of blood soon seeped out of the side of Yonathan's torn chain mail.

Lithar had not escaped unhurt, however. He felt his own black blood, cold against his chest. Lithar glanced down at his armor in surprise; it did not even have a scratch on it. So, he thought, if this human wants to play with magic, so be it.

The evil warrior clapped his hands together, and then split into three identical figures who rushed at Yonathan.

Yan spat out his dragon fire hot enough to boil rock and Marhyn flung up her wand and sent her own blue fire to counteract it. Yan stopped as he quickly realized that this would be fruitless, and instead darted his head in and snapped a bite of the black dragon's tail, whipping his head back to avoid her counterattack. The people on the ground could barely make out the movements of the lightning quick dragons. It was said that dragons lived in their own time—that was why they could move so fast and live such long, long lives, spanning centuries and ages. Whether this was true or not, the two dragons were in a fierce contest.

Yan rose, seeking to gain the upper altitude. He hovered there for a second, and then dove straight for Marhyn. The black dragon rolled out of the way, but Yan got a slice of its soft underbelly. Blood dripped for a second on those below, then stopped as the wound closed itself. It appeared that Yan would have to exhaust this dragon's supply of magic first.

Yonathan stared at the three Lithars now facing him, and actually he was glad. Where before he was only able to destroy this hated enemy once, now he could do it three times. He rushed toward the one on his left, who swung his sword horizontally, as if to cut Yonathan in half. Yonathan not only parried the blow, but he hit Lithar's sword so hard that he knocked it from his hand. Unhindered by any danger, Yonathan brought the Light Sword down, slicing through armor, flesh, and bone as easily as air. No scream of anguish rewarded Yonathan. Lithar turned into a puff of smoke, and vanished. The middle Lithar laughed shrilly, then split into three again. There were four now. Yonathan knew he would have to guess the right one...

...But how to do it? Dragons had an almost infinite supply of magic. If this one could heal itself so easily, Yan might never be able to destroy it. Unless...perhaps his healing magic only covered small wounds? Yan flew backwards, into a cloud. Under his cover, he slowly sank, keeping quiet. Marhyn could probably sense him, but perhaps...

He would get the right one with luck. Yonathan faced two more of the Lithars, who were now surrounding him. He used the Light Sword on one, cutting him in half and watching as the cloud of smoke rose to greet him. The other one sliced at him from the back, but Yonathan was able to partially block it. Lithar struck his sword into Yonathan's thigh. The blood ran out, reminding him of the other cut in his side. Yonathan sliced the Light Sword through the creature, leaving his armor and sword that he had vainly attempted to use as part of the dust cloud. So apparently even the fake ones could hurt. Yonathan needed a plan to decide…

How to attack? From the bottom, of course. That was the one weak point of a dragon, and it made them nervous to have another dragon underneath them. Yan filled the air around him with his cloaking magic, thickening the cloud and the night so that the other dragon could not tell where he was. The other one could sense that he was using magic, but she could not pinpoint Yan's location exactly. Yan was about to burst upwards in a powerful stroke when he saw a white light emitted from Marhyn. It spread outwards in an oval shape, burning away the cloud and exposing the star filled night sky. Everything was clear…

…Around Yonathan and Lithar, the other members of their armies had respectfully moved aside, leaving a forty foot circle for the dueling combatants. Yonathan still didn't have an idea. He could slice through fake Lithars all day, but each time more of them sprang up. How could he tell which one was real? A pile of stones at his feet grabbed Yonathan's attention. He picked one up and hurled it at the nearest Lithar. The stone went through him without stopping. This gave him an idea…

His idea was to create several sections of cloud large enough to hide a dragon and when Marhyn illuminated the wrong one, to attack her while she was using the illumination magic. That way, she would be weaker. Yan sent out four clouds, himself in one of them. The clouds swirled around him, in the way of a magician with a ball under one of three cups, making it indecipherable into which cloud the shapeshifter had originally ventured. Then Yan had another idea. This one would surely work…

To defeat his hated enemy, Yonathan had waited since the destruction of Freeton. Dreams of his citizens, the citizens he was supposed to protect, filled his every sleeping hour. He saw their pain at being used by the evil wizard, their hatred of their false lives, and at the same time their helplessness. He saw their salvation at the hands of Tarthur and Derlin, their hope under Kandan, and then their deaths, horrible and graphic. Their charred, cut up bodies followed him everywhere. No punishment would be fitting for those who did this, but he would now deliver the ultimate punishment that he could. He would kill Lithar. Yonathan stumbled into the dirt, pretending to fall and instead picked up a handful of rocks, which he hurled at the various Lithars. All of the rocks hit against the Lithars' armor and bounced off. Lithar chuckled inwardly. He had anticipated Yonathan's ploy. This boy was smart, though, and it made Lithar glad that he had had a chance to do battle with him that day. The boy could not last much longer, though. There were fifteen Lithars now, and the boy was tiring quickly. Soon it would be all over...

...If Yan's plan worked, that is. He transformed a small part of himself into wind, and sent the invisible wind into the next cloud. Dragon Yan became a shade lighter, more transparent. The wind moved the second cloud around under Marhyn and her dragon and made it look as if Yan was in that cloud. Marhyn's dragon twitched imperceptibly when he noticed the cloud with the wind in it. Marhyn nodded as she prepared to send a bolt of fire into the cloud and Yan tensed his muscles, waiting...

...For the right moment, the Light Sword had lain dormant during the entire fight. Now, the blade began to glow yellow, and the ruby that formed the eye of the dragon began to burn with an unearthly fire. The exhausted Yonathan glanced down at his sword and he felt its warmth pulsing through his veins, giving him new strength. The sword jerked upwards, pointing to a Lithar a little bit off to the right. Yonathan felt his vision clearing, he saw the other Lithars as only thin shells of magic, while the real one looked every bit as cruel as he was. Then the vision vanished. But he had seen enough. Yonathan charged forward...

Into the cloud filled by Wind Yan, Marhyn sent her full fury. The attack and loss of part of his essence hardly disturbed Dragon Yan at all. He had already begun to launch his attack from behind Marhyn's right. Screams of warning from her troops died in their throats as Yan tore into the black dragon, his claws ripping apart its soft underbelly, a dragon's most vulnerable spot. Dragon entrails fell to the field below, hissing and burning the grass when they fell. Yan's forked tail sliced into the black dragon's wing, ripping through tendons and causing the dragon to hover precariously for a moment and then fall to the field below...

...Where Yonathan was charging forward at Lithar. Lithar threw his sword at Yonathan who barely dodged it as it cut into his shoulder. It bled, but he did not feel it. Unconsciously, he switched his sword to his other hand and then continued his charge. Unthinking, he rushed forward and brought a slice down diagonally across Lithar's chest, and then another one across the other side. Yonathan spun his sword in a circle, and then came vertically down through Lithar's helmet, stopping when he had reached the evil general's midsection, where he turned his blade and ripped it free on his left, only to double back and slice through Lithar's right leg, whirl in a circle, slice again through his midsection, spin once more in the same direction, and with all his might bring the sword down in a vertical arc, leaving a pile of body parts where the evil general had been. Yonathan looked at his shoulder, which had now begun to tingle. The black, frothy mixture around the wound told him one thing. His vision becoming blurry, Yonathan collapsed from exhaustion and the poison.

Dragon Yan mustered the effort to land, roar in the direction of Marhyn's already fleeing troops, and then he too collapsed into a heap of dragon flesh. His strength would return when the fire-heated air returned to normal and was able to rejoin him, but for now, he just lay there in an exhausted heap. Marhyn's mangled body lay underneath the carcass of her dragon. They had won the day!!

CHAPTER 17

▼

THE PLAN

The plan to make Valena enamored of Derlin was going nowhere. For one thing, Derlin would acquiesce to nothing unless it was absolutely perfect. He had rejected several ideas that Tarthur thought would work, and everyone was becoming frustrated. The planning was, however, a welcome diversion from the military drills that they were subjected to every day. The army was new and green, and King Garkin was making sure that everyone was trained and ready to go. He also wanted to make sure that the troops were well rested, however, so he gave them a few hours a day to do as they wished, relaxing and becoming friends with the people from all around the world. This time is when they planned.

Everyone brought something different to the plan. Tarthur, of course had the magic he had learned from Akin and that which he had learned on his own. He also had much experience with little tricks and subterfuge. Derlin brought an impassioned desire to make the plan perfect and a knowledge of the subject. In the weeks that Cilio's army was engaging Marhyn in the South, Derlin had gotten to know Valena better, in fact, the two had become good friends. Valena seemed to like Derlin very much. Yvonne brought a feminine touch to the planning, and both boys had to admit that they would have been lost without her suggestions on what colors went well together and what words would make a girl's heart beat faster. Yvonne threw herself wholeheartedly into the planning, and it seemed the poor city girl was somehow trying to make up for the childhood that she had never had. She would never admit it to anyone, but secretly she envied Valena. As a child Valena had had dolls and dresses and friends to play with her hair and share secrets with, in short she had had all the things that little girls treasure. And now, she was going to be romantically courted by Derlin. Years of living side by side with reality had numbed Yvonne to prettiness and had robbed her of girlish diversions. Yet she cared for Tarthur very much…

When the day of the plan finally came, Derlin was more nervous than ever. He combed his hair at least a dozen times with a wooden comb, and worried incessantly whether or not he had chosen the right outfit. (He only had two, one dirty and one clean, so no one else could understand his worrying.) By the time he went to pick Valena up for their daily horse ride and learning session, he was practically dripping with sweat from his armpits and various other parts of his body. When he arrived at Dalin's tree, he was barely able to stammer out a greeting and mumble something about Tarthur having to meet with Akin and study some magic, so it would be just the two of them alone. Valena smiled and nodded, and Derlin relaxed slightly.

Elven horses were slightly different than those in the rest of the world, being both smaller and more agile. This was necessary because they had to dart in between the trees without getting stuck. After his weeks of training, however, Derlin had become used to riding them and had even become quite skilled. So it was that Derlin suggested a far away clearing for them to ride to that evening. Valena agreed, and soon they were on their way.

Derlin was nervous throughout the ride, but he began to calm down when Valena wrapped her cool, soft arms around his waist to avoid falling off. He began to wish that the ride would never end.

The Creator apparently had more pressing issues to attend to at the moment, and consequently the ride did end. Derlin dismounted, then grabbed Valena's hand and helped her to dismount. They walked over to the middle of the secluded clearing and Derlin pointed to a strange looking species of flower. "What's that flower," he tried to ask as nonchalantly as possible.

Valena seemed puzzled. "What? I've never seen that flower before." As she went over to take a closer look, the flower opened up and a small roll of parchment was revealed. Valena took the parchment, unfolded it, and read.

To the one whose beauty is endless like the stars,
This night is dedicated to you and you alone
Relax, dear, and enjoy your dinner.

"It must be for you," Derlin said, blushing. Yeah, it was sad, he reflected, but he couldn't come up with any better poetry than that. Oh well, it would have to do.

Valena smiled, confused. "Enjoy your dinner?" she questioned. Derlin turned around and where before there had been only an empty clearing, now there was a tree stump with an elegant white tablecloth spread across it. On the table were the finest foods of the elven kingdom, prepared almost to perfection by Tarthur and Derlin themselves. Accompanying this was a bottle of elderberry wine, a delicacy even to an elven princess. "Oh," Valena gasped. "You picked all of my favorite foods." Derlin had spent the weeks attending on Valena's every word, finding out which dishes she liked, how she liked them prepared, and had made everything exactly to her liking, even down to the right amount of herb seasonings.

The meal was superb. Derlin didn't know it at the time, but Tarthur had even put a little magic into it to taste it. Nevertheless, the boys had never cooked a better feast. They had even had a little help from Suie, one of Valena's maids, who was an excellent cook. Yvonne hid in the shadows and played the violin, adding a perfect touch to the meal. Whenever something was needed, it floated in from the forest and landed perfectly on the table. Two intertwining *Poeloe* plants grew up around where they sat and sprayed their delicious and sensuous aroma into the night. Everything was unfolding perfectly.

After dinner, they lay out in the clearing and watched the stars. "I want to thank you for a wonderful night, Derlin. I will truly remember this night for as long as I live. Yet, I want to ask you something. Why did you go to all this trouble just for me? I have taught you much about my people, but I remain ignorant about your customs. Do you often do this for your friends?"

Derlin waited a moment before replying, letting her words soak in so he could fully appreciate the beauty of her voice. In that moment, crickets began to chirp musically, filling the air with their sweet harmony. That hadn't been part of the plan, but he had to admit it was a nice touch. It appeared that the Big Guy Upstairs might even be helping him out. "Valena," he began. "You must understand that you are a very special friend to me. No, I would not do this for just anyone."

"But why me?" she wondered. "It's not as if I'm…"

Derlin put a finger to his lips and pointed skyward. "Watch there," he whispered.

The stars in the sky glittered in their places for a moment, and then began to change. Some became brighter, some twinkled out of existence, and some began to move. They swirled around and then began to form a shape. It was pointy at the bottom, and soon Valena saw what it would become; Tarthur had made the stars into a heart. Inscribed in the heart were the intertwined names Derlin and Valena. Derlin turned his head towards her and softly but firmly said, "Because I love you, Valena."

Valena collapsed her head in her hands and began to cry. "What's wrong," Derlin said, worried. "What did I do wrong?"

"Nothing," Valena sobbed. "You're the sweetest, nicest, best person I know, and I would love to be with you."

"What's the problem, then?" Derlin asked, confused.

"I'm already betrothed to Hano. We're getting married in six months."

*　　　*　　　*　　　*

The sound of running water that woke him made Yonathan want to go to the bathroom. Even before he opened his eyes, he could sense the peacefulness and tranquility of the place he was in. He did not remember how he had gotten there or why he had come. An overwhelming sacredness permeated the place, and his memory came back in a rush. He hoped Lithar had not defeated him and sent him to the Eternal Vale. Fearfully, he opened his eyes. He was in a room with white walls and a white ceiling. His bed was warm, but a cool breeze came through the window. An oak door was shut on the opposite side of the room. At this point Yonathan remembered that he did not know what the Eternal Vale looked or felt like, so he wouldn't know if he were there or not. It certainly felt like a holy place. Yonathan could take it no longer, though. He had to get up and find an outhouse or at least a tree. As he got to his feet, he felt a dizzying sensation fill his head and force him to sit down again. He eventually made it to the door only to find that it was locked. In desperation, he searched around until he found a bedpan, and then used that. The sound of the trickling of water was all around him. Feeling much better, Yonathan went back to sleep.

When he woke up again a small man came into his room, and informed him that he was not, in fact, dead, but rather very much alive and at the holy spring of Treshin. He had been brought there by advance riders from Cilio's army and had almost died twice in the first week. His wounds had not been bad and had in fact almost healed, but the poison he had been infected with was extremely potent. Yonathan had been very lucky to live. The miracle workers at Treshin were the best in the world, but even they had almost been unable to save Yonathan.

Yonathan had wanted to set out for the king's army in the North as soon as he healed, but he was stopped by another transient resident of Treshin. Kandan Ironsmith had been there ever since the battle of Freeton. He had been charred and burned and his injuries were healing very slowly. So Yonathan had decided to stay and help nurse his friend back to health. All the while, Cilio's regiment advanced northward and the Death Lord readied his troops for a final showdown.

✳   ✳   ✳   ✳

In the days following the failed plan, neither Tarthur nor Yvonne had been able to rouse Derlin from his melancholy. He had stayed in the tree that the elven authorities had loaned to Tarthur and Derlin and he had sulked around inside. The only one who was able to get him to say a few words was Dalin, who had come in on the second day. He had tried to explain things to Derlin; Valena had told him everything. He explained that while he thought Derlin was an extraordinary boy, elven custom required her to wed someone of noble birth.

"Hano is my very dear friend," he explained. Derlin already hated the man. "Hano and I have been friends since childhood. He is very proud of his elven heritage and is a very smart and courageous warrior. I think he will make a fine match with my sister."

"I don't like him already," Derlin countered. "I don't care how courageous he is."

"Derlin," Dalin reminded him softly. "You cannot hate someone for trying to do what you wish to do also. If anything, you should admire his good taste."

Derlin nodded grudgingly. He didn't want to listen to reason, didn't want to believe Dalin, he just felt like hating Hano at the moment. But he knew that Dalin was right.

"I guess later I'll be able to accept him, right now I'm just angry. I do want her to be happy, and I guess she's out of my league anyway, as long as she really loves him…" He trailed off and looked at Dalin for an answer.

The elf prince turned his head away. "She wasn't asked."

After nearly a week of sulking, Derlin was ready to put the incident behind him, at least outwardly, and begin life normally again. News of Cilio's courageous and narrow victory had come from the South, with the army not far behind. Tarthur and Derlin had each shed a tear for Freeton. It seemed strange to the boys that the entire town was gone. It seemed so removed, like if they were to travel south they would find the town intact and all the people still alive. Those people, whom Tarthur and Derlin had only a few months ago saved, were already dead and would never see the world again. It made all view the coming struggle with the Death Lord with apprehension.

Derlin had seen Hano in a chance meeting with the army. They had both walked up to talk to Dalin simultaneously, and the elf prince had no choice but to reintroduce them. Derlin had already met Hano once in Tealsburg, but didn't remember him very well. The coldness in Hano's eyes startled Derlin. He could tell Hano was furious at him for trying what he did. It seemed to Derlin that the whole of the elven kingdom had heard about it. (Actually, Tarthur had only given the illusion of rearranging the stars, and not actually done it, for such a thing was well beyond his fledgling powers; consequently, only a few elves had heard about it, and were keeping it secret. But to Derlin it seemed like everyone knew.) In Hano's eyes and in his voice was more than just anger at one trying for his future wife. Hano cared very much about Valena, that is sure, but while he had a fiery temper, he was at times cold toward her. He tried everything he could, and indeed, he had thought he made her happy.

When he went to see her the day after Derlin's plan, though, he saw something new in her eyes and face. It was beautiful; it was a love of life and a tender joy that he had never been able to unlock. Even though he knew the old elven rules were like iron, and he had a firm lock on wedding Valena, he still felt uneasy and threatened by this boy. It was a fear that he would marry Valena and love her all of his life, but that her love would be for someone else. He could control everything about her, except her heart. Oh, he knew very well that she liked him and respected him, that she would be a faithful wife, do anything he asked of her, even give her life for him, and he knew he would do the same for her. Hano feared nothing more in life than going to sleep with her many years from their wedding day, and seeing her turn away from his body to gaze out at the stars, hoping for a duplication of that feat of so many years ago. It tore him up inside. Hano felt as if this human had come to take everything he had ever worked for, and destroy it.

Accordingly, their meeting was composed of a few unmeant pleasantries, no mention of the most important thing in both of their lives, and cordially worded goodbyes in a bitter tone. Fortunately for them, advance units from the army had already arrived and the bulk of the army would be arriving for the next day or so. They would have a few days for rest and resupplying, and then they would be off to attack the Death Lord's hopefully unmobilized forces and steal the Water Orb. In the business of war, they could forget the personal issues until after.

Finally the rest of the army arrived, and everyone was in Breshen, King Garkin, General Cilio, Zelin, Addyean, Tarthur, Derlin, Yvonne, Dalin, Yan, Sir Terin, and all of the knights. The only one missing was Yonathan, who was still at Treshin. Tarthur and Derlin were praying for his recovery. Once the army arrived, there was much to talk about. Zelin revealed that the Rune Sword had unexpectedly become hot during the time of the battle with Marhyn. A common soldier had said that Yonathan had suddenly pointed the sword at the real Lithar and then charged him. The sword had glowed white-hot. Zelin was extremely interested in this, because it seemed that the Rune Sword was giving some of its power to discern truth to the Light Sword. Such a transfer among weapons of power had been theorized, but had never been observed before. If it had happened, then it meant that they shared something in the way that they were made, and maybe had other similarities as well.

Derlin was armed with the Light Sword, on specific instructions from Yonathan, and General Cilio had agreed. Derlin would be in the front. Tarthur, who very much wanted to fight, would be in the middle, in the most protected spot in the army. He was assigned a contingent of three members of the Guard to be with him at all times. They would be the ones, along with Yan, who would make the assault on Darhyn's castle to recover the Water Orb if they got the chance. Tarthur kept a copy of the spell with him at all times, Zelin kept another copy, and they had left one in Breshen and one at the capital. They had carefully chosen how many copies to make because they couldn't chance one falling into the wrong hands, yet at the same time they didn't want to lose the ones they had.

Derlin went to bid farewell to Valena before they departed. He waited outside her tree until he saw Hano and Dalin exit, and then knowing she would be alone, stepped inside. A cool, woody smell emanated from the room. The door to Valena's room was open, so Derlin knocked softly on the oak as he stuck his head inside. Valena looked up quickly, and Derlin could tell she had been crying.

"Perhaps I should come back later," he said hurriedly, already on his way out.

Valena stopped him with a distant sounding word. "No, I guess it's better to get it over with all at one time. Goodbyes are so horrible sometimes."

"You're going to miss him very much, aren't you?" No one needed to be told who him referred to.

Valena nodded softly. In her sadness, Derlin thought she looked more beautiful than ever and he felt another ache in his heart. "We have known each other since we were children. We were born only one month apart. Ever since we were young, we've known that we were meant for each other."

Derlin nodded back. "It must be very special to know someone your whole life and then share everything with them in marriage."

"When I was a little girl," Valena continued, and Derlin almost thought that she hadn't heard him. "I used to play with Hano and my brother, although he was always older, almost every day. Yet I wondered why it was so empty, I love Hano as a friend, but I never felt something special, like I felt with you that night. I always thought that it was just because I was too young, and later I wondered if such a feeling ever existed. I have read about it, in stories of long ago."

"Oh Derlin," she sighed, looking through his eyes and into his soul. "It felt like my heart melted and I felt lightheaded and it was the most wonderful feeling in the world!" Then she sighed and looked sadly away. "Yet, apparently, it was not meant for me."

"Well," Derlin suggested, "you can always come with me, after the war. We can make our own lives. It's not up to some rules made long ago for no good reason."

Valena was almost mad. "You don't see it, Derlin. There is no way out of it for me. And even if there were, I am not sure I could just leave Hano and run away with you. I don't even know you! How can you say you know me even? You have known me for only a few weeks, yet you think you want to spend the rest of your life with me? There is more than love in a marriage. There is respect, admiration, and security. And traditions are not traditions because they are observed only when convenient. Traditions are traditions because they are never broken. Never."

"It's just a feeling I felt, the first time I saw you, Valena, and if you could feel only a tenth, no a hundredth of what I'm feeling now then I would have no trouble convincing you, you would know it for sure in your heart. Think with your heart, not with your head."

Valena softened a little bit. "Here, Derlin, take with you my ribbon," she said, undoing it from her hair and letting her dark locks fall about her shoulders. "It is green, the color of life. Wear it next to your heart in the battle, and think of me praying for you. Fare thee well, and may life prevail…"

Derlin could not meet Valena's gaze, as she started crying again. He slowly kissed her salty cheek and left, each wondering if it was the last time they would meet.

*   *   *   *

King Garkin was glad that he had General Cilio as head of his army. He feared a lesser man would have been destroyed by Marhyn's well-placed trap in the South. The Dark Lady was extremely cunning, and had almost been able to defeat King Garkin's southern force. If that had happened, she would have had a free attack on the capital, and from there she would have been able to wreak havoc on the whole country. The Death Lord would probably not be as cunning as Marhyn, but he was certainly much stronger and his evil was of a deeper and darker nature. With Marhyn defeated, however, spirits picked up. The king's army would not have to face an alliance of Marhyn and her brother. The commanders had been nervous that Darhyn would try to attack Breshen while Marhyn was attacking from the South, and thus face a split army. But scouts had reported no signs of any movement around Castle Rathskellar. Indeed, the fortress seemed deserted. If Darhyn had just awoken, he would not have much time to gather an army to combat the king's men. If he was still asleep, then Tarthur would have an easy time stealing the Water Orb.

Cilio had come back with his force and had immediately begun to deal with the organizational problems that his return had caused. The king's men had not been idle at Breshen, however, and all that lacked was rest for the troops. After two days, the vast war machine was ready. Cilio had decided to keep the whole army together because he didn't want to take the chance of waking the Evil One. If he was awake, he already knew of their coming, and any advance unit would be quickly defeated, if he was asleep, an advance unit could wake him and give him time to summon forces to his aid. Although, since it had been many months, more than likely he was ready.

On the day the army left, it was raining and cold, even though it was still spring, the time when evil was weakened. This is an inauspicious beginning, Tarthur thought. He had learned the word from Akin and now used it all the time. Tarthur had a limited vocabulary so the big words he did know he used often.

The rain cleared up during the afternoon and the rest of the day passed without much incident. At a normal meandering army pace, the trip to the gates of Castle Rathskellar would have taken almost two weeks, but since every day possibly counted, Cilio hoped to make the trip in shortly over one week. The army was organized into patrols of ten men headed by a patrol leader and an assistant patrol leader. Groups of ten patrols were organized into squadrons with a squadron commander and two assistants. Ten squadrons were grouped together into a battalion of a thousand men, and two battalions together formed a company. The company leaders were the Duke of Walis, the Duke of Breswick, Sir Terin Ironfist, and the fourth had been offered to Addyean, but he had renounced it in favor of a knight named Sir Tali, who was Cilio's pupil and handpicked successor to Cilio himself. Dalin was also in charge of a fifth company comprised solely of elves. The few token forces of other races like dwarves and gnomes were also segregated in the army. Zelin was the leader of a group of magicians, and General Cilio was put in charge of the whole army of slightly less than eleven thousand. Higher than General Cilio was an executive council of King Garkin, the elven king, Warren, Zelin, Cilio, Addyean, Dalin, Yan and Sir Terin. They gave day-to-day control over the army to Cilio but would debate all major decisions.

They traveled until after it was dark, posted sentries, and rested. The next morning, they awoke, and the juggernaut rumbled on.

*   *   *   *

Sir Stephen was almost nauseous with excitement. He had expected to be picked as a patrol leader, but he had also been chosen to be first assistant to his squadron commander. None of the men in his patrol were knights, and none of them had ever fought before either. There were three farmers, two blacksmiths, an unemployed bum that they had picked off the streets of the capital, three merchants, and Sir Stephen himself. He had had a hard and frustrating time teaching them how to handle their weapons properly during their extended stay in Breshen, but eventually he had taught them passable skills. He had become good friends with his men, and he knew that they trusted him with their lives.

His squadron commander was none other than Sir Undbar, the gruff old knight he had known since he began his training with the Royal Knights. Sir Stephen admired him and Sir Undbar took him into confidence on all matters of the squadron. If Sir Undbar fell, it would be up to Sir Stephen to assume control of the hundred men. Although it was less than one percent of the whole army, Sir Stephen took his responsibility very seriously.

The glory of war burned inside Sir Stephen as his horse jostled him up and down during their journey. He reminisced over the stories he had been inundated with since he was a child. He was already on his way to becoming the greatest knight that ever lived; he would help destroy darkness wherever it reared its ugly head. He would chase the forces of shadow from the land and the evil ones would quake in fear when they saw him approaching. He could see it already. In the horrible conflict, the forces arrayed against his army would be immense, but through courageous acts, Sir Stephen and his patrol would hold fast, and if he had to take command of the squadron, well, a finer squadron would not be found on that day of bloodshed. It was time for the men to stand up and be counted, to find what they were made of. He knew his patrol would stand with him.

They stopped for twenty minutes at noon to rest and eat lunch. The hot sun was already beginning to beat down on them mercilessly, and there was no shade or cover of any kind in the Savannah Plain. They had left the last source of fresh water behind them a day ago, and now were on the rations that each had and what was brought by the supply wagons. One of the blacksmiths wiped the sweat from his forehead as he took a swig from his canteen.

"This weather's just like the forges back home, eh?" Sir Stephen greeted.

"Don'ta remind me of home," He said in the gruff and heavily accented voice Sir Stephen had gotten used to. "This placea's more like hell. Home is a placea of love and warmth. Anda her." With this, he opened a clasp of a necklace he wore around his neck. Inside was a magic image of a little girl, barely five years old. The girl danced a small jig and then spoke, pleading. "Daddy, daddy, come play with me."

Sir Stephen was touched. He had no family in the world except his parents, whom he did not know very well.

"Aye, dona think I'ma complain'. I know why weare heare. I see the need to kill that bastard. But I dinna say'd like it."

The man took one look at the glittering image, and the girl spoke again. "Daddy, daddy, come play with me."

The man nodded, "I willa darlin. Just as soon as the bad things are gone. It'll be like before, you and mommy and I will play all day long." With that, he snapped closed the clasp and tucked it back into his shirt.

Sir Undbar received word to resume marching, called it out to Sir Stephen, and the army moved on.

*   *   *   *

Tarthur was using the trip to get to know his bodyguards better. He did not know that they were part of the Guard, or even what the Guard was, but from the first moment he met them, Tarthur was impressed. They showed him all sorts of neat tricks and sleight of hand that made Tarthur gape. He liked these guys already.

There was Gyeun, a half-elf who was like the leader. He always seemed open to whatever Tarthur might tell him and was always anxious to talk. Next was a man named Thon, a man almost as big as Yonathan but much more agile. The last was Youin, a girl who Tarthur thought might be pretty. He wasn't sure, of course, since he had given up looking long ago. He had been beaten so many times by Yvonne that his body now had an involuntary reflex that made him look away from whatever girl he saw. All three seemed to know all about Tarthur, or at least whatever he had ever told to anyone else seemed to wind up in their brains somehow. And they never seemed to forget anything. They even knew about the incident with the pie, and about several other disciplinary incidents that had occurred back in Krendon. Only, they knew the wrong versions, so Tarthur assumed that they had been talking to the baron. He therefore took great pains to straighten them out on some things.

One example was the time that Tarthur and Derlin had decided to pretend that they were knights out of old stories. No one could ever accuse the boys of not having an imagination, but they could not imagine everything. They would need swords to play at this game. So they had just meandered over to Baron Erc-rilla's house and found his sword neatly packed up with the rest of his provisions including food and clothes. The only logical explanation was that the wise baron had obviously known that he was coming and since he had set all of his things out in one place, he apparently wanted Tarthur to help himself not only to his sword but to some food as well. (Actually, he was packing for his hunting party that was leaving the following morning.) Tarthur and Derlin had been hesitant at first to just take the food and sword, but as Tarthur pointed out, they really had no choice and had better obey their proper legal authority. Tarthur shuddered to think what the baron would do if he came back and found that Tarthur had not taken any of the things he had spent so much time getting ready for him in a nice and neat pile. It was good to know that they had a ruler who was so concerned with the safety of their town as to loan out his personal sword for military train-ing of the less fortunate townsfolk. The food might even rot if left out too long.

When the situation was analyzed from this obviously true and rational view-point, it was downright absurd that that old cranky knight Erso had found Tarthur and Derlin, innocently practicing their fighting skills, and brought them to the baron. The baron, much to the surprise of any objective observer, was actually angry. He had probably been drinking, or under the spell of some ghastly trickster gnome, (they abounded in that part of the world, living only to cause mischief. Tarthur himself had been blamed more than a few times for things that they had caused) so that he had misinterpreted his own magnanimous act.

Tarthur and Derlin had been sent to bed without dinner, and he was to miss breakfast the next morning. That night was when the dream had come…the dream that had started all this. Tarthur looked around him, amazed. Thousands of people were together, were risking their lives, all because of his dream. He felt suddenly powerful, for it was his dream that had set everything into motion, and then helpless. He was being caught up it events that were sweeping him away just as the water wave had swept away those evil things in his dream. He felt as if the dream was so long ago, centuries ago, or even as if he was hearing about it happening to someone else. He just hoped he would be able to use the Water Orb when the time came.

Gyeun chuckled when he heard Tarthur's story. Tarthur had only known these people for a short time, but he already felt like they were his friends.

*   *   *   *

On the fifth day they caught sight of Castle Rathskellar. Derlin, Dalin, Yan, and Tarthur were the only ones who had seen Marhyn's castle in the South, and even they gaped at the awesomeness of the Death Lord's fortress. Even seen from far away it was terribly forbidding. The rest of the army was totally unprepared. Fortunately, they were still far away, so it did not look as terrible as it really was. They could see no sign of any evil forces, yet they could feel the evil. The heat waves that beat down over the king's army were relentless, and everyone was uncomfortable. During the night, the desert cooled off and water froze. Men huddled in blankets to keep warm, as there was nothing to build fires with in this land where nothing lived. Morale was low but the men were still loyal, though talk to the effect of "Let's do this and then get home" was heard throughout the ranks.

After they caught sight of the fortress Cilio doubled the sentry, but it didn't really matter because no one got much sleep anymore. They traveled most of the day and night because the men weren't likely to get much rest in the desolate land. They had good and well protected supply lines coming from all over the world to Breshen and then to the army along their route. The wagons were plentiful and kept the army well stocked.

They slowed up on the seventh day because they were almost there, and no one wanted to begin the attack at night. On daybreak of the eighth day they stood on the hill overlooking the castle. Men tightened their armor, took swigs of water, and stretched out their muscles in anticipation. As of yet there was no sign of anything moving within the castle. The army's plan was simple, to go in and destroy any opposition. If there was none, they would search the castle until they found the Orb and alert their commanders who would alert Tarthur's group.

Tarthur was ready with his group of Gyeun, Thon, Youin, and Yan. They were to go in on foot with the army and then Tarthur would try to navigate them through the fortress to where he had found the Water Orb and the Death Lord. From his dream, he remembered nothing more than that he had taken alternating right and left turns. Yan was nervous; he would have to fend off Darhyn if they encountered him until Tarthur found the Orb.

Cilio rode back and forth through the ranks screaming out a speech he had prepared earlier. It told of bravery, of history, and of the chance these men gathered here today had to make the world safe from evil. Those few had already conquered the evil to the South, now only one remained. "We might die today," he extolled. "Yet how many people can say they have truly lived? Is a safe, boring life on a farm truly living? Some would pity us who have to bear hardship and who will defeat the evil, for there is no doubt we will win. But I say, let us pity them! They will never feel the blood rush through their veins, feel adrenaline, feel the excitement of war, the thrill of victory. Thousands of years from now they will look back upon this day with wonder and amazement. Ours is not to listen to tales of bravery and great deeds done by others in some far away land, once upon a time. Ours is to stand up and fight and leave it to others to listen to legends written about us! We know the quickening of the heart, the turning of the stomach, which I am sure all of you feel now. We know what it is to be alive! We know what it is to be men! We will show Darhyn what the men of Daranor are made of!!!"

Cilio was shouting now, galloping back and forth on his horse and filling the men with his excitement. "For king!" He screamed.

"For king!" They echoed.

"For good!" He shouted.

"For good!" They echoed again.

"To live!!" He screamed, thrusting his sword in the air and then leveling it toward the hated fortress.

"TO LIVE!!!" They screamed, drawing their weapons and charging down the hill and into the still empty fortress of the hated Death Lord.

CHAPTER 18

▼

THE TRAP

A bone chilling sound echoed from within. The men were almost at the gates when they magically swung open and a hundred skull knights came marching out. Creatures of every size and shape burst from the battlements and turrets. A skull knight on horseback led the columns of the undead. A chill filled Tarthur when he remembered the terrible time in the forest when Yan and Yonathan had saved Tarthur and Derlin from the skull knights and the reaper. But now there were a hundred of them. The king's men would have trouble killing the unkillable.

Tarthur's group was to wait and see if the king's men could obtain a victory before starting off into the fortress. If the enemies were too strong to be defeated easily, Tarthur's group was to wait until they had a good opening and then break through. His stomach was all in knots and Tarthur felt like vomiting. It was possible that he would decide the fate of the battle this day.

Horrible things kept swarming out of the dark fortress. Derlin was even surprised that all of them could have fit in it before. The lines were only about a hundred yards apart now, and they were closing fast. Derlin was a patrol leader and he ordered his group to follow him as he charged into a five-headed monster. The monster flung up his claw but Derlin sliced his Light Sword through it and down through its arm, cutting it in half lengthwise. The creature didn't seem to notice, and it swung its other claw at Derlin. Derlin ducked, and brought his

Light Sword sweeping across the monster's legs. The hideous being collapsed and the other members of Derlin's patrol were quick to finish it off.

Zelin's magicians had immediately scanned the battlefield and decided that the skull knights were the biggest threat. The magicians closed in on them and began to attack. A black clad magician brought his hands up out of his long, billowing cloak and sent a burst of fire that blew off the heads of several skull knights in a row. Another magician folded his hands intently in his cloak, murmured a few words for a second, and then brought his hands up and faced them towards the decapitated heads. Immediately, they were encased in three foot thick ice, and useless to their bodies, which were already beginning to fall down. But the ice was melting in the hot sun.

Zelin himself stuck out his hand, which for a moment quivered as a fireball began to grow in his palm, then abruptly straightened his elbow and sent the ball of fire shooting out into the air. It split into four pieces, each of which went directly for a skull knight. The fires hit them square in the chest, exploding and sending fragments of their bones for miles around. It would be some time before those got back together.

The battle was going much worse for Dalin and his company. Hideous monsters were killing the elves whose bows and arrows, even when dipped in neurotoxins, were not having much effect. A grim looking giant charged toward Dalin. Dalin's friend rushed out to meet him. The giant stopped where he was, and his eyes turned red and began to glow.

Two red streams shot out of the giant's eyes and into Dalin's friend, who screamed in agony. He kept screaming, and Dalin saw that the streams of red were not killing him, only burrowing around in his insides until they had caused all the pain they could; only then would they finish the job. Dalin tried to break a stream of red with his sword, but it was useless and only caused his friend to cry out all the more. The frightened elf looked up into his prince's eyes and the message was crystal clear. A solitary tear running down his cheek, Dalin raised his sword and in one stroke finished it.

The elf prince turned angrily toward the giant, who was only laughing. Dalin rushed forward, dodging to the side when the giant fired again. Dalin brought his sword up against the creature's thigh, and then sliced it back across his ribs. The giant hunched over in pain then reached up and knocked Dalin across the face with a backhand slap. Dalin reached up to feel his face and he felt his own blood running from his nose. He turned to look at the creature whose eyes once again began to flash red...

Before it could fire, a red-cloaked elf jumped up from behind it and smashed his hammer down on the creature's skull. Black and green slime oozed out and then Hano drew his sword and poked both of the creature's eyes out. Then he rained down blow after blow and destroyed the creature's skull. The two red eyes jumped around, looking for a new place to live. Hano squashed them with his hammer repeatedly, until they were nothing.

"Let it flow through you, Dalin," he said. "It's the only way to beat them. Hate makes you strong." Before Dalin could reply, Hano was gone to another area of the fray, destroying evil wherever he went.

As the battle wore on past midday, Cilio knew he must do the one thing he had hoped to avoid. His men were tired, hungry, soaked with their own sweat and blood, and the ferocity of the evil army's attack had totally surprised them. Darhyn had known for quite some time that they were coming. They had walked into a trap.

But it was not a trap in which they were helpless. They still had Tarthur and the king had the Power of Earth on their side. Although, King Garkin could not use it until Darhyn used his Power of Fire, and perhaps the Power of Water as well. It was just too dangerous to send Tarthur. The enemy lines were too thick, and even with his escort of the Guard, he could never even hope to break through.

So Cilio would order the retreat, they were too weakened in the Savannah Plain anyway. Evil was very strong here, and the heat weakened the King's soldiers. When they retreated, every step they took away from the heart of evil weakened their enemy. If they had to make it to Breshen, they would be able to use the trees for cover. Hopefully, they would not have to go that far. Retreating would spread out Darhyn's army enough as to allow Tarthur and his escort to pass through undetected and have a shot at Castle Rathskellar. Cilio knew that he must order the retreat soon or risk fighting at night, one thing that he desperately did not want to do, especially here.

The king's men fell back orderly, not so quickly as to break lines, and not so slowly as to make no progress whatsoever. Whenever a group of monsters would pursue too quickly and cut themselves off from the support of their comrades, they would be soon cut to pieces by the king's army. The farther away the army got, the faster they went, and soon they had achieved complete separation from the Death Lord's forces. Cilio soon gave the order for his men to eat and rest and sleep if they could. It was just after seven o'clock in the evening, and the general told the men to rest quickly, for he anticipated another attack after dark.

In this he was not disappointed, for shortly after the setting of the sun the evil ones came again. They were more organized now, and they were starting to use their powers in combination to achieve deadly results. In this new battle, one hideous creature would scream forth in some ancient and guttural language, freezing whoever heard it; helpless, the king's soldiers would be easily finished off.

The battle began when a group of the swifter members of monsters: centaurs, flying creatures and the like, cloaked themselves with darkness and swept two hundred yards out to the right of Cilio's forces, to try to attack their backs. Cilio didn't see them, but Zelin detected magic being used, so Cilio sent Sir Terin's company to deal with them. They were now fighting back to back with the rest of the king's forces.

Next came a charge to the front, which was met by the unified force of the allies. Darhyn had put some of his deadliest monsters up there. Some, once killed, would turn into acid and burn anyone within fifteen feet. Others would explode, and still others would turn to stone with the attacker's blade still within their bodies, leaving them weaponless. In this way, they continued to inflict damage even after they were killed.

The executive council was having a tough time. Firstly, they could have no reasonable estimate of Darhyn's strength. His army was composed of mercenaries, goblins, trolls, orcs, and many members of smaller races like black dwarves, mountain gnomes, dragons, and snakes. But in addition to these that were alive and could be killed normally, he had his host of skull knights who would do his bidding and would continue to pursue the king's forces forever. The real problem, however, were the creatures that Darhyn had summoned from unknown realms. Zelin had explained that there were other known worlds where Darhyn could have gone and recruited monsters for his work, but interworld travel such as this was difficult. Zelin himself knew for certain that there were three of these other worlds, up to ten had been theorized, but it was possible that there were some that had been discovered by Frehu or Darhyn and known only to them. As if this wasn't enough, Darhyn was also capable of creating creatures to do his bidding, as he had created the skull knights. This process was slow, but no one knew how long Darhyn had been awake, or even how long he had been preparing.

The other problem that they faced was that of the command of the opposing army. Zelin had suggested that since Darhyn would be weakened when he left the heart of evil in the Savannah Plain, he was probably just sending out his mind in a remote control of his army. He would be sending it through three or four generals who would be responsible for executing his commands. Cilio asked if it would be possible to kill these generals, and thus confuse the army. Zelin hastily replied that they would be some of the toughest monsters to kill, and if they did kill them, Darhyn would just devolve the control onto someone else.

Sir Terin's group was having a tough time with Darhyn's cavalry, they were just too quick. Zelin himself had stayed in the front, but he had sent Polu, another magician who was his second in charge, to the rear with half of the magicians to help out. Yan was also back there to aid Sir Terin. Polu had immediately ordered his magicians to send fire to burn off the darkness spell that Darhyn was using to hide his men. It worked somewhat, but since it was night they could still only make out faint shadows of the monsters they were fighting.

Sir Undbar's squadron was a member of Sir Terin's company, dealing with the attack on the rear of the main army. Sir Stephen heard a sound in front of him and yelled for his men to dive, swords in the air. They did and soon felt contact with their outstretched blades. Sir Stephen rolled, and saw a huge leathery bird lying injured on the ground. His patrol stood motionless for a second and then remembered to rush forward and finish it off.

Sir Terin's company was holding, but it was becoming tight. Horses galloped through the lines, their riders cutting down men right and left. A huge fleshy ball of spikes came rolling around and bouncing into men, sticking them and rolling free to kill again. Sir Undbar charged the nightmare, which changed course to meet its attacker. The ball rolled forward, and then jumped up into the old knight's face. Sir Undbar swung his sword across its body and then spun out of the way. The ball skidded in the dirt, kicking up a big cloud of dust, and then jumped up to attack Sir Undbar once again. This time, the gruff old knight jabbed his sword straight forward, into the creature. The creature quivered, then shot out all of its spikes in every direction, sending three into the one who had killed it. The valiant old knight gasped once, and then breathed his last.

The battle on the front was going much better, but there again the evil ones were combining their strength to cause enormous damage. The skull knights spread out and would begin to attack in the front lines, where the fighting was thickest. They could afford to take unlimited damage, and as soon as they could secure a breach in the king's lines, the other creatures would rush in. In this way, the dark ones gained valuable strategic positions without the loss of life.

Hano was fighting like crazy, and even a few of the creatures made of fear itself were beginning to shy away from him. His emotions were overwhelming him, but not to the exclusion of his reason. He rushed forward right into the path of a skull knight, then hacked off its arm with one blow of his sword. The skull knight calmly reached down to pick up his limb, but before he could the red-cloaked elf bent down and grabbed the severed arm at the shoulder, then using all of his force slapped the knight with his own arm so hard that his head fell off. The knight grimly walked over to pick up his head as Hano turned to meet one of the stone creatures. They were fat little dwarves, with yellow putrid teeth and reeking breath. Hano had an idea. He sliced at the monster with his sword enough to wound it, but not kill it. The creature screamed in pain and attempted to hit Hano with a hammer that had spikes sticking out all over it, but Hano easily dodged the slow and sloppy attack. Then, he jabbed the skull knight's severed arm into the creature's wound, turning and twisting it until he could feel the life leaving the creature, feel its blood beginning to harden. Soon, he was dead, and the skull knight's arm was encased in the granite. The skull knight, now without his arm, began to try and reattach himself, but it was futile. His arm was now a part of the stone.

Hano screamed out the plan to the elves, and Dalin sent a messenger to tell the rest of the army immediately. Kill the stone creatures with the skull knights and they will be as good as dead. Before this second battle, General Cilio had hoped that his forces would at least be able to fight evenly with the dark ones, but this estimate was proving woefully inadequate. At night, deep within the heart of the Savannah Plain, they could not hope to defeat the evil ones. Yes, they could force a roughly even battle where almost everyone would die, and that they had a small chance of winning, but Cilio was not ready to risk that. That was just what the Death Lord wanted, and Cilio would not play into Darhyn's hands further. They would retreat until they could spread out the forces enough for Tarthur and his group to slip through. Then they could keep falling back and slowly destroying Darhyn's army as it overextended itself. The strength of Darhyn's army had radically altered Cilio's plan. Now, he was content to just fall back and create time. For this he did not need to sacrifice a large number of his men. If Tarthur and the Guard failed, then things would be different, but they could reasonably hope to fall back as far as Breshen without suffering any real damage. But to begin the strategic retreat they would need to defeat the unit at the back of their army, and cover the front. Cilio sent a rider to relay orders to the Duke of Walis to have his company join that of Sir Terin in the rear. He also sent orders for Dalin and his elves to withdraw into the safety of the interior and ready their longbows. The elves were famous for their archery. The king also had a battalion of a thousand archers, and he sent word for these also to be ready on the flanks with arrows in string to begin the retreat.

Chaos reigned in the rear of the army. Men had been cut off from their support all around and the battle had turned into little more than a wild free for all. Men had to be careful to avoid hitting people on their own side, such was the confusion and darkness all around. Sir Stephen hadn't seen Sir Undbar fall personally, but one of his patrol members had told him. Now was his chance. Sir Stephen was the leader of a wrecked squadron of one hundred men.

Sweat rolled down his face and into his eyes, blinding him until he wiped it away with his forearm. Sir Stephen couldn't think of anything else to do, so he got up on his horse and screamed for his squadron to rally to him. The clamor and overall confusion of the battle made him seem like a tiny ant calling out for them to hear him. It was not working, and if he didn't do something soon, the whole back of the army was in danger of collapsing. Frantically, the young knight looked around until he spotted a magician. Sir Stephen spurred his horse onward to the man and told him to make the signal. The magician understood, and sent a symbol of the king's crown made out of fire into the sky over Sir Stephen's head. The signal burned brightly, illuminating the area around him.

The other soldiers knew that they badly needed a rallying point, so they had been looking for one. They flocked to Sir Stephen, who massed the king's soldiers together and then used them to attack Darhyn's monsters as a unit. Monsters that could kill a solitary human over and over again without being injured now found a much different story facing five or ten at once. Sir Stephen led his men onward through courage and even a little skill, and soon he saw the red and gold banner of the Duke of Walis come up to join his squadron. With the reinforcement of two thousand men, they were able to finally destroy enough of Darhyn's rear attack force for Cilio to order the archers in place on the flank. They had arrows dipped in powerful neurotoxins, which would at least slow the most ferocious monsters. The archers were ready to cut to pieces any of Darhyn's monsters who were stupid enough to try to pursue King Garkin's rapidly fleeing army. The army went backwards at a sort of jog, which was much too fast for the skull knights. By morning, they were far enough away to rest for a few hours, before they spotted Darhyn's monsters in the distance again. They hastily retreated the whole of the second day, slept a few hours at dusk, and retreated again during the night, then slept and prepared again at daylight. Cilio decided to let the men rest until Darhyn's forces were spotted again, then to begin another battle. During the retreat from that battle was when he would try to let Tarthur and his escort slip through.

The king's men were tired, and the rest was badly needed. Fortunately, their fatigue was not compounded with lack of food or water, which were both plentiful. Their supply lines were holding well, and the king's soldiers were refreshed by hearty meals of bread, meat, potatoes, cheeses, wine, fish, and rice. They had plenty of water, but it was made hot by the relentless sun that beat down on them. They were well armed, had plenty of arrows and other single use commodities, and would have the advantage of defending their position. This was a welcome advantage indeed. Cilio decided to use this opportunity for a small attack when the battle started.

At two o'clock in the afternoon Darhyn's forces were spotted in the distance again, and by three o'clock they were ready to attack. Tarthur thought he had been nervous on the first day they were about to attack Darhyn, but it was nothing compared to what he felt now. He was with Gyeun, Thon, Youin, Yan, and Derlin. General Cilio had just told them to be ready, that they would be in a charge on the wing of the army, who would die to let them through. People were going to die, just so Tarthur could have a chance. When they were deep within Darhyn's army, they were to continue to slip through the rest and walk until they got to Castle Rathskellar, there to search for the Orb. Derlin was not going with them. The more people they brought, the easier they could be caught. So it was just the five of them. And Tustor, of course, but he could only send out his mind to Tarthur infrequently and then for short duration. The whole army was counting on the five of them. He felt as if the army was making a big mistake placing their hopes in him. What could he do against the Death Lord himself?

Derlin looked at Tarthur, and neither of them needed to say what they were both feeling. They knew that there was a good chance that this day would be the last time they saw each other. Derlin was going to tell Tarthur about his responsibility, about Yonathan, about everyone counting on him—but one look into Tarthur's face told him this was unnecessary. Looking at the person he had known all his life, Derlin saw something unfamiliar. Tarthur had become a man. Tarthur, looking into Derlin's eyes, saw the same. They were ready.

Words didn't come easily to either. "Hey," Derlin said putting a firm hand on Tarthur's shoulder. "Take care of yourself. We've been through too much together. We got to get one more thing to show Morty up with."

Tarthur reached forward and hugged Derlin, then separated and slapped his friend on the shoulder. "Hey, let's kick some ass!"

The battle started much in the way of the others, with the evil ones charging the middle of Cilio's line. Cilio had anticipated this though, and archers were already ready to cut the skull knights to pieces with their arrows. The magicians had given the archers a powder to place on the ends of their arrows that exploded when it reached their target. Exploded skull knights took hours to reassemble themselves. Next came some ferocious monsters, with projectile weapons of their own. These forced the archers to fall back and be replaced with soldiers with shields. Soon, the lines had closed and the archers shed their now useless bows for weapons that worked better in close combat.

When the lines had been closed for about half an hour, Cilio sent his charge on the left wing. In a normal battle, the charge would serve to cause Darhyn to divert some of his strength from the front to the sides and thus give the allies a greater chance to break through in the middle. But this charge's main purpose was to get Tarthur and his escort safely across enemy lines. Tarthur and his group were in the middle, protected by a wall of soldiers. They pushed forward through fierce fighting, and it seemed as if Darhyn's monsters were having the advantage. After fifteen minutes they had pushed two hundred meters into the enemy lines when a group of fifteen ogres and a midsize dragon came up to stop their advance. Tarthur saw men dying all around him, and when he looked at Yan, he knew that this was the time. Gyeun gave the signal, and they quickly rushed past their protection. Tarthur woefully noted that it would be the last protection they would have for quite some time.

$$* \qquad * \qquad * \qquad *$$

She wished Yvette were here. Yvonne had been able to busy herself with organizing the supply wagons going to the front, and nothing helped the days creep by more than having something constructive to do. Still, her anxiety was overwhelming her. She felt so restless; she wanted to be out there doing something. Here the greatest events of her lifetime were transpiring, and she was sitting around organizing food and weapon shipments. It wasn't as if she had no right to be involved, either, especially since her boyfriend was one of the main people involved! It was funny to call him that. While she had admired boys before, Yvonne had never had a real boyfriend. She smiled when she thought of Tarthur, and inwardly cursed herself for submitting to him before he had left. Against her violent objections, he had made her promise that no matter what she would stay in Breshen and away from the fight. There were only two people in the world that could make Yvonne promise something like that, and actually keep it. That was all the more reason she wished her twin were there to comfort her, and to knock some sense into her about the whole Tarthur issue. If she didn't know better, she would probably say that she was in love! Imagine, the head of the Guild of Thieves in love, just like some ordinary teenager. What was the world coming to?

At least she had been able to get permission to accompany the next set of shipments to the outskirts of the forest. She would honor her promise and not set foot outside the trees, but she could still be as close to the front as possible. They weren't too informed about the progress of the war, but from what she had been able to determine, the Death Lord had hidden in his castle preparing an army, and the king's men had walked into a trap. The army was losing ground every day, but destroying a substantial part of the Dark One's forces. She supposed it was only a matter of time before the king's men won.

While she only stayed back because Tarthur had asked her, as long as she was staying, she had agreed to a favor from Derlin. Even after Valena had revealed that she was betrothed to Hano, he still cared very much for her. She had a brother, fiancé, and father all out in the front lines leading their people. Yvonne had grown up without any of these, but she knew what it would be like for Valena to lose them. The elf princess's life would be shattered. Of course, Yvonne reflected sadly, if we lose this war and our army is all killed, everyone's life would be shattered, and all life as they knew it would be destroyed. So Derlin had asked Yvonne to check in on Valena periodically and make sure the stress of having so many people who were so close to her in constant and grave danger wasn't more than she could bear.

Valena for her part was handling her duties well, but the fatigue showed on her face. Elven society did not permit women to be rulers, and consequently Valena had never received the training in the arts of organization and commanding others that were required of a leader. The head of the elven nation in Breshen was an elf named Geriyo, but Valena found herself taking over many of his duties. He was only too willing to let her, as he had more than enough to do. Even though she had never received any formal training, always being around the leaders of her people had taught Valena more than a few things.

So it was that Yvonne found Valena in her favorite spot. She was sitting on a log and watching a small stream that wound its way through the forest. The hideaway was a little apart from the main section of Breshen where most of the elves lived, and was very secluded and very pretty. As Yvonne felt the calm that permeated the place, she knew why Valena came here. Yvonne knew the elf princess came here almost every day, but Valena had never seen her follow her.

Yvonne felt a little awkward, but then went to sit next to her. Valena did not act startled as Yvonne had expected, and almost seemed to not to notice Yvonne's presence. Valena knelt gazing into the river.

Suddenly, she spoke. "Why do we do it?"

Now Yvonne was a little startled, thought for a minute, and realized she didn't have the foggiest idea. "Why do we do what?"

Valena turned to look at her. Yvonne could tell that she was indeed beautiful. "Live. It's like this stream here. Look at it. We're leaves in the stream. We start out up there," she pointed to a pool that formed the beginning of the stream. "Then we fall, and we keep going down steadily. But we never go according to ourselves. The river is always driving us. Sometimes, we go slowly for a long time and we think that is normal. Then," she said, pointing to a place where the water was beginning to pick up speed. "We get hurled along faster and faster, unaware of even where we are going, let alone why. And it only leads to that, where we all fall and everything ends up in a mess and those that we love who were around us before are scattered forever, and some not even floating anymore." She finished by pointing to a little five foot waterfall. "And nothing is ever the same again."

Yvonne took a deep breath and shrugged. "Perhaps we do it for the ride. I mean, we may be going fast, but the sights and the scenery are worth it. And we do it because we don't know what's ahead. Perhaps a shake up can even be good. For those of us at the bottom half of society, if God decided to repartition everything, we might make out better after the fall."

"Not me," Valena sighed softly. "I have everything I could want, money, power, a loving family, a faithful husband-to-be…" She trailed off slowly.

"Then maybe we do it for the uncertainty," Yvonne countered. "Maybe because we don't know what is coming up around the riverbend."

"But we do," Valena said sadly. "The end is always the same for all of us. We all live, eat, breathe, sleep, and then we die. We all know what the end is going to be."

"We may know the end, but we don't know the journey. We don't know which way we will go. If my leaf brushes up against someone else way back there and he floats away, how will I know if I will meet him again or not? Maybe our paths will cross again later in life, and maybe not. But that is one thing I don't know."

Valena thought about it for a moment. "And what if your leaves cross, and you don't want to chance meeting again somewhere down the stream?"

"Ahh," Yvonne said, understanding. "Then you must catch the other leaf, and bind them together. That way, you float as one entity. That's really the only way."

"You brought some strange friends with you," Valena changed the subject. "How did you meet them, anyway?"

"Well, you see, there I was one day standing at the fountain, and this boy came up to me talking about how pretty I was. So, I was a little bit flattered, but then I decided to try to steal some money from him. Believe it or not, I stole ten thousand gold pieces off of him! Then, my twin sister and I fooled him into thinking he was chasing only one thief and he never got me back for that. Well, that's almost the way it happened. Or rather, that's the way that Tarthur would tell it. It was a good plan, though. Yvette and I are like this." Yvonne finished by crossing her fingers.

Valena chuckled. Of course, Derlin had told her the real story before, but she liked to hear Yvonne tell it. She could see a lot of Tarthur in her. "Yes, I know what it's like to be so close to someone that you can feel them, even though they are far away. I know my family is okay; I can sense their life-forces burning strong, but I'm still worried."

Yvonne understood. Somehow, she knew Yvette was all right as well. Although, she was back in the capital, so she wasn't in any more danger than usual.

Yvonne started as Valena suddenly cried out. She reached forward and grabbed the elven princess, whose eyes were full of fear, looking for a second like some wild animal. Yvonne followed the direction her shaky finger pointed, straight for the waterfall.

*   *   *   *

Back in the council, they were hurriedly debating whether to continue to fall back to Breshen or not. Sir Terin had suggested they stay and fight this one day, and Cilio was in agreement. The monsters would be expecting another hasty retreat and would not be fighting cautiously. It gave the allies a chance to possibly hold them on that day. The elven king, however, was suggesting that they hold out indefinitely, out of concern for his homeland. He did not want even the fringes of his beloved forest to be destroyed.

"We must fight today and then we will retreat," Cilio was saying. "I don't wish to see Breshen destroyed either, but it is better a few trees than lives. We need to give Tarthur time, and they are too strong for us."

"You wouldn't understand," the elven king responded sadly, "but trees are lives."

"Yes," continued Hano, always quick to defend his revered leader. "And we can beat them here. Many will die, yes, but it is a sacrifice we must make. I myself will be the first to die to save our homeland."

"*I have an idea*," came the voice. Everyone was startled. The voice was coming from Warren but it had lost its annoying nasal tone. His eyes were flashing red.

Before anyone else reacted, Addyean had plunged a dagger into his back. Warren seemed unaffected. *"I said, I have an idea, why don't we all die?!"*

Zelin shot a barrage of ice from his fingertips into Warren, who seemed to be struggling with his body. The ice hit him and his eyes flashed back normal again. "What are you doing?" he cried frantically. "This wasn't part of our deal. Master, please!" He was breathing haggardly now, terrified of what was happening to him. "Please, no...NO!!!" Warren's screaming was slowly being replaced as his eyes began to flash red again. Now, his body was beginning to melt and be replaced by leathery thick skin. Addyean's dagger clanged uselessly on the ground. Warren's skin began to stretch and stretch until it snapped, covering the emerging monster with a warm putrid ooze.

The council was staring at the figure in horror. It spoke with the Death Lord's voice.

"So, you have come to defeat me??? I will destroy your army. I will destroy your boy. He has something I need and my minions will sweep over the land destroying wherever they go. I grow off your death."

With this, the monster who had taken over Warren's body charged forward for General Cilio. Zelin threw himself in front and sent another barrage of ice into it. This barrage knocked him backwards but he stood up again and charged forward straight for the elven king. Hano stood in his way, defending his king. The monster swung a huge slimy paw at Hano, who sliced at it with his sword. The monster's paw sent the elf sprawling, however. Unobstructed, he ambled forward and with a huge mouth full of razor sharp teeth bit the elven king in half.

Zelin had now had time to weave a powerful spell, and he stretched out his hands, sending a net that engulfed the monster who struggled wildly to break free. Zelin had designed the spell, however, so the net would become stronger the more the captive struggled. Soon, the creature toppled to the ground where, enraged and tear-filled, Dalin and Hano jumped on it and began to destroy it. Sir Terin, Addyean, and King Garkin even helped get some blows in. By the time it was done, the monster crumpled into dust and then disappeared. The battle still raged on in the front.

"What was that?" Cilio hurriedly called out to Zelin.

"Darhyn took over Warren's body and sent one of his monsters to kill us and throw our army into confusion," the wizard replied. "This is horrible..."

The rest looked puzzled, then Zelin finished. "The spell to do this kind of transformation requires great power and a willing subject. It means..."

Sir Terin could finish from here. "It means, Darhyn is near the peak of his power, Warren has been a traitor for a long time, and he's waiting for Tarthur."

"And the worst part is," Zelin had recovered from the initial shock. "Darhyn doesn't have the Water Orb spell. He can't use the Orb now, but if he steals the spell from Tarthur he can. If they fail then the whole war is lost. All our hopes depend on them now."

*   *   *   *

Yan surrounded the party with a cloaking spell but they still needed to move quickly. The lines of monsters were not thick and the diversionary charge had worked well. Most of the monsters were concentrating on the enemy in front of them and did not notice the tiny cloud of dust that was Tarthur and his escort. The other four had formed a ring around Tarthur. Once, a creature sensed the magic, and had turned to rush at them. As Tarthur was turning to look at it Gyeun had already taken out two long steel spikes and thrown them into the creature's eyes. The monster slumped over dead. Being with these men, Tarthur felt almost safe. He knew he would feel safe against anyone, anything…except Darhyn. No one could make him feel that way.

Tarthur was tired, but he knew he must press on. The hopes of the world were riding on him now. The lines of monsters thinned. They were pretty much out of Darhyn's army. They would pass a few stragglers every now and again, but by walking a few hundred yards out of their way they could avoid them. At night when they started to rest, Tarthur could see that even the usually cool and relaxed Yan was showing signs of extreme fatigue.

Gyeun, Youin, and Thon divided up the night into three watches, and let Tarthur and Yan sleep. Indeed, those three didn't even seem tired at all. They let Tarthur sleep for eight hours; it was the best sleep he had had for a while, and then they started on their way again. They would travel this day and then sleep, that way they would be able to begin their attack in the morning.

The day was passing without problems, until they saw a company of monsters coming straight at them. They didn't have time to evade them, so Yan turned into a monster and quickly tied up the other four. As he walked by Yan called out something about the master needing some captives for his personal use. The monsters snickered as they passed. Yan desperately hoped this was not some grim foreshadowing of their end.

The rest of the day passed quickly, and they were in sight of Castle Rathskellar by sunset. They ate, even though Tarthur felt like he would throw the food right back up. Gyeun gave him a pill that he said would help him regain strength when he got tired the next day. Tarthur hoped it would work.

They settled in for the night, and although Tarthur thought he would never sleep, soon he was snoring loudly. That was when Tustor came to speak with him...

"*So,*" the aged merwizard said after a pause. "*We are finally here. You don't know how my people have been waiting for this day for so long...*" Tustor trailed off, and then seemed to regain his composure. "*But for now we have work to do. I will explain to you what you must do tomorrow. I will try to be there with you when you are close to the Orb. Normally, Darhyn would be able to prevent me, but if you have the Orb in your control, I may be able to establish the connection. But to get it, there are a few things you must know.*"

Tarthur nodded, looking up at the figure that he respected so much. He wished Tustor were here in person to help him.

"*You will feel strong when you come upon it, but you must not try to control it. You must be like the water is. You must flow with it. Water is the most patient element. It can form gorges by running for millions of years. It can fit into any container. In that way you too must be flexible and patient with the Orb. It will come to your aid. I have put a marker on you that tells it you are our representative. It will seek you out. Yet, Darhyn is strong. You will need all your courage and wits.*"

Tustor started to trail off, even as his image began to become more transparent.

"No! Don't go," Tarthur pleaded. "I need you here with me. I need your strength. I need your wisdom..."

Tustor was fading away quickly. "*No, Tarthur, you must do it alone now, I can't stay for long...remember...be flexible and...patient...show the Orb love...flow with it...*" Tustor faded away completely, leaving Tarthur once again alone and cold in the night.

The five awoke to a cold morning. The sun was already beginning to burn away the chill and turn it into blistering heat. They would have only about an hour of bearable temperatures, but they were only a mile away from Darhyn's gates. They covered the distance quickly. Tarthur wondered if they were going to go through the front, but Youin led them around to the side, where she walked up to a seamless wall and found an imperceptible crack. She put her fingers into it, and flicked a switch. Tarthur heard a scraping as a slab of stone slid away to reveal a cobweb-filled stairway. Gyeun went in first followed by Thon, Tarthur, and Youin, while Yan brought up the rear. Tarthur was amazed. These guys even knew about secret passages in the heart of evil. It seemed like they knew every-thing.

Gyeun stopped to explain the situation to the rest in hushed tones. "It is as I had hoped. This keep is organized into twelve rings of defenses. Each is guarded by a door with magical protection. Darhyn himself is sure to be in the center. As for the Orb, it's anyone's guess. If we follow this path, it will take us up right inside of the tenth door. I suggest that we leave two here to guard Tarthur and the other two of us will see if the Orb is anywhere in the perimeter. It's possible Darhyn has the Orb with him, and is waiting for us. We would do better to look around first in case he has just made a trap with himself in the center and the Orb is somewhere else. If this is the case even if we defeat him, we may die before reaching the Orb. Since we know the way, Youin and I will…"

"Stop," Tarthur interrupted. Gyeun looked at him puzzlingly, and then saw that his face was glowing with a radiance that Gyeun recognized as magic. "The Orb is that way. I can feel it calling me. I feel…so very certain. More certain than anything ever before in my life."

Gyeun nodded sadly. "Okay, let's go."

Yan looked puzzled. "Why, what's wrong, Gyeun? Isn't it good that Tarthur can sense it?"

Gyeun nodded softly with his iron face. "Yes, it's just that Tarthur pointed straight in the direction of Darhyn. It's time for a showdown."

CHAPTER 19

▼

INTO THE HEART OF EVIL

As the companions wound their way through corridors of stone, Tarthur was more nervous than he had ever been before in his life. Like no other time, he wanted to run and run and never stop until he was back in Krendon. He wanted to hide there and let other people worry about themselves. He wanted to leave the world alone, and all he asked for in return was that the world leave him alone also. But then he thought of Yvonne, of Derlin, of Dalin, Yonathan, Yan, the people of Freeton, and all of the people all over the world that he had seen dying. All of these people were now counting on him. And do whatever he would, he could not let them down. He could not let himself down.

Soon they emerged from a cellar into a courtyard. The whole area seemed deserted, and it was so still, not even a lonely tumbleweed blew through the eerie stillness. Any hopes of the fortress being abandoned, however were never even realized. They could all feel the evil in this place. At the end of a courtyard was a door. Tarthur could feel that it was wrapped with magic runes of protection that would kill anyone foolish enough to open it. Yan went forward and began to disable it. Youin also knew magic, so she helped. Tarthur was about to volunteer to help also, but Gyeun stopped him. Tarthur would need his strength for later. They went through it, and into another courtyard. Then they went to the last door, and this one was wrapped with so many intricate seals of death and protection that Tarthur knew he would be needed to help undo it. That is, if they could undo it at all. Yan went up and put a simple, non-evasive explore spell to see what spells guarded it, and he was almost sent flying by the explosion that rocked the chamber. Yan stood up, brushed himself off, and shook his head sadly. They would have to find another way in. Gyeun was about to insist that there was no other way that he knew of when he was cut short.

The door swung silently open on its own.

"Welcome," a voice echoed inside each of the heroes' heads. *"I've been expecting you."*

Tarthur looked up and saw the hideous form of the Death Lord Darhyn. It was the same one he had seen in his dream, but now he was bigger, darker, and more terrifying. In his hand he was holding a black sword that glowed red where there was no light. Next to Darhyn was a glistening orb that swirled with different hues of blue and black. Tarthur had never seen the Water Orb before, but he had no doubt as to what was lying before him.

"You have come to bring me the Water Spell, boy," Darhyn said it with such finality that Tarthur himself almost believed it. *"If you wish, you may join me by handing over the spell willingly. Then we will rule this land together. If you resist, I will kill you and take the spell. Decide now."*

"You idiot," Tarthur yelled out. Why would he have come all this way to join someone who had been trying to kill him for the last year? "I will never join you, and this day you die!" Tarthur was becoming enraged. He remembered all the pain that Darhyn had caused, and now he would get even.

"As you wish," Tarthur felt the words. *"I have saved your pitiful life enough times. Now it ends."*

Tarthur was lost in thought. Saved his life? The thought was soon banished as he saw Gyeun rush forward and attack Darhyn from the side. The Death Lord turned at this annoyance, but as he did, Youin had already sprung forward and grabbed the Orb. She tried to lift it, but was having trouble. Finally she got it, but Darhyn turned away from Gyeun and saw her as the new threat. He sent a barrage of fire from his fingertips right into the girl. She screamed for a second and still on fire managed to toss the Orb to Thon. The girl immediately dropped to the ground and rolled, but the white-hot fire had done its damage. She rolled three times and then was still.

Thon ran with the Orb as Tarthur pulled out the spell that would allow him to banish this nightmare. Darhyn sensed the danger and sent another barrage of fire straight for the big man. His red fire was met by the blue fire of Dragon Yan. In the confusion, Yan had shifted shapes and was now facing Darhyn with his own fire to counteract that of the Dark One.

Darhyn sensed the trouble he was in and with a snap of his fingers monsters flooded into the room. They headed straight for Thon. The big man knew he was in trouble, so he hefted the Orb with all of his strength and threw it straight for Tarthur, who reached out his hands to grasp it…

A winged creature darted in front of Tarthur and grabbed the Orb before Tarthur had the chance. The monster beat his wings once and screeched in a high-pitched whine. He never finished it though. Gyeun leaped up as high as he could and rammed his sword into the creature's soft underbelly. The monster toppled over and the Orb fell from his grasp.

Tarthur hurriedly spoke the words of the levitate spell, and sent his force out to grab the Orb. It bounced once in the middle of the air as if it had fallen on a mattress, and then Tarthur reached out his spell and caressed the Orb. Fluidly, he called out to it and brought it near to him. Tarthur could feel himself succeeding. He could feel all of his doubts, insecurities, and problems of the last year being washed away. Tarthur felt the wild exhilaration surge through every part of his being, felt it fill him up and lift him off of the floor.

Tarthur saw Darhyn fold his hands together in his cloak and bring them out with a tongue of flame floating above his palms. The Death Lord reached inside his cloak and brought out a yellowing scroll, nearly identical to the one Tarthur had. This fight was just beginning. Darhyn read aloud the words, and then a blast of fire shot directly at Tarthur. Tarthur rolled out of the way, and commanded the Water Orb to come to his aid. He screamed at it for it to help him, to wash away Darhyn with its powerful floods.

Nothing happened.

Tarthur didn't know what to do. He couldn't command the Orb. Darhyn sent another stream of fire at him, and this time Tarthur actually got burned. He quickly rolled it out. But, why couldn't he use the Orb?

From far away, the memories of the merfolk and the words of their gentle leader came back to him. *"Be flexible, be patient, flow with the water."* Tarthur reached inside of himself and let go. He relaxed; he yielded his control over the Orb. He allowed the power to flow over him, carrying him along wherever it would go. And the Orb responded.

Huge waves swept over the chamber of the Death Lord. Darhyn spread his hands, and sent waves of fire lancing out in all directions, evaporating the water and turning the room into a scalding sauna of steam. The steam cleared out of the vents and soon the room was as before. Darhyn called more monsters.

Tarthur saw that one of these who came was a majestic knight, with a white horse and white banner, but the surprising thing was that he was dressed all in white armor. Tarthur had never seen white armor before, and this knight had a counterpart, dressed all in black. Instead of attacking Tarthur and Yan, they actually attacked the monsters themselves, helping Tarthur. The boy only briefly noticed, things were moving so fast.

Now it was the Dark One's time to attack. He sent huge torrents of fire out from his person, but Tarthur threw up the Water Spell to counteract them. They were evenly matched, but Darhyn had the monsters. There was no way they could win.

Yan saw this quickly, and he beckoned for Tarthur to come out of the room. Gyeun was already there and as Tarthur glanced about the room he saw the body of Thon, lying in a heap of monsters that he had slain. The three ran from the chamber, and Gyeun led them along the right paths so soon they had at least a moment's respite. All three had haggard breathing. Yan turned to speak to Tarthur.

"We did it," he said, but the exhilaration somehow was not in his voice. Tarthur still clutched the Water Orb. "Darhyn is too strong for us to beat right now. But, if we can escape with the Orb and bring it back to the front, we can combine it with the Power of Earth that the king has. It will be a long and hard battle, but we would win eventually. Then with both powers we could kill Darhyn and regain the third."

Tarthur didn't really like that plan very much. It involved a lot of ifs and a lot of lives would be lost. They would have to make it out of the palace alive, sneak through Darhyn's army which would be looking exclusively for them, and make it back to the king's side. Tarthur sighed, "Well, if there is no other way…"

*   *   *   *

The battle had been raging fiercely on the front lines. Ever since the devastating death of the elven king, the allied forces had lost a little morale, but gained a new and fiercely tempered determination. They had followed Cilio's plan of cautiously dropping back and were now only one day out of Breshen. They had been fighting hard, and it showed. In the battles since Tarthur and his escort had set out they had inflicted more damages than they had suffered. Yet, in the battle that had let Tarthur through they had suffered greatly, and almost the whole diversionary charge had been wiped out. But they had bought their chance.

Sir Stephen was doing well with responsibility. He bore it like a fine cloak, and the duties seemed to fit him like never before. He was actually doing things very carefully, always taking time to make sure that they were done right. Yet, for all his attention to detail, his excitement had not waned. He was ready for this war, and he knew that they would win. His squadron was actually one of the better ones, even though it now had only sixty members in it. At Breshen, the rumor was that General Cilio was going to reorganize the army to account for the loss of life and even up the ranks a little bit. Sir Stephen held high hopes that he would get a good post.

The battle that day opened almost as usual. The Death Lord's armies were getting to be more habitual now; they would always attack toward late afternoon and force Cilio and his men to retreat at night, rest during the morning, and then prepare to be attacked again later that afternoon. Sir Stephen hoped that he was not just lulling them into a false sense of security, only to explode later. He also hoped Cilio would do something surprising. He seemed to be waiting for something.

The next charge of the monsters cut short the young knight's reverie as he galloped forward on his black horse, calling out for his troops to follow after him. Sir Stephen met the first charge of mercenaries and rained down a blow from his sword on the nearest man's head. The mercenary flung up an iron rod to deflect the blow, but the force of it still hurt the man's arm. Sir Stephen wheeled up his horse and with a snap of the reigns the horse sent the man flying. Sir Stephen galloped straight for another man and swung his sword at this one also, but this time faked high and then sliced it across the mercenary chest. As the man doubled over in pain, Sir Stephen smashed the pommel of his sword down on his enemy's face.

The battle was going about average for a few hours, both sides trading positions. Cilio gave the order that they would try to hold here for at least two days before retreating, and when they got to Breshen they would hold there indefinitely until they could gain the advantage or it would be strategic suicide to stay longer. No one was even thinking of falling all the way back to the king's castle, although that would be the ultimate and last resort stronghold.

Both armies had been decimated in the long, hard battles that they had fought. If either army now faced the other army at full strength as they had in the beginning, it would be certain who would lose, and lose easily. Nearly forty percent of each army had been killed in one manner or another. Sir Terin's company was finally making headway in the battle, and had succeeded in cutting off a sizable section of Darhyn's forces. Cilio sent Dalin's elven company over to cut off their retreat, and Tali's company to reinforce the attack on their front. If the rest of the army could hold, they would destroy a large section of Darhyn's force.

The monsters realized the trap that they had been led into, and turned to break free. If Dalin's company could stop them, it would be all over for those monsters. The monsters charged into the elves, but the courageous warriors held their ground. Hano was rushing about, a red streak as his crimson cloak mingled with blood. He killed whatever he could, and smashed the legs of those he could not, so at least they would not escape, and someone could come along to finish them off later.

A huge ogre came charging forward, offering a shield to his companions. He was trying to break the elven line and let the rest of his compatriots through to the safety of their other force. Before he knew it, he felt a shooting pain in his left knee. He looked down to see an elf screaming obscenities at him. Hano's hate was complete. The monster looked down in annoyance and got a sword thrown in his eye for his trouble. Hano took a flying leap onto the monster, climbed up his back and grabbed hold of his mane. Tugging with all his might the elven warrior reached around, grabbed his sword back and decapitated the creature. His head rolled in the dust as blood oozed all over the field.

Dalin came to fight side by side with his childhood friend. The pair relentlessly dispatched monster after monster. It was working. Darhyn's entire right wing had been cut off and was nearly all destroyed. The tide of the battle was finally turning.

A black shadow form came to fight Dalin. The shadow weaved and bobbed around, waiting for his chance. With a lightning quickness he shot right into Dalin's chest. The elf prince tried in vain to bring his sword up in defense, but the monster was too quick. The monster entered Dalin, until he was completely inside of him.

As quick as it had entered him, the monster shot out of Dalin's chest, leaving him stunned. The black shape screamed in frustration, then turned to look for another target. Its eyes fluttered around, then turned to Hano and smiled a hideous, eerie smile. It had found what it needed.

Before anyone could respond, it was inside the red-cloaked elf. Hano screamed in agony and then in rage and exhilaration. He turned to Dalin, and Dalin saw his friend's eyes roll back into his head and reemerge black. When he spoke, it had a demonic echo to it.

"Now, my hate is complete." Hano reached across with his hammer and brought it smashing down on an elf's skull. He laughed shrilly and the sound chilled Dalin to the very bones. As Hano raised his hammer to strike another surprised elf, Dalin knew what he must do. Tearfully, he raised his bow and notched an arrow in the string…

…And fired. The arrow pierced both of their hearts. Dalin ran over to his friend, and cradled him in his arms. Crying freely, he heard shouts of victory. As he looked around, he saw that they had held long enough, that the king's men had been able to destroy Darhyn's entire right wing, and now Darhyn's entire army was retreating. Dalin didn't understand why they were going, the battle was far from over, and he didn't care. He just sat there, cradling the foreign looking face of his lifelong friend. Hano's features were distorted with rage almost beyond recognition, but Dalin thought he saw something of the good underneath it all. Just then, the shouts of victory turned to shouts of surprise, and then to horror. Staring up through tears, Dalin saw the real reason for the retreat of the Death Lord's forces.

To the East, across the plain, was a gigantic army, an army that could easily defeat both the king's and the Death Lord's forces. Dalin thought he was seeing things, but at its head was none other than Queen Marhyn herself.

$$* \qquad * \qquad * \qquad *$$

"Actually," said Yan with a sigh, looking once again tired and old. "There is one other way." Tarthur and Gyeun looked up at him curiously. "There is another way," he repeated softly to himself. "When they empowered me as a shapeshifter, they gave me the power to turn into anything that I have once seen, touched, or felt."

Yan paused to let his words take effect. "A long time ago, before I was imprisoned by Queen Marhyn, I saw Tivu, and I was allowed to touch the feather from Firewing."

Tarthur looked at him slowly, letting the meaning of his words dawn on him. "So, you are saying that you'll transform into the Power of Air for me to use? Then with the two powers we can beat him. Why didn't we think of this before? We could have been using the Air Spell since the beginning."

"I was hoping it would not have to come to this, since nothing of this nature has ever been done before, we can't know the results. You must also be careful, because I think that you will only get one use."

"What will happen to you?" Tarthur questioned suspiciously. "Won't you be sent into the dimension of used magic?"

"No," Yan said quickly, and a little harshly. "Trust me Tarthur, I know much more about magic than you do. I'll be just fine. Now, let's go. Every minute we waste good men are dying."

Tarthur nodded and set out ahead, but Gyeun stayed back and looked at Yan. Yan nodded, and then spoke. "Right, don't get yourself killed; the boy may need an escort back to the army. Oh, I'm too old for this."

The trip back to Darhyn's chamber seemed quick compared to the harrowing flight from it. Tarthur somehow knew that he was now about to finish what he had started so long ago in his dream. It all ended here. They burst into the chamber with Dragon Yan spraying fire wherever he went. The monsters were still there, but the ghost knights were still in battle with them. Gyeun hung back, hesitant to join the fray.

Darhyn looked mockingly at Tarthur and then began anew. Darhyn commanded the beams of fire that shot out from his person, and Tarthur called out softly for the Water Orb to come to his aid. Instead of relinquishing the flames as he did before, this time Darhyn kept them up, sending his essence out along the battle lines at Tarthur. Tarthur could feel the Dark One trying to take him over. He could feel his evil and wanted to drop the Orb and run. Out of the corner of his eye, Tarthur saw Dragon Yan become silver and then shimmer, and then he saw a huge feather float down and land in his waiting palm. Darhyn's force was strong against him, but Tarthur reached down and asked Yan to help him.

Tornado-like winds swept the chamber, knocking everyone from their feet. Gyeun had somehow anchored himself to a marble pillar with a chain, but even that was coming loose. Tarthur stood in the center of the tempest unharmed, unfeeling. The elements did not touch him, but he felt dangerous power like none he had ever felt before.

Darhyn flew against the throne and the winds died down in the rest of the room as they converged on him. The Dark One screamed, for once feeling the agony he had inflicted on so many. The winds intensified in power and focus, even as his screams intensified in volume. A black portal opened in the back of his throne. Struggling, and vainly trying to hold onto anything that could stop him, Darhyn was sent flying through, the wind pushing him in. The portal slammed shut.

Tarthur collapsed from the strain, and looked around the eerily empty throne room. The monsters were all dead or had fled the keep. The black and white knights had vanished into thin air. Yan was nowhere to be seen. The only one left alive was Gyeun, who came over and lifted the exhausted Tarthur up. Tarthur forced himself to stand and walk forward. On the throne of Darhyn danced a single tongue of flame on top of a yellowed scroll. The flame did not consume the scroll. Tarthur reached down, picked it up, and then collapsed once again in Gyeun's arms. Gyeun started to carry Tarthur out of the room, but Tarthur was trying to wait for Yan. Gyeun had to insist they get out this instant. Yan, he told Tarthur, could take care of himself. He would meet them with the army. Right now, they needed rest, and they were not about to rest here. Gyeun turned to look at the room where he had lost two of the Guard, and did not wipe away a tear as he dragged Tarthur out.

CHAPTER 20

▼

THE END OF BRESHEN

Complete pandemonium reigned supreme as the three armies battled for control of the barren ground, in what would in turn decide who would control the entire world. Marhyn's attack had caught both armies completely by surprise. No one could imagine that after she had destroyed the merfolk she had actually sailed east with her troops to her secret base on the Volcano Island, where they had trained and waited. If there was anyone who thought that even Marhyn would not sacrifice part of her troops in the South, in an attempt that had from the beginning been destined to lose, indeed, created for the sole purpose of tricking the king's men into thinking that they had defeated her once and for all, he would have been fooled when she had used a replica of her body at the head of her troops, a replica that also had died. Even the troops of the Death Lord Darhyn, her own brother, had been completely taken by surprise. Marhyn had waited while the two armies, thinking that they were alone, had fought and destroyed themselves, and now she was ready to attack them both, while they fought amongst themselves.

Marhyn had positioned her army so that she had the Death Lord's troops between her and King Garkin. That way, she only had to fight a one front battle, and her two enemies would keep destroying each other on the western side of the field. Her deception was perfect. Well, almost perfect, she had not wished to lose Lithar, but he was only a man anyway. So what if he died? He had been a good servant, though.

General Cilio immediately ordered the retreat to Breshen when he saw how he had been fooled by Marhyn for the second time in as many months. His tired force would soon be annihilated if they were forced to fight Marhyn's numerous and well rested monsters and men. Darhyn's forces were slightly more confused, but soon reorganized themselves and followed the king's men in their retreat. They had only two places to go, and they too did not want to face Marhyn right off the bat. The flight to Breshen was harrowing, everyone in the army was calling out to his superior for answers, for help, for reasons why this was happening, and no one was being answered. Derlin stumbled on, the Light Sword glowing powerfully at his side. It was ready for a confrontation.

Derlin wondered what had happened to his friend Tarthur. He hoped he was all right, but now he was worried that Tarthur had gotten killed by Darhyn, and Marhyn would win and take control of the world. He could not bear the thought of that possibility. He knew he would die first. Although, he also knew that even if he did his best and gave his life, it probably wouldn't end up meaning much in the grand scheme of things. It was troubling for Derlin to think about death, both his and Tarthur's. It was not usually a subject that young people thought about often. Death was something only for old people to worry about. But the events of the last year had forced him to consider the reality of his own mortality. Derlin had never thought he would die, but then again, he had never thought he would kill, either.

They made it to Breshen by the middle of the night, but even so there was no time for rest. Marhyn's fresh troops had traveled almost as fast as the king's troops so they only had about two hours to prepare for the onslaught. They were on the outskirts of the town, so fortunately there were only a few houses. Cilio stationed archers and anyone well enough to shoot but not well enough to fight in the trees as well. The thick undergrowth would help to provide at least minimal cover. As part of the general preparations, General Cilio had ordered those among the elves who could not fight to build barricades at the edge of Breshen as a precautionary measure. But since the attack from Marhyn was so completely unexpected, the barricades were in substandard condition. They were at least better than nothing, however.

The courteous troops of the Death Lord had withdrawn to the North, so as to give Cilio's army the first chance to fight with Marhyn. They would wait north, and either retreat or try to attack Marhyn and force her to fight on two fronts. Although, since this would help the king's troops immensely, Darhyn's troops couldn't be expected to fight until they were attacked. Cilio guessed that Marhyn would concentrate on the forces one at a time. He hoped that Marhyn would attack Darhyn first, but since the king's men had their backs to the forest, he

assumed that Marhyn would turn first towards Breshen, and then deal with Darhyn's army later.

Cilio sent one third of his army to the back so they could try to get some rest.
If all went well, they would be able to rest and the first group would receive
enough cover from the trees to be able to hold off her armies. It was a risky plan,
though.

The first charge came quickly and sloppily. Marhyn had the superior numbers
and rested troops, and she was willing to sacrifice a little efficiency if she could
just get the chance to attack quickly.

Her haste cost her, as arrows rained down from all sides and cut her first
charge to pieces. Frightened elves attacked by throwing whatever they could,
chairs, tree limbs, and rocks down on the attackers. A few of the Dark Lady's
men succeeded in breaking through, and soon they were engaged in fierce battle
underneath the trees. Sir Stephen had volunteered his group for the front line.
He personally didn't feel the fatigue that many of his companions did, and he
knew that they could serve best where they could do the most damage. Marhyn's
forces were mixed with monsters, goblins, and men. As Sir Stephen met the
charge, he tightened his grip on the pommel of his sword.

A burly goblin ran at him, but then tripped over a root that had moved into
his way. Sir Stephen reversed the grip on his sword and plunged it into the goblin's back. Blood squirted all over the ground. Next, a mercenary ran up to face
him. The man swung his sword to slice the knight diagonally across the chest, but
Sir Stephen brought up his own sword to block it. The resounding clang echoed
through the forest, mixing with the screams of the dying. Sir Stephen came out
from the rebound swinging high, and the man swung low. The man's sword
sliced across Sir Stephen's calf even as Sir Stephen's sword cut into the man's
neck. The man fell over, but was still alive, and Sir Stephen realized he had just
done what his instructors had told him never to do. Never miss a killing stroke.
Sir Stephen looked down and saw the man in pain as a bloody bubble came up
from his lips. Closing his eyes, Sir Stephen finished it. But before he did, the look
in the other man's eyes unnerved him. It scared him, and it seemed to the young
knight that he had just killed a human, someone who could have been his
brother, or someone's father. The reality of war began to hit him, that it is the
most hideous thing possible on earth, and that glorious battles are just tales told
by people who were never there. Yet, looking across the field, he also saw why war
was sometimes necessary. They would send the fiends back were they belonged.

Derlin was doing well for his part. He too was in the front lines, as the Light
Sword would always have to be. He sliced through monsters, goblins, and men,

whoever was stupid enough to fight him. His skill was improving, (having an invincible weapon certainly helped) and for the last few battles he had become a rallying point for the king's troops. In this way he was also learning how to command. It seemed weird to him that grown men would follow his every order, back in Krendon they just used to yell at him and tell him to go do something useful. If he would have reached up and felt his face, he would have felt the faint stubble of a beard coming in. Indeed, he was a man.

The pain in Sir Stephen's leg was not too bad, but the cut sure looked nasty. He knew that he should probably go to the healers' tent, but it would be overflowing with much more serious cases, and besides, if he did that he would be out of the fight for at least a couple of hours. The king needed him most here.

So he tore off a piece of his dirty cloak and wrapped it tightly around his calf. It wouldn't do much for the wound, he knew, but it would at least keep him from losing too much blood. After a few minutes of bandaging, he was ready to rejoin the fray. Sir Stephen looked up to see a huge bear-like monster charging for him. He thought quickly, then ran up a stump and leaped high in the air, grabbing hold of a nearby tree branch. He swung himself over the top, and then waited for the monster to stop, looking for his vanished prey. Sir Stephen dropped from the sky, sword pointed downward and thrust it into the bear. The monster snarled in rage and then scratched Sir Stephen's side with his claw. The claws only scratched a little, and soon Sir Stephen ripped free his blade and blood squirted everywhere. The creature lumbered on, and then fell and didn't move again.

The elven forest was alive, and even the trees were helping out, sliding in the way of someone here, taking a sword slice or an arrow for another there, but Marhyn's troops had brought poisonous powders. They sprinkled them at the base of the trees and the roots curled up and died, felling the trees and killing whoever happened to be lodged in them.

But the worst was the fires. Marhyn had ordered men to set fire to the trees. The elven trees didn't burn easily, since they were alive and there was much green vegetation, not to mention the fact that the trees were able to draw water from other lakes in the forest and through an interconnected network extinguish the fires at their bases, but Marhyn had brought flammable materials that burned with unholy heat and refused to go out.

Yvonne was there too. She had just arrived from the heart of Breshen with her supply wagon. She had never anticipated fighting, but now that the battle was all around her she wasted no time. The monsters were the ugliest thing she had seen in her life, but living as she had in the streets, she had seen many things and had become desensitized to ugliness.

She saw a raggedy man turn to her and look lustfully over her body. Frightened, she cocked her head towards him and waved. The man rushed over and went to grab her, but as his hand came out he felt a dagger in his stomach. He plucked it out, and Yvonne cautiously retreated, not knowing what to do.

Suddenly, a tree branch came down and fell into her hand. The tree gave up a part of itself, and Yvonne swung, knocking the man across the face. She picked up her dagger and made sure he never got up.

The high council was in a panic. The retreat through the forest to the main part of Breshen that could be used as a fortress would take time, and in order for them to do that, they would need to hold. They would need to hold at least until Marhyn gave up for the day. Cilio was doing his best to organize the army into traps and counter traps, and his mobile forces were at least giving them a chance in the battle. It was up to the men of the kingdom to show what they were made of.

Sir Stephen was showing what he was made of, namely blood. It was oozing all over his leg, the exertion had caused his heart to beat even faster and pump more blood out of his body. He tightened the wrapping, and the flow seemed to slow down a bit. He rushed forward and hacked at a rude little goblin who was trying to set a tree on fire. The monster saw Sir Stephen coming, and cowardly threw his conflagration kit at the nearest tree, where it exploded and began to burn hotly. Sir Stephen quickly killed the creature, but was soon forced to retreat from the ferocious flames, even though they were almost ten feet away. He felt a dizziness in his head, but fought on.

Sir Terin Ironfist was in the middle of his army astride a horse. He carried the banner of the Royal Knights, and was riding about, combating monsters wherever he went. His company was now almost completely destroyed, but they were still fighting as well as they could. He swung his sword down on a dwarf, and then tried to gallop out of the way as he recognized it as one of the acid-spitting ones. He was too late; acid sprayed on his leg, ate into his armor, and burned his ankle a little. It hurt, but he grimaced and fought on.

Dalin's company had been put in charge of putting out the fires in the trees, and was having marginal luck, but the fires were popping up in more and more places. Cilio had realized that if the fires spread, they would be trapped between Marhyn and the fire, in which case they would surely be annihilated. Dalin was shuttling forth barrels of water, in connection with the trees. The elven trees were helping, but there were three areas of uncontrolled fires now.

A huge ogre charged forward, and two men came to face it. Sir Stephen waved them aside, this one was for him. Today was his day, the day he finally served his king and became a real knight. He would remember this day as long as he lived.

A little faint, he ran forward and sliced the ogre across the leg, cutting flesh but not drawing much blood. The ogre turned, and took out a staff and swung it at Sir Stephen's head. The young knight ducked, but then the ogre brought it back around and vertically down. Sir Stephen blocked it, but the impact hurt his sword arm. He switched hands and continued. Again, he went forward, faking, and managed to stab the ogre through the center. This caused the ogre to squeal in pain, but bring the staff down across Sir Stephen's face. Sir Stephen got up again, and went forward dizzily. The ogre laughed, and once more smacked him hard with the cudgel. Sir Stephen fell hard, and started to get up...

Before he could do so, the ogre came forward and kicked him in the ribs, breaking several. Sir Stephen remembered having one last thought as he saw the ogre raise his staff once more, "No, I don't want to die..."

Derlin was engaged in fighting a troll, when he saw it suddenly break off from the confrontation. Finally, he thought, they're beginning to get scared of me. But as he looked around, he saw that it was not a unique phenomenon. All the monsters were running away, back to central points. Derlin dared not hope for a retreat and the respite that would accompany it, even for a moment. He was right not to. Soon, they charged forward again, and they were each carrying something. He came forward to face one of them, but the monster ran around him and for the trees.

Derlin was confused, and then he understood. They were now using their whole army to set fire to the forest. Dalin saw it too, but it was too late. Flames roared up everywhere, lighting up the morning, starting to destroy the forest. Marhyn's forces ran back, and now Cilio's men had nowhere to go. The flames were advancing in all directions, forcing the king's men toward Marhyn's army. Derlin looked back, and he wondered how they were going to get out of this one.

All around, he could tell his people were thinking the same thing. He saw lifelong friends saying goodbye to each other, nodding softly and clasping hands firmly. They turned to face their ultimate foe, who had outsmarted and outmanned them. Tarthur didn't matter. The battle would be over within a few hours.

Cilio drew the men together, and the message was the same for all. They would fight as long as they could, but when it came to the end, they would end it all with one ferocious charge up the middle. After this day, there would still be a resistance to Marhyn, and if Tarthur had gotten the Orb, then perhaps the resistance might have some chance of success. They would have to fight in the mountains. Yonathan would join when he was healed, and maybe Tustor could get more help from the council now that the situation was urgent. The eyes of the men held this little hope, yet one thing was certain—none of them would be around to find out how it ended.

Marhyn didn't wait, she began the next charge, and the king's men looked around at the field of dead and dying, of fire and blood, and tightened their grips on their swords. The first charge came ferociously and mockingly. Derlin faced a three-headed monster, cut off two heads in a single swipe, and then was startled to find that two spikes grew out of where the heads were. The creature came at him now, but this time it was a little off balance, and Derlin dove and cut off a leg. Now it flipped over, and a head grew out of where the leg was, giving it more balance and sense of direction. It faced Derlin, waiting…There was a rumble to the east, and what Derlin saw nearly made his heart stop.

Huge waves swept across the battlefield, sweeping away the monsters. Everyone looked up, startled. There at the head of the battle stood Tarthur himself, except that he was so changed that even Derlin almost didn't recognize him. Tarthur was glowing with power, and there was a wide circle around him where no monster dared go. Queen Marhyn's army shrunk back in fear, even as he blasted them with a twenty meter wide swath of fire.

They fell blackened and lifeless.

Cilio lost no time in seizing his advantage, for even though Tarthur was powerful, the battle was far from over. Cilio ordered his men into Marhyn's army, whom they began to tear apart viciously. The center parted, and Marhyn herself on a black dragon came through to face Tarthur.

"So, boy, you think to ruin my plans after I have come this far? I should have crushed your pitiful body a long time ago. But now, you die."

Tarthur stood motionless. "That reminds me of what Darhyn said to me. Look at this war! Look around you! You fiends have caused this suffering; you have caused these good men to die! You do not feel remorse?"

"I do not feel. I feel only hatred, hatred for you!" Marhyn sent a burst of fire out at Tarthur. Tarthur brushed it away with a flare of his own.

"You do not feel? Yet you will pay with your life. This ends here." Tarthur said it with such finality that even Marhyn hesitated to look at him. He had so much power in his face, so much strength.

Tarthur sent fire out, burning the dragon that Marhyn was on and sending her sprawling. She caught herself with a levitate spell, but then seemed to think the better of fighting this boy and decided to run away.

Huge towers of water grew up around her, stopping her from passing. Frantically, she looked around inside but saw no one. She whirled, and Tarthur stepped through the torrent. Inside it was quiet, completely cut off from the rest of the army.

"Spare my life, please," she pleaded. "I can rule with you…I can do anything you want me too…" her clothes began to melt away, revealing a beautiful half-naked woman, who pressed her body against Tarthur. She reached behind her for a dagger, even as Tarthur threw her to the ground.

"Why don't you ever understand? You cannot offer me anything, except your life, which I take now." Tarthur reached forward, and sent fire lancing into Marhyn's body, which shuddered once and then became still, still smoldering on the ground. Tarthur stared at her without pity for a moment, and then began to weep at all he had witnessed, all the pain that had been caused, over and over again.

A thin wisp of blue smoke, the color of the marble in Marhyn's fortress, wafted up from the corpse as Tarthur was crying, head in hands. He looked up, felt the life-force, and nodded softly. With a sweep of his hands he let the walls of water crash down, obliterating any trace of the smoke, or the body.

Tarthur turned to look at the flaming elven forest and sent another set of waves into it to extinguish the fires. There was a gigantic hiss as the fires gave their heat to the water, and colossal columns of steam rose up to the sun.

Zelin was destroying the Death Lord's army. Instead of fleeing, as they should have done, they had decided to stay and fight it out to the end. The monsters there just wanted to kill anyway. A few of the men had deserted, but for the most part, they were there to kill or be killed.

Most fell into the category of the latter. With two elements of power, they were no match for Tarthur. The rest of the king's army began to fight on soul now too. Their bodies were absolutely fatigued beyond all belief, but they saw the end in sight, and nothing could turn them back from their aim now. Before twilight fell, the entire force of the Death Lord and that of his sister had been obliterated.

Tarthur was dead tired. How he had gotten the Orb, or made it back so quickly, were stories that had to wait for another day. The first thing he did when he got back was to seek out Derlin. The two looked at each other and began to cry together as men. They embraced, and that is where Tarthur collapsed.

The healers' tents were overwhelmed that night, and the army did not leave the sight of the battle for almost a week, except to move a little inside the trees to escape the stench. Yvonne insisted on caring for Tarthur herself, and there was no one who would argue with her. She only allowed Derlin and a doctor in for a few minutes. Tarthur was very near death, he had used all of physical strength to return so quickly and use the magic. Yvonne sat up all night, wiping his head with a cloth and exhorting him to hold on.

People came up, Yonathan and Kandan among them, and others that had not been able to fight came up to staff the healers' tents and bury the bodies. There were many serious cases of men whose bodies simply gave up. They had lost blood and sweat, and driven themselves to extreme fatigue. There were widespread infections and diseases that most of the army doctors had no way of fixing. Tarthur himself was in bed for three days before he finally rose.

Upon leaving his tent, Tarthur received a standing ovation from the crowd. It was time to tell his story. Yet, what could he tell? He got up, told them of his meetings, told them of Yan and his ultimate sacrifice, for he had learned that Yan was once again outside of the world, lost in time. After the battle with Darhyn, Yan might have been able to retransform himself, but instead he had used all of his power to meld Tarthur's body with the wind, and fly him back to Breshen. Yan had given up everything, and so had so many others who had given their lives in the fight against evil. Then a strange thing happened. For the first time ever, someone would have said that Tarthur was modest. He didn't see himself as the hero, at least no more of a hero than anyone else who had stood together on the field that day, or those who had fallen before. He did, however, use his moments of fame to call for better relations among the races. They had been lucky this time, but they must be united since the threat could come again. And for once in his life, Tarthur told the story exactly the way it happened, without embellishment. It needed none.

Later that day the council met to discuss everything and make sure that there were no loose ends. This time when they met, they were in high spirits, and there was none of the tension that had marked their earlier meetings. Tarthur began. "So after all this, I really still don't understand everything. Why did Darhyn choose me? I mean, what was his plan?"

The members looked around hesitantly at each other and shrugged their shoulders. Finally it was Zelin who spoke. "We have been hard at work trying to determine this for over a year now, and I think we finally have some answers, though not all. Why it was you...that we don't know."

Tarthur spoke again, suddenly remembering something. "One thing he said to me surprised me. I had forgotten about it, until now. Darhyn told me, 'I have saved your pitiful life enough times.' When did he ever save my life?"

Zelin sighed. "This is indeed important. It might fill in some gaps that I have been wondering about. For instance, why were you allowed to escape so easily from Marhyn? Why did she not simply kill you when she had the chance, or put you under maximum security? Why have you been so incredibly lucky? Here is what I surmise. Whether it is what truly happened or not, only Darhyn knows…

After the last war, Darhyn sent the Water Orb out of the world so we would not be able to reclaim it from him. He was preparing to set up an army and attack us, but before this he sent his mind out to find some humans who could do his bidding. He found Warren, and he found you. He probably found others too, although, they are no threat to us now that their master is gone. He began to help them rise in power and status, so they would be where he needed them when the time came to attack. But you, Tarthur, you messed up his whole plan. For you, you wounded him. Yet much more importantly, you destroyed the Water Spell. Yes, when you read aloud the original spell, you destroyed it and took away Darhyn's ability to use the Orb. But luckily for us, you copied down the spell in your sleep, and so it was not lost to us. Little did you know that one act would be so important.

After this, Darhyn's plan changed. Without the aid of the Water Orb, he couldn't march into Breshen and take it and take the whole kingdom like he could have with it. Far from the heart of evil, he is weakened and his monsters cannot fight well. He would have had a chance if Warren had killed King Garkin, and he probably would have been able to stop, or at least delay a mobilization. But Addyean thwarted that plan. So he had to wait and build up an ambush in Castle Rathskellar, knowing that we would go in after the Orb. He meant to destroy our army there and kill you, taking the spell. That way, he would have no trouble defeating us."

Tarthur was puzzled. He didn't want to believe that all this time they had only been walking into a trap. "But, what about the skull knights that attacked us?"

"Did they ever attack you directly? Or did they attack Yonathan, Derlin, and Yan only? Remember back, when you came to us, you had no wounds from them. They were probably trying to keep up the charade, or they were trying to kidnap you and bring you and the spell back to Darhyn."

"But Darhyn wasn't the only one protecting you. The Orb itself has the power to control things. When we met in the Vale, Tustor revealed that it had placed a marker on you, and this is what protected you from coming to harm from Marhyn. The Orb wanted to come back. It sensed that it was needed, and now with the destruction of the merfolk, it has come to pass. It will be needed to help them rebuild."

Now the question came from Addyean, and it was directed more at King Garkin than the others. "Why did Warren slip past us? Did he have some kind of marker as well? Considering recent events, I wonder why I did not learn that he was evil at Treshin."

Zelin replied. "No, Warren did not have any kind of marker. I myself sensed that he was evil, but I did not imagine that this would happen."

Dalin spoke up. "Perhaps it didn't have so much to do with Darhyn as with other things. My father once told me that he would die from a monster biting him in half. It had to do with something that had happened earlier in his life. Still, I wonder how he knew..."

The council fell silent at this revelation. No one spoke for a few minutes, and the General Cilio broke the silence. "I have sent units of the army to Castle Rathskellar to go and destroy the infernal fortress once and for all, and to try to till the soil. The same will be done in the South with Marhyn's castle. I believe that these two will never trouble us again, and we can set up memorials on the spots and set up cities nearby. That way, others who would be like they were will have no place to set up fortresses, and if they do we will have plenty of advance notice."

Zelin spoke with satisfaction, but his oldness and frailness were apparent. "From Tarthur's accounts of the deaths, I think we can believe that Darhyn and Marhyn have really been defeated and destroyed. If Darhyn has in fact made it to another dimension, we may have to worry about him coming back at any time, so we must be always in a state of perpetual readiness. We will have magicians watch the gates, and we will be ready if he comes again. But with Water, Earth, and Fire on our side, even if he comes at the peak of his power, we should be able to defeat him. Now that we have the Water Orb, we can also take the self protect spell off of the Earth Grain, by attacking, and using the Earth Grain to defend ourselves. Polu and I will take care of this."

That settled, the council decided to retire, and Tarthur couldn't help feeling very lucky.

*   *   *   *

The days rolled by, and gradually everyone went their separate ways. Sir Terin and General Cilio went back to the capital to run the city in the absence of the king, who stayed with Derlin, Tarthur and the elves in Breshen. It was approaching midsummer, the elven time of grieving.

Tarthur and Derlin once again went to stay with Dalin in his tree. When they came back, Valena rushed out, grabbed Derlin tight in her arms, and held him there, as if she would never let go. She had already heard about Hano.

Derlin reached inside his vest and pulled out the green ribbon that he had kept ever since the last time they had met. It was stained red in a few spots with blood.

The meeting between the two started awkwardly. "I'm sorry about what happened to Hano and your father..." Derlin began softly. "I know they meant a lot to you..."

Derlin looked into her deep eyes and saw the pain there burning so intensely. He could tell the death of her father and fiancé had hurt her tremendously. Without speaking, she put a finger to her lips and held Derlin tighter.

In the time that they stayed in Breshen, Derlin and Valena grew closer than ever before. They talked all night long, about their stories, about pain, and about what it meant to be alive. Derlin had never realized that it was so tough to be a princess. Sometimes they fell asleep in each other's embrace. Dalin smiled but said nothing.

The ceremony honoring the dead was beautiful. King Garkin stood beside Dalin as they mourned Hano, the elven king, and the forest itself. The trees that had died in the fire were called by name, and an account of them was told by the other trees. They started out on the sacred lawn, where an elven caller described the dead. He told of their childhoods, their loves, and their sacrifices. The elven community was close. Everyone knew everyone else. When it was done, they walked silently through the forest, contemplating the passage of time. The leaves were already beginning to turn gold and as they fell they formed a carpet of color for the mourners to walk on.

For a few days, no one said anything. The whole group lived in silence, and then abruptly King Garkin announced that he must go back to the capital, and Tarthur and Derlin knew that they must go with him too. Derlin was having terrible problems trying to decide what to do. He wanted to spend his life with Valena, and it looked as if she wanted to spend hers with him as well.

One night when they were talking, Dalin walked into the room. He looked a little sterner than usual, and Derlin and Valena turned to greet him.

"I don't know if you've heard, Derlin, but the king plans to leave for Tealsburg tomorrow at sunrise. He was hoping that you would join him and Tarthur."

"Actually, your majesty," Derlin began to reply. It felt weird to think of Dalin as a king. He had not formally taken the title. Everyone just seemed to call him that. "I was kind of hoping to live here for a while. If that's okay..."

"Well," Dalin replied. "You know that the elven rules about marriage are very strict. In the present situation, they have become even stricter. She is the princess, you know. If anything were to happen to me...you'd be next in line for the throne."

"The throne? I don't want the elven throne, I wouldn't have a clue what to do with it!"

"I know that, Derlin. I know that you are a good and honest man, and there is no one that I would rather wed my sister to. However, you still have a few responsibilities in the world to take care of first. And things around here are very hectic right now. I think it would be best if you returned to Krendon with Tarthur for a little while, just a few months. Then after that, if your heart is still true, you could come back. I should have established a more firm control by then, and if you two love each other as much as it looks to me…then there'll be no problems. That's as long as you agree to give up the throne, of course."

Derlin sighed. Being separated from Valena for even one minute was torture. He didn't even like leaving her to go to the bathroom. But Dalin was right. He did have responsibilities to the rest of the world for a while longer. The war had caused such terrible devastation, and he would be able to help inspire the people to have hope in the future. He nodded. "I guess you're right again, Dalin."

He turned to Valena. "You know I'll miss you dearly, precious. So let the time pass swiftly until my return."

They talked all that night, and once again fell asleep in each other's arms. Derlin rose to go early in the morning, and, afraid to touch what appeared to him to be a beautiful statue, he gently moved a stray lock of hair from her face. She stirred, and then awoke. The look in Derlin's eyes told her that it was time for him to go, at least for a little while, and she reached up her hand softly, and gave him a cool kiss on the lips, whispering, "I love you too" into his ear. It was the first time she had told him.

Derlin was smiling the whole way back.

$$*\qquad*\qquad*\qquad*$$

In Tealsburg, the festivities were grand. Tarthur couldn't help feeling a little bad for the people who weren't there, those who had given up everything for the others to survive. Tarthur met Yvette again, and she actually seemed rather impressed by him. He should have noticed it, but the whole town was amazed. Already the legends were beginning to grow about the man who bore two elements of power. "Seven feet tall," he was. He had come from some "remote northern province, where he killed cougars and minidrakes with his bare hands," and "spat into the eye of Darhyn," who had "quaked in fear and run away from the vicious hero." Tarthur himself actually admired some of the stories, they were quite well told. He decided that he should have thought of them himself earlier in Krendon.

The formalities and court presentations didn't give either Tarthur or Derlin as much pleasure as they had always imagined that they would. Before, he would have loved to have known a real knight, but that day Tarthur had every rank of knighthood, every conceivable title of generosity and magic and every beneficial adjective heaped on top of him until he thought he was going to be buried. It was weird for the boy who had always been poor to ask for anything and have it immediately granted by the king. An earldom? Sure, why not? Horses, swords, gold, food? Whatever Tarthur asked for was provided him free and immediately. Just for the heck of it, he had himself promoted to Earl of the North, and Derlin as his lieutenant earl. There was no Earl of the North, and Tarthur had never even heard of a lieutenant earl before. They both just made up those titles, but now he was the direct supervisor to Baron Ercrilla. Not that any of this mattered now, though. Tarthur was unsure of what to do with his life now. He didn't know where he would live permanently, but he knew that he must at least return to Krendon for a while. And he knew that he wanted to take Yvonne with him. Yet before that, he had some places to stop by.

✻   ✻   ✻   ✻

In the grasslands in the shadow of the hideous fortress of Queen Marhyn, two figures stood silently with their heads bowed. They had been standing through the entire night, neither talking, both lost in their own private thoughts. One was a big man, and the other one a little smaller, was missing his right arm. Day broke, and the one handed man nodded to the other one.

"It is indeed time, my friend," Yonathan nodded back. Kandan went over and picked up a shovel, and with his good hand began to turn the soil lose and shovel it out of the hole. "It will be hard, you know," Yonathan trailed off. Nothing like this was ever easy...

"I know," Kandan replied. "Yet, this town will live again. If we die trying, this town will live again. As God is my witness, this town will live again!"

Yonathan stuck a banner in the ground with a grim determination, and spoke aloud. "I hereby declare this the new home of Freeton, the town that like the phoenix will rise from its ashes to create itself anew..."

✻   ✻   ✻   ✻

Tustor was ready to see Tarthur, and the look on his face when Tarthur humbly begged the revered leader of the decimated mermen to become the keeper of the Water Orb and to use it to help rebuild their shattered race was like none other that he had ever seen. Tustor wept huge salty tears of joy, and hugged the Orb and caressed it tightly. Girn came forward; he had been with them all this time, and Tarthur felt a little embarrassed and sorry for his friend. Yet, Girn too had grown through the ordeal, he had lost his stammer, and Tarthur could see he was perfectly happy staying with the mermen. Tarthur offered to take Girn back to Krendon, and Girn thanked him. Girn would return to Krendon often, but he would make his home in the sea for now at least.

Wera came up to talk to Tarthur, and handed him a flask of *kokhor*. "Thank you for winning, Tarthur. Because of you, my husband did not die in vain. There is so much that I wish I could give you, but...all I have is this *kokhor*. I know Truin wanted you to have it."

Tarthur nodded solemnly as he went forward to receive the gift. "It is because of people like your husband that I was able to do what I did. It is I who owe him so much. Rest assured, I will not forget him."

*   *   *   *

Tarthur and Derlin had long anticipated their return to Krendon, but as it happened the reality of it was much different. It was only the five of them now, Derlin, Tarthur, Addyean, Yvonne, and Zelin. Baron Ercrilla and the rest had returned earlier. King Garkin had given Addyean another year off, and he chose to stay in Krendon.

Tarthur enjoyed seeing all of the old people whom he had known, and all of them were glad to see Tarthur. Some of them he flattered. Judith, for example, he told that while the dinners he had shared with the king were scrumptious, they were nothing compared to her mincemeat pies. Tarthur reminded the black-smith, however, that there were indeed such things as dragons, and he had a very good friend who was one, and was personally offended at the man's disbelief. Tarthur sternly warned him to be careful, lest a dragon should choose to prove it to everyone. This time, the man didn't argue.

The one person that Tarthur didn't see however was Morty. He was nowhere around when Tarthur came into town. While Tarthur hadn't exactly expected Morty to meet him on the way rejoicing, he did think his absence was a little bit peculiar. Tarthur and Derlin had been discussing how to treat Morty on the trip to Krendon. While it certainly wouldn't be appropriate to blast him with tongues of fire, they had to make sure that he knew who had won.

The town banquet arrived, and bolstered by Tarthur's praise, Judith had cooked up a doozy. And this time the best food went to Tarthur first, even though he politely demurred to Baron Ercrilla, who of course gave it back. They were in the middle of this exchange when Morty walked in and a hush fell over the whole town. They all remembered how Morty had talked after Tarthur and Derlin had left. Of course, back then most of them had been on his side, but now that Tarthur was the hero, allegiances shifted.

"Uh…welcome home, Tarthur and Derlin…" he managed to stammer out.

"Morty," Tarthur responded. "Good to see you. I was beginning to wonder where you were." At this, the tension left the room. Apparently, Tarthur either hadn't heard about the rumors, or had just decided to forgive Morty.

Morty walked up to Tarthur and began to feel a little more comfortable. "I was a little afraid that you'd be mad at me for all those past episodes and misunderstandings. I was um…kind of trying to avoid you."

Tarthur grabbed Morty around the shoulders and began to talk to him in the old buddy sort of way. "That's ridiculous. I tried to leave those petty quarrels behind me a long time ago. And besides, it should be you forgiving me. I usually got the better of you, you know." Morty was about to argue vehemently, but then thought better of it, and just nodded in agreement.

Tarthur smiled generously. "See then, you were scared for nothing. I'm glad we got that all cleared up."

Morty smiled. "Yeah, me too."

Tarthur went over to the table, poured them a couple of glasses of wine with his back to Morty, and came back with a twinkle in his eye. "And to prove that there's no hard feelings, how 'bout a drink?"

THE END

Coming in 2005

DreamQuest 2: ProphecyQuest

Fifteen years after the fall of Darhyn, the world is in a state of relative peace and prosperity. A scholar stumbles on an old prophecy regarding a child who can see himself as he really is, and thus pass through the Wall of Glass separating the Eternal Vale from the Lands of Daranor. An apparition of Tivu the Cloudwalker signifies that the age has now come to pass, and the child now walks among men. The prophecy dictates that with the opening of the gateway, the lost Power of Air will return to the world. Tarthur sees this as a chance to rescue Yan and sets off in search of the child. But, unbeknownst to him, another mysterious creature is also hot on the trail. He is relentlessly pursuing the Power of Air for his own ends, and soon Tarthur begins not only to fear for his own life, but for that of his young son, who seems to be inexplicably caught up in the prophecy every step of the way.

*　　　*　　　*　　　*

It wasn't unheard of to see someone out and about at this time of night, but this man seemed not to fit. For one thing, Gerthoud had never seen clothes like that before. The stranger wasn't going about his business but just stood there, eyes fixated on Gerthoud, as if he were looking straight through him. That was especially odd, as the young man was the one who was transparent.

"*It is time.*" When he finally spoke, Gerthoud was shocked by the pleading urgency in the other's voice. Gerthoud looked down at his watch, forgetting that he didn't own one.

"Time for what?" Gerthoud was about to add, 'Time for you to leave me alone!' but thought better of it. Something about this figure frightened him.

"*The One walks among us! It is time for him to enter.*" The figure began walking closer to Gerthoud. He was only a few meters away now.

Gerthoud instinctively stepped back, but this only caused the other to increase his anxiety all the more. His eyes called out to him, beckoning Gerthoud to help him. "*The age is here. The time is now! I cannot do this alone!*"

Gerthoud rubbed his eyes, trying to erase the specter of the vision he saw. That 'house brew' must have been a lot stronger than he realized. When he looked again, the figure was gone.

Cautious now, Gerthoud continued walking home, his pace slightly quickened. After he had gone a few hundred more meters, he couldn't stand it any longer. He quietly ducked into an alleyway and began to relieve himself against the wall of a building.

The previous scare had almost been forgotten, and he happily urinated on the wall. He thought to write his name, but then sadly remembered that he knew neither how to read nor write. It was amazing how alcohol could manage to magnify one's perceived possessions and abilities. Once, he had even jumped off a table, believing that he could fly. His constant limp was to serve as an eternal reminder that he could not. He was almost done when he noticed with alarm that his urine had a green tint to it. What had Rowen put into that vile concoction this time? As he looked around, though, he saw that the green tint was coming from a mist that was slowly wrapping around his ankles. Confused, Gerthoud turned to see a new figure blocking the alley. This just wasn't his night for drunken hallucinations!

The new figure was dressed all in dark black robes and seemed to float on the green mist. Suddenly something made Gerthoud very afraid.

"What did he tell you?" The figure spoke with a raspy voice that grated on Gerthoud's eardrums.

"Who?" He asked his question boldly, daring the vision to challenge him.

If the figure was annoyed, Gerthoud couldn't tell. "The one who came to you before. The Cloudwalker." His voice sounded the same as before.

Gerthoud had been pretty drunk before, but he never remembered his hallucinations talking to him about each other. Something was seriously wrong here. Gerthoud decided to play along. He didn't know any Cloudwalkers, or even what one was, but he instinctively knew who the dark figure was referring to.

"He said something about the time. Time for 'the One' to do something he couldn't do by himself." After speaking the words, Gerthoud almost wished he hadn't. Something was not right.

The figure seemed pleased. "Did he say anything else?" Now Gerthoud was beginning to get annoyed again, his moods quickly changing as he felt threatened.

"He said that you should get out of here and leave me alone!" Gerthoud almost shouted the words.

The dark wizard nodded. It seemed that he was satisfied with his interrogation. He turned to leave and then turned back. "I almost forgot something. You should be rewarded for your help. I will make you great...I will make you powerful." He was almost panting with anticipation. "But first...I need something from you."

At this he brought his hand up over Gerthoud's chest, and then his fingers abruptly stiffened as a green glow began to form in his palm. Gerthoud felt the worst pain of his life. It felt as if the very cells of his body were being ripped from him, his life-force being torn from his chest. The pain cut through the haze of drunkenness and allowed him to feel the last few moments of his life with astounding lucidity. This was real. He screamed with all his might, but his voice was quickly sucked out as his life drained from his body.

The wizard's breath was haggard, full of weakened excitement. He grabbed the dead body and slumped it over his shoulder. Before he left, he paused for a brief moment to savor the sensation of the warm life he felt within him mix with the cold night air. So the One now walked the earth. His goal had never been closer. The race was on.

www.dreamqueststory.com

0-595-26804-8